Get Caught

Duets

Two brand-new stories in every volume... twice a month!

Duets Vol. #51

Popular Natalie Bishop makes her romantic comedy debut with a charming romp about two couples who start out mismatched, but work it out by story's end. Joining her this month is Darlene Gardner who spins "a delightful tale with an engaging set-up and lovable characters," according to *Romantic Times Magazine*.

Duets Vol. #52

Jennifer LaBrecque returns with a wonderful tale in the Diapers & Detectives miniseries. *Romantic Times* notes that this author always writes "humorous dialogue and lively scenes." And talented Sandra Paul is back with a zany story about "mooning." Ms. Paul never fails to give readers "lots of humor and romance," says *Rendezvous* magazine.

Get Caught Reading both Duets volumes today!

Get caught reading Harlequin.

"Kisses always makes boo-boos better," Molly said innocently.

Sloane disagreed. Jo obviously didn't want him to kiss the lump on her forehead, which was fine because he didn't want to kiss her. Did he? "Oh, I think it already looks much better."

Molly's big brown eyes filled with tears. "Aunt Jo's never gonna get better, 'cause you won't kiss her boo-boo." Little Tara joined the sob squad, too.

Sloane groaned. He'd collared hardened criminals. He'd engaged in Marine skirmishes. And now he was being done in by two bawling little girls.

"For goodness sake, just kiss me," Jo said in a low voice.

Sloane's lips nuzzled the velvet smoothness of her forehead. He lingered longer than he should have and only released her when she pulled unsteadily away from him, confusion in her eyes.

Miraculously, the wailing stopped. "I tole you that would make it better," Molly crowed triumphantly.

Sloane suddenly realized he'd just witnessed junior manipulation in its finest form.

For more, turn to page 9

Kids + Cops = Chaos

Jennifer LaBrecque

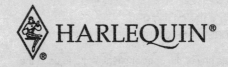

HARLEQUIN®

TORONTO • NEW YORK • LONDON
AMSTERDAM • PARIS • SYDNEY • HAMBURG
STOCKHOLM • ATHENS • TOKYO • MILAN • MADRID
PRAGUE • WARSAW • BUDAPEST • AUCKLAND

ABOUT THE AUTHOR

Jennifer LaBrecque loves to laugh—usually at the most inappropriate times. Her passion for reading, writing and laughing, combined with her tendency toward inappropriateness eventually led her to write romantic comedy. However, she definitely took the circuitous route. Along the way, she waitressed in a barbecue joint, telemarketed family portraits, hawked athletic footwear and wrote dry-as-dust articles for business publications. Jennifer lives in northwest Georgia with her inquisitive daughter, heroic husband, four bad cats and a cherished dog.

Jennifer would love to hear from you. You can write to her at P.O. Box 801068, Acworth, GA 30101.

Books by Jennifer LaBrecque

HARLEQUIN DUETS
28—ANDREW IN EXCESS

"The Mooner has a very small waist with a sharp indent between her hips and ribs."

Jason's gaze lingered on Dee as he spoke, and he stepped closer. To her shock he reached out and placed his hands above her hips, gathering her jacket and blouse tightly against her. "Your waist is so tiny," he murmured, his husky voice filled with an odd satisfaction. "My hands span it with no problem."

Neither moved. Jason appeared deep in thought; Dee was frozen with fright.

She could almost see his brain ticking away like a mental time bomb. In another few minutes— seconds!—he'd reach the correct, fatal conclusion that she was the Mooner. And then he'd explode.

She had to stop him. How could she escape? *Diversion! That was the answer!* Say— No! *Do something!*

She flew up on tiptoe and flung her arms around his neck. Her fingers slid into his thick hair, pulling his head down until his lips were within reach.

Then she kissed him.

For more, turn to page 197

RECYCLED PAPER · RECYCLED PAPER

HARLEQUIN DUETS

ISBN 0-373-44118-5

KIDS + COPS = CHAOS
Copyright © 2001 by Jennifer LaBrecque

MOONSTRUCK
Copyright © 2001 by Sandra Novy Chvostal

This edition published by arrangement with Harlequin Books S.A.

® and TM are trademarks of the publisher. Trademarks indicated with ® are registered in the United States Patent and Trademark Office, the Canadian Trade Marks Office and in other countries.

Visit us at www.eHarlequin.com

Printed in U.S.A.

This is dedicated to Gail Balcomb, Lee Epperson, Ellen Gallagher, Laurie Hutwagner, Billy Lugar and Liz Maxwell. Mucho thanks for ensuring my own little demon spawn had a great summer while this book took form. Friends are one of life's most precious treasures and you guys are priceless (close to ancient, too!).

Prologue

"I'M A COP. Not a baby-sitter," Sloane Matthews declared.

"Listen, Matthews, you know more about this case than anyone else. You're also the best in the department. I need you to go undercover on it." Vic rubbed a hand over his balding pate.

"I can't go undercover as a nanny. I don't know anything about kids." He and Vic weren't exactly friends but they respected one another professionally. Vic ran a tight department and Sloane always solved his cases.

Vic, father of seven, eyed him with skepticism. "Sure you do. Don't you have any kids in your family?"

Sloane pushed his hands through his hair. "I'm an only child of only children. Kids are a mystery and I want it to stay that way. Even if I had kids, I wouldn't leave them with me." Sloane wasn't about to admit it to Vic, but there were only two things that scared the hell out of him. Thus far he'd managed to avoid both.

Marriage and children. They constituted totally alien, unknown quantities that left him feeling out of control. And Sloane was very much into control. He kept his relationships with women casual and, truth be told, he'd rather face a felon than a kid any day.

Vic shrugged. "They're little people. They eat, sleep and play. Only difference between them and us is they're too little to drink beer and work with a bookie."

"Jeez, Vic, you make childhood sound poetic."

"You want me to give it to Blakely? He'll run with it."

Sloane bristled. He and Blakely had been engaged in an unspoken rivalry since the academy. This job would be a piece of cake for Blakely, uncle to numerous nieces and nephews. Worse, it would be a feather in Blakely's cap. Competitive nature aside, Sloane had worked this case damn hard for the past eleven months. Vic had played him and played him well. He wasn't about to turn it over to Blakely. "Over my dead body."

"That's the spirit, Matthews. Anyway, how hard can it be? It's only three kids."

"When do I start?" Sloane asked, shoving aside his qualms. He had a job to do and he'd do it well. He always did. Eating, sleeping, and breathing his job ensured success. Failure wasn't in his vocabulary.

"We'll have you in Cheltham's house by next week. It should be easy enough. The last nanny just gave her notice. Cheltham's days of getting rich off smuggling pre-Columbian artifacts is about to end. With him and the missus out of the country for a week, you'll have this nailed in no time. Especially since he's got a home office."

Sloane had been waiting for a break in this case. But as a nanny? Much as he hated the way the scenario was shaping up, Vic was right. Max Cheltham ran his shipping empire from a home office, which had made it hard to infiltrate. Now with Cheltham and his wife out of the country for a week, he should be able to put this case to bed.

He'd investigated Cheltham and could pinpoint exactly the balance in his business account, but he'd never paid any attention to Cheltham's children. Sloane squared his shoulders. "So, tell me about these kids."

Vic scanned the sheet on his desk. "Okay. You got a boy named Connor. Age six. First grade. Extracurriculars are Boy Scouts, soccer team, piano lessons, and junior finance club. Busy kid."

Sloane doubted he'd heard that last part correctly. "Junior finance club?"

"Yep."

"But the kid's only six." What had happened to baseball in the sandlot?

Vic shrugged and turned his attention to the sheet once again. "Kiddo number two is three. Name's Molly. No school for little Molly but she does have Kindermusik once a week and a play date every Thursday."

Sloane quelled the panic lurking at the edge of his control. Once he got this terminology down, he'd be fine. "What's a play date?"

"Yeah, I asked Gladys about that. She says it's like a coffee klatch where the kids play while the women yack." Vic grinned evilly. "Uh, sorry Matthews, where the *caretakers* yack. Keep your ears open and you'll probably pick up all kinds of pointers."

He ignored Vic's gibe and made a mental note to contact Vic's wife, Gladys. With seven children of her own, Gladys could prove to be a valuable resource. "What about the third one?"

Vic scanned the sheet. "Another girl. This one's named Tara. One and a half. She doesn't do anything." He sat the sheet of paper on his desk. "Be ready to begin Operation Undercover Nanny this Sunday when Cheltham and the wife leave the country. The nanny service promised a replacement could start that day."

Sloane pushed back his chair and stood. "So, that's it?"

Vic leaned back and planted his feet on his desk, all traces of his wise-guy persona gone. "I need you to nail Cheltham and nail him quick. I'm starting to get some heat on this one from the muckety-mucks. You're the best man I've got so don't let me down. There's a lot riding on this one."

He knew Vic had caught some flak over the Cheltham case but for Sloane, there was a lot riding on *every* case— his professional integrity. "Consider it done."

He let himself out of Vic's office, already planning. Sloane had great organizational skills and he was re- sourceful. He had two days to prepare. A couple of child reference books and a phone call to Gladys and he'd be set.

After all, how hard could it be to take care of three kids?

1

"YOU SHOULD BE stretched out in a hammock enjoying sex on the beach."

At her grandmother's exasperated proclamation, Jo Calhoun hit the brakes, nearly taking out the fountain in her sister's driveway. That was precisely what she'd planned, but how had Nora known? "Sex on the beach?"

Nora snapped her fingers. "Get with the program, girl. It's a drink. All that stuff about sex in a hammock—" she waved her hand in dismissal "—way too much swinging and swaying. Anyway, my point is, you ought to have your workaholic fanny parked on a beach instead of mopping up your sister's mess again. You finally decide to get away from that business of yours and take a bona fide vacation and then Cici has to go and mess things up." A concerned frown settled between Nora's brow.

Jo and her twin sister Cici had formed some type of symbiotic relationship in vitro. Cici was the beauty. Jo the brains. Cici the romantic. Jo the practical. Cici answered the call to marriage and procreation. Jo courted an M.B.A. and her own business. Cici made messes. Jo cleaned them up. It was a relationship they'd spent thirty-three years perfecting.

"Cici said it was an emergency. She had to accompany Max and she needed me to check in on the new nanny." Jo squashed the frisson of resentment she felt at Cici's not bothering to clear it with her first. Jo took care of things. It was what she did. What she'd always done. Just because she'd begun to question the route her life had taken didn't make her a new woman.

She jumped out of her little red convertible, still a little in awe that she, practical, plain-Jane Jo Calhoun, had actually traded in her sedate sedan for a sexy sports car. Turning thirty-three had pushed buttons she hadn't known she had.

Nora exited the car at a slower rate. "I still say you shouldn't have canceled your vacation to pick up Cici's slack."

She'd booked her first vacation since…since…well, forever. She'd planned an entire week away from the computer software company she'd started six years ago. Only after spending so long nurturing the company into thriving success, maybe she'd angsted into an early mid-life crisis.

And what had she wanted in a vacation? Sun, sand and sex—not necessarily in that order. Staid, sedate Jo Calhoun in those conditions? It was hard for even her to imagine. But after all, on some tropical island, she could be whoever and whatever she wanted to be. Sort of like going to a costume ball and letting loose. She could get this sense of dissatisfaction out of her blood and get back down to business. So, she'd booked a vacation. But then Cici had needed her, suddenly, there went the vacation.

Jo retrieved a bag of doughnuts from the minuscule back seat. "I can go to Jamaica anytime. How could I enjoy myself if I was worrying about the kids?" She adored Cici's children. She loved their mischievous, rambunctious ways—especially when she could give them back to their parents. But lately, the serenity of her life was becoming a bit mundane. Boring, in fact. She'd developed an ill-defined itch that begged to be scratched. Jamaica had seemed a good place to scratch.

Her unused plane ticket sat on her dresser at home. Now, instead of boarding Flight 325, Jo mounted the front steps to Cici and Max's plantation-style home, with Nora muttering behind her. Doric columns flanked the stairs and supported the wide veranda. Late-blooming clematis hung in fragrant bowers. Bound by a sense of duty and carrying just a tinge of attitude over foregoing sun, sand and sex in the Caribbean, Jo fit her key into the lock of the massive front door. The only staff member to work on a Sunday was the unfortunate nanny in question.

Jo and Nora stepped into the marbled foyer that showcased a soaring, curved staircase reminiscent of *Gone With the Wind.*

"Every time I come through the front door, I expect Rhett Butler to saunter out of the library," she observed to Nora. Jo's comment echoed in the massive foyer.

Nora rolled her eyes and refused to be coaxed out of her case of the sulks.

The immense quiet weighed the house down. It struck Jo as sort of eerie. "Do you hear what I hear?"

"I don't hear anything."

"That's just it. Neither do I. Have you ever known Connor, Molly, and Tara to be this quiet?" Jo raised her voice and yelled up the staircase. "Hey, munchkins! Jo-Jo and Norrie are here."

Quiet settled back over the house like a blanket falling into place.

If they'd been in the backyard, she and Nora would've heard them when they'd driven up. "Hey, kids. Come on. I've got doughnuts. Jelly-filled." That'd bring them down.

The desperate silence gave way to a muffled thud in the library to the left of the grand staircase. With her heart thumping in trepidation, Jo marched across the foyer and yanked open the library door.

She froze in the doorway, eyeing the large, bare-chested, duct-taped man in front of her. Furious green eyes glared at her from above the silver tape that sealed his mouth shut.

No nanny. No kids. Just one big, very angry, semi-naked man with weird tattoos sat in the middle of the room. Panic threatened. She pushed it back. Max and Cici were out of the country. And she was in charge.

Where were the kids? She forced herself to calm down. Hyperventilating wouldn't accomplish anything. Jo shoved her grandmother behind her. "Looks like Cici was right to be concerned."

"Who's that man, dear? Where are his clothes? And why's he all taped up?" Nora peered around her, and Jo threw out a protective arm. Until she knew the situation, the best place for her grandmother remained behind her.

"I don't have a clue. But I'm about to find out." Adrenaline surged. She flipped open the top of her pepper spray and tossed Nora her cell phone. "Go out onto the veranda. Call 9-1-1 and get the police over here." Panic flared in the man's eyes. He shook his head frantically. Who, except a criminal, would object to police presence? Certainly not an innocent guy in duct tape.

Tamping down her panic, she called for her nieces and nephew once again. "Connor? Molly? Tara?" Except for objecting grunts from the stranger and Nora's muted voice, silence reigned. He'd have a whole lot more than pepper spray to worry about if he'd harmed one hair on their precious little heads.

Almost immediately the wail of a siren sounded in the

distance. The man slumped in resignation. Aware that help was on the way, but not content to wait another minute to locate her nieces and nephew, Jo squared her shoulders and approached the stranger. Well-groomed, he didn't look like a criminal, except for those weird markings on his face. Friend or foe? She'd know soon.

She'd never removed duct tape from a body part—actually, she'd never had a duct tape experience. Probably best to treat it like a big, ultra-adhesive bandage—just grab a corner and rip it off. Approaching only close enough to work loose a corner of tape, Jo made her intention known. "I'm going to pull this off. If you know where the children are, you'd better tell me."

She closed her eyes and gave a mighty yank.

SLOANE DIDN'T have the luxury of running his hand over his stinging mouth and upper lip. His hands remained taped behind his back.

There hadn't been anything about bondage in either of the two child-rearing books he'd read. But he didn't think these three qualified as children. Any number of more appropriate names came to mind. "Demon spawn" topped the list.

"The children are—"

Three of his fellow police officers charged in with weapons drawn, cutting short his revelation.

"You can relax now, ma'am."

She continued to train the pepper spray on Sloane's face. She didn't as much as blink in the direction of Blakely, Sloane's nemesis, who led the charge. Not particularly a stellar start—duct tape and now Blakely. "Not until I know where my nieces and nephew are."

Sloane nodded toward the drapes flanking the French doors. "Last time I saw them, they were over there."

The long velvet shifted and rippled. A small boy's blond head popped around the side. "Hi, Aunt Jo."

His little sister squirmed out from underneath the floor-length fabric. "Jo-Jo."

The woman—"Aunt Jo"—sagged on the spot, letting the can of pepper spray drop to the ground. She moved and scooped up the little girl, burying her face against the child's neck. "Where's Tara? Where's your new nanny? Do you know this man?"

The child, Molly, shoved a finger up her nose. "Me'n Connor put Tara to bed cause it was nap time. She was grumpy. And that's our new nanny." The finger came out of her nose to point directly at Sloane. She smiled angelically in his direction. Of course, she'd smiled angelically the entire time she'd rolled him in duct tape and drawn all over him with marker.

"He's the nanny?" She squeezed her eyes shut briefly. "Oh, my God."

"Sloane Murphy at your service." He'd changed Matthews to Murphy for this assignment.

An older woman with bright red hair stepped out from behind "Aunt Jo." "Connor, what's going on here?"

The kid shuffled out from behind the drapes avoiding eye contact. "We were just playing a little game."

"You know better than that, Connor." Disappointment came through in Jo's voice.

Blakely swallowed a smirk. "According to 9-1-1 you're the grandmother and you're the aunt, am I correct?" he asked pointing. "And he's in charge while the parents are away?" The brunette nodded curtly. Blakely turned to Sloane. "Sir, perhaps you can explain this situation. Why don't you tell us how two small children managed to tie you up?"

"They took me by surprise. I didn't want to hurt

them.'' It galled Sloane to admit a mistake to Blakely. Blakely's skeptical look pronounced that *he* would've known how to handle the situation. Sloane would never, ever, live this one down. Three kids and one phone call had reduced his professional reputation to hash.

''We was playing, and we made Mr. Sloane an indignant just like we saw on TV yesterday.''

Damn straight, he was indignant.

Connor rolled his eyes and pushed his wire-framed glasses up on the bridge of his nose. ''Indigenous, you moron. He was an indigenous tribe member found in the lower basin of the Amazon. According to the Discovery Channel, they're on the verge of extinction due to a loss of habitat.''

''Don't call your sister names,'' the redhead corrected.

The kid was a regular walking encyclopedia.

The brunette turned her attention to Sloane. ''What happened to your shirt?''

He indicated the shredded mass in the corner. ''They cut it off after they tied me up.'' Thank goodness they'd stopped with his shirt and he wasn't sitting here bare-ass naked in front of everyone with other parts duct-taped. Some things were too painful to contemplate.

Blakely, Upshaw and Dickerson emitted strangling noises. Damn, if they weren't enjoying this.

The two women shared a horrified look. ''Connor. Molly. You know you're not supposed to play with scissors.'' The older one took them to task.

Warped. The whole bunch of them were whackos, from granny down to the little one. The kids had assaulted him, tied him up, cut his clothes off and hid while the police rushed in, and these nutty women took them to task for name-calling and playing with scissors.

Jo shifted Molly to the older woman's arms. ''Nora,

why don't you take Connor and Molly upstairs and check on Tara?''

Nora snagged Connor's collar as he hustled past. "What a good idea. Connor and I can chat while you two get to know one another." She nudged Jo's shoulder. "He's cute. Don't let this one get away."

The brunette turned bright red.

Not to worry. Duct tape aside, he wasn't going anywhere until he had the evidence needed to nail Cheltham.

En masse, Nora and the children moved toward the carved, walnut staircase. Molly's voice drifted back over Nora's shoulder, "Norrie, it was so fun. And after Connor taped Mr. Sloane's mouth, it wasn't even too loud."

Blakely and Upshaw smirked. "It looks like you've got everything under control, ma'am. If you don't need us, we'll just leave and file our report."

Sloane knew exactly what kind of report they'd file. His duct tape debacle would be all over the station within minutes.

"Thank you for responding so promptly. Sorry to have bothered you."

"All in a day's work. Call us anytime." Sloane's buddies in blue started toward the door.

The brunette thrust a paper bag emblazoned with a local doughnut shop logo toward Blakely. "Here. Take these for your trouble. I brought them for the kids but they obviously don't deserve them now."

Blakely accepted the bag with a smile. "Thanks, it'll save us a trip." He inclined his head in Sloane's direction. "It's probably fine to untape him now. You'd better tell those kids to go easy on him for a little while, too. We'll see ourselves out."

Jo stood rooted to the spot until the click of the front door indicated they'd gone.

"Right. So let's get you untaped and out of that chair." Brisk and business-like, she moved behind him. The Terrors from Hell had dragged a straight-backed, spindly legged chair that matched the fancy desk in the corner of the room to the middle of the thick Oriental carpet when they tied him up.

The woman's hands were cool and steady against his wrists as she worked at the tape. But her breath whispered against his back in small, warm gusts and her hair tickled his shoulder as she struggled. Her fragrance surrounded him. Sloane found both sensations distractingly, inappropriately, erotic.

"I'm so sorry about all this. The kids can be a handful."

Her comment brought his attention back to the matter at hand, namely his hands still bound by tape. A handful? *That* was the understatement of the year. They were more like hellions. He bit back the comment and tried to muster a nanny-like response. "Kids will be kids." He'd been reduced to clichés.

"Maybe I should just cut though the tape and let you pull it off." She grabbed the scissors off the desk and in a matter of seconds his hands were free. He made quick work of untaping his ankles, then, gritting his teeth, he snatched the tape off one wrist and then the other.

She winced as dark hair came off, as well.

"Once again, I'm so sorry about this whole thing…you know, the kids, the police." She extended a square, capable hand, her nails short and unpolished. "I'm Jo Calhoun. Cici's my twin sister. And don't bother to say it—there is no family resemblance. The other woman is Nora Ferguson, our grandmother."

Training kept the surprise off his face. Cici Cheltham sported a mane of blond hair, a big pair of baby blues, and a whole lot of curves. No one would ever miss seeing Cici Cheltham. Conversely, Jo Calhoun would make a great undercover cop because she was so average. Shoulder-length brown hair, unremarkable brown eyes, medium build, all added up to just another face in the crowd.

He took her proffered hand and started at the accompanying tingle. It was probably just a little static electricity. Although her touch threw him slightly off kilter, she didn't seem to notice a thing. "Sloane Murphy from the Nurturing Nannies Network," he offered.

She pulled her hand from his and took a step back. Her sharp, practical gaze raked him from head to toe, lingering on the dragon tattooed on his belly. "Sorry for the earlier mix-up, but no one mentioned you were a man, and you don't exactly look like a nanny."

He deserved a little retaliation for that phone call that had just ruined his reputation. And Sloane, who never mixed business with personal interest, found himself perversely piqued at Ms. Calhoun's cool attitude. "Usually, there's very little confusion that I'm a man. And I love being a nanny." Any bigger lie and he'd choke on it.

"Uh, right." She looked from his wrists, now missing a band of hair, to his shredded shirt. "I can see why."

He caught sight of himself in a small mirror between two framed prints of hunting dogs. Spiraling circles and straight lines adorned his face and neck. "Wow. That's some art job." He grinned in spite of himself. With his hair standing on end, he resembled some odd cult member.

"Connor and Molly did a number on you."

"Tara helped, as well." He recalled a passage from *Learning and Loving with Kids* that Vic's wife had loaned him. "Kids need an outlet for their creativity." Of course, these three needed a keeper. Or a straitjacket!

Jo Calhoun's brown eyes announced she thought he sounded like a nut. Hell, *he* thought he sounded like a nut. "So you're not quitting?"

"Absolutely not." Not until he had the evidence he needed to put Cheltham out of commission. He'd never had a case or a crook best him yet. He didn't intend to start now. Sloane noted Jo's silent sigh of relief. He'd bet these brats ran through nannies almost as fast as the little one ran through diapers. "Actually, they did quite a good job. Notice the symmetry between the designs they drew on the right side and the left."

Aunt Jo bent and picked a marker up off the floor, exposing him to a remarkably remarkable backside. He revised his earlier opinion. Okay, so folks would remember her if they got a look at her tush outlined in those shorts. He wasn't likely to forget for some time, himself.

"It's a good thing you appreciate their artistry." An evil grin lurked at the corner of her mouth.

He had a bad feeling about this.

She placed two markers in his hand. "They're permanent."

Sloane hazarded another look in the mirror and swallowed hard. "Permanent? As in…"

"As in…it'll have to wear off." She gave way to a full-blown smile.

Now he knew where the kids got their sadistic streak. They'd inherited it from their aunt.

Jo STRETCHED OUT on Molly's double bed while Molly resided over a tea party with her stuffed bears. Connor had wisely retreated to his room, supposedly to work on a project for his junior finance club. Jo suspected he'd made himself scarce to avoid further tongue lashings.

She eyed the white rodent in a corner cage. Mephisto,

the family cat, sat outside the cage and stared balefully at the creature inside. "That rat gives me the willies," Jo said. Why couldn't Cici's kids have a nice normal pet like a hamster?

"Actually, Hermes is a white mouse. Not a rat. He's okay." Nora shrugged. "But I wouldn't want him snuggling up with me in bed at night."

Jo shuddered. Although she adored her sister, she and Cici definitely had different taste. Pets. Careers. Homes. She never felt comfortable in Cici's house. In Jo's humble, non-decorating opinion, everything seemed overdone, except Molly's bedroom. "I love this room."

Nora nodded from her perch on the window seat that formed a tiny turret. "It's lovely isn't it? Every little princess should have her own castle."

Gazing at the ceiling, Jo fancied she could almost see the fluffy white clouds actually drift where they were painted against a robin's-egg-blue sky. On one wall stood a unicorn, saddled in finery and tethered—a mythical steed for an absent prince. Jo didn't just love this room, she adored it. An adoration she'd never quite reconciled with her pragmatic nature. Speaking of not reconciling….

She propped up on one elbow. "I don't know about this new nanny."

"Well, I don't know much about him, either, dear. But he is a looker. And the children seem to like him."

Jo's eyebrows shot up. "I don't want to see what they do when they decide they don't like someone. Nora, they bound and gagged him."

"Exactly. He was vulnerable and they didn't harm him."

"Well, something doesn't feel right. He's huge and…well, such a man."

Nora's blue eyes shone with satisfaction. "You *did* notice."

"Of course I noticed." Jo slapped a finger against her wrist. "Yep. There's a pulse. I'm not dead yet." She'd noticed a lot more than she'd wanted to when she'd untaped him.

"I'm glad to hear it. I haven't been too sure lately."

Nora appeared demure, but Jo knew better. At eighteen, she and Cici had moved in with their grandmother when a corporate transfer had sent their parents to California. Living with Nora meant finishing their senior year in Savannah. Two years later, Cici had married Max Cheltham. Twelve additional years after that, Jo moved into the house next to Nora out on Tybee Island.

"Very funny, Grandma." That'd get Nora. They'd had only one rule from the time she and Cici were tots—they were never to call Nora "Grandma." Her social life whirled far too fast for that tag.

"Josephina Wilhelmina Calhoun...."

Oh, God. Anything but her unabridged name. "Truce. Anyway, Mr. Murphy strikes me as an unusual nanny."

Nora rubbed her hands together. "Makes me wish I needed baby-sitting myself. Darling, did you see that chest and those shoulders? Well, of course you did. You were right there, too. And those green eyes. Such an unusual shade—reminds me of those lovely jade earrings my second husband gave me for our first anniversary. Or was it my first husband for our second anniversary? Anyway, they're lovely. And that brown hair with all that subtle shading. Just like a mink coat I had before those animal rights people told us we shouldn't wear them."

Jo'd noticed. As she'd pointed out, she wasn't dead. She'd stopped one step shy of ogling his bare upper body after the police left: defined muscles, a hairy chest, and riding on the flat planes of his belly, a tattoo of what appeared to be a small, fire-breathing dragon. She simply didn't have Nora's romantic nature to wax poetic. "Earrings and a coat—do you want to wear him or admire him?"

Nora dropped a suggestive wink. "Sugar, if I was thirty years younger, I'd go for both. I suppose I'll have to leave it up to you to carry on for me. I've got a feeling you should go for this one."

Without being thirty years younger, Nora'd still probably have a better chance with him than Jo would. Jo didn't possess a romantic, seductive bone in her practical, pragmatic body.

And that suited her just fine. Most of the time. Until recently when she'd begun to fantasize about what it would be like to be a wild, far-from-practical-and-pragmatic woman. Once she had realized he posed no threat, a tied-up and half-naked Sloane Murphy had only increased the newfound beat of her libido drum.

She sat up on the bed and crossed her legs in the lotus position. "How old would you say he is? Early to mid-thirties? No wedding ring. Do you think he's gay?"

"Get with the new millennium, girl. A male nanny? You bet. But gay?" Nora fluffed her short red hair and snorted. "Trust me. I know these things. Honey, he's no more gay than you or me."

The last statement came out one decibel below a shout. Despite internal radar and other physical attributes, at seventy-three, Nora's hearing wasn't what it used to be, which resulted in her sometimes talking overly loud. Like now.

Footsteps paused outside Molly's door. A slight knock preceded Nanny Murphy letting himself in. Nora'd nailed every detail. Sloane Murphy ranked as a hunk. Even with a shirt on and the weird face art. One glimpse of his jade eyes put to death any hope he hadn't overheard Nora's last statement. A slow heat leisurely crawled up her face.

"Well, thanks for discussing Cousin Jeff with me, Nora." Lame, lame, lame and then some.

"Excuse me for interrupting, ladies. I just wanted to check on Molly." Sloane strode over to the corner where Molly sat with her bears. He hunkered down until he was level with her.

"We need to discuss what happened earlier today, Molly," he said, his tone patient.

Molly smiled happily and stuck a finger up her nose. Jo cringed from the bedside. Cici assured her the finger-up-the-nose trick would soon lose its appeal. It couldn't happen soon enough.

"You're not mad, are you? You're happy, aren't you? Aunt Jo-Jo just asked Norrie if you was gay. Norrie said you wasn't. Gay means happy, don't it?" Molly disengaged her finger, pleased as punch with her deductions.

Really, if a shred of enchantment existed in this bedroom, perhaps it could manifest itself now and the bed would swallow Jo whole. No such luck. She remained planted on the comforter and pasted on a sick smile.

"Molly's such a clever thing. Jo had just told me what a pleasant disposition you had in light of what you'd been through and that's what got us onto the topic of Cousin Jeff." Nora couldn't lie worth a hill of beans.

He shrugged off the pitiful explanation, obviously comfortable with his own sexuality, and shifted his attention back to Molly. "I'm happy as a clam. But let's make a new rule. It's much more fun if everyone gets to play. So, the rule is—no more tying anyone up, okay?"

"Okay."

Clanging from across the hall cut short their exchange. A muffled chant arose. "Out. Out. Out. Out."

Molly jumped up gleefully. "Tara's up. That means she wants you to get her out of her crib, Mr. Sloane."

Jo steeled herself. Connor and Molly were a handful. And they'd taught Tara everything they knew.

SLOANE FACED the golden-haired cherub and recalled some of his most important training—the enemy could not be taken at face value. She appeared beatific. She looked harmless. He knew better.

Gladys had advised him to be firm but gentle. He employed caution as he approached the crib. "Are you ready for Mr. Sloane to get you out of bed?"

Halfway across the room he stopped in his tracks, a foul odor rendering him motionless.

The little tyrant shook the rail for good measure. "Out," she commanded, as if concerned he might change his mind.

He forged forward. He'd served in the marines. He'd faced down drug dealers. How bad could one baby's crappy diaper be?

Just as he reached the rail, Tara plopped down on her diapered fanny and scooted across the crib. The stench further assaulted him.

"Come on. I can't just leave you in there like that." He couldn't, could he?

She giggled and flung herself at him. Sloane hefted her out of the crib. Even though she stunk to high heaven, she felt soft and plump and cuddly.

Just as she reached for his nose, he placed her on some kind of table with a plastic cover and a bewildering array of products. Gladys had told him something really important about this diaper changing business, but he couldn't remember. He already had too damn much to remember. He unsnapped her pajama legs and freed her pudgy, little limbs. The fetid smell ripened.

He took a deep breath. Stay calm and focused, he instructed himself. Calm. Focused.

He squatted to search for something to clean her with once he removed the diaper.

"You're s'posed to tie her down." Molly, speaking from the doorway, startled him.

He looked up and saw Tara leaning precariously over the table edge. Sloane leaped up and settled the baby away from the edge. Yeah. Now he remembered Gladys's pointer—strap the baby down. He clipped the strap into place. "Thanks. I was just about to do that." Great. Now he was explaining himself to a three-year-old.

Tara protested her confinement with an ear-shattering scream that settled into a sob.

Molly ambled over and handed him a plastic canister. "Here's her wipes."

"Thanks. I was just about to get them." He shouted to be heard over the miniature banshee's wail.

Nothing for it. He braced himself for action. Sloane released the diaper tabs. What a mess! He glanced from her dirty tush to the box of wipes and back again. He was supposed to clean her up with those thin, little wet tissues? Not in this lifetime.

Quick as a flash, he unhooked the strap and unsnapped the rest of her clothes. He tucked her under one arm—a naked, wiggling, poop-covered football—and sprinted toward the bathroom. The wailing ceased immediately.

He turned on the faucet. Making sure the water wasn't too warm, he plunged her dirty little butt under the spigot. Tara laughed and blew a spit bubble.

"Yeah? Well, I'd feel better with all that sh—stuff off me, too."

He glanced up and caught Jo and Nora's reflections in the mirror. He hadn't realized he had an audience. Good thing he hadn't botched the job.

JO SHOOK HER HEAD as she and Nora left Tara's smelly bedroom behind. She knew next to nothing about kids, but even she knew a lack of experience when she saw it. "I'm calling the Nurturing Nannies Network and checking his references. If that man's got experience as a nanny, you can butter my butt and call me a biscuit."

2

"BRING ON THE BUTTER. I'm a biscuit." Jo replaced the receiver and sank back into the leather chair, mildly shocked. Even though the door to the library remained closed, she leaned closer to Nora and lowered her voice. "The director at Nurturing Nannies says he's one of their most highly recommended employees. She did mention his methods were often unorthodox." Yeah, she'd second that after watching him carry Tara like a stinky football and shove her little tush under the faucet.

"As long as you're satisfied, then so am I."

"The problem is, I'm not satisfied." What she'd been told didn't reconcile with what she'd actually witnessed. The ledger simply didn't balance.

"I'm glad you're finally admitting it, dear." Innuendo laced Nora's voice, and her wiggling eyebrows settled the inference.

"Nora, why does everything come down to the lowest sexual denominator with you?"

"Well, why not dear? Don't knock it till you've tried it."

And what exactly did one say to that? She'd been all set to try it in Jamaica. Hey, she'd seen "How Stella Got Her Groove Back," but the truth of the matter was she wasn't Angela Bassett and she'd never possessed a groove in the first place. Best to return to the subject at hand.

"I've got a funny feeling in my gut about Sloane." She dealt daily in calculated outcomes. Which made her "intuitive read" regarding Sloane all the more baffling. She didn't do the intuitive thing. At least, she hadn't until now.

"A funny feeling's a start."

"For goodness' sake, Nora, not *that*." God help her if Nora ever found out she'd experienced a surfeit of *that* when she'd wrestled with his duct tape earlier. Really, it was unsettling to find herself so captivated by the scent and texture of a stranger's naked yet well-formed back that she had wanted to test the taste and touch of him against her tongue. Jo disliked feeling unsettled. "First and foremost, I want to make sure everything's okay with the children. Cici mentioned things had been strange around here lately."

"What kind of strange? Why didn't you tell me before?"

"I didn't want to alarm you. She couldn't tell me anything definitive. Just that she'd had bad vibes. Actually, Max had begun to act strange."

Nora frowned. "Hmm. Cici had a feeling, huh? And Max is never strange."

Everyone in the family had learned long ago to not ignore Cici's vibes. What her sister lacked in common sense, she made up for in instinct. Cici had intuition out the wazoo.

"Yeah, I know. That's why she insisted on traveling to Bogota with him. I think we should at least stay through dinner and then play it by ear."

"Wonder what they're having?" Food ran a close second to sex on Nora's list of favorite things. Mrs. Price, Cici's and Max's housekeeper and cook, produced mouthwatering meals. Nora jumped to her feet. "I'll let Mrs. Price know."

"Sorry. You're out of luck. Sunday's her day off. Didn't you notice she wasn't around?"

"Heck. There goes a good meal." Nora headed for the door. "Well, come on. Let's go check out the kitchen. My stomach's about to meet my backbone. Maybe there's something decent to eat around here."

"Wow! I wish we ate like this all the time." Connor dropped his sullen demeanor.

"This is my favoritest dinner ever." Molly had her finger out of her nose.

Even demanding little Tara seemed content to push the food around on her high-chair tray.

Sloane beamed with pride at the feast in front of the three demons—uh, children—and himself. He'd found some revolting casserole concoction in the refrigerator that the kids had protested. It'd been up to him to prepare their meal. This was more like it. He had a handle on things now.

Too bad "Aunt Jo" with her cool brown eyes and aspersions on his sexuality couldn't see him now. Sloane tried to shake off his rancor. What difference did it make if that brown wren of a woman questioned his sexuality? It meant he'd done a great job in hiding his true identity. Just because the brush of her hair and the feathering of her breath against his back in the library sparked an awareness of her in him that intensified when he found her sitting on Molly's bed, didn't mean anything. Actually, it meant he needed to keep his mind on his investigation.

As if his thoughts had conjured her up, Jo marched through the kitchen door, trailed by Nora. At the sight of their feast, she stopped abruptly, leaving Nora to bump into her.

"Care to join us, ladies? There's plenty." Now he'd impress her with his organizational skills.

"It's yummy." Molly licked her fingers to emphasize the point. "Aunt Jo-Jo, you can sit with me and Norrie you sit there."

Nora slid into the dictated seat. Jo settled the little girl on her lap and sneaked a quick kiss behind Molly's ear before she surveyed the table. "I have never seen anything like this before."

Sloane knew how to lay out a feast. "What can I pass you first? Cheese Doodles? Potato chips? We have three kinds of dip. Or, are you ready for a root beer float?"

"Is there anything green on this table?"

"Sure. Right here." He passed the bowl of pistachio pudding topped with miniature marshmallows.

"Uh, thanks."

Nora tucked into the smorgasbord with gusto. Tara banged a cup with a lidded spout, leaving a trail of apple juice down the side of his face. In the span of one afternoon he had these kids pegged. Connor was a veritable whiz kid who'd offered Sloane a stock tip by way of apology for his earlier role in the let's-duct-tape-the-new-nanny routine. Molly was the director. She took everything in, analyzed it, and then directed. And Tara found trouble like a heat-seeking missile.

"Hey! Watch the liddy cup." He wiped the juice off his face with a paper napkin. Jo and Nora exchanged a look. Were nannies supposed to let kids slop drinks all over them? Too bad. He had to draw the line somewhere.

Tara stared him straight in the eye and slammed the cup down again. The entire table stopped eating to watch.

Sloane recognized a challenge, even if it was a liddy cup and not a glove she'd thrown down.

"That's it, young lady. The liddy cup is mine." Amazingly, she gave up the sticky plastic without protest.

Connor and Molly giggled at each other across the table. The women swapped another look.

"What?" One minute everything seemed fine and the next he felt lost. It was like crossing the border into a foreign country.

"Sippy." Connor resumed his one-boy war on the Cheese Doodles.

"Huh?"

Molly giggled again and shoved her finger into a bowl of pistachio pudding. Better the pudding than her nose. "You're funny, Mr. Sloane."

Jo Calhoun leveled her brown eyes at him. At close range, he noted they weren't ordinary brown, as he'd first thought. Instead, milk chocolate flecked with caramel came to mind. But so far, he hadn't encountered anything sweet about her. He'd wager some acerbic comment sat on the tip of her tongue.

"Do you sideline as a comic, too?" She widened her eyes in mock admiration.

Maybe he'd developed psychic tendencies. More like psychotic with this group.

"Excuse my granddaughter, Mr. Murphy. She's cycling." Nora dabbed at a blob of onion dip on her upper lip.

Jo choked on a chip and grabbed Molly's root beer float.

Molly eyed Nora dubiously. "You don't have that old-timer's do you, Norrie? Mama said even if you get the old-timer's, Aunt Jo would never put you in one of those homes 'cause she's one of those people that takes care of other people.''

"It's Alzheimer's." Connor rolled his eyes in disgust at his sister's mispronunciation. "You could at least say it right."

"No, dear, I don't have Alzheimer's. What put that ridiculous notion in your head?"

"You said Aunt Jo was cycling, but she's sitting right there."

"PMS, dear. She has PMS." Nora threw her hand up, fending off the question before it could leave her mouth. "Ask your mother when she gets home, since she's so free with opinions and information."

Perhaps he knew next to nothing about kids, but Sloane knew plenty about women with PMS. He never dated long enough or got involved enough to experience the dreaded syndrome, but he'd had plenty of buddies who'd fallen into the steady girlfriend and/or marriage trap. Second-hand, he'd learned two common symptoms among PMS women—total irrationality and a craving for chocolate. He eyed Jo with trepidation. "I saw a can of chocolate syrup in the refrigerator. Can I get you some?"

The premenstrual avenger rolled her eyes. "I don't have PMS, and I don't want any chocolate, thank you." She turned her eyes in Nora's direction. "However, any more comments along those lines, and Cici will need to revise her opinion."

Nora snorted, but Connor cut her off. "Hey, if she doesn't want the chocolate syrup, can I have it? Chocolate increases the levels of serotonin in the brain, increasing a general sense of well-being. So, can I have it?"

The kid was a walking, talking fact sheet. Sloane shrugged. "Sure."

Tara sucked on a potato chip and played with her pudding. Why was he still clutching her sticky, plastic cup? He placed it on the table.

Molly pointed at the cup and batted her brown eyes with caramel flecks just like her aunt's. "Sippy, silly."

Had he spoken in code when he was a kid? "What?"

"She's telling you it's a *sippy* cup, not a *liddy* cup." Challenge and suspicion glinted in Jo's eyes.

He couldn't blow his cover before he made any headway on the case. The kids he could handle. He needed to get rid of Jo Calhoun and her suspicions. "Of course. I knew that. I just prefer the term liddy. It seems a more accurate description."

She didn't believe him. Not even for a second.

Connor poured chocolate syrup over his marshmallows and burped loudly.

Sloane ranked it. "Five."

Molly applauded at the same time Connor protested. "Hey, no fair. Molly got a five and mine was louder."

"Molly's also younger. I know you're capable of better." Sloane and Connor had reached a truce after their rough start this afternoon. Sloane recognized all the signs of a boy who needed a male role model who was around more than his father. God knows, he knew all about how it felt to be a boy desperate for a busy father's attention.

The boy grudgingly accepted his decision. "Okay."

"Connor, don't you need to excuse yourself?" Jo prompted with a raised brow.

Molly jumped in. "We're in training. Mr. Sloane's judging our belches. He's our mental."

Undercover or not, he felt oddly compelled to make a positive difference in these kids.

"Mentor. He's our mentor, Molly." Connor corrected her, still obviously miffed over belching no better than his kid sister.

Jo's mouth opened but no sound came out. A frown tugged her dark brows together over her straight nose. She didn't appear particularly happy with the news of his mentoring efforts. Nora hooted from the other end of the table.

"Look. Tara's green just like the pudding." Molly pointed past Sloane's shoulder to where Tara sat on his right.

"She's probably wearing the pudding," Sloane quipped.

He turned just in time to intercept as the kid projectile hurled. Linda Blair couldn't have done a finer job. And he stood corrected. *She* wasn't wearing the pudding. *He* was. The second time around.

JO SHOOK HER HEAD at the squeals coming from behind the bathroom door for the second time today. She'd braved the girl's bath time once before and it had proved a sobering, frightening experience. Screwing up her courage, she cracked open the door and stuck her head inside. She ducked as a wet sponge sailed past her cheek and squelched to the floor. Molly and Tara were in the bathtub together, splashing and creating general mayhem.

Sloane glanced at her from his perch by the tub, his hair wet and standing on end. From his soaked state, she'd hazard half the water in the bath had found him. He resembled a deer caught in headlights—certain he should do something but too immobilized by shock to take action.

Despite the appealing cling of his wet T-shirt and the unspoken plea for help in his green eyes, sanity and self-preservation led her to promptly abandon him to his small charges and close the door.

She wandered down the hall to Connor's room and

offered a perfunctory knock before letting herself in. Already ensconced in bed, he put his book and his glasses on the nightstand when she came in.

"Oh, hey, Aunt Jo. What're you still doing here?"

"Norrie and I thought we'd spend the night. Is that okay?" She and Nora were staying just to make sure Sloane Murphy knew what he was doing with the kids.

"Yeah. Sure."

Jo stood at the foot of Connor's bed. He looked so young and vulnerable in his big bed, wearing superhero pajamas. And more than a little down in the mouth.

"What's the matter Mr. Man?"

Connor squinted at the solar system mobile suspended from his ceiling. "Nothing."

"Nothing as in nothing or nothing as in…" She left the sentence open, hoping he'd finish it if he had something he needed to get off his thin, pajama-clad chest.

"Nothing as in nothing." He glanced at the clock on the wall. "Did you know that even though it's eight-thirty at night in Bogota, same as it is here, it's springtime there while it's fall here?"

"Is it now?" So, that accounted for the long face. Connor missed Cici and Max probably more than his extroverted sisters, but wasn't nearly as forthcoming with his feelings. Her heart ached for the desolate look in his cornflower-blue eyes.

"Yeah, it is."

"Well, ever since I was a little girl, I've known there was only one cure for a case of the nothings." Jo slowly maneuvered around the foot of the bed.

Connor's eyes began to gleam in answer to the teasing note in her voice. He clutched the covers fast beneath his chin and squirmed farther down the bed. "No, Aunt Jo," he protested weakly.

"That's right, Mr. Man. Prepare yourself." She held up her hands and wriggled her fingers. "The best thing for a case of the nothings is a tickle-a-thon." They each launched at one another with shrieks of anticipatory laughter.

Jo immediately went for Connor's tickle spot, just below his rib cage. Being younger, smaller and generally more wiley, he circumvented her fingers and tried to get to the area behind her knees. Jo fell on the bed and they rolled around. In mid-assault, Connor stopped.

What kind of sneaky diversionary tactic was he trying now? Breathless from laughing so hard, Jo poked her head out from beneath the covers. Sloane stood in the doorway, a hint of amusement and something more intense in his eyes. It was pretty hard to muster any dignity when you were rolled up in a sheet and your hair had taken on a life of its own. Unfortunately, sticking her head back under the covers and playing possum wasn't an option. Instead, Jo sat up, pushing her hair out of her face, unable to look away from him.

"Uh, yeah?"

Sloane glanced from Jo to Connor and back to Jo. "Lights out in five minutes, okay? It's important to stick to a schedule. Children need routine and constants in their life." He sounded as if he'd read a book and memorized parts of it. A hint of a smile softened the directive.

"Actually, recent studies have shown..."

Jo poked Connor in the ribs and cut him off. "No problem. We'll have his lights out in less than five minutes." She eyed Sloane's wet hair and damp clothes. "Are the girls in bed?"

"Tara's down for the count. Molly's picking out stories." Sloane stepped through the doorway and directed his attention to Connor. "Anything you need?"

"No, sir. I'm fine."

"Well, good night." The door closed behind him.

Jo flopped onto her back.

"Why'd you poke me, Aunt Jo?"

"Because regardless of the latest study, your light needs to be out in five minutes, Mr. Man."

Connor made a face but then dove across the mattress for the bedside lamp. "Actually, stay right there, Aunt Jo. I've added two constellations." Jo had given Connor a junior astronomy kit for his birthday when she'd discovered the subject interested him as much as it did her. He clicked the switch and plunged the room into darkness, except for the gallery of fluorescent stars on his ceiling.

Jo stared at the constellations glowing on the ceiling and felt Connor inch over until he snuggled at her side, his head nestled against her shoulder. "Can you tell which ones are new?"

She slipped one arm around him and pointed with the other. "Let's see Cassiopeia and…right there, Orion."

"Yep." She felt his smile against her shoulder and knew a moment of soul-deep contentment, watching the shimmer of fluorescent stars with Connor. This was as close as she'd ever come to having children. Cici had chosen motherhood. She had opted for career. For the first time, she questioned if she'd made the best choice.

"Aunt Jo?"

"Hmm?"

"I like Mr. Sloane."

Jo hid her surprise at his admission. Connor usually held his feelings close to the vest. "Do you?" She looked at him in the faint glow cast by a night-light.

"Well, he's okay." He shifted his attention from her probing gaze to his curtained window. "I wouldn't mind if he stayed instead of leaving like the rest of our nannies have."

She shifted onto her side and brushed her hand across his short cropping of blond hair. "I imagine that would be up to you, in large part. You might not want to repeat this morning's episode."

"Yeah, Mr. Sloane said he couldn't recommend the duct tape." He had the good grace to look sheepish. "He said we did a good job decorating his face, but he wished we'd picked a washable marker."

"Hmm. So is that why you want him to stay? Because he didn't yell at you?"

Connor traced a rocket ship on his sheet with his thumbnail. "I guess. I think he likes me."

Jo would've liked to jump in with the assurance that all of his nannies had liked him, but she'd never lied to him and she wouldn't begin now. She couldn't fathom loving any kids more than she did these three, but she also didn't have her head stuck in a pile of sand. In truth, Connor and his sisters had behaved like little monsters and driven all of their nannies away. Discipline seemed to be the only thing Cici denied her kids.

"If you think he does, it's probably true." Jo shifted off the bed and tucked him in.

"Yeah. Isn't it cool?" He snuggled deeper in his bed, and smiled sleepily.

"That is cool. 'Night, Mr. Man." She kissed the smooth down of his cheek and wrapped him in a soft hug.

"'Night, Aunt Jo."

She walked across the room and opened the door. "Sleep tight. Don't let the bedbugs bite."

She closed the door behind her, relieved he'd lost that desolate look. She'd peek in on the girls and then she'd meet with Sloane Murphy to see if she could put her niggling disquiet to bed, as well.

HER STEPS FLAGGED as she made her way down the hall to the nanny's suite.

She disliked confrontation. Cici thrived on drama, which accounted for all the scrapes she mired herself in. Not Jo. Jo liked everything to run smoothly. But Cici had charged her with overseeing the kids, and she wouldn't back down until she felt they were properly cared for. She sucked in a breath and knocked on Sloane's door.

He opened the door and finished tugging a dry T-shirt into place, offering her a teasing glimpse of that darn dragon hiding behind a smattering of dark hair on his flat belly. Her own belly felt all fluttery. In general, men simply did not affect her this way. Why this one, and why now? Her hormones and Cici had monumentally bad timing.

"What's wrong? Does one of the kids need me? Has anyone else barfed?" His green eyes reflected anxiety, not annoyance, as she'd anticipated.

But then again, he'd been surprisingly gracious when Tara had thrown up all over him and then again during the girl's bath time splashing bonanza. So, he was a nice guy. That still didn't prove competence.

"No. Everyone's okay. But we need to talk."

He stepped back and to the side. Jo looked past him but didn't comply with his unspoken invitation. Cici had decorated the bedroom and sitting room with a woman in mind. A very frilly, fussy woman. Gold and cream brocade overlaid with cherubs—wishful thinking—covered the bed and swathed the windows. Gilded Louis-the-something-or-other furniture with spindly legs littered the room. She didn't belong in this room, but neither did

Sloane Murphy. The overtly feminine decor emphasized his masculinity to an almost unbearable degree.

She was acutely conscious of the width of his shoulders straining against the white cotton of his T-shirt; the faint stubble shadowing the flat planes of his face and rugged line of his jaw; the worn denim riding low on his hips; and the sprinkling of dark hair on his bare feet. Sequestering herself in a bedroom with him didn't seem the smartest move.

"Why don't we meet in the library?"

"As long as you promise to not tie me up and cut off my clothes." His edgy smile tripped her up.

Such a thought would never have occurred to her. Unfortunately, the power of suggestion played out the scene in her mind....

"I think I can manage to restrain myself." She sounded far more confident than she felt.

"When do you want to get together?"

The man played havoc with her equilibrium. It had to be a combination of Nora's constant sexual harping, her own errant hormones, and having seen him in a partial state of undress twice in one day. She, Josephina Wilhelmina Calhoun, was not given to these flights of suggestive fancy. She didn't find it a comfortable fit.

"How about now?" She just wanted to get this over with and retreat to the guest room. A little yoga and a shower would set her to rights.

"I'll be right down."

Jo didn't wait for him. She hurried down the stairs, taking advantage of the time away from him to marshal her wayward thoughts. A flick of the switch by the door bathed the library in soft, recessed light, leaving the room with a far more intimate feel than it had earlier today. Jo promptly turned on the lamp between the matching leather chairs in an effort to dispel the cozy privacy of the shelf-lined room. A harvest moon offered further illumination as its light slanted through the mullioned panes of the French doors leading to the veranda.

She stared at a row of books without seeing any of the titles. Some internal alarm tripped her sensory switch the instant Sloane stepped into the room, even without the snick of the well-oiled door closing behind him. She turned to face him.

Shoes. He'd slipped on a pair of deck shoes before coming downstairs. That's what he'd stopped to put on. Jo took a deep breath, unintentionally inhaling his male scent. She whooshed out the air, as if she could rid herself of this attraction to him that easily.

"Mind if I sit down?" he asked rhetorically as he dropped into one of the chairs.

"Go ahead." The quicker she spit this out, the quicker they could go their separate ways. "I think I can safely speak for Cici and Max when I say encouraging the children to belch and then ranking them is inappropriate, Mr. Murphy." She faced him from across the room, separated by the thick, wool carpet.

He leaned forward, bracing well-developed forearms on his knees. A slow heat curled through her and she struggled to bring her attention back to the matter at hand. "Did you ever wonder why your nephew spearheaded such an aggressive game today? Wrapping me in duct tape isn't a normal kid's game. But I'm guessing it's pretty run of the mill for Connor. And it's gotten worse lately, hasn't it?"

Sloane's insight took her by surprise. From recent conversations with her sister, she realized Connor's "pranks" *had* escalated in the past month or so. "Yes, it has."

"I didn't ask him why he'd done it. That's obvious. I asked Connor why he was so angry. Any idea what he told me?"

"Uh, no." She hadn't even recognized his anger. Her oversight left her feeling more than a little inept that it had taken a total stranger to point out what she should have seen.

"A group of kids at school call him a sissy."

"What? Why didn't he talk to anyone about this? Our family sticks together. If one of us has a problem, we all have a problem. Pardon my bluntness, but why would Connor confide in you?" Perplexity, not resentment, drove her thought processes.

A shrug rippled an impressive number of muscles beneath his T-shirt. "He said he tried to talk to his dad, but his dad never has time." If he felt any censure, he didn't show it. His expression remained impassive. "And as for you or his mom, I don't know. Maybe he wanted a guy's input."

His explanation sat uncomfortably on her shoulders, but she recognized the truth. "That makes sense. Max is a good guy, but he spends most of his time empire-building. I still wish Connor had confided in me or Cici."

Once again Sloane shrugged, setting off another byplay of muscle. "He and I talked. He's a pretty smart kid. He said he doesn't really care what they think, but he's tired of hearing it—he wants to shut them up."

"Okay?"

"Connor came up with a plan. He figures a few good belches will shut them up. I figure it's worth a try."

Absolutely, positively, a guy thing, 'cause she didn't understand. "Only Connor could concoct such a scheme. He's going to belch them into submission? That's a classic."

Sloane leaned back in the chair and smiled. "It's brilliant. Few things carry more weight with young boys than an outstanding expulsion of gas."

It was certainly innovative. She'd give them that. A snicker or two escaped her. "Thank goodness he decided on belching as opposed to..."

His smile segued to a grin that crinkled his eyes at the corners. "Really, Ms. Calhoun, I'm shocked."

"Don't be, Mr. Murphy. I've lived next to Nora for over ten years. I'm fairly conservative, but I'm not a prude. And I've never shocked anyone unless you count the time I refused to dissect a frog in biology. But that wasn't really shocking, just good sense." She also didn't normally babble but his smile reduced her to mindless mush.

His green gaze pierced her to the core, leaving her feeling vulnerable and more than a little exposed. She shifted her back against the bookcase, but didn't look away from the intensity of his gaze. The flare of desire she read in his eyes quickened her pulse. Jamaica could've been here and now. The thick carpet beneath her feet became shifting sand. The lazy whir of the ceiling fan was a warm breeze blowing in from the exotic expanse of the Caribbean. The muted light was the tropical sun filtered through a canopy of towering palms. Jamaica or Georgia? Did anything really matter outside of the primordial attraction swirling between them?

Without a word, Sloane pushed himself out of the chair and crossed the rug. He placed one hand on the bookcase behind her. Awareness arrowed through her, heightened her senses. The recessed lighting shadowed his eyes, but threw the lower half of his face into stark relief—his stubbled jaw, the slight cleft in his square chin, the line of his lips, and the fading ink marks. The slow, measured rhythm of his breathing whispered a seductive promise. Even without contact, his heat wrapped around her. No aftershave masked his clean, male fragrance.

Jo could've easily sidestepped away from him. If she'd wanted to. She didn't. She wanted to test the silkiness of his hair against her fingertips, taste the pleasure of his mouth, and absorb the heat and strength of his body against hers. She, who had never shocked anyone, stunned herself with her salacious desire.

He raised his other hand to grasp the shelf on the other side of her. It was a confinement as much her own making as his.

"And for the record—" he leaned forward until she saw herself reflected in the soft green of his eyes and felt the feathering of his breath against her face "—I'm strictly heterosexual."

Even with her senses heightened and the tension thrumming between them, she rationalized her options. He attracted her. In all probability, he appealed to her as an unknown. One kiss. One concession to Jamaica. It would serve as an indulgence and a cure. Her fingers curled against his T-shirt, the supple cotton warm from his body heat. A matching heat spiraled though her. Inexorably, she tugged him closer until his breath became her own. "I know."

The last word lost itself against the hard line of his mouth. She enjoyed the touch of his lips against hers, the faint scrape of his beard against her face, but a marked lack of fireworks quelled her ardor. Mission accomplished. Time to retreat. She released his T-shirt and ended the kiss, her equilibrium restored. That had been pleasant enough, although mildly disappointing considering the sensory hype.

"Now it's my turn."

"Turnabout's fair play." Her voice was even. She'd taken a kiss. Now he'd take his.

He bracketed her shoulders in his hands, moving the pads of his thumbs in small circles against the fabric of her shirt. She shivered at his light but sure touch. "Ah, but sometimes fair play isn't the best play." What could've easily sounded threatening, came out as a sexy promise. A slight tug from Sloane brought them toe to toe, thigh to thigh, and chest to breast, leaving her tingling and eager for more.

She tilted her head slightly upward, indicating her willingness to play. His mouth descended and rained a series of teasing kisses upon her lips. Each nip and taste stoked the heat building inside her until she moaned her impatience for more. He took everything she offered and then asked for more with the relentless slant of his mouth against hers.

Logic abandoned her to the storm that swept through her. Jo opened herself to closer contact. Sloane groaned into her mouth, his tongue meeting hers in a game of pursuit and surrender. She tugged his shirt from his jeans, desperate for the touch of his skin against hers. Thought ceased to exist as sensation ran rampant.

Cupping her buttocks in the palms of his hands, he pulled her tighter against him. Jo welcomed his hard ridge against the apex of her thighs. Finding no relief for the consuming need that manifested itself in her wet heat, she tugged his hips closer in a fervent quest.

The resonating gong of the doorbell brought a return to reason. Jo reluctantly pulled away, her breath coming in ragged gasps. The rapid rise and fall of Sloane's chest told its own story.

"I'd better see who's at the door before the bell wakes

up the kids." Her voice sounded as shaky as her legs felt.

Sloane shook his head as if to clear it. "No, let me. It's late for visitors."

Jo glanced at the impressive thrust of the soft denim covering his crotch. "You're not in the best shape to answer the door."

The mouth that had so recently rocked her world with just a kiss, thinned in resolve. "I don't care what shape I'm in. It's late, and as far as anyone knows, Mr. and Mrs. Cheltham aren't home. You wait here." Before she could answer, he stalked out, leaving the library door open behind him.

Jo should have protested his high-handed, macho-male manner. She really should have. And she might have raised more of a ruckus, if she hadn't seriously doubted her ability to walk. She managed to cross the room and to drop into one of the chairs. How odd to have someone taking care of her. It held a strange measure of comfort.

Nora's voice echoed in the foyer. "Weren't asleep, were you? I locked myself out on the veranda. Thanks for letting me in." Even after twenty years of kicking the habit, Nora still occasionally sneaked outside for an illicit smoke. "Goodness me. That must've been some dream. Sorry to get you up. Good night, now." Of course Nora would notice his arousal. And of course she'd comment on it.

She let out the breath she'd held when Nora's footsteps continued up the stairs without checking out the open library door. Jo focused on her yoga breathing exercises to restore her composure. Too bad she hadn't theorized impotency.

3

SLOANE TOSSED the wet towel onto the bathroom floor and pulled on a pair of briefs. Nothing like a cold shower to get his head back where it belonged.

He'd made a supreme ass of himself over Jo Calhoun. He had no business approaching her in the library. He knew she hadn't thought he was gay. That had been apparent in the way she'd looked at him when she'd come by his room to summon him. No, he'd used the issue as an excuse. He should never have let her kiss him. And he'd damn sure made a mistake kissing her back. What the hell was wrong with him?

If Nora hadn't rung the doorbell when she had, he wouldn't have given them another five minutes until they wrestled one another to the floor and finished what he'd started. They'd been combustible.

God, what was it about her? She didn't boast beauty or a great body—usually two sure magnets. She was snippy, aloof, sarcastic. He didn't particularly like her. And he'd hazard she felt the same about him. But something in her tugged at him as steady and strong as the undertow accompanying the tide. And it was just as dangerous.

Sloane recalled the high-stakes lesson of Charlie Gallagher. Gallagher had been a great undercover cop until he'd gotten emotionally involved with a suspect. He'd blown his cover, leaving one cop dead and Gallagher stripped of his badge.

Jo's sister could be involved in his case up to her eyeballs. His job demanded he discover the truth and bring the culprits to justice. "Doing" one of the suspect's sister in the library wasn't part of the deal. He wouldn't repeat tonight's mistake.

Against all rationale and reason, he wanted to. And he had the ache to prove it.

He sat on the side of the bed, not bothering to pull back the blankets. Exhaustion sent him flopping onto his back. Keeping up with those kids had damn near killed him today. He'd been bound, gagged, markered, had his shirt cut off, annihilated his professional reputation, had his sexuality questioned, changed numerous diapers, played father confessor and counselor to a young boy, prepared dinner, been puked on, bathed three kids, read bedtime stories, and his day wasn't over yet. In a couple of hours, when Jo and Nora were asleep, he'd check out Cheltham's office.

How much did nannies make? He didn't have a clue, but it couldn't possibly be enough.

When he mustered the energy, he'd sit up and make a note that Vic should nominate Gladys for canonization. The poor woman had seven kids. She was either a saint or insane. Maybe a little of both.

Jo TWISTED in the sheet for the umpteenth time. Frustrated, she punched the pillow in an effort to make herself more comfortable. Sleep played an important role in her life. She loved to sleep. She embraced it. She required at least seven hours to maintain a semblance of civility. Sleep never eluded her.

Jo couldn't sleep.

She checked the clock by the bed. Eleven fifty-five glowed in the dark. A whopping five minutes since she'd last looked. She couldn't get comfortable. She couldn't relax. She rolled onto her other side and cursed Sloane Murphy. She was too restless, almost feverish. And he'd done this to her with just one kiss. None of it made sense.

She didn't trust him. She'd witnessed his kindness to the children, but he also bordered on inept. He resented her being here. Sloane Murphy was hiding something. Something about him didn't ring true.

However, the hungry way he'd devoured her mouth hadn't been a lie. Nor had he faked his jutting response. Hours later and no longer caught up in the throes of a passionate kiss, Jo continued to feel out of control. She felt like a spring wound too tight. On edge. Dysfunctional.

A faint cry sounded in the quiet. Had she imagined the noise? No, there it was again, only louder and longer. Within seconds, it gained momentum. Tara.

Jo waited. Any second now, Tara would quiet when Sloane checked on her. Seconds dragged by, and still the baby cried. Jo threw off her covers, concerned Tara might feel abandoned.

She crossed the landing that linked hers and Nora's rooms, on the other side of the house, with the children's bedrooms. Just as she reached Tara's room, Connor appeared, holding the baby. Tara continued to wail.

He passed her over to Jo. Jo tried crooning. Jostling. Bouncing. Nothing worked. She didn't know how to soothe her niece. She knew how to play with the kids. She knew how to spoil them in typical aunt fashion. Only she didn't know squat about taking care of them. But she knew someone who supposedly did.

She thrust Tara toward Connor. "Hold her while I get help."

She didn't stop to knock on Sloane's door, but burst in. She paused while her eyes adjusted to the dark and the dim glow of a hall night-light penetrated the inky black. Sloane lay stretched on top of the bed, close to naked save a pair of briefs, sleeping like a baby. But that was the problem. The baby wasn't sleeping.

She approached the bed and called to him. "Sloane. Sloane, wake up."

He mumbled in his sleep and rolled his head in the other direction. So far, she'd spent her night tossing and turning because of him. He could've at least had the common decency to lose some sleep, as well. And now she had a crying baby to contend with and she was at a loss. Jo didn't like being at a loss.

She stepped between his outstretched legs, terribly aware of the expanse of bare, sinewed chest and the lean lines of muscular thighs in front of her. Even though she appreciated the view, she'd appreciate her niece finding solace more. She took another step and poked him in the chest. Hard. "Wake up, Sloane."

His eyes flickered open. In that instant, before comprehension displaced sleep, he smiled sexily and reached for her. "Hey, baby."

Wrong time. Wrong place. Wrong woman? Had he mistaken her for someone else? She backed out of his reach.

Reality dawned before he made contact. "What's wrong?" He sat up on the edge of the bed.

"Tara's crying."

"I hear that." He dropped back to the mattress. "Make her stop."

"I've tried. I don't know how." He must still be half asleep. "That's your job," she reminded him as she grabbed his hands and tugged. "Get up."

Sloane sat up again. This time he shook his head, as if to clear it. "What's wrong with her?"

"If I knew, I wouldn't be in here, would I?"

His look assessed her quickly but thoroughly, making her aware of the short nightgown she'd borrowed from Cici's closet. His brows met in a frown. "Unfortunately, I don't think you would."

Jo moved aside, out of the dim but illuminating light from the hall.

Sloane stood and grabbed a pair of jeans from the floor at the foot of the bed. Jo should've looked away. Looking away was the decent, respecting-his-privacy thing to do. Instead, she chose a most un-Jo-like path and watched—ogled, to be more precise—the impressive display as he tugged worn denim over his lean flanks and a cotton T-shirt over his broad shoulders.

Sloane started toward the door. Jo followed. "Didn't the former nanny brief you on the kids?"

"Yeah, it was very brief. She wished me good luck and walked out." Sloane tossed the answer over his shoulder.

Connor met them in the hallway. He eagerly gave up his screaming charge. "I've got to get some sleep. I've got school tomorrow."

Sloane held Tara on his shoulder and awkwardly patted her back. A resounding belch echoed in the hall.

"Ten." Connor and Sloane spoke in unison. Connor grinned sleepily as he stumbled back to his bedroom.

Gas? All that ruckus for gas? Sloane definitely had a way with the children.

JO GAVE UP pretending sleep would come. The house had settled back into quiet. Apparently Sloane had put Tara back into her crib without further mishap.

Jo had returned to her bed. However, instead of the welcome relief of slumber, she was cursed with reliving those few seconds when he'd reached for her, greeting her like a lover. Jo, supreme commander of her own mind, couldn't dispel the scene or the unfamiliar throb of sexual tension he'd awakened in her. She'd even resorted to mentally singing "Ninety-Nine Bottles of Beer on the Wall." By the seventy-third bottle she'd realized the futility.

She had a particularly challenging bit of software she'd been working on last Friday. Even though she'd planned her vacation time away from the company, work always took her mind off of everything else because it tended to consume her. She'd use Max's computer to dial into her P.C. A difficult round of programming logic would set her to rights. Or, at the least, she'd accomplish more than writhing around in bed alone.

Jo slid out from under the covers. Barefoot, she crossed the landing and made her way down the stairs. Max's office sat adjacent to the back of the house, linked by a passageway off the mudroom of the kitchen. She tried to remember the code for the doors on either end of the passageway. You'd think he ran Fort Knox instead of a shipping business.

Moving cautiously, she navigated the long, dark hallway to the kitchen without mishap. She entered a series of numbers into the lighted keypad and the doorknob clicked beneath her hand. She stepped into the passageway.

Running lights similar to those on airline aisles saved the space from total darkness. The mudroom door closed behind her with a muffled thud. The doors closed automatically, ensuring the door to Max's office was never left open.

She walked the short passageway. She entered the code on the next keypad and pushed against the knob. The door swung open. She stepped forward, then stopped. How odd! The green glow from the computer monitor illuminated the room eerily. Max and Cici had left this morning. Why would his computer be on? And why wouldn't a screen saver be up instead of a ledger?

The door swung behind her, catching her shoulder as it closed. Jo pitched forward, her arms flailing in a vain attempt to right herself.

The edge of Max's desk rushed to meet her head. She had time for one thought—this was going to hurt. And it did. Until she sank into dark oblivion.

"NOW, TELL ME HOW YOU got that whopper on your head in the middle of the night." Nora settled an ice bag over the goose egg nesting on Jo's forehead, and plunked herself down on the opposite side of the bed.

"I'm not sure what happened. I couldn't sleep, so I thought I'd dial into my P.C. from Max's computer. You know those doors are weighted and on a timer?"

"Yeah?" Forget about the doors being weighted and timed. Nora took note that Jo couldn't sleep. Nothing ever came between her granddaughter and sleep. But then again, this particular granddaughter had never been caught in the throes of good, old-fashioned sexual tension. Nora had said three Hail Marys and a hallelujah that Jo had finally met a man who could shake her up a little. Indulging in a little post-dinner smoke, she'd seen Jo and the nanny lip locking in the library as if there was no tomorrow. She'd tried to wait them out, but finally had to ring the doorbell. Aging in general was one big pain in the derriere, but this incontinence business was a bitch.

She realized she'd missed Jo's reply. "Sorry, dear. What'd you say?"

"I didn't move in time, and the door caught the back of my shoulder when it closed. I couldn't catch myself before I hit the edge of the desk."

"You know about those doors. Why'd you stop in the doorway?" Nora quizzed her, positive Jo hadn't told all.

Jo hesitated, as if she doubted her facts. "I stopped just past the doorway because I'd expected the room to be dark, but it wasn't. Would Max leave town and not turn his computer off? And instead of a screen saver, his ledger was up on the monitor."

Nora waved her hand, annoyed. "I don't get all that computer mumbo jumbo. Give it to me in plain English."

"The whole computer thing is odd. Especially since the ledger was gone when I woke up." Jo shifted the ice pack on her knot. "Maybe Max dialed in from Bogota. It's the only reason I can think of that would make the screen change after I passed out."

Nora still didn't understand the computer thing but Jo seemed to think it was a big deal. The real big deal, in Nora's opinion, was Jo had finally met her match in Sloane Murphy. She felt it in her bones. But given half the chance, Jo would skedaddle back home and things would fizzle out between her and Sloane before they ever got a chance. Jo had planned a week off in Jamaica. Whether she knew it or not, what she was looking for was right here, staring her in the face. Nora just needed to keep her there long enough to figure it out.

"That's probably what happened, dear. But maybe we should stay a few days, until things settle down. You've already arranged the time off from work."

"I can work here from my laptop. I'll pick it up tomorrow. If Max plans to dial in, I can't tie up his line." Jo stifled a yawn.

Nora pulled out a deck of cards. "Forget going to sleep. With a bump like that on your noggin, you've got to stay awake." She shuffled the deck with the skill of a Vegas dealer. "Name your game."

"Great. I couldn't sleep earlier. Now you won't let me." Jo sat up straighter. "Rummy. Go ahead and deal."

Nora beamed. She knew exactly what had kept Jo awake earlier. And she loved a good game of rummy.

4

A WET WARMTH permeated his layers of sleep, dragging Sloane into reluctant consciousness. He winced as he opened his eyes, momentarily disoriented at finding himself in a rocking chair in Tara's room. His neck had a hell of a crick in it, but things like that happened when you fell asleep in a chair instead of a bed. And he wasn't even one step closer to getting the goods on Cheltham.

Tara squished in his lap and smiled up into his face.

"Morning, miss." Funny. He'd never been around kids. His parents considered him "an accident" from which they'd never quite recovered. Absorbed in one another, they hadn't made room for anyone else. They'd never encouraged him to bring other kids home with him. It wasn't until he joined the police force that he found a sense of belonging and family.

But he'd never gained any experience with kids. They were foreign territory he'd never wanted to explore. Only this one almost made him forget about the pain in his neck.

He smiled at his small charge.

Tara rewarded him by flinging her diaper past his head.

"Hey, you're s'posed to wear that—" Sloane stopped in midsentence. One dry diaper off of one baby's bare butt accounted for his warm, wet feeling. The blue denim on his left thigh was distinctly darker than the rest of his jeans. So far, she'd thrown up on him and peed on him, which only left....

Sloane quickly deposited Tara on the floor and stood from his cramped position in the rocker. Muscles he hadn't thought about in years protested. Quite a feat, considering he worked out at the gym on a regular basis.

Molly wandered into Tara's room, trailing a worn blanket behind her. "Uh-oh. You had a naccident."

Only this assignment so far. "Morning, Molly. I didn't have an accident. Your sister did."

"It's okay. I have naccidents, too." She lowered her voice. "But you shouldn't blame it on Tara. Mama says that's when you get in trouble. You got to take sponsobility for your own nactions."

"She took off her diaper." Once again he'd reduced himself to arguing with a three-year-old.

"That's 'cause they feel icky. I used to wear 'em and they feel icky when they're wet." Molly spoke with the supreme authority of one who'd been diaper free for at least a year.

Sloane could vouch firsthand for the "icky" cling of wet clothes. He needed to change out of his jeans. He ran his hand over his bristled jaw. In fact, a shower and a shave sounded pretty good.

He stepped out into the hall with Tara and Molly in tow and literally bumped into Jo. He grabbed her arm to steady them both, a surge of attraction arrowing through him at the feel of her warm flesh beneath his palm. A purple knot the size of a handball stared back at him from the center of her forehead. Dark circles shadowed her eyes.

"What happened to you? You look like hell."

"Hell's a bad word. You said hell. You're not s'posed

to say hell.'' Molly admonished him before Jo could answer.

Concern and surprise at her appearance had caused his careless tongue. ''Heck. I meant heck. Sorry.'' He looked back to Jo for an answer. She *did* look like hell.

''You don't exactly look so hot yourself this morning.'' She scowled, which elicited a wince. ''I tripped and hit my head. Then Nora felt compelled to keep me up all night playing rummy. According to her, she wanted to make sure I didn't have a concussion. I think it's because she wanted to play rummy. So, I knocked the dickens out of my head and I've had no sleep.''

And she was in a primo bad mood. He almost asked her if she was sure about the PMS thing but mustered enough brains cells to not go there.

''What'd you hit to give yourself a knot like that?'' He strove for the right mixture of sympathy and concern to get an answer to a question he had no right to ask.

''I hit the corner of Max's desk. The office doors close automatically and I didn't move quickly enough.'' She touched the big knot on her forehead.

Damn. He should've been snooping around in Cheltham's office instead of snoozing the night away. And just why was Jo prowling around Cheltham's office after midnight last night? No amount of concern and sympathy would allow him to get away with asking that question.

He'd noticed the keypad yesterday in the mudroom. The doors closed automatically? Yet, Jo had access. Cheltham's wife was perhaps part of this. Maybe Jo, as well. Hadn't Jo told him last night that the family stuck together through thick and thin? Did that extend to criminal activity?

''You gots a big boo-boo, Aunt Jo. Did you cry? Does

it hurt bad?'' Molly asked, her lower lip trembling. Aunt Jo ranked high in her affections.

Jo squatted to the girls' level, wrapping her arms around them. "Don't cry, peanuts. Aunt Jo's fine. It only hurts a little, and it already feels a whole lot better than it did."

Still sporting a frown of concern, Molly dug in her nose for inspiration. She turned her face up to Sloane, having found it. "Mr. Sloane can kiss it and make it better."

Jo looked as if Molly'd just suggested Chinese water torture. Well, she could lose the pained look. Kissing her last night had shown poor judgment. While it hadn't done anything to advance his investigation, it had muddled his mind. He didn't plan to repeat the mistake, even under the directive of a miniature dictator. And why would he want to kiss some lump on a prickly pear of a woman, anyway?

"No, that's okay." Her face flushed. The red, combined with her purple goose egg, lent her a rainbow appearance.

Molly's mouth set in a straight, obstinate line. "It needs a kiss. Kisses always makes boo-boos better."

"Why don't *you* kiss it? That'd sure make it feel better," Jo suggested.

Sloan's ego took a beating at the desperation tinging her voice. She certainly hadn't objected to him kissing her last night.

"Okay." Molly slopped a wet one in the vicinity of Jo's forehead. Tara copied her sister.

"Thanks, sweet pies. That's just what I needed." Jo stood, her hand trailing affectionately over the top of their heads. "What happened to Tara's diaper?"

If she hadn't noticed his peed-upon thigh, he wasn't

going to point it out. The Cheltham kids and adult dignity
didn't exactly go hand in hand. "Don't ask."

With a display of obstinacy any mule might envy,
Molly turned to Sloane. "Okay, it's your turn. A
growned-up kiss is what really makes it better."

Sloane didn't think so. Jo obviously didn't want his
kiss, which was fine, because he didn't want to kiss her.
Did he? "Oh, I think it already looks much better."

Molly's big brown eyes filled with tears. "Aunt Jo-
Jo's never gonna get better cause you won't kiss her boo-
boo." A series of sniffles followed her proclamation.
Tears began to flow down her cheeks. Tara joined the
sob squad.

They wailed in unison as if he'd stomped on their tiny
hearts. He'd collared some of the most hardened criminals you might care *not* to meet. He'd engaged in skirmishes in the marines. But the fact that two little girls
stood bawling their eyes out and he was partially responsible—well, that just about did him in.

Jo attempted to console the girls. They wailed louder.
With a sigh of resignation, she stepped closer to him.
"For goodness' sake, just kiss the stinking thing," she
lowered her voice, "or at least pretend to, if it'll make
them stop crying."

Who'd have thought such little lungs could generate so
much noise? But then again, who'd have thought that one
adult woman who'd shown so much enthusiasm last night,
could show so much reluctance now? He cupped Jo's
shoulders and pulled her to him, the soft feel of her at
odds with her sharp tone. He'd just get close enough that
the girls would think he'd kissed her. Or so he intended.

The warmth of her skin lured him beyond intent. His
lips nuzzled against the velvet smoothness of her fore-

head, wisps of her hair teasing his skin. He lingered longer than he should have and only released her when she pulled unsteadily away from him. He recognized confusion in the depths of her caramel-flecked eyes. Apparently she found their chemistry as confounding as he did.

The crying continued. ''They're so busy crying, they missed it.'' She tapped Molly on the shoulder. ''Look, honey. Mr. Sloane's going to kiss it now.''

He repeated his performance. Miraculously, the wailing stopped and the tears dried up.

''I tol' you that would make it better,'' Molly crowed in triumph.

Realization dawned. He'd just witnessed junior manipulation in its finest form.

Kid Number Three opened his bedroom door and stumbled bleary-eyed into the hall. ''I overslept. I have to leave for school in thirty minutes and it's our turn for car pool this morning.''

Half an hour? No problem. Sloane could easily shave and shower in half that time.

Molly tugged at the dry leg of his jeans. ''Mr. Sloane, I'm hungry.''

Tara toddled over. ''Food. Food. Food.'' Or, to the best of his ability to decipher her baby babble, that's what it sounded like. At any rate, her chant could become a tirade at any moment.

Molly continued to tug. ''Can we have chocolate cake for breakfast? Please. Pretty please, with sprinkles on top.''

''Cake. Cake. Cake.'' Tara circled him, her chant for food taking on an urgency.

''I need a favor,'' Jo shouted over the ongoing cake-for-breakfast lobby. ''I actually came to beg a lift. My car won't start this morning. Connor's school is halfway to my house. I need to swing by and pick up my laptop and some clothes.''

''Some clothes and your laptop?'' he parroted with a sinking feeling.

''Yep.'' She smiled a challenge his way. ''Nora and I have decided to stay for a visit. Maybe a week or so.''

Chocolate cake momentarily forgotten, Molly danced a little jig. ''Yeah. Aunt Jo-Jo and Norrie for a whole week. Cool.''

Tara joined in the dance.

Oh, yeah, cool. Real cool. Downright peachy.

He mustered a smile, ''No problem.''

An entire week of having Jo underfoot, messing up his investigation and his mind.

''We can't be late this morning. There's a big test first thing,'' Connor informed him, as if he doubted Sloane's efficiency. He eyed his sisters. ''None of us is even dressed. And we haven't had breakfast, either.''

Tara leaped back onto the breakfast wagon with a vengeance. ''Cake. Cake. Cake.''

Molly burst into tears, abject misery written on her small features. ''I had a naccident.''

Sure enough, a little puddle marked the carpet between her feet.

Connor yelled above all of it, ''We'll get zeros on our tests if we're late. We can't be late. I have to maintain an A-average to belong to the finance club.''

Sloane met Jo's eyes above the sea of tiny-mite-generated pandemonium. He read the challenge in her brown eyes.

He squared his shoulders and scooped up a dripping toddler under one arm and a diaper-free cake fiend under the other. Surprise silenced both the girls. He instructed

Jo and Connor, ''Meet me at the garage at seven-thirty. We'll have breakfast on the way. You won't be late.''

He wished he felt as confident in his promise as they'd looked. And they'd both looked pretty damn skeptical.

''YOU'RE THE NEW NANNY? And the children are skipping breakfast?'' Mrs. Price, the housekeeper/cook glanced from Sloane to the girls to the steaming bowls of oatmeal in the breakfast nook.

Jo hung back in the hallway, not feeling the least bit guilty about eavesdropping. Sloane wasn't exactly the poster boy for nannies. He'd thrown on a pair of khakis and a polo shirt, but he hadn't shaved and one piece of dark hair stood straight up on top of his head. Unfortunately for her hormonal state, he looked sexy and slightly disheveled. But he didn't look as if he should be taking care of three small children.

Molly and Tara didn't do much to improve Mrs. Price's first impression of Sloane. Molly still sported a morning rat nest on the back of her head that could house her mouse Hermes and a number of his rodent friends. Tara's hair obviously hadn't seen a brush, either. Tara wore a pink shirt—inside out—with red-checked shorts. Molly sported a turquoise shirt scattered with orange frogs over a pair of shorts tie-dyed in pastel colors. She wore the shirt backward. Did all of Sloane's former charges look like little fashion refugees? Cici—given her slavish devotion to clothes and style—would have a heart attack!

Sloane flashed Mrs. Price a disarming smile that planted a dimple square in the center of his left cheek. Lord, the man had oodles of charm when he chose to. ''Yes, ma'am, I was sent by the Nurturing Nannies Network. Breakfast looks wonderful. Maybe the girls can have it for a snack today.''

Mrs. Price appeared appropriately charmed. Jo couldn't watch an ''Andy Griffith Show'' rerun on late-night TV without thinking of Mrs. Price every time she saw Aunt Bea. Except Aunt Bea never simpered at a man the way Mrs. Price was doing now.

Tara stuck out her tongue at the cooling, congealing oatmeal on the table and expressed herself with a rude sound, ''Plllt.''

''I hate awfulmeal.'' Molly expounded on the subject.

Jo had to throw her vote in with the girls. She'd rather skip the oatmeal altogether.

Sloane jumped in as Mrs. Price's lips quivered at having her breakfast maligned. ''Girls, we'll talk about it later. Mrs. P., I'll try to get a better grip on the schedule from here on out. Maybe if you help me...'' Another one of his lethal smiles and Gwen Price turned to putty.

Connor chose that moment to tear down the hall, tucking his shirt into his pants as he ran. ''Come on, Aunt Jo.''

Sloane hustled them all toward the door. Mrs. Price suddenly noticed Jo. ''Goodness, what happened to you? Can I get you some ice?''

Jo lacked the time and inclination to relay the story one more time. And until she found out exactly what had happened in Max's office, keeping quiet seemed the best course. ''I slipped and hit my head. Nora's upstairs asleep. We'll be staying over for several days.''

Mrs. Price appeared momentarily nonplussed, but quickly recovered. ''Very well.''

She'd detected Sloane's lack of enthusiasm regarding her and Nora's decision to stay earlier today. Mrs. Price, too, had been perturbed until she masked it. This was getting weird: First she takes one heck of a tumble and then her car won't start. Had the door caught her between the shoulders last night or had she surprised someone in Max's office? A shiver chased down her spine. Things were getting curiouser and curiouser. And she wasn't going anywhere until she had some answers.

SLOANE PULLED AWAY from the red light and accelerated down the tree-lined avenue. The late-model, high-end SUV handled with surprising ease.

"You might want to slow down through here," Jo cautioned him. She'd climbed in next to him on the passenger seat. Tara and Molly squabbled over jelly donuts in the center seats, giving Connor and his car pool buddies the rear. Having Jo share the front with him lent the whole situation a surreal sense of family—a great big family. She even sounded like a wife, telling him how to drive. It didn't annoy him nearly as much as it should have.

"It'll be fine. Those boys can't be late for their test." He shouldn't have ever let her talk him into going through the drive-thru for a dozen jelly-filled doughnuts. He should've just kept driving, so he could drop Connor and his buddies at school and get back to the Cheltham estate and his investigation. But no, one genuine smile from Aunt Jo and he'd wheeled into the drive-thru.

"If we can just beat this light, we'll make all the rest." He sped up. He'd caught every red light since they'd picked up the last kid.

Blue lights flashed in his rearview mirror, the wail of a siren piercing the chaos in the SUV. Sloane swallowed a curseword and glanced over at Jo as he pulled onto the right-hand shoulder of the road.

She didn't laugh outright, but there was a distinct

gleam in her brown eyes. ''I don't think you're going to beat the light.''

At least she'd brought along a sense of humor.

Sloane groaned at the number on the squad car behind him. Blakely. Anyone but Blakely. What had he done to deserve this cursed streak of bad luck? Sloane rolled down his window and waited.

''I don't want the policemens to take Mr. Sloane to jail,'' Molly wailed from the middle seat.

''They won't take me to jail, honey,'' he reassured her.

''They'll take you instead,'' Connor threatened. He and his buddies dissolved into a snickering fit.

''Connor....''

There wasn't time for more. Blakely approached the vehicle, already writing on his clipboard, ''Sir, do you know how fast—'' He stopped in midsentence when he recognized Sloane. If Blakely grinned any bigger, he'd hurt himself. ''Ah, Mr. Murphy, we meet again. Glad to see you're not wearing duct tape today.''

Sloane handed over his driver's license and the vehicle papers without comment. Being a smart aleck with Blakely wouldn't accomplish anything.

''Thirteen miles over the posted speed limit. I'd say you wore your lead shoes this morning.''

Beside him, Jo made a choking noise. Well, she could go ahead and laugh. Blakely looked past him and sent a smarmy smile Jo's way. Jeez, he hated those guys who thought you had to see each one of their teeth when they smiled. ''Hello, ma'am. We've got to stop meeting this way.''

And she smiled back at him. Sloane had worked damn hard to get past her cool demeanor and now she beamed at Blakely's cornball comment. And just when she'd been sounding so wifely to him earlier. Sloane recalled a locker room discussion on Blakely's recent divorce.

"If we could get a move on..." Sloane interrupted. He had to get the kids to school. Let Blakely make goo-goo eyes on his own time.

Wrapping up his comedic routine, Blakely returned Sloane's papers, along with a speeding ticket. Sloane checked the dashboard clock. The delay hadn't helped, but he still might make it.

Molly and Tara leaned over the back of his seat. "One, three, four. Go!"

Suddenly two blobs of raspberry jelly dripped down Blakely's uniform front.

"Go, Mr. Sloane. Make your getsaway before the bad man 'rests you," Molly screeched into his ear as she and Tara fired off two additional rounds of jelly.

In absolute honesty, Sloane could've halted the attack, but he also figured Blakely deserved it. Sort of. Let him get a taste, no pun intended, of what these kids were capable of.

Jo stopped the girls as they prepared to squeeze off another volley of raspberry goo. "No more, girls. Give Aunt Jo the doughnuts. Sergeant Blakely gave Mr. Sloane a ticket for driving too fast. He's not going to arrest anyone." Having disarmed the children, she shifted her attention to Blakely. "I'm sorry about the mess. They were just trying to defend their nanny."

Blakely wiped a blob from his eyebrow. "No real harm done, ma'am. Those little gals have quite an aim."

"We're gonna be late!" Connor shouted.

"If that's all, Officer, we'll go." Sloane shifted into drive and couldn't resist adding, "—before the situation gets any stickier." He didn't try to check his grin. Now who was the comedian?

Jo bit into the confiscated weaponry. A red smear of raspberry decorated her lip. "Hmm. A jelly doughnut is a terrible thing to waste." She glanced behind them to where Blakely still stood on the shoulder of the road, dripping raspberry filling. "Now, that guy has a great sense of humor."

Her comment wiped the grin right off Sloane's face.

"You're back already?" Nora quizzed from the bedroom.

Jo backed out from underneath the Queen Anne writing desk in the guest room where she'd plugged in her computer and squinted at the bedside clock. Only midmorning and it felt like midnight. "We got back about half an hour ago. We'd have been back earlier if Sloane hadn't been stopped for speeding." She connected the printer to her laptop and grinned. "He wasn't a happy camper. It was the same policeman—I think his name's Blakely—who responded to our 9-1-1 yesterday." She relayed the pastry attack.

Nora chuckled. "They're creative little devils, I'll give them that. How's your head?"

"A little achy, but okay. I'm just really tired. Some of us didn't sleep in this morning after playing rummy all night." She speared Nora with a pointed look.

"Honey, if you'd play your cards right, you could be up all night dancing."

Nora looked as if she was up to no good. Jo knew that look. Jo knew Nora. Jo knew better. She took the bait, anyway, since Nora seemed to thrive on "shocking" her conservative granddaughter. "Okay, I'll bite. Dancing?"

"Mattress dancing."

"You're out of control." Jo indulged Nora's role of outrageous grandmother and played along at being suitably shocked, even though Nora's suggestion held great appeal. Nora had never pushed Jo so hard or so fast on a man. God help her if one of the kids mentioned Sloane ministering to her boo-boo this morning. Kids had short memories, didn't they? She ardently hoped so. "And there are a whole list of reasons why that's a bad idea." Actually, a reality check might serve her well now. Because her brain seemed to have gone on vacation and left her body behind.

"Name 'em."

"For starters, he's the kids's nanny."

"I never knew you were a job snob, Josephina."

Jo possessed excellent communication skills. She seldom encountered problems communicating with her employees or customers or even the check-out person at the grocery story. Nora, however, had a knack for twisting her words around. Jo ground her teeth. "I'm not a job snob. How about the term 'sexual harassment'?"

"He doesn't work for you."

"It would be awkward afterward."

Nora plopped onto the bed and pulled a bottle of fire-engine-red nail polish out of her vest pocket. "Annabelle Tinsley's dating Nathan Biedelmyer." She opened the polish and began painting her nails as if her pronouncement settled things.

"Uh, okay. That's nice. What do Annabelle and Nathaniel have to do with me?" Sometimes Nora's conversational train pulled out of the station and left her standing on the platform.

Nora blew on her fingernails and waved her hand in the air for a quick dry. "Nathan, not Nathaniel. We're all in the same bingo club. And if things don't work out with Nathan and Annabelle, we're still all in the same bingo club. We'll all deal with it. In the meantime, Annabelle says Nathan's a hottie.''

"A hottie? Where do you get these terms?" It bordered on humiliating that her seventy-something grandmother was more in tune with Jo's generation than she was.

Nora applied polish to the nails on her other hand. "I read a lot." She examined the magazine on the bedside table. "And it's not *Software Entrepreneur.*" She rolled her bright blue eyes in Jo's direction. "Trust me, Sloane's a hottie. Wonder if he's got an available father or grandfather? Maybe we could double date."

Maybe Jo'd just find a bridge and jump first. "Don't go there."

Nora pretended to pout. "Party pooper. Well, let's get back to you and Sloane. Those kids—God love 'em—will run him off in no time. Better make your move while he's still around."

"Something about him doesn't feel right." Actually, part of her problem stemmed from Sloane feeling all too right. This morning in the car, she'd discovered with something akin to relief, that he'd fallen asleep holding Tara in the rocker and had stayed in the chair all night. Before his admission, she'd wondered if he'd snooped in Max's office last night. Tara had unwittingly supplied him with an alibi.

Nora shrugged off her reservation. "You checked him out with the nanny service. They said he's great. What more do you want? That's part of your trouble."

News to her. She didn't know she *had* any trouble.

"You make up your mind how something should be and that's it," Nora continued. "This poor fellow doesn't look like what you think a nanny should look like or act the way you think a nanny should act. Therefore he can't be a nanny. You've got to learn to think outside the box, Jo.''

In the entire span of their lives, Nora had never seriously lectured Jo. The uncomfortable ring of truth behind Nora's words left her feeling a little defensive. So she'd managed to get into a little bit of a rut. Hadn't scheduling a hot vacation in Jamaica proved she could think outside the box? A nasty, insidious voice inside her head reminded her she'd immediately jumped back into her comfort zone the minute Cici called for help.

Jo had lived with Nora long enough to recognize her moods. There was no arguing her down on this one. She'd have a ready rejoinder for the rest of Jo's list.

''You're right. I'll just march up and say—'' she stepped on something soft and furry ''—'Hey, Sloane, how 'bout we do a little mattress dancing?''' She bent and picked up the teddy bear Molly'd left in her room. A red light glowed on the back of its furry head. Absently, she flipped the button off to save the batteries.

Nora played dumb to Jo's sarcasm. ''That's it, girl. I knew you had some zip buried in you somewhere.'' Nora hopped off the side of the bed and hurried out of the room. ''I'll be right back.''

Lovely. Nora made her sound as if she were a boring old maid with one foot in the grave and the other slipping! She had plenty of zip and a little bit of zap, too.

Didn't she?

Nora returned and tossed a magazine onto Jo's bed. A sultry brunette wearing a pin-striped suit cut to her navel, sans bra, pouted on the cover. Make Him Bonkers In The Boardroom headlined as the feature article. Okeydokey. This definitely wasn't *Software Entrepreneur*.

Nora turned on her heel. ''And make sure you take notes.''

5

JO USUALLY ENJOYED the gardens behind Cici's house, spectacular with colorful flower beds, brick pathways and a screened gazebo. Now she rushed past them, hurrying along the path that led from the back of the house to the street-side entrance of Cheltham Shipping. On a good day, she disliked the claustrophobic passageway linking the house and Max's office. Her mishap last night had her feeling ''creeped out,'' to borrow one of Nora's terms. And that was especially disquieting for Jo because she wasn't the easily creeped type.

She opened the ornately carved door and stepped into the elegant interior. Surprise stopped her only a few steps onto the polished rosewood floor.

Sloane Murphy sat with one hip propped on the desk of Max's very buxom secretary, Tiffany Burns. Sloane leaned so far toward her, his dark head nearly touched Tiffany's blond hair. Tiffany displayed the same sexually confident air as the woman on the cover of Nora's magazine except, mercifully, her suit wasn't cut to her navel and Tiffany had managed to harness her breasts with a bra. Of course, Jo would need only about half the harnessing power if she ever worked up the nerve to take that particular plunge.

Instead she killed the urge to apologize for interrupting and slapped down the green-eyed monster rearing its ugly head. Just because Sloane had kissed her witless last night didn't mean he couldn't cozy up to Tiffany. Sloane straightened, but never moved from his perch on Tiffany's desk. No doubt still enjoying a bird's-eye-view of Tiffany's obvious assets. What business did he have here, anyway?

"The girls are napping and I have a monitor." He patted a device clipped to his belt. "I just wanted to introduce myself to everyone. Ms. Burns has a fascinating job. So much responsibility for someone so young." Sloane explained his presence, as if she'd asked the question out loud.

"Oh, Ms. Calhoun. What can I do for you this morning?" Tiffany had never called her Ms. Calhoun a day in her life. Until now. Perhaps she should check her cane at the door. "Wow, that's an ugly knot on your head."

Tiffany's crisp, blue linen suit emphasized her enormous, long-lashed blue eyes. Jo glanced down at the rumpled T-shirt and shorts she'd worn yesterday and now again today. Lack of a shower, sleep and fresh clothes didn't improve her disposition. Now, not only did she feel old, she also qualified as frumpy.

Jo widened her eyes in surprise and felt along her hairline. "There's a knot on my head?" Now she could add bitchy to her other attributes. Old. Frumpy. Rumpled. Relatively flat-chested. Bitchy. And one ugly knot on her forehead.

Tiffany looked at her as if she feared the bump on her head had affected her good sense. "Yeah. It's a really big purple knot."

Jo cut to the chase. The sooner she could get out of here, the better. "Has Max called in yet today?"

"About an hour ago. They were exhausted. There were all kinds of delays and they'd just arrived."

"What delays?"

"Flight delays and once they arrived…" Tiffany paused for dramatic effect, "Mr. Cheltham was mugged in the airport."

The drama wasn't lost on Jo. She dropped into a chair. "He's okay? Cici's okay?"

"They're both fine. Some kid snatched his laptop and ran. Mr. and Mrs. Cheltham spent hours at the police station, but they weren't hopeful it would be recovered."

"You're sure they're both okay? They only took Mr. Cheltham's computer?" Sloane's brows furrowed into a single line over his nose.

Tiffany waved her hand, her long pink nails emphasizing her point. "That's right. Just his computer. Oh, it could've been much worse. What if he'd snatched Mrs. C.'s Gucci bag? That thing's worth a small fortune and she keeps all her makeup in there." Tiffany glanced at Jo, woman-to-woman, horror etched on her face. "Can you imagine being in a foreign country without your makeup? You'd have to go emergency shopping and they might not even carry your brand."

Uh…yeah. Was Tiffany for real or just kidding? Her horrified expression spoke volumes. Max's laptop—worth a couple of thousand dollars and his link to his business—gone and Tiffany was worried about Cici's war paint? Jo slapped on eye pencil and mascara each morning simply to avoid frightening small children. "Yeah, the makeup was a close call."

Sloane, out of Tiffany's range of vision, wagged a remonstrative finger at Jo. His green eyes glittered with mirth. He read her loud and clear. Sharing a silent laugh with him felt almost as intimate as sharing a kiss. And was equally disquieting.

Sobering his expression, he turned to Tiffany, "What about Mr. Cheltham's computer?"

"Oh, that was easy. I found a computer store in Bogota. They're delivering it this afternoon and we'll download all the files by modem."

Tiffany possessed a warped perspective, but she was efficient.

Max couldn't have dialed into his computer last night because he hadn't had his laptop. Perhaps Tiffany had worked from home. "Do you ever dial in?"

Tiffany wrinkled her nose. "Mr. C.'s the only one set up for remote access. But I wouldn't mind. I could work in my pajamas." She batted her eyes suggestively at Sloane.

"Now there's a thought." He smiled, relaying his appreciation of the mental image.

Jo suppressed the desire to smack that smile right off his face. Anyway, she didn't have time to watch Tiffany make cow eyes at Sloane. Ledgers didn't appear and disappear on their own. A chill ran down Jo's spine. Someone had been in Max's office last night. That same person had sent her flying into the desk. But who was it?

"Were you in the office yesterday?" Jo tried to sound casual as she quizzed Tiffany.

"No." She frowned. "Was I supposed to come in? I almost never work on Sundays and I had a date yesterday." Tiffany glanced at Sloane from underneath her lashes. "Nothing serious, though. We're really just friends."

Oh, brother! Jo barely managed to not roll her eyes. "Do you have a number where I can reach Max and Cici?"

"You want me to put through a call for you?" Tiffany offered.

Jo wanted to talk to them, but she didn't want an audience. "I won't bother them now. Just give me the number and I'll get in touch with them later."

Tiffany paused, considering Jo. "You know, a green-based concealer would work wonders on that yellow and purple bruise."

A helpful makeup tip when she already looked like something the cat had dragged in. Her humiliation was complete. "Thanks. I'll keep that in mind. Can I get the number?"

Tiffany scribbled a number on a notepad. "Good luck getting through. The lines are iffy down there. They were out all morning." She leaned in close to Sloane while passing the paper to Jo.

He intercepted the note and stood. "I'll walk back to the house with you."

Jo plucked the paper from his fingers. "Don't leave on my account." She sounded exactly the way she felt. Testy. Out of sorts. Not her usual collected self.

"I need to go up, anyway, to check on the girls." Sloane walked to the door with her. Jo fought to regain the equilibrium that seemed determined to flee every time she got within spitting distance of Sloane Murphy. She liked her equilibrium. She resented the fact he could destroy it effortlessly.

At the door, Jo turned once again toward Tiffany. "If either Max or Cici call in before I reach them, can you patch them through to the house? Nora and I are staying here for a week or so."

Had she not been watching closely, Jo might've missed the slight frown her words evoked.

Tiffany nodded her head. "I'll let them know."

Three for three. Sloane. Mrs. Price. and now, Tiffany Burns. None of them wanted her and Nora there. Was it simply a case of the mice wanting to play while the cat was away? Or was there more at stake?

"WHAT DO YOU MEAN you haven't snooped in Cheltham's office yet? What the hell were you doing last night? Or did the little kiddies tie you up again?"

Sloane was holding the cell phone away from his ear, but Vic still almost deafened him. Blakely had spread the story around the precinct in double time. He'd love to see Vic or Blakely stuck in this nanny gig.

"Someone else was in Cheltham's office. I didn't think we needed to make it a party." Between Jo Calhoun shaking up his libido and those three kids running him ragged, he'd been too damned exhausted to even remember his assignment. His lack of headway on the case was frustrating him.

The echo of Vic's feet hitting his desk came over the phone line. "Okay, Matthews, you've got my attention. What gives?"

"Cici Cheltham's sister and grandmother dropped in and spent the night. The sister was in Cheltham's office after midnight. Now they've decided to *visit* for a week or so." Was Jo involved in this? Was she deliberately trying to throw him off kilter?

Vic grunted on the other end of the line. "Timing seems odd, huh?"

"Yeah. And Cheltham's office has a coded entry system, with the doors weighted and timed." Sloane paced over to the window and pushed aside the heavy drape. A circular driveway fronted the house with a gurgling fountain standing between it and the street. Elaborate wrought-iron gates flanked the driveway, where a small red sports car sat parked. The car was a surprising choice for Ms. Calhoun. He'd have guessed a sedate sedan. But he suspected Jo wasn't what she seemed. She seemed calm, cool and collected, but that certainly wasn't how she kissed.

"So what was the broad doing in there?"

A van turned in off the oak-lined street and parked behind the red car. Eddie's Auto Repair was lettered on the side of the van. Jo walked out of the house to greet the repairman. The mesmerizing sway of her hips killed his concentration. "What'd you say?"

"You aren't coming down with something, are you, Matthews? We need you in top form."

Maybe he *was* coming down with something. That'd explain a lot. He dropped the curtain and turned away from the window, shaking his head to clear it. "I'll be fine. I'm always in top form."

"Glad to hear it. My ass is hanging out the window on this one along with yours. Now, what was the chick doing in Cheltham's office last night?"

"I don't know." Why wouldn't her car start this morning? Why had she stopped in the doorway when she obviously knew the doors closed automatically? He didn't have those answers, either.

"What do ya mean, you don't know? Why didn't you find out?"

"Vic, I'm the nanny. She's already suspicious. If I ask too many questions, I'll blow my cover."

"You think she might be involved? Is she trying to cover for her sister?"

Those same two questions had chased around in his head all morning. The circumstances surrounding Jo Calhoun's visit were suspicious. She'd dropped by and then decided to stay. She'd been snooping in Max's office when she'd gotten that nasty bump. And what about the way she'd quizzed Tiffany Burns?

Was she involved? He shouldn't care one way or another, but instinctively he hoped not. Logically, his professionalism demanded he find out.

"I don't think so, but have Wiggins run a background check and pull her bank records. She could be covering for her sister. They're a tight family and they take care of their own."

When they'd discussed Connor's problems with the school bully, she'd revealed the bond their family shared—if one of them had a problem, they all had a problem. Was she running interference for Cici and Max?

"According to the secretary, Cheltham was mugged when he arrived at the airport in Bogota." Sloane relayed the details. He left off Tiffany's views on makeup. Maybe he was coming down with something, after all. Tiffany, batting her big baby blues and sporting an impressive set of attributes, still hadn't set his motor humming the way Jo could with just one scornful glance. Maybe he'd sign up for a flu shot this year.

"What do you think's going on with that? Just a coincidence?"

Too many years in police work left Sloane skeptical of coincidences. "Seems unlikely. It could be a diversionary tactic on his part. Or maybe he's crossed the wrong people. Or maybe there was something in that laptop. Then again, maybe it *was* just a kid off the street who saw a chance."

"Out. Out. Out." The demand came through the monitor on his belt loud and clear. Duty of a different kind called.

"Gotta go, Vic. One of the kids is up from her nap."

"Get into that office, Matthews."

"I'll check back in tomorrow."

"Yeah, you do that. And, Matthews?"

"Yeah?"

"Me and Gladys might want to talk to you about some baby-sitting when you're done with this assignment." He choked on his own laughter.

"Very funny, Vic." Sloane hung up with Vic's laughter ringing in his ear.

JO PULLED A DIET COLA OUT of the fridge and popped the top to celebrate having a functional car once again. Eddie had jiggled some wires and told her she needed a new starter.

Mrs. Price poked her head out of the laundry room off the kitchen. "How's the head, dear?" Motherly concern creased her round face.

"Fine."

"It looks painful."

"It looks much worse than it is." What a comforting thought—to know you looked much worse than you felt. "Really, it doesn't even hurt."

"You know a little green-based concealer would work wonders on that," Mrs. Price offered while folding a bath towel.

Jo nearly spewed her diet cola. It was one thing to have Tiffany mention the concealer, but Mrs. Price—a woman well past her prime—pushed the envelope. She, Josephina Wilhelmina Calhoun, had obviously been standing behind a rock when feminine mystique was being doled out. She vowed then and there to read Nora's magazine cover to cover as soon as possible. She had a knot the size of New Zealand on her forehead, an itch just begging to be scratched, a man-size case of lust in the form of one nanny who she still couldn't believe was a nanny at all, someone had hacked onto Max's computer and then pushed her into a desk, and to top the whole stinking mess off, she hadn't had any sleep in more than twenty-four hours.

A double ring on the house phone rescued her from a reply. Jo didn't answer it. Mrs. Price took her duties very seriously. Attempting to make your own sandwich or answer the phone offended more often than not. Mrs. Price bustled out of the laundry room and picked up on the third ring. "Cheltham House. She's right here." Mrs. Price turned and held the phone out toward Jo. "It's for you."

"I have Mrs. Cheltham on hold for you. Can you take the call?" Tiffany announced.

Jo glanced toward the open laundry room door that showcased Mrs. Price's backside as she reached into the dryer. "Tell Cici to hold on. I'll take the call in the library."

"Just buzz me when you're ready."

Jo hung up the phone and hurried to the library. She closed the door behind her. She rang Max's office and Tiffany patched her through to Cici.

"Jo? How's everything? Are the kids okay?"

"The kids are fine."

"How's the new nanny working out? She hasn't quit already, has she? Is that why you're at the house?" Cici finally paused, whether for a breath or a reply was anyone's guess.

Jo chose her next words carefully. She needed some answers but she didn't want to alarm Cici. "Nurturing Nannies Network has a good reputation?"

"You know how Max is—only the best. They provide the crème de la crème of nannies. We've been very pleased so far, except that none of them seem to appreciate the kids's joie de vivre. They can't seem to handle their sense of adventure and high level of creativity. Why?"

Visions of Sloane naked from the waist up, bound and gagged, came to mind. Yeah, the kids had joie de vivre in spades. She plopped into one of the armchairs, swamped by relief that Sloane was what he claimed to be. Once again, her instincts had failed her while her logic prevailed. "The new nanny is…" How to describe someone who orchestrated a belching contest? "Well, fairly unorthodox. And no, he hasn't quit yet."

"Unorthodox is good. I don't have a problem with unorthodox. He may be just what my kids— He? The new nanny is a he?"

Oh, baby, he was definitely a he and then some. "Uh-huh."

"How cool! Is he some crusty, middle-aged fellow named Jeeves?"

"Uh, no. He's not your typical nanny. That's why I wanted to make sure *you* trusted the agency."

"Have the kids been good?" A note of futile optimism threaded Cici's voice.

"Good is a relative term."

"Well, for goodness' sake, we're relatives cause we're family. So tell me, have my little angels been good?"

"They tied him up with duct tape, cut off his shirt, and painted his face with permanent marker."

"I'm so glad they're having a good time and getting along with him. But he shouldn't let them play with scissors."

Her sweet, marvelously free-spirited sister didn't have a clue. Jo could only shake her head at the phone while Cici continued. "Max is so stressed already, he doesn't need any more problems. I'm really worried about him."

"Why is Max so stressed?"

"He says it's nothing. But when that kid stole his computer, he freaked out. And you know, Max doesn't usually freak out."

A gross understatement if she'd ever heard one. In the twelve years Max and Cici had been married, she'd never seen staid, solid Max anywhere close to *freaking out*. Now Cici was another cup of tea altogether. Cici and freaking out were intimately acquainted. "Are you sure you aren't overreacting?"

"I'm telling you, he almost hyperventilated. And you know I recognize a good case of hyperventilation when I see it. If I can just smooth things over for the rest of our trip here and you make sure the nanny doesn't up and leave, I think he'll be fine."

"Don't worry about things here. I'll take care of it." So much for confiding her suspicions to Max that someone had been snooping in his office. There wasn't much he could do from Bogota anyway. Besides, she was fully capable—she'd handle it on her own. However, without alarming him, she could have Max confirm or negate her suspicion that someone had been in his office.

"Is Max around?"

"He's working on the new laptop. Hold on. Thanks for watching out for the new nanny." How telling that Cici thought the nanny needed looking after rather than the kids. "And give my little angels a hug and a kiss from their mommy. And tell them to stay away from scissors."

Jo supposed the duct tape qualified as play material. "Don't worry, Cici. I'll take care of everything."

"I know." Cici's breezy voice backed her statement.

Max's voice came across the line almost immediately. "Jo."

He'd always been a man of few words, possibly because Cici offered so few opportunities for him to get a word in edgewise. "Hi, Max. I just wanted to check something with you. Do you mind if I use your computer while you're gone? Nora and I may spend a few days at the house until the new nanny gets the feel of things."

"Sure. Just make sure it's set up so I can dial in." Max sounded distracted.

"No problem. How's work?"

"Waiting for a computer left me out of pocket." Max confirmed what she suspected. No ledger should've appeared on-screen last night.

"Does anybody else have access to your office? I don't want to get in anyone's way."

"Tiffany, but she can work around you. Anything else?"

"Max, I went into your office late last night. A ledger was up on the screen and later it was gone."

"I dialed in from the plane. Maybe I didn't log off the remote when I shut down. It would've just timed itself out. I wouldn't worry about it."

Max wanted off the phone and Jo had a lot to think about. His remote would've timed itself out long before she'd arrived in his office. They exchanged goodbyes. Jo heard the click as Max broke the connection. Deep in thought, she didn't move as quickly to hang up on her end. Another click carried clearly over the line. Someone had listened in on her conversation. Tiffany, who had patched the call through, immediately came to mind.

She replaced the receiver, her hands shaking. Anyone with good sense would be a little frightened. However, good sense had seemingly deserted her approximately twenty-four hours ago. Jo breathed deeply, trying to calm down. Because right now, she was mad enough to spit nails.

SLOAN WHISTLED TUNELESSLY as he went down the stairs. The kids were all asleep. At last. What a day— hustling to get the kids ready for car pool, that speeding ticket with Jo in the car, getting chewed out by Vic, homework with Connor, bath time, bedtime. Only the end of day number two and he was exhausted again. But not too exhausted to catch the playoffs on that big screen TV he'd spotted earlier. He might as well watch the game while he waited for Nora and Jo to retire. He didn't want to have to explain his presence in Cheltham's office to either one of them.

He opened the fridge and pulled out a beer. Then he snagged another one. Insurance. Once he sat down, he didn't want to have to get up.

He heard the game before he reached the door, yet it still surprised him to find Jo slouched on the leather sofa watching baseball. He stopped in the doorway. Engrossed in the game, she didn't notice him. She'd propped her feet on the coffee table, and was munching popcorn with the intensity of a pitcher staring down a batter. Her face reflected a the-rest-of-the-world-might-be-going-to-hell-but-I'm-watching-baseball enthrallment.

Suddenly, inexplicably, he felt awkward. Only because he hadn't expected to find her here. He cleared his throat, "Mind if I watch the game, too?"

Startled, she scooted up on the couch and swung around to face him. Surprise, wariness, and perhaps an inkling of pleasure all reflected in the brown depths of her eyes before she recovered her composure. "Uh, sure, go ahead. Have some popcorn. I always make too much."

Sloane settled on the other end of the sofa and held out one of bottles he'd carried in. "Want a beer?"

"Sure. Why not? Thanks." She took the bottle from him.

"I thought you'd be asleep."

"I thought you'd be asleep."

They'd spoken simultaneously. Jo laughed, her eyes sparkling. "I thought the kids had worn you out again."

Sloane almost lost track of what she said. She seemed different tonight. More relaxed. She also had the sexiest little mouth. Her upper lip was a little wider than her bottom lip, giving her mouth a slight petulance. "Uh, yeah. The kids. They did." He gestured toward the screen. "But I didn't want to miss the game."

She nodded in agreement. "I know what you mean. I think I could sleep standing up right now if it wasn't the playoffs."

Spoken like a true die-hard fan. Go figure. Jo Calhoun, a woman he'd originally labeled as average now seemed anything but. "I didn't know you liked baseball."

"How would you? We don't know anything about one another." A tired smile robbed her words of any sting. Her head drooped against the back of the sofa.

With a start of surprise, Sloane realized he knew more about Jo Calhoun in the span of a day and a half than he knew about most of the women he'd dated sporadically. "That's not true. I know your nieces and nephew adore you. You're smart and savvy enough to own your own business and run it off-site." He thought of her facing him down, armed only with pepper spray and guts. "You're independent, resourceful, and loyal." He also knew the taste and feel of her. "You think a jelly dough-nut is a terrible thing to waste. And now I know you like baseball."

"Wrong. I love baseball. Max knows the marketing

director for the Braves. He's promised to get me tickets if they go to the series."

He grinned at her enthusiasm. "Remember me if you get an extra ticket. I can always hold your beer and hot-dog."

"It's a deal."

A runner made it to first base. For the next several innings, they talked baseball, complained about bad calls, and finished off the bowl of popcorn. Jo knew more about the sport than most of his buddies.

At the top of the seventh inning, he realized she'd grown very quiet. He glanced over. Sleep had triumphed over baseball.

Sloane tried to concentrate on the game, but Jo looked so uncomfortable half slumped against the back of the sofa with her neck at that awkward angle. What the hell? Here he was missing the game, because sleeping beauty might wake up with a stiff neck.

He rationalized his next move. She was kind of testy without enough sleep—he'd witnessed that today. Waking up with a gimpy neck guaranteed a testy tomorrow. On behalf of himself and the kids, he owed it to everyone to make her as comfortable as possible. So he did the only decent, self-sacrificing thing a man in his circumstances could. He settled her head on the couch. His Boy Scout duty done, he resumed watching the game.

She wiggled around for a moment until her head found his lap and settled on it as if it were a pillow. He clenched his teeth, determined to ignore the sexual pull of having her head on his lap.

She snuggled against his thigh, sending all his good intentions straight to hell. Only sheer force of will and a good measure of military and police training kept him marginally focused on the big screen. He studied her face in repose. Nice straight nose with a light dusting of freckles. The smooth curve of her cheek. The discolored knot on her head. She looked softer. Gentler. Almost sweet. She shifted and rolled over. Her face now pressed against his crotch. Jo smiled in her sleep. His crotch lobbied for the opportunity to smile back.

Sloane concentrated very, very hard on the game. He settled his head back against the couch and stared in determination at the big screen. He'd like to see *someone* score tonight.

NORA LET HERSELF INTO the house and followed the sounds from the TV. She'd tried halfheartedly to harass Jo into line dancing tonight. Lucky for her, Jo had turned her down to watch the ball game instead. Sometimes Jo cramped her style.

Nora skidded to a halt in the doorway. *Well, it was a start.* Jo slept with her head parked in Sloane's lap while he snoozed with his head thrown back, his left hand resting against her hair. Nora shook her head. Leave it to Josephina to waste a perfectly good opportunity.

She prodded Sloane's shoulder until his eyes blinked open. ''Hey, Murphy. I hate to interrupt the slumber party, but Jo's gonna be madder'n a hornet if Mrs. Price comes in tomorrow morning and finds her like that.''

''Huh?'' He blinked sleepily.

He was a nice boy and serious eye candy, but a little slow on the uptake. ''One of you needs to get up and go to bed. Jo sleeps like the living dead, so you're the lucky duck. Vamoose.''

''But I can't just leave her here.'' He eyed Jo protectively.

Nora shrugged. ''She'll be fine. But I'm telling you,

she'll be hopping mad if she wakes up staring at your crotch with an audience.''

"Can you turn down her bed?" He slipped one arm underneath Jo's neck and the other arm under her knees. Sloane struggled to his feet. Jo wasn't fat. But she wasn't a delicate, petite thing, either—a little heavy in the derriere department. Cici had the boobs; Jo had the butt.

Nora stifled a grin. "I'll get it ready." She raced ahead while he staggered along behind her.

Whether he knew it or not, the boy had it bad.

Jo EXPERIENCED the most curious sensation of being watched. She blinked her eyes open. Two sets of blue eyes stared at her above the edge of her mattress, at very close range. Jo smiled a welcome and pulled back the edge of her covers. "Morning, sweet pies. Want to climb in with me?"

The girls squealed gleefully and scrambled onto the bed. Jo had never considered how terribly lucky Cici was to wake up to their cute little faces every morning. They sandwiched Jo between them.

"Do the piggies, Aunt Jo. Pleeease." Two sets of small toes were thrust her way with the requests.

Jo obliged with a rousing rendition of "This little piggy…" for each girl a number of times. Finally satisfied, they put their feet back under the covers and snuggled up to her.

"Norrie said you was extinguished."

Jo laughed and kissed Molly's fall of dark hair. "I think you've inherited your mother's instinct for vocabulary."

"Exhausted, you little rascal. I said your aunt Jo was exhausted." Nora stood in Jo's bedroom doorway. "Mr.

Sloane set up a tea party in the playroom for you girls, if you're ready.''

Molly and Tara abandoned Jo's bed in record time. Their squeals echoed across the landing as Molly skipped toward the playroom with Tara toddling behind her on chubby legs.

"Feeling better after a good night's sleep?"

Jo's brain began to function when she sat up in bed. "How'd I get here? The last thing I remember was watching the game."

Nora preened, as proud as a peacock. "Prince Charming carried you."

Mortified, Jo dropped back to the mattress. "Please tell me you're teasing."

Nora held up two beringed fingers. "Scout's honor."

Jo squeezed her eyes shut and pinched the bridge of her nose. "He probably permanently injured his back. I weigh a ton."

"Don't be silly. You're just half a ton. And he only groaned a few times."

Jo searched for a silver lining. "It could've been worse. He could've suffered severe stubble injury if I hadn't shaved my legs yesterday. But he should've just left me."

"He refused to leave you there."

She didn't trust Nora even a little bit when it came to men, sex, and/or food. "What were you doing in the den?"

"Oh, I heard the ball game and dropped by to say nighty-night. For which you should be supremely thankful." Nora paused for dramatic effect. "You were both sound asleep."

Not nearly worthy of the build-up Nora had worked so

hard to achieve. "What? Let's have it. Was my mouth hanging open? Was I drooling?"

Nora snickered. "You should've been drooling, honey. You're face was buried right in that man's crotch."

Think outside the box, Nora had said. Maybe she'd give Nora a dose of her own outrageousness. "Damn if I don't sleep through the best things—Sloane's crotch and the final score." Wow. She'd actually shocked her shocking grandmother. "Close your mouth, Nora. You look like a trout."

Nora snapped her mouth shut and then promptly re-opened it to hoot. "Jo, you're just full of surprises this morning."

Jo looked at the bedside clock. Nine thirty-five. She never slept past six. "I've been asleep a long time."

"Yes, you have. Longer than you think." Nora paused at the door on her way out. "I'm glad you're waking up."

Jo prided herself on being a fairly intelligent woman. She read Nora's message loud and clear. Had she been asleep all these years? Did that account for her general restlessness and discontent?

Nora closed the door behind her. Jo reached for the magazine her grandmother had left behind yesterday. She'd take notes.

6

TARA SQUEALED and kicked her legs, demanding for
Sloane to push her higher in the baby swing at the park.
Beside her, in a regular swing, Molly pumped. Sloane
alternated pushing the two girls. He'd brought them to
the park after picking Connor up at school. Now Connor
sat at a picnic table, intently piecing together a toy boat.

Even though some of the trees had begun to show fall
colors, it was a warm Indian summer day. He couldn't
do a damn thing on the investigation until late tonight
after everyone was in bed. He might as well be here
letting the kids wear themselves out. And putting some
distance between himself and Jo.

Looking through Cheltham's office was much more
difficult with Nora and Jo staying at the house. Was that
Jo's plan? Was driving Sloane crazy with her challenging
looks, hot kisses, and snuggling up to his crotch part of
her plan, as well?

"We wanna play in the sand." Molly cut into his silent
speculation, dragging her feet on the ground to slow her
swing.

Tara mouthed one of her most-used phrases. "Out,
out."

Sloane stopped Tara's swing and lifted her out over
the safety bar. Molly leaped out and ran over to the sand-
box where she promptly dumped a bucket of sand toys.
Having settled the girls in the pile of sand, he ambled

over to Connor. The more he was around the boy, the more Connor struck a chord of recognition in Sloane. As a kid, Sloane had been a bit of a loner—hell, he still was—and he recognized that same quality in Connor. But it was more than that. Sloane had also hungered for attention from his father, often misbehaving and getting into trouble because any attention was better than no attention. Again he saw the same thing here.

Keeping an eye on the girls, he dropped onto the bench opposite the boy. "How's it going?"

Connor feigned a nonchalance belied by his hunched shoulders. "Okay."

"How's the belching going?"

A snaggle-toothed grin momentarily relieved his gloom. "Cool." He fiddled with the sail of his boat, his grin gone as quickly as it arrived. "Now I've got even worse trouble."

Sloane leaned back and propped his elbows behind him on the picnic table. "Maybe I can help."

"I doubt it." Connor looked miserable.

"Try me." What could possibly be so bad in a six-year-old kid's life?

"I've got girl problems."

Sloane grimaced. He could relate. In spades. And he wasn't so darn sure he could help. "What's going on?"

"Melanie Marcum likes me." Even the tips of Connor's ears grew red.

"Do you like her?"

"Gross. No. She's a girl."

Sloane spotted Molly raising a bucket of sand over Tara's head. "Molly don't pour that on Tara, it'll get in her eyes." Molly grumbled but put down the bucket.

He shifted his attention back to Connor. "So she likes you, but you don't like her?"

Connor abandoned the boat model to trace his toe in the sandy soil. "She's not bad for a girl." He pushed his glasses farther up onto the bridge of his nose. "Actually, I sorta feel sick to my stomach when I'm around her."

"That's a tough one." He didn't feel sick to his stomach when he was around Jo, but he damn sure felt out of sorts. Sloane sighed and rubbed his hand over his chin. "I know how you feel."

Connor brightened. Misery loved company. "You do? You've got woman troubles, too? Do you feel like you're gonna throw up when she's around?"

"Something like that." It was darn close for a guy who prided himself on always being in control of a situation.

"So what are we gonna do?"

He checked his watch as the sun began to dip toward the horizon. Time to get the kids back to the house and then dinner. "Molly. Tara. Get your sand toys together." He forestalled impending mutiny with a bribe. "We'll pick up jelly doughnuts on the way home. You can have them for dessert if you eat your dinner." Strictly a coincidence they were Jo's favorite. He helped Connor snap the model boat sail into place. "We're gonna do what guys have been doing for a long time. We're gonna suck it up and hope it goes away."

Connor eyed him dubiously. "That doesn't sound like much of a plan to me. What if it doesn't work?"

Sloane, who always had a plan and then a backup plan just in case, found himself at a loss. He stood and hoisted Tara onto his shoulders. She clutched at his hair and shrieked in delight. Sand trickled down the collar of his shirt.

Molly carried her sand pail in one hand and clutched his hand with the other. Connor picked up his boat and walked beside him. Instinctively, Sloane reached for the boy's hand. He wasn't sure whether he surprised himself or Connor more with his action. But Connor gripped his hand in return as they traipsed toward the SUV. With each step, sand sifted into his shorts.

On the path to the parking lot, they met a young woman pushing a baby carriage. "Ya'll sure do look like your daddy," she called to the kids as they passed her.

Molly burst into a fit of giggles. Tara kicked her feet against his chest and tugged on his ears. Connor rolled his eyes, but grinned all the same. Sloane experienced a flash of pride and an emotional wrench that surprised him.

Connor tugged at his hand. "So, what's the backup plan if sucking it up doesn't work?"

Sloane didn't have a clue. Damn. Between Jo and the kids, he couldn't seem to regain his equilibrium. "If it doesn't work, then we punt."

"MR. SLOANE'S IMPOTENT."

Jo darn near sucked down the entire Brussel sprout she'd forked into her mouth.

Sloane made a pained choking noise.

Nora seemed the only adult at the dinner table unperturbed by Molly's announcement. "And where did you hear that, dear?"

"Mama said it on the phone today. She said 'Mr. Sloane's a impotent part of our family now. You kids be sure you behave.'"

Connor rolled his eyes with all the disdain a six-year-old could muster for a younger sibling. "Molly, you moron. She said he's important."

Molly glared back and stuck out her tongue, mashed potatoes and all. "That's what I said. Impotent."

"Mr. Sloane, Molly made a face at me."

"Mr. Sloane, he called me a mo-ron."

Jo watched the spectacle unfold.

Tara, for once, didn't join in the fray. Possibly due to the fact that she was busy stuffing Brussel sprouts down the front of her diaper. Jo had eaten her Brussel sprouts in a misguided attempt to set a good example for the children. Besides, she'd heard about the jelly doughnuts for dessert. Although, stuffing the stinky little vegetables in a diaper actually struck her as a better idea—or at least more appropriate.

"Hey, you two. Let's skip making faces and calling each other names, okay? Mmm, Mrs. Price sure makes good mashed potatoes, doesn't she?" Sloane took a big bite in a not-so-subtle attempt to change the subject.

"Norrie, do you think Mr. Sloane's impotent?" Molly, predestined genetically, proved herself just like the other women in their family—incapable of dropping a subject.

Nora helped herself to another biscuit. "Ask your aunt Jo, she knows a lot more about that kind of thing than I do."

In a pig's eye.

Molly promptly posed her question, "Is he, Aunt Jo?"

Five sets of eyes turned to her expectantly. Even Tara ceased her diaper stuffing. Sloane shot her a look, half warning, half challenge.

Jo always behaved. Jo was always very circumspect. Normally, she would close the discussion then and there. However, some impish impulse prodded her to provoke him. "Oh, I believe Mr. Sloane's very, very impotent." She smiled sweetly in his direction. "So you kids should behave."

Sloane's laughing eyes promised retribution. Anticipation tingled along her nerve endings.

"Now if we could just get the adults to behave," Nora murmured to no one in particular.

"Starting with the oldest." Jo addressed her meat loaf. Perhaps that bump on the head had affected her more than she realized. She'd never talked to her food before. Or made comments intended to stir up trouble. She hadn't even known she possessed this flirtatious teasing side. She'd always left those things up to Nora and Cici.

"Aunt Jo, your head looks like a science experiment we did at school." Connor stared at her yellowing goose egg from across the table.

For Pete's sake, couldn't he comment on the new wallpaper in the kitchen or ask about dessert or something? Instead he had to point out for the entire table how gruesome she looked. "Thanks, Connor. I always wanted to resemble a science experiment."

"She just needs Mr. Sloane to kiss it again." Molly, not to be usurped as the dinner table authority, put her brother in his place.

"Yuck," offered Connor.

"Again?" Nora arched an inquiring brow toward Sloane, who developed a tremendous interest in his iced-tea glass.

Molly patted Jo's hand. "Maybe he can kiss it when you do your dancing."

Dinner settled in the pit of her stomach like a lead ball and dread crept up her spine in premonition. She had heard a similar version of this conversation earlier. Her cool head took a hike. She leaped up from the table, desperate to shift conversational gears. "Who's ready for some dessert?" She grabbed her plate to clear it. "I know I am. Molly, it's our favorite, jelly doughnuts."

"Hurray," all the kids cried in unison.

Whew! Jo placed her plate in the sink and sagged with relief. What a close call.

Jo turned back to the table. Sloane scrutinized her speculatively. A gleam in his eye foreshadowed his intention.

He wouldn't.

He did.

"I love to dance. I'm a regular Fred Astaire. What kind of dancing does Aunt Jo like, Molly?"

"You know, mattress dancing. We heared her ask you."

Judging by the stunned expression on his face, he'd expected the tango. How had the girls overheard her conversation with Nora? Humiliation overloaded her brain. She should do something—anything—to save the situation. Instead she stood rooted to the floor, floundering in embarrassment.

Things couldn't get worse.

They did.

Molly pulled out a stuffed bear sharing Tara's high-chair. "Jo-Jo broked it."

Jo recognized the bear she'd stepped on yesterday.

Tara's pudgy little fingers prodded a top button.

"Hey, Sloane, how 'bout we do a little mattress dancing?" Jo's voice spilled out of the bear, loud and clear, and echoed throughout the room. Not just once, but over and over. Son of a gun. The stinking little bear contained one of those damned recording devices.

Molly repeated her earlier accusation. "You broked it."

Unfortunately, she hadn't. Too bad she hadn't crushed it when she'd stepped on it. Jo located the off switch in the middle of the sixth rendition of her proposition. "I'll fix it, honey." A couple of good stomps could take care of that. Although, then the kids would think she was really a bad sport.

"Do you like to mattress dance, Mr. Sloane?" Molly quizzed innocently.

Connor's face wrinkled as if he smelled something bad. "What *is* mattress dancing?"

"I haven't had a lot of practice, but I hope your aunt Jo will teach me all the steps she knows. Oh, and you kids should just call it by the name most people know—the cha-cha. Otherwise folks might think you were..."

"Stupid?" Connor supplied, horrified he might earn that label.

"Well, yeah, they might think you were stupid if you referred to it as mattress dancing. So you shouldn't ever say that again."

Outrage at having the kids consider her stupid warred with horror at having them repeat the phrase. Stupid seemed the better option.

Nora barely contained herself. Tears threatened as she laughed into her napkin.

"What's wrong with Norrie?" Connor eyed his great-grandmother.

"Is she okay?" Molly seemed worried.

Nora's outrageousness had resulted in perhaps the singular most humiliating experience of Jo's life. This was even worse than when Darlene Nielsen had told everyone Jo stuffed her bra in high school. She didn't feel a shred of compunction about skating. "Don't worry about Norrie. She's just enjoying a senior moment."

SLOANE SLIPPED through the French doors of Max and Cici Cheltham's darkened bedroom and stepped onto the patio, closing the door behind him with a soft click. With the kids asleep, Nora out for the evening, and Jo in the

shower, he'd swiftly but thoroughly searched Cheltham's
bedroom. He knew Cheltham favored black tasseled loaf-
ers and Cici owned a ton of makeup, but he'd discovered
no trace of the stolen artifacts. Nada. Nix. Zilch.

He stalked down one of the brick paths and then
stepped under the gnarled arms of a moss-draped oak.
While he had a clear view of the house, the tree kept him
out of sight. A light shone in the kitchen window downstairs. He recognized the faint glow in Molly and Tara's
respective rooms as night-lights. On the opposite end of
the house, a light shone in what must be the bathroom.

He punched in the precinct number on his cell phone,
anxious to get the info on Jo's background. Wiggins liked
working late hours, so he might catch him. Wiggins
picked up on the second ring.

"Matthews here. Find out anything on Jo Calhoun?"

"Lady looks like a regular straight arrow. Makes a
decent amount of money. Socks most of it away. Very
predictable woman."

The straight arrow in question appeared, silhouetted
against the slats of the shuttered bathroom window.
Sloane watched in fascination as she bent forward and
toweled her hair. Sloane deliberately looked away. Not
out of any misguided sense of decency. Hell, no. He
looked away because he wanted her so badly he could
almost taste her. Watching her bend over like that severely limited his ability to carry on a conversation
with... Who was he on the phone with?

"Matthews?" Wiggins prompted in his ear. Oh, yeah.
Wiggins had just pronounced her a straight arrow.

"Yeah. I'm not surprised to hear it. Thanks for the
check."

He could feel Wiggins's hesitation on the other end of
the line. "There was one thing. It's probably nothing but

you might as well know. She recently booked and paid for a vacation she didn't take. One of those all-inclusive deals down at a singles resort in Jamaica.''

Unbidden, jealousy seared him, swift and hot. ''Was she traveling with anyone? Meeting anyone?''

''Not that I can tell.''

Sloane unclenched his jaw as the light in the bathroom extinguished. ''Any idea why she didn't go?'' A trip to a singles resort in Jamaica didn't sound like Jo. Paying and not going certainly didn't sound like her.

''No clue. Her flight was booked for last Sunday but she was a no-show.''

Last Sunday. The same day she'd turned up at the Cheltham house unannounced and stayed. The same day she'd begun to unhinge him.

JO WALKED with measured steps, her footfalls echoing against the polished wood of the floor. She'd avoided Sloane like the plague since dinner, excusing herself from the table as soon as decently possible. She couldn't forestall the reckoning any longer. She was in bad shape— she couldn't stay away any more than she could forego breathing. A woman shouldn't feel it so deeply—it bordered on obsession.

Even if it meant facing Sloane, she couldn't miss the second game of the playoffs.

He sat on the couch, the requisite bowl of popcorn on the middle cushion. Even wearing a pair of worn jeans and a T-shirt, he looked good. But then again, he would look good in anything. *Or nothing,* a naughty voice whispered in her head.

''Mind if I join you?''

''Oh, I planned on it.'' He smirked, much like a cat toying with a mouse. And she knew just who he'd cast in the role of the ill-fated rodent. "I didn't think you'd miss the game."

The one they played or the one on the big screen? Jo straightened her spine. She wasn't a mouse. She didn't even like Hermes, Molly's pet. Perhaps she'd behaved like a mouse after dinner, scurrying away, but no longer. She had taken notes when she'd read Nora's magazine. If he was a cat, so was she. And if her analogies and thinking seemed a little convoluted right now, she attributed it to the unannounced leave of absence her ability to think logically had taken.

"I wouldn't miss this game." She practically purred. She read acknowledgment in his green eyes.

A rock star belted out a tortured rendition of "The Star Spangled Banner" on-screen. Jo waited. Every gaze and gesture Sloane sent her way promised retribution.

Finally the waiting ended.

"I'm flattered at my status as an extended part of the family, but that impotency thing...." He gave her an affronted expression. A teasing note in his voice belied any hurt feelings.

"It's just a little matter of semantics. It's not a big deal." She played his game.

"Trust me. It's a very big deal."

Based on their close encounter in the library, she could vouch for that. "I suppose it's all a matter of perspective."

"You owe me."

"You're right. I apologize."

Sloane shook his head reluctantly. "I'm afraid a verbal apology is inadequate after questioning my virility. I think I'm entitled to exact my pound of flesh."

A frisson of excitement shivered through her. Jo felt like someone with an aversion to heights peering over the edge of a precipice. Except she stood on the ledge, far more excited than frightened, a bit awed at her daring. And eager to push forward.

"Name your price." Did she sound breathless? She *was* breathless.

The batter stepped up to the plate.

"Let me think about it."

Let him think about it? What was there to think about? She knew the payment he'd demand. She employed deduction and reason every day. He'd ask for a kiss.

The pitcher wound up and released. And so the game began.

The intensity on-screen didn't compare to what played out between the two of them. With each inning, tension keyed Jo tighter and tighter. Every time she shifted in her seat, crossed her legs, drank a swallow, she felt the heat of his gaze brush her. And felt an answering response thrum inside her.

Neither spoke a word.

Top of the ninth. Bases loaded. Two outs. Three balls. Two strikes. The pitcher delivered a curve ball. The batter slammed it out of the park. The fans cheered wildly.

The tension thickened between Jo and Sloane. In her mind, she'd already kissed him. Many times. Many ways. She'd traced her lips along the square line of his jaw, nibbled at his firm lower lip, and even licked that little fire-breathing dragon residing on the planes of his belly into submission.

Anticipation pooled into a liquid heat between her thighs and tightened her nipples. Sloane defined the ephemeral discontent that had plagued her recently.

The game was over. *Want* had walked out the door some time ago. She *needed* to scratch this itch. Jo turned to face him.

Sloane slid his arm along the back of the couch until his fingers brushed against her arm. The rasp of his fingertips against her bare flesh jolted her already heightened senses.

"I know what I want." His voice, low and edgy, echoed her feelings.

Good. So did she. "Name your price."

The distance between them narrowed as they moved toward each other, drawn by an attraction she didn't particularly want but couldn't seem to control.

He ran his fingers against the sensitive skin of her neck. She shivered at his touch. "I want you to say what I heard earlier tonight."

His thumb traced the hollowed plane of her cheekbone. So sure she'd anticipated his request, she doubted her hearing. But who could think straight now? "What?"

"I want you to reissue that dance invitation. I want to see your face," he caressed her mouth with his fingertips, "and feel my name against your lips when you say it."

Instinctively she licked his finger with the tip of her tongue. He shuddered in response. "Say it. Now," he encouraged hoarsely.

"Sloane, how would you like to mattress dance?" Jo didn't feel at all ridiculous uttering the invitation. She felt womanly and sexy and desirable, especially when his eyes darkened with arousal.

She captured his finger and took it in her mouth, savoring his taste and texture. He closed his eyes and groaned. "Honey, you are killing me."

He hadn't seen nothin' yet. Jo released his finger with a naughty smile. "And I wanted to make it all better."

A thin wail followed by Molly's voice interrupted them through on the monitor he'd placed on the side table. "Mr. Sloane? Mr. Sloane, I don't feel so good."

Sloane leaped from the couch and ran, taking the stairs two at a time. Jo kept pace right behind him.

When they entered Molly's room, Molly reached out for her. Jo sat on the edge of the bed and scooped the child into her lap. Molly's sturdy arms wrapped around her neck.

Sloane squatted beside them, smoothing his hand over Molly's back in a soothing motion. "What's the matter, Molly?"

"My tummy doesn't feel good."

"Do you need to go to the bathroom?" Jo asked, at a loss, never having dealt with the children when they didn't feel well.

"I don't know."

When in doubt, find the bathroom. Jo stood with Molly in her arms.

"I'll carry her if she's too heavy," Sloane offered.

Before Jo could reply, Connor appeared in the doorway, clutching his stomach. "I don't feel very good."

Jo and Sloane's exchanged looks over Molly's head. The acknowledgment of impending disaster ended abruptly when Molly spilled the contents of her stomach down the front of Jo's shirt.

"STOMACH FLU. There's a minor epidemic. The good news is after one or two really miserable days, they'll be right as rain." The doctor gave them a hearty smile.

Jo cuddled Tara in her lap and stared across at Sloane, dismay evident in her caramel-flecked eyes. "That's the *good* news?" She squared her shoulders and faced the doctor. "Go ahead, give us the bad."

Dr. Thomason grimaced. "Unfortunately, it's highly contagious. Connor probably picked it up at school. I'd suggest a mini-quarantine. I'd say it's highly probable that you and Mr. Murphy will come down with it, too. You've already been exposed. If you can keep any other members of the household from catching it, you'll be ahead of the game. It's especially tough on the old and the very young.''

Tara whimpered against Jo's chest while Molly lay listlessly on Sloane's lap. Connor sat propped against his side. Concern for Nora darkened Jo's eyes. "Don't worry,'' Sloane told her. "We'll send Nora home. I'll take care of everything.''

Jo sat a little straighter, as if he'd lifted a load off her shoulders. "So, what do we do for the kids?'' she asked Dr. Thomason.

"Give popsicles and keep them comfortable. It'll be a long two days, but then it should be over.''

"Even I can handle that.'' Her mouth curved into a rueful smile. Jo was a trooper. A good player to have on your team.

Unfortunately, he wasn't sure whose team she was on.

SLOANE COLLAPSED in the spindly legged chair in his room. Damn, if he wasn't tired. Taking care of the kids and Jo with the stomach flu while pursuing the investigation had drained him. Thank goodness he'd avoided the flu.

He punched Vic's home number into his cell phone. He wanted Vic to know they'd made some headway on the case.

"Yeah, hello?''

"You're even personable at home, Vic. Good to know you're consistent.''

"I hope you got some news and aren't just calling me to chat, Matthews.''

"I got a look at some of the financial records today

while the secretary was out to lunch. I also pulled up Cheltham's schedule and the shipping schedule. There's definitely a pattern between the three.''

''Good. But it's circumstantial. We can't arrest him on that.''

''If there's dirt, I'm gonna find it.''

''So, how are the kiddies? Have the little hellions tied you up lately?''

Protective instincts that had nothing to do with being a cop came out in spades. ''Actually, the kids are great. I don't know what the hell was wrong with all those other nannies. They're really not bad kids—well, not that bad— they just get into stuff.'' He recalled some of their dinner conversations. ''And they're very outspoken.''

''Jeez Louise! Have we got a new recruit for the Daddy Brigade or what, Matthews?'' Vic came as close to cordial as Sloane had ever witnessed. What was with him? Just because Sloane liked the Cheltham kids didn't mean he was looking to sign up for the Daddy Brigade. ''But we got to find a volunteer for the Wife Brigade first,'' Vic continued. ''If you're gonna do it, Matthews, do it right.'' Kids. Marriage. Frightening propositions— both of them.

Even scarier was how quickly Jo's face—ghastly green from the stomach flu—came to mind. Desperate, Sloane tried to plug Tiffany Burns into his mental picture. She had those great big…eyes. But stubborn, aggravating, entertaining, captivating woman that she was, Jo wouldn't budge.

If he was this messed up from Jo and her bunch, just how out of control would his life be with a wife and kids of his own? ''Not gonna happen, Vic.''

''You oughta think about finding a nice girl and settling down. I could introduce you to my niece, Vicky.''

Vic, offering fatherly advice, was one thing. Vic offering his niece on a blind date conjured up terrifying images. Sloane needed to dump this conversation.

"Uh, I think I hear one of the kids crying."

"Yeah, well mine are all in bed so me and Gladys are gonna have a little private time. The youngest one just started kin-de-garten and the wife's been making noise about missing a baby. Hey, a man's gotta do what a man's gotta do to keep the missus happy, eh, Matthews?"

Thank God his imagination didn't carry him far enough to envision that. "Uh, yeah. Catch you later, Vic."

"I'll have Gladys find Vicky's number and you can give her a call."

"Sure thing."

Yeah, maybe when hell froze over.

Jo DROPPED THE PHONE in disgust. She'd tried unsuccessfully all morning to get through to Max and Cici. So she decided to take a walk down to Max's office. Maybe Tiffany had heard from them. Even if she hadn't, the fresh air and exercise would do Jo good.

The house was empty until she ran into Mrs. Price in the kitchen. Jo was pleased to see her kindly face, having been sequestered in her room with the stomach flu for the past two days.

"Feeling better, dear?" Mrs. Price diligently stirred a pot of soup on the stove.

"Much better. Thank you." Although Sloane had handled all the dirty dishes in an effort to minimize spreading germs, Mrs. Price had kept a steady supply of broth and dry crackers available for the sick ones. Jo hoped Mrs.

Price didn't catch the awful bug. "You aren't feeling sick, are you?"

"Good heavens, no. I'm healthy as a horse. Now that you're feeling better, will you be going home?" Mrs. Price didn't look up from her pot.

"Oh, no. I think we'll stay until Cici and Max return." Or until Jo found some answers as to who was snooping around Max's office and why.

"Just wanted to know how much food to prepare. I'm sure the children will enjoy you being here."

Jo nodded as she opened the back door. "It's nice to spend time with them."

"You don't realize how much family means until they're taken away from you." A faint sniffle followed.

Jo let herself out the back door, not wanting to pry into Mrs. Price's business. Jo realized she didn't know anything about Mrs. Price. It sounded as if she didn't have much family left and missed them. Jo's heart ached for the older woman.

It was hard to feel melancholy in the wash of autumn sun warming the rear garden. A butterfly winged gracefully past. Jo paused to soak up the sun and warmth, her eyes closed, her face lifted to the sky.

In the still of the moment, Tiffany's voice drifted through the open window of her office. "Be sure to park on the street and meet me here at midnight tomorrow night." Tiffany paused. "Yes. I've got a key and it's safe. I can get us into Mr. Cheltham's office. Just make sure you use the street entrance. 'Bye."

Jo carefully retraced her steps. It didn't matter if Tiffany had heard from Cici or Max. Far more important was who she was meeting in Max's office tomorrow night—and why.

"VICKY? Hi. My name's Sloane Matthews." Sloane heaved a sigh of relief that she'd actually been home. "Your uncle Vic gave me your number. I thought maybe you'd like to grab a bite to eat and a movie."

"Hi. Uncle Vic mentioned you might call. I'm not a big movie fan, but I'd love to do dinner." The voice on the other end of the phone sounded like a female version of Vic. But at this point, Sloane didn't even care if she looked like Vic.

"How about tonight?"

"I know girls aren't supposed to go out if someone only gives them one day's notice—" *That was news to him.* "—but I am available."

"Uh, great. How about I pick you up around seven?" He jotted down the address she gave him. "See you then."

He hung up and wiped the sweat off his brow.

Hell had not frozen over. Oh, no. It was far, far worse than that. He'd had the most horrifying dreams all night. Jo Calhoun decked out in a wedding dress, enticing him down the aisle. Jo holding a baby and looking at him with shining eyes. Jo, himself, and three kids in a mini-van driving to Disney World singing that song about wheels on a bus. Finally he'd woken up in a cold sweat and a blind panic.

Something was happening to him and he didn't like it. Not one little bit.

7

"SO, HOW'RE YOU FEELING?" Nora dropped onto the other end of the sofa.

Jo leaned back on the buttery-soft leather. "Fine. Much better. Incredible how one day you feel so sick and the next you're back on your feet."

"Are the kids in bed?"

The starting lineup for the game appeared on-screen. "Yeah. They were worn out. After two days in bed, they played hard today."

"Sloane's lucky he didn't come down with the bug."

"Uh-huh." Jo stared at the screen, reluctant to discuss Sloane. She refused to admit she was in a funk because he wasn't here watching the game with her. Surely even Nora could take the hint.

She couldn't. "He certainly took good care of you and the kids while you were sick."

"Yep." He'd taken great care of the kids. He'd been wonderful to her, too. Solicitous. Caring. Tender. Now he'd decided to skip the game. Fine. She did not miss him. No. That would verge on ridiculous. And Jo Calhoun never even entertained ridiculous—much less verged on it.

"Where is he?" Nora looked around, as if she'd just noted his absence. She didn't fool Jo for a second.

"He took the night off."

"What?"

"Time off. He's entitled to time off, Nora."

"So, what was he doing?" Nora pulled a nail file out of her pocket and worked on a hangnail.

"I believe he had a date tonight."

Nora flipped the file over and buffed, her eyes narrowed, her lips pursed. "He *told* you he had a date?"

"Oh, yeah. A blind date. Wanted to let me know he wouldn't make the game tonight. Wasn't that thoughtful?" Her voice quivered. Really, this had to be the result of residual flu symptoms and some hormonal surge.

Nora tucked away her nail file and stood. "Buck up, Josephina. This is good news. You've got the boy running scared."

"I don't get it." What purpose would prevarication serve? She knew very little about men and what made them tick. Nora could write a book.

"It's simple. If he hadn't mentioned it, that would've meant he didn't care if you knew or not. But the fact that he told you—not just that he'd be out, but out on a *date*—means he cares. And he's running scared because he cares."

Jo massaged the ache in her temples. "Okay." But she still didn't get it.

"Big bingo tournament tonight. I'll be out late. Do you need anything before I leave?"

"No. I've got the monitor for the kids, water, popcorn, and baseball." And her own company, which had always proved adequate in the past. Jo forced a smile. "Have a great time."

"How about, I won't do anything you wouldn't do?" Nora winked from the doorway.

The long-standing joke between them coaxed a genuine smile from Jo. Unbeknownst to Nora, that particular gap had narrowed considerably.

Jo vowed to blot Sloane from her mind for the remainder of the game. However, she spared him one last thought.

She hoped he had a miserable time.

SLOANE CLOSED the back door behind him. He smacked his leg with the rolled-up magazine in his right hand. What a miserable evening. He heard the television set. With any luck, the game was still on and Jo was still up.

He hurried down the hall and into the den. Jo had stretched out on the couch, a wicked-looking knitting needle poking up through a ball of yarn sat in the spot he usually occupied. Incidental or deliberate?

She didn't acknowledge him.

"Long game, huh?" He shifted from foot to foot, but she didn't sit up to make room for him on the couch.

"Yeah. Short date, huh?" Her tone made him think of a chilled mug at Tyrrell's Tavern. Definitely frosty.

"A disaster. Mind if I sit down?"

"Sure. Go ahead." She remained planted and looked pointedly at the armchair across the room.

He settled instead on the arm of the sofa, ignoring the fact that she ignored him. Faint circles shadowed her eyes. "Do you feel okay? Were the kids too much tonight? You look a little pale." Damn, he shouldn't have stayed out so long.

"Did you hurry home to tell me how awful I look?" That put a rosy glow in her cheeks.

Guilt washed over him. He didn't even have a ball and chain and he still felt like a wandering husband. "We just went to dinner before I took her home. We didn't even have dessert."

"What was so disastrous? Was she hideously unattractive? Was she boring? Were you embarrassed to be seen with her?'' Jo sat up and paused in her diatribe for breath.

Sloane took advantage and slid off the arm into his spot, moving the instrument of torture to the coffee table.

"What? What was so awful about her?'' Jo demanded.

Sloane unfurled the magazine and tossed it on top of the coffee table. He indicated the cover with a flick of his wrist. A gorgeous brunette pouted on the front. "Vicky Finelli. My date tonight.''

Jo glanced from Vicky's photo to him and back to the magazine. Good thing they'd already established he wasn't gay. Otherwise he felt sure Jo would pull that out of her bag next. "You didn't stay for dessert with *her?* What could possibly be wrong with her?''

He shrugged. "She was great. Entertaining. Gorgeous. Smart.'' With each descriptive, Jo's mouth grew a little tighter. "But I…I wanted to get back for the game. She isn't a baseball fan.''

Jo's brow cleared in understanding. The band of tension across his shoulders eased.

"Should I grab some more popcorn and a couple of beers?'' Sloane offered.

"Okay.''

He didn't need additional encouragement. He made the trip to the kitchen and was back in record time.

He passed her the opened bottle. She didn't drink it immediately, but turned her attention to the game.

She stroked her fingers up and down the length of the long neck. Sloane lengthened and hardened as surely as if she were touching him.

Jo covered a yawn. "Excuse me. If something doesn't happen soon, I may not be able to stay up for the whole game.''

She might not make it, but if she didn't stop rubbing

that damn bottle, he'd be up the whole night. The game. He should just concentrate on the game. That was why he'd come back early, wasn't it?

"Has anyone scored yet?"

"No, they can't get their balls in hand." She stopped fooling around with the bottle. Thank goodness. He couldn't take much more of that. His reprieve lasted only seconds. She put the bottle to her lips, then tilted her head back and took a long drink. She sighed with satisfaction. "Hmm. That's good."

Sloane could barely breathe. He certainly couldn't think. All the blood in his body had gravitated to one spot.

The announcer's voice called out, frantic with anticipation and excitement, "Is he gonna score? Is he gonna score? Bases are loaded. Just one ball could get Maddox from third base to home. Oh-hh, no. He struck out." The crowd groaned in disappointment and frustration. Sloane knew the feeling. "It was so close, folks. But the game's not over."

Jo finished her beer and stood. "I'm going to get a glass of water. Can I get you anything?"

Talk about a loaded question. How could she stand in front of him with her chocolate-brown eyes so serious and not know how she affected him?

Jo must have read a hint of what he'd really like in his expression. "From the kitchen. Do you want anything from the kitchen?" She edged toward the door.

One second she was edging, the next, her foot caught the leg of the coffee table and she fell sprawled across him. She upended the bowl and popcorn rained down on both of them. An instant after the shock of impact—she was no tiny woman—Sloane absorbed the feel of her against him: her bare leg thrust between his, the rounded,

plumpness of her buttocks wedged against his crotch, the
lean line of her back against his chest, the weight of her
head against his shoulder.

"Are you okay?"

She nodded against his shoulder. "Just winded." She
wriggled against him. "And your beer bottle's poking
me. We're both lucky it didn't break." Her hand felt
beneath her, intent on moving his bottle.

Sloane stilled her questing hand. A man could only
stand so much. "That's no beer bottle, honey. And yeah,
I feel very lucky it didn't break."

"Oh." That one word that spoke volumes. Then making no effort to get up, she rocked back against him.
Buttered popcorn nestled between the skin of her neck
and shoulder.

In the back of his mind Sloane knew several good
reasons he shouldn't do what he was about to do. But
for the life of him, he couldn't remember them. He bent
his head forward and nibbled a piece of popcorn off of
her shoulder. He licked the smear of butter from the
heated velvet softness of her neck. She tasted of salt and
woman. He dipped his tongue into the indentation at the
base of her throat, savoring the taste and texture of her
skin. "That was the best popcorn I ever had."

Jo slid off his lap and onto her knees to face him. Her
hair hung in loose disarray about her shoulders. Her eyes
glittered with a fire he knew he'd started.

She leaned forward. "I know there's a very good reason I shouldn't do this—" her voice held a husky note
"—but I can't remember why."

This chemistry between them had also killed her memory. "Neither can I."

She leaned toward him, her lips slightly parted. Her
hair brushed against his jaw and tickled his neck as she

leaned toward the open vee of his popcorn-littered shirt. Anticipation ripped through him, tightening his gut. He wanted—no, needed—to feel her mouth against his skin more than he needed his next breath.

Incredible. Her hot mouth nuzzled against his chest, eating the pieces of popcorn one at a time. She raised her head to gaze into his eyes, her breath coming in small measured pants. "I like the butter and salt best."

She dipped her head and swirled her tongue against the sensitized skin of his chest. She lapped at him like a kitten feasting on cream. With each stroke of her velvet tongue, he grew harder. As she leaned forward, her hardened nipples brushed against his belly. He massaged her thigh, his hand slipping beneath her shorts to knead the full roundness of her magnificent butt.

The intensity of his want shook him. He wanted to drive deep inside her, fill her with himself. He couldn't tell her who he was and why he was there. But he could offer one measure of honesty. He pulled her onto his lap. She sat astride him, facing him, the rhythm of her breathing in sync with his. He rocked against her and she gasped when she rubbed against his erection.

"Jo, I didn't skip dessert with Vicky tonight because of the game." He slipped his hands under the edge of her T-shirt and explored the satin plane of her back. He closed his eyes and rested his head between her breasts. "I came back because she wasn't you."

She winnowed her fingers through his hair. "I could've cleared that up for you before you left. There's usually very little confusion between me and a cover model."

He spanned the indention of her waist with his hands and inhaled the clean, womanly scent of her. He dropped back against the couch.

"Not once did I want to touch her the way I'm touching you." The smooth heat of her skin quivered beneath his splayed fingers. With his thumbs he traced rhythmic circles against the lace underside of her bra. Her lids lowered to half-mast.

"I didn't want to learn the taste of her skin..." He dipped his head to nuzzle the soft flesh at the base of her throat. One of them shuddered, perhaps both. "Or memorize her scent..."

He didn't just want a quick roll, a release from the sexual need that gripped him. He could've had that with Vicky Finelli. He'd received the message she'd relayed with her hand on his thigh under the table. Vicky meant far fewer complications and probably a good time. Only neither Sloane's flesh nor his spirit had been willing. He wanted Jo. This would be complicated. Hell, it already was. Probably unethical. He recognized Pandora's box, and still he ached to open it.

He tugged her shirt back into place and folded his hands over his belly. "I came back because I want you."

A secretive, seductive smile curved her lips. "Good."

Good? He'd bared his soul for good?

"Nora's out for the night—or at least a good portion of it." She slid off of his lap and the sofa to stand in front of him. She picked the monitor up off the table. "The kids are asleep."

"Your room or mine?"

"Neither."

"Huh?"

"You'll see." She walked toward the door.

He staggered to his feet, rooted to the spot by the mesmerizing sway of her hips. Jo turned at the doorway, and held out her hand in supplication, "Sloane, are you coming?"

He certainly hoped so. He tried not to limp, but walking in his condition presented a challenge. She laughed, a low throaty sound that indicated her appreciation of his finer points. He grinned down ruefully at his tented khakis. He'd crawl if Jo, with that promise in her eyes, was the prize.

JO LED SLOANE down the garden path. Literally. She carried a quilt tucked under her arm and in one hand, she clutched the monitor. The fingers of her other hand were entwined with Sloane's.

Booking a vacation in Jamaica was as close as she'd ever come to giving in to impetuousness. The word ''daring'' wasn't in her vocabulary. So if she was going to discover it now, she'd do it in a big way. This wasn't the real Jo Calhoun, this was the fantasy she'd sought.

Neither she nor Sloane spoke. The velvet heat of a warm Southern night wrapped around them. A symphony of crickets and the occasional tree frog offered a serenade. Stars littered the inky blackness of the sky, a sliver of a moon holding up one corner. The perfume of flowers lining the bricked path hung heavy in the still air.

The path ended at a screened gazebo set amid gnarled oaks festooned with Spanish moss. Still in sight of the house and well within monitor range, the gazebo seemed a world apart. They mounted the two steps and entered their own private fantasy.

Sloane took the monitor from her and placed it by the screened door. Jo spread the quilt over the plank flooring. She straightened and turned to face him, marvelously sensually aware of herself as she'd never been before, the slight abrading of her bra against the hard tips of her breast, the throbbing flesh at the juncture of her thighs.

"Do you know what I want?" He leaned against one of the posts, his hands tucked into his pockets.

Jo laughed quietly into the soft dark of the night. "I have a pretty good idea."

Although he stood in the dimpled shadow, she felt his answering smile. "I want to see you naked." His smile faded. "I want to watch you strip off every layer until there's only you. Will you undress for me?" His voice washed over her in a harsh rasp. His words inflamed her, emboldened her beyond anything she'd ever imagined.

She slipped off her sandals. Grasping her T-shirt at the hem, she slowly pulled it up her body, feeling the brush of cotton against her skin with almost painful intensity. Tugging the shirt over her head, she tossed it aside. Moving with a slow languor, she unfastened her shorts and slid them down her legs. She stood in the puddle of cloth, wearing only a lace bra and panties.

"Go ahead, Jo. Take the rest off." Strain threaded his voice.

The musk of her arousal mingled with the scents of the night. "Do you know what I want, Sloane?" She reached for the front hook of her bra.

"Tell me. Tell me what you want."

She unsnapped the bra and shrugged it off. "I want to get to know that dragon on your belly. Intimately." Hooking her thumbs in the waistband of her panties, she skimmed them down. She stood naked in front of him.

Unmet needs and raw desire pulsed between them. Sloane pushed away from the wall and walked toward her. "Baby, you're perfect."

Desire convulsed low in her belly at his rough reverence. "Now your turn. Take your clothes off for me."

He stripped off his shoes, shirt, khakis and briefs with

sensual deliberation, pausing to extract a foil wrapper from his wallet and drop it on the quilt. All Jo's coherent thought fled. He was magnificent—broad shoulders, hair-roughened chest, that dragon hiding on his belly, lean hips, powerful thighs, and an amazing display of virility. Jo's thighs clenched and her nipples tightened in eager anticipation.

Urgency replaced languor as they came together. Tongues stroked against one another as their sweat-slickened bodies strained together. Sloane cupped her buttocks, kneading her, lifting her against his erection. Jo clutched at the broad expanse of his shoulders, reveling in the clench of muscle beneath her hands.

Of one accord, they stretched out on the quilt. His hands shaking, Sloane ripped open the foil package and donned protection. He rolled onto his back. With his hands guiding her hips, Jo slid on top, sheathing him within the tight folds of her body.

Moonlight slanted across the flat planes of his belly, that fire-breathing dragon teasing her. Sloane nearly drove her mad as he coaxed and encouraged her to find completion. She rode waves of pleasure that crested higher and higher until she clenched around him and found a release that seared her to her soul.

Sloane answered her cry with his own, as if he'd waited on her satisfaction before seeking his own.

Replete, she stretched out on top of him. His arms enfolded her as satiation weighted her limbs, leaving her deliciously lethargic. Sloane rolled onto his side, taking her with him. The cadence of his heart beneath her ear lulled her deeper into a state of relaxation. Sloane nuzzled against the damp edge of her hair as her eyes grew heavier and heavier.

Drifting off to sleep in his arms, she had the oddest sensation of homecoming.

SLOANE STROKED HER damp hair off of her forehead and watched Jo sleep. Wasn't it his job as the man to roll over and go to sleep following sensational lovemaking? He grinned into the dark. But no, she had to beat him to it. Leave it to his Jo.

His Jo? Was she? In the most absolute sense of the word, she had been. He'd never felt that any other human being belonged to him, with him. He'd never experienced the emotional connection to another person he felt to this woman.

Light filtered through the draping moss and dappled the alabaster of her skin. He subdued the urge to explore the slope of her breast and its dark crest. Just the thought turned him on, but he didn't think his ego could take it if Jo slept through his advances. And as he knew from previous experience, once Jo fell asleep, nothing woke her.

Sloane stood and dressed, clipping the monitor to his belt. He collected Jo's clothes and stacked them on top of her before he gathered her up in the quilt. He staggered as he navigated the stairs from the gazebo to the bricked path.

"Baby, you're gonna have to start falling asleep where you plan to stay for the night, cause I can't keep hauling you around."

She snuggled closer to his chest in response.

He grinned and automatically surveyed the back of the house. His attention riveted to Cheltham's office. The green light of the computer monitor glowed behind the pulled shade. A figure was silhouetted in front of the glow.

Sloane silently apologized to Jo as he shifted her to a fireman's carry and took off at a trot. Someone was in Cheltham's office. As soon as he took care of Jo, he'd take care of his case.

8

"SO, WHAT ARE YOU telling me, Matthews?" Vic asked.

"At 12:05 last night, someone was in Cheltham's office, at his computer. I spotted the light and silhouette in the office window."

"Male or female?"

"First impression—female."

"What about the young broad and the old lady?"

Sloane winced at the terminology. Jo and Nora would have a piece of Vic if they ever heard him refer to them that way. "Cheltham's grandmother-in-law was out playing bingo. The sister-in-law was asleep."

"You sure?"

"Positive." And then some.

"Maybe it wasn't them, but they could be working with someone. Where'd they think you'd be?"

"I thought about that. Whoever it was probably knew I'd be out late last night. But remember I told you that Cheltham's sister-in-law knocked the hell out of her head in his office? That weighted door sent her flying and she hit the edge of his desk. After last night, I think someone pushed her because she was about to see something she wasn't supposed to. I think someone else is working with Cheltham." A surge of anger ripped through him. If his theory proved true and he got his hands on the person responsible for hurting Jo....

"So, who do you think was in there? Why were they

there? And how the hell they'd get by you, Ace Ventura?''

"There're two ways to gain access to Cheltham's private office—through the house and through his secretary's office.''

"What about the window where you saw this person?''

"Decorative iron bars. Anyway, I secured the house and made sure the kids were okay. I returned and approached the office from the house. By that time, the mystery guest had vanished into thin air.''

"So, you got a theory as to why someone's bumping around in Cheltham's office while he's out of town?''

"Looks like a partner to me.''

"Then why the secrecy and late-night visits?''

"Maybe his partner wants to keep it hush-hush. Maybe it's a double cross.''

"So what's the plan, Matthews?''

"Cheltham's mystery partner seems to prefer arriving around midnight. I'm going to stake out the office tonight.''

"What makes you think they'll show?''

"Just a hunch. Cheltham's only out of the country for another two days. When I compared his travel schedule and the computer entries, there's always a flurry of activity right before he returns.''

"Hope you're right. Time's running out, Matthews. Need any backup tonight on this?''

"I can handle it.''

JO LAY VERY, VERY STILL in her bed, her eyes closed. She'd had the most incredibly erotic dream. In it, Sloane Murphy had been the perfect lover. If she could just get back to sleep, perhaps she'd be able to tap back into the fantasy.

The shrill of her alarm shattered any hopes of drifting back to sleep. Jo fought the urge to weep with disappointment. She usually dreamed of hardware hookups and software links. Dreaming of hookups and links of another nature had brought her intense satisfaction.

She reached over to hit the snooze button. *Owww!* Muscles ached in places that hadn't ached for a long time. She blinked and looked toward those aching muscles. Naked flesh greeted her gaze. She lay on top of the quilt that lay on top of her still-made bed.

Last night wasn't a dream. It had been real. Jo had often thought sex overrated, but now she revised her opinion. Or perhaps, she'd discovered the difference between having sex and making love with someone you connected with on a soul-deep level.

Jo never looked at herself naked. It simply wasn't a situation that came up. She stripped down twice a day— once to shower, once to don a T-shirt for bed—but she never stopped to look at herself. She didn't need to scrutinize her flaws or to examine too closely where she fell short of the mark. She'd always considered her butt too big and her boobs too small.

Now she saw herself through Sloane's eyes. She recalled the way he'd admired and complimented her body, the pleasure he'd found there. She took stock of herself bared. Suddenly, all her parts seemed just right.

A wail and a banging on her bedroom door catapulted her out of bed. Wrapping the quilt around her, she threw open the door. Molly stood outside, gesturing frantically across the landing.

"Save him, Aunt Jo-Jo. You gots to save him."

Jo finally calmed her down enough to figure out Hermes had escaped his cage.

"He scaped from his cage and 'Phisto ran after him. Don't let him eat him, Aunt Jo-Jo."

Jo shook her head, resigned to doing the good aunt thing even if it meant saving a rodent that icked her out. She dressed in record time and ran down the hall to save Hermes.

Jo crossed the landing and stood in the hall. "Do you have any idea where he went?"

Molly pointed toward Sloane's room.

Jo rapped on the bedroom door that stood cracked open. No response. She turned to Molly, "Where's Mr. Sloane?"

"Tara wasn't through with breakfast, so he stayed in the kitchen with her." Sniffles punctuated her answer.

Entering his room without his permission seemed invasive. "Let's wait. I'm sure Mr. Sloane can find Hermes when he brings Tara up."

Tears flooded Molly's eyes. "'Phisto followed him in there. 'Phisto's gonna eats Hermes."

As if the cat took pride in his role in this debacle, he yowled from inside the room. Molly wailed. Jo wavered. She hated that damned rat—mouse, technically a mouse—but she loved her niece. She couldn't stand around and do nothing. Molly might face psychotherapy years from now because the cat ate the rat and her aunt Jo let it happen.

She squared her shoulders. She was going in. "Molly, go get Hermes's cage and bring it here."

While Molly fulfilled her part in the mission, Jo entered Sloane's room. Mephisto sat atop the mirrored dresser, staring down at the top drawer, evil intent etched on his kitty countenance. The top drawer hadn't been closed all the way. She recognized the beady eyes taking cover under socks.

Jo scooped the cat off the dresser and suffered his baleful stare. She exchanged cat for cage with Molly, then closed the door. "Mr. Sloane can get Hermes when he comes back." And she wouldn't have to touch the furry little rodent.

Molly glared at Mephisto. "You're a mean, bad ole kitty."

Jo agreed with the general sentiment but not the reasoning. "Oh, honey. Mephisto's not bad because he chased Hermes. That's his instinct."

Molly thrust out her bottom lip, "Well, he's got a bad stink."

Out of the mouths of babes….

"It's the way he's made. It's his job in life." Molly appeared marginally satisfied. "Cats were meant to eat rats."

The moment the last phrase left her mouth, she knew she'd said too much. Far too much. She should've quit while she was ahead.

Molly embarked on a fresh bout of crying. Her little shoulders shook as she pleaded, "Please go get Hermes, Aunt Jo. Pretty please. He's scared a death."

Jo glanced down the hall desperately. Where was Sloane? How long did it take Tara to finish eating? Dumb question. She'd witnessed firsthand how Tara refined the art of dawdling at the table. Jo resigned herself to rat retrieval.

"Wait right here. I'll be back in a minute with Hermes."

Jo left Molly in the hall and closed Sloane's door behind her. She didn't need the darn rat running somewhere else. She opened the cage and placed it in the spot Mephisto previously occupied on the dresser. She opened the drawer to catch Hermes. Hermes scurried beneath a mound of socks. Jo shifted them aside, her fingers closing around metal. Handcuffs. Bright shiny handcuffs. Right next to a bright shiny badge labeled S.P.D., engraved with the name Detective Sloane Matthews. Right next to a nasty-looking gun.

A wave of nausea washed over Jo as implications battered her.

"Did you gets him, Aunt Jo?" Molly called from the other side of the door, mobilizing her.

Being lied to took the edge off touching the little varmint. She snatched Hermes up from the corner he'd backed into and tossed him in the cage. "Oh, yeah. I've got him now." Very carefully she restored order to the sock drawer. A quick glance around the room revealed the closet door standing ajar. She'd say she found Hermes in there.

Cage in hand, she strode across the room and threw open the door. Molly threw her arms around Jo's waist. "Thank you, Aunt Jo. You're the bestest."

Sloane appeared at the top of the stairs, Tara propped on his hip. "What's going on?"

"Aunt Jo-Jo's the bestest in the world," Molly proclaimed.

"Oh, I'll agree with that. She sure is." The lazy heat in his gaze swept her from head to toe, lending a whole different meaning to his words. "But what's she doing?"

Two minutes ago, Jo would've delighted in his private banter. Now she itched to slap that sensual regard right off of his handsome, deceptive face.

Jo smiled as sweetly as possible. "I just tracked down a rat."

SLOANE WATCHED JO pour herself a second cup of coffee and serve up a first to Nora. Things felt awkward between them. But then again, he'd never experienced a "morning after" that included kids, a grandmother, and pets.

Connor came in, carrying a bucket with a ventilated lid and a pair of long, plastic tweezers. "I gotta catch some bugs for a science project. Want to help, Mr. Sloane?"

Tara jumped up and down.

"I wanna hunt bugs, too." Molly invited herself.

"I don't want the girls to come," Connor appealed to Sloane.

The problem wasn't as much the girls as it was a matter of sharing attention. Sloane stood. "How about we all go on a bug-hunting expedition and you're the leader?"

"I'm in charge?"

"You're in charge."

Molly's expression threatened mutiny.

Sloane negotiated. "It's his project, Molly. Maybe you could carry the notepad"

Her brow cleared and she danced around the kitchen with Tara. "Let's go now."

Nora grabbed Jo by the elbow and herded her along with him and the kids. "Come on, Jo. We can have our coffee on the patio while the kids search."

When Jo hung back, Nora prodded her out the door. "It's nice outside. Not too hot yet. And I want to hear all about last night."

Jo emitted a hybrid choking/strangling sound. Nora slapped her on the back.

"What's wrong with you, girl? Did your team get skunked in the ball game last night?"

Sloane didn't hang around to hear the rest. He'd rather track down bugs any day than withstand Nora's grilling. He herded the kids down the same brick path Jo had led him last night. The gazebo caught his attention. He glanced back at Jo. Without any difficulty, he anticipated a repeat of the previous evening with a few minor variations. And maybe a shirt. Splinters could be painful. He didn't need to think in that direction now. Later. He deliberately looked away from the gazebo.

Sloane dropped to his knees and joined in the search for roly-polys. Five minutes and several bugs later, he and the girls stretched out on the grass and indulged in a little cloud gazing. Connor, their fearless bug leader, continued to track down insects.

"That looks like a dog with a bone." Molly pointed to a cloud formation.

"Hey, it does." Sloane didn't have to feign enthusiasm. This was fun. He'd never spent much time around kids, even growing up. They were fun. "Look, right there. It's a double scoop of ice cream in a cone."

"Mmm. Yummy." Molly slid her hand into his.

Sloane knew a moment of soul-deep contentment. The lazy drone of insects, the kids' laughter, Molly's small hand clutching his, the murmur of Jo and Nora's voices on the patio—it would be a lucky man who could call this his. But he was not that man. An insidious voice inside his head whispered that he could be, one day. With the right woman.

Molly sang out a number of creative cloud interpretations. Tara rolled around on her back. How would their carefree lives change if their father went to prison? Sloane hated the idea of what it would mean to these three kids, but dammit, he wasn't the criminal. It was his job to find criminals and to bring them to justice. If Cheltham was guilty, he'd take him in.

Tara tired of their game and wandered off to the gazebo. He let her roam, confident she couldn't get into anything in there.

Minutes later, he realized just how wrong he could be.

Tara toddled down the stairs and danced along the brick path wearing a pair of white lace panties on her head.

Molly spotted her at the same time. "Look. Tara's a cloud. Tara's a cloud."

Dammit all to hell. How had he overlooked Jo's panties last night when he gathered up her clothes?

Connor dropped his tweezers. "That's disgusting. You've got panties on your head."

"Poo panty clouds." Molly dissolved into giggles. Tara, still dancing, joined in the giggles.

Sloane knew as surely as he knew his name, he shouldn't look over at Jo and Nora. He tried. He really did. He couldn't help himself.

He looked at Jo.

Nora looked at Jo.

Jo left.

But not before he'd caught a glimpse of her face. She would kill him for this.

"So, IT LOOKS LIKE YOU lost something last night." Nora followed her into her bedroom, closing the door behind her.

More than Nora would ever know—dreams, fantasies, trust, fledgling self-esteem in her femininity. All things considered, what was a pair of panties? "It looks that way."

Jo walked to her bedroom window overlooking the backyard. Sloane and the kids remained in the garden. Jo's underwear no longer adorned Tara's head.

"Are you going to tell me what happened or do I have

to drag it out of you?'' Nora laughed but Jo recognized it as no idle threat. Nora could worry a subject to death, until you begged to give her details.

Jo paced from the window to the bed and back again. The whole sorry mess and all its implications had chased around in her brain since she'd discovered Sloane's true identity. Why were the police here undercover? Why was Max so stressed? Who had been in Max's office last Sunday night? Why was Tiffany meeting someone at the office tonight?

She still didn't have any answers. But she'd formulated a loose theory and a plan. Part of the plan included getting Nora and the kids out of the house. If Nora knew everything, she'd insist Jo take the kids and leave. Jo wouldn't exactly lie, but she wasn't exactly going to tell Nora everything she knew. And the stinking phone lines were down between here and Bogota so she hadn't even been able to quiz Max and Cici.

Jo sat on the bed and propped herself against the headboard. Her bright blue eyes alight with interest, Nora settled on the end. ''You tried a little horizontal rhumba, didn't you?''

Jo felt a blush creep up her face. It was one thing to participate in the horizontal rhumba, but quite another thing to discuss it with your grandmother—regardless of how liberated she was. ''Uh, yeah.''

Nora slapped the duvet cover with glee. ''Girl, I saw the chemistry between the two of you from the beginning. It was powerful.''

Powerful didn't begin to describe what had transpired between them last night. But Nora was right—there'd been chemistry between them from the beginning.

''Max and Cici are back tomorrow. Do you think you could take the kids to your house tonight?'' Jo kept her fingers crossed that Nora wouldn't suggest Jo and Sloane go away.

"Sure thing, honey. I've been waiting a long time for you to meet the right man." Nora winked, ready and willing to aid and abet. "When should we leave?"

Nora seemed so excited, Jo hated deceiving her. "Uh, the sooner, the better."

"Give me half an hour to pack the kids's bags and then the coast'll be clear." Nora stood and started for the door only to retrace her steps and envelop Jo in a hug. "I'm so happy for you, Josephina. I've been worried about you the last couple of years. Worried you wouldn't find happiness. But Sloane's a good man."

Right. Sloane was a two-faced, lying, rat. But now was not the time to break that news to Nora.

9

SLOANE FELT IT in his bones. Today was his lucky day. He waved to the kids as they piled into the car with Nora. They wouldn't be back until tomorrow.

He closed the front door and turned around to find Jo standing on the bottom step. He damn near forgot to breathe when he saw the invitation in her eye. He walked over to the stairs, her vantage point from the step, leaving them at eye level.

Jo scraped a fingernail down the front of his shirt and he sucked in a breath, his muscles clenching in response. She leaned into him and he slid his hands beneath her shirt to mold against the warm satin of her back. He tested the sensitive skin of her neck against his lips. A faint shudder rippled through her, yet she pulled away and stepped back from him.

"Let's go upstairs." She caught his hands in hers.

"If that's what you want, then that's what we'll do." Upstairs. Downstairs. On the stairs. He didn't much care as long as he was with her.

They mounted the stairs in silence, Sloane following the mesmerizing curve of her bottom. She didn't hesitate at the top of the stairs, but led him across the landing to her room.

The heavy curtains were drawn, leaving the room dim and intimate. The sheets were turned back on the bed and she'd mounded pillows against the ornate ironwork headboard. Even though they had the house to themselves, she closed the door with her toe. She'd obviously put some thought into this scenario.

Today *was* his lucky day.

Jo left him there and walked to the other side of the bed. She began to unbutton her blouse. "Why don't you undress and meet me in the middle?" she offered huskily.

Sloane watched as she shrugged off her T-shirt. His mouth grew dry at the pout of her nipples through the purple lace of her bra. He was hardly aware of taking off his own clothes. He stretched out on the bed and propped on his side, already aroused to an aching point. Jo smiled as he voiced his approval of the matching scrap of purple lace panties beneath her shorts.

She climbed onto the mattress, braced on her hands and her knees.

"Aren't you going to take off your bra and panties?" His voice sounded strained even to himself.

"All in good time." She straddled his leg and reigned a series of tiny kisses from his knee up his thigh. He reached for her and she batted playfully at his questing hands. "Just lay back and enjoy."

With pleasure, he complied. Her tongue swirled against his hip, and he thought he might explode when her shoulder brushed against his erection.

He closed his eyes and absorbed the feel of her mouth moving against his belly, the flick of her tongue against his nipple, the brush of damp satin panties against his thigh. He sighed as she tugged his arms over his head, her lips following the path of her hands. She sat astride his chest, leaning forward and he inhaled her womanly scent. Her warm, satin-covered breast hovered a short distance from his mouth.

He heard a familiar click but it took a moment for the

sound to register in his brain. By then the press of cold steel effectively trapped his hands to the headboard.

Incredulous, Sloane tried to pull his hands down. Police-issue manacles bit into his wrist.

She'd handcuffed him to her bed with his own damn cuffs.

She sat up and rolled off of him and the bed in one lithe movement. "Was there something you wanted to tell me?"

Damn, how had she found out? When had she found out? And just how angry was she?

One glance at her face, answered his last question. She was pretty damn mad.

"Okay, so I'm a cop. Uncuff me, Jo."

"No. Not until you tell me why you're here pretending to be a nanny." Her eyes glittered and damn if she wasn't magnificent wrapped up in her anger and that purple underwear.

"You know I could charge you with obstructing a police officer in the line of duty."

"And you know I could call 9-1-1 and let your buddies find you naked and handcuffed to the bed."

A part of him had to admire her guts. The part of him that wasn't howling in protest at her threat. "You wouldn't."

She picked up a cell phone. "Want to bet on that?"

No. No, he didn't want to bet on that. That was an absolute worst-case scenario.

"I'll tell you when you uncuff me."

Jo shook her head, her hair brushing against her bare shoulders. "Sorry, I can't do that. I'll uncuff you when you tell me."

Sloane considered his position and his options. His position was pretty clear—naked and handcuffed to her bed.

His option was pretty basic—tell her the barest facts that would get him by or have her call in Blakely.

"Someone's smuggling pre-Columbian artifacts out of South America and selling them on the black market." Sloane watched her carefully, gauging her reaction.

Her face blanched, putting to rest any lingering suspicion he had that she had any knowledge of the operation. "And you think that someone is Max?" She sank to the edge of the mattress.

"I'm sorry, Jo, but all the evidence points to him." He hated to see the knowledge register in her eyes that if Max was guilty, Cici might be, as well.

She raised her chin. "You're wrong. Max isn't smuggling artifacts."

"I know it's your family and you don't want to believe it, but everything we've found indicates he is."

"Maybe you haven't found everything then." She knew something. He read it in her face. "Someone was in Max's office last Sunday night. The ledger was up on the screen when I came in."

"He could have a partner."

"He could also have an enemy. I think someone's setting him up." She sounded so sure.

"I'd like to believe that, but who and why?" And he would. He cared about Cheltham's family more than he should. He didn't want to see their lives ripped apart. But it was pretty awkward discussing his case wearing handcuffs. "Why don't you uncuff me now?"

"How do I know I can trust you?" Sloane watched the byplay of suspicion wash her face. "How do I know you won't arrest Max when he gets home tomorrow?"

"How do I know I can trust you? How do I know you won't tip Max and Cici off?" He tossed the ball back in her court.

Jo tortured her bottom lip with her teeth, obviously torn.

"We can work together, Jo. I just want to find out the truth. If you're so sure Max is being framed, help me prove it."

"Okay. I guess we have to trust one another." She wasn't happy about it, but he read the resolve in her eyes. She retrieved a key from the desk drawer and moved over to the bed.

Climbing back up on the mattress, Jo leaned over him to fit the key in the lock. He stared in fascination as the pulse at the base of her throat accelerated.

Sloane closed his eyes against the tantalizing sight of her breasts wrapped in purple lace. Unfortunately, closing his eyes only heightened his awareness of her musky fragrance.

"Damn." She swore as her bare stomach pressed against his cheek.

He wasn't sure how much more of this he could stand. "What are you doing, Jo?"

She climbed farther up the bed, leaning past him. "I dropped the stinking key." She stretched, bringing her thigh temptingly close to his mouth.

Sloane gave in to temptation. He pressed his mouth against the soft flesh in front of him. She froze with a whimper.

"Forget about the key, Jo." He muttered as he nuzzled against her, heady from her fragrance and her taste. He caught the edge of her panties in his teeth and tugged.

"But what about the key?" She breathed huskily.

Another tug and the delicate lace holding her panties together ripped. "We'll find the key later."

Jo clung to the iron headboard and rubbed his thigh with her instep. "What key?"

Jo FOLLOWED SLOANE into Max's office. They'd agreed to work together, but she didn't know whether he really wanted to discover the truth or to merely gather enough implication to make a case against Max. As he'd proposed, they each had to trust the other. And Jo had to trust that the truth would prove her theory that Max was being framed.

"What exactly are we looking for?"

Sloane grimaced and rubbed the back of his neck. "An artifact or two laying around would be a nice start, but he—" Jo poked him in the back. "Okay, okay, whoever the culprit is, they're too smart for that. Since you're convinced Max is being set up, who do you think it is?"

Sloane had shared the circumstantial evidence against Max, which merely reinforced her suspicions about Tiffany. Jo leaned against Max's desk. "The ledger entries shifting money always occur when Max is out of town, right? There's no sign of forced entry into his office. The manipulated files are pass code protected. I'd say that all points to Ms. Burns."

Sloane scanned the contents of Max's file drawer. "That's pretty good, but you're missing one critical component."

Jo refused to divulge her ace in the hole—Tiffany's assignation at midnight tonight. That stretched her trust factor a tad too thin. "What? I thought that about covered it."

"Motive. Why would she frame her boss? If he goes to jail, she's out of a job." Sloane returned a sheaf of papers to a manila folder.

"And Max's motive?"

"Money. It's one of the big criminal motivations."

Jo simply didn't believe it held true in this case.

Money definitely motivated Max, but he seemed more driven by the scent of success.

"You said 'one' of the motivations. What are some of the others?"

"Revenge runs a close second. Men in Cheltham's position usually step on a few toes along the way. Anyone come to mind?"

Jo tried to recall any mention of disgruntled employees or suppliers, anything that might provide a lead, but came up blank.

"There's a piece missing somewhere." Sloane closed the drawer with finality. "Unfortunately, I don't think we're going to find it here now."

Jo suspected Sloane was right. She'd probably find the missing piece when Tiffany showed up at midnight.

Jo VACILLATED to the point of annoying herself. She wanted to see the game, *but* she *didn't* want to see Sloane. He shattered her control. She wanted to see the game, *and* she *did* want to see Sloane. Control was severely overrated. The game was a given. She could watch it on any number of TVs in the house, but there was nothing like seeing it on the big screen. Did. Didn't. Did. Didn't. She shoved the pillow over her head. A little oxygen deprivation couldn't possibly worsen matters.

Where was the clearheaded businesswoman who owned and ran a successful enterprise? She needed her back.

She tossed the pillow aside and stood. She'd go down and watch the game. She'd project an image of cool. Cordial. In control. She'd be herself. She smoothed her hands over the skirt of her sundress. So, she wore a dress instead of a T-shirt and shorts. Big deal. She deliberately didn't pull a brush through her hair, loathe to give the impression she'd primped to watch the game.

Resolute, she marched downstairs and into the den. Sloane grinned at her, flashing that right-cheeked dimple. The big goof! Did he have to act like a puppy with a new playmate?

She stifled the urge to grin back. Good thing she knew the real deal, otherwise she'd mistake his delight at seeing her as genuine. *Cool. Calm.* She sat on her end of the couch.

Sloane nudged the bowl between them. "I made us some popcorn." He thrust a long-neck her way. "And I brought you a beer."

She took the beer from him. "Thanks." Jo shifted her attention back to the screen. "It should be a good game."

"Yeah." He shifted closer on the couch, touching her hair tentatively. "Your hair looks nice. Sort of messy and sexy. You did something different to it, didn't you?"

Jo hardened her heart and thought with her head. "Yeah. I didn't brush it."

"Oh. Well, it looks nice, anyway." He shifted on the sofa as if seeking a comfortable spot. "Jo, about last night…"

"What about last night?" If he dubbed last night or this afternoon a mistake, she wouldn't be responsible for her actions.

"I want you to know I would've never left your panties behind on purpose. They were with the rest of your clothes when I picked you up. I think I lost them when I stumbled coming down the stairs because you're sort of heavy—" He floundered at the look on her face.

Normally even-tempered, Jo felt as if the top of her head might blow off at any moment.

"Only a little heavy. Really."

"Shut up."

"I didn't mean…"

"Just shut the hell up, Sloane." Jo stared steadfastly at the starting lineup.

The seconds dragged by.

"I've got a solution, though. One I think you'll like." His voice dropped to that husky cadence she found so hard to resist. She shifted, trying to ignore the tingling awareness between her legs. Pathetic when a man could make you ache merely with the sound of his voice.

"A solution infers a problem. What's the problem you've solved?" Okay, so maybe exciting rather than pathetic.

"The problem is misplaced panties. The solution, don't wear them."

His tone was low and provocative. His suggestion, naughty. And arousing. Very, very arousing. She swallowed hard. She should end this right now. Just get up and walk out. She should.

She didn't. She sat riveted to the sofa as liquid heat dampened the garment in question. Despite who he was and why he was here, she wanted him. Fiercely.

She looked at him. A febrile desire danced in the green depths of his eyes, echoing her own.

He twined her hair around his hand, his fingertips rubbing the sensitive skin of her neck. She arched like a cat seeking solace against the backs of his knuckles.

"Are you wearing any panties now, Jo?" His voice was a husky rasp that quivered through her, leaving her trembling.

She ran the tip of her tongue over her lips. They felt swollen, aroused. "Yes." She couldn't say more.

"Would you take them off for me?" He tugged gently on her hair, until her head rested against the back of the sofa. She turned her head to face him, her breath coming in shallow pants. She was on fire and only he knew how to quench the flame. "Now. Will you take them off now, baby?"

She ran her hands up under the edge of her sundress, raising it to the tops of her thighs. She hooked her thumbs under the elastic of her bikini briefs. Jo shifted her hips upward and skimmed the panties down, as requested.

With a harsh groan, he captured her mouth, shifting her until she lay across his lap. Sloane moved his hand beneath her dress, teasing and tormenting her. His clever fingers promised paradise as his hardened length nudged erotically against the backs of her thighs. Jo dropped her head to the arm of the couch and savored the double play of sensation.

Pleasure gathered at her center, building in intensity like the steady lapping of waves against the shore until it crashed over her, drenching her. Her eyes drifted shut as satisfaction rippled through her, the calm following a storm.

SLOANE SHIFTED Jo's sleeping form to a more comfortable position as he navigated the stairs. Her head lolled against his shoulder, the warmth of her breath teasing his neck. She was an incredible woman. Smart, sassy, strong, sexy, and very much asleep.

Carefully, he deposited her on her bed, the sheets still rumpled from their earlier lovemaking. He pulled the covers over her, admiring the graceful line of her legs and the full curve of her bare bottom.

He brushed a kiss against the faint bruise still marring her forehead. A wave of tenderness washed over him. Disconcerted, Sloane straightened, deliberately pushing aside the emotion.

He crossed the room and closed the door behind him. His muffled footsteps provided the only sound in the house as he strode across the landing to his room. Sloane strapped on his holstered gun and checked his handcuffs before heading down the stairs to stake out Cheltham's office.

He was a little early, but he didn't want any more surprises tonight.

JO BLINKED SLEEPILY at the digital readout of her bedside clock—11:43 flipped to 11:44. Ah, several hours of sleep left. She rolled over.

Tiffany. Midnight. Max's office. Jo jackknifed upright in bed. How'd she get in bed.... Never mind. She knew.

She threw off the covers and jumped out of bed, shaking her head to clear it. She had to hurry to get in place before Tiffany arrived. Her stomach roiled with a grand case of nerves. Jo pushed aside her trepidation. She didn't have time for the jitters.

This operation called for a T-shirt and shorts, not a dress. She shucked her dress. Heck. She'd left her panties behind once again. No time for a retrieval mission. Her panties would just have to wait till later.

She pulled on another pair. She couldn't keep doing this. She either had to resolve to keep the damn things on around him or, as he suggested, give up wearing them altogether.

She knew which idea was far more sane. She also knew which idea was far more fun.

Jo dressed as quickly as she could in the dark, not willing to alert Tiffany and her cohort by turning on a light.

Armed with a video camera, pepper spray, and her cell phone, Jo slipped out of her room and down the stairs.

She flipped the cell phone to silent mode and pushed aside her fear as she approached the passageway linking the house and Max's office. Focus. Concentrate. Her family needed her. She could do this.

Punching in the code, Jo hurried down the passageway. She flipped the top open on her pepper spray and took a deep breath. If Tiffany had arrived early, Jo was out of luck. She punched in the code and pushed open the door. She sagged with relief at the empty, dark space. She'd beat Tiffany to the office.

"What're you doing here?" Sloane's voice rasped from across the room.

Jo swallowed a shriek and barely checked her finger on the pepper spray. The floor-length curtains fronting a dummy window on one wall rippled as Sloane stepped from behind them.

"You almost scared me to death. You're lucky you didn't get a face full of pepper spray." Jo kept her voice low.

"You're lucky I didn't shoot you. Get your fanny back upstairs before you screw up my stakeout," he ordered in a furious whisper.

Get her fanny back upstairs? Of all the high-handed... Her finger itched to use the pepper spray. "No. This is my stakeout. If anyone's leaving it's you."

"You're interfering in police business."

"This is my family's business."

The sound of a door opening followed by voices cut short their argument. Sloane tried to drag her to the curtains with him. Jo pulled away. "No, I'm going to the bathtub."

Jo had decided hours ago the bathtub offered the optimal cover. If she adjusted the shower curtain just so, she had a clear view of Max's office in the bathroom mirror. Besides, criminals engaged in nefarious activity wouldn't be looking to shower.

"Well, be quiet and be careful," he cautioned as they rushed in opposite directions.

Jo had barely settled into the bathtub when Max's office door opened. Jo started videotaping via the mirror. Tiffany Burns giggled as she entered Max's office. "Come on in, Brad. Welcome to the inner sanctum." Brad, a tall, blond, twenty-something young man followed her in.

Tiffany flicked on the lamp on the credenza. She'd traded in her business suit for a short skirt and halter top. Jo's heart raced. Any minute now Tiffany and her cohort would incriminate themselves.

"Hey, shouldn't we leave the light off? What if someone sees it? I don't want to get caught." Brad sounded nervous, as well he should.

Tiffany pushed him down into Max's executive leather chair. "Don't worry, Stud Boy. They're all middle-aged or babies. They're probably all asleep by now."

Middle-aged? Had that bimbette just called her middle-aged? Jo came precariously close to giving up the gig for the satisfaction of showing Tiffany just how alert she was at her advanced age. And Molly would take her down if she knew Tiffany had referred to her as a baby.

"It wouldn't have occurred to me to come in here, if Mr. Cheltham's sister-in-law hadn't asked me about it. I'd never thought about it before, but after she asked, I decided, what the hey?" Tiffany hopped on top of Max's desk.

Great. Blame her. Make it sound as if she'd put the idea in Tiffany's empty little head.

"This sure is a big desk." Tiffany leaned back on her elbows, and walked her toes up Brad's chest. Brad didn't seem nearly as nervous as he had before. "Can I take some dictation for you?"

Ugh. Jo almost groaned out loud. Please, someone tell her what she thought was going to happen wasn't about to happen.

"Why don't you get comfortable first, Ms. Burns?" Brad got into the game.

Tiffany reached behind her and untied her halter. Her breasts sprang free. Good grief. There was an awful lot of her. Maybe she'd smuggled artifacts to pay for a boob job. Jo clicked off the video and squeezed her eyes shut. She refused to watch. She sent a hostile, telepathic message to Sloane—he'd better not be watching, either.

"Oh, my, what a big dictaphone you have."

Jo barely managed to swallow a laugh. She didn't want to hear this. She checked her watch before she shoved her fingers into her ears. Jo checked the urge to announce herself. Tiffany *seemed* too stupid to mastermind a scheme implicating Max in criminal activity. On the other hand, perhaps she worked with someone.

She'd take her cue from Sloane. She wouldn't be the one to blow this stakeout. Maybe Tiffany and Brad just wanted to get in some extracurricular activities before they got down to their crooked business.

Resigned to remaining in the tub, Jo steered her mind in a direction other than the muffled sounds from the next room. Her life had taken on a carnival quality in the last week. Right now she should be working on the software project for Newsome and Long. Not sitting in a too small bathtub, trying to avoid listening to Tiffany Burns and Brad-the-boyfriend have sex on her brother-in-law's desktop. She should be losing weight. Instead, she kept losing panties. She should know the score of each of the playoff games. Instead, she knew the score of one green-eyed, dimple-cheeked cop posing as a nanny. This week proved the adage: you had to be careful what you asked for. She'd wanted one week of excitement—of being someone other than herself. Forget Jamaica. She'd gotten it in spades right here.

Tiffany hit a high note in the next room. The girl would need another job after tonight. She should look into opera—she had the lungs and the volume.

Jo pulled her finger out of her ear to check her wristwatch. Forty minutes. Come on, already. Couldn't they finish up? Her backside had gone to sleep.

A final heave-ho wrapped up the show in the next room. Thank goodness. Now, if they'd just leave, she could escape this porcelain prison.

"Let's enjoy a little shower together before we go, Stud Boy."

Just say no, Stud Boy, Jo mentally urged enduring Brad.

"Could you do that thing with the soap you did at your house last weekend?" Brad sounded very eager about the soap thing.

Jo didn't want to know. She scrunched her knees up to her chest, but didn't give up hope. Maybe his pager would go off. Maybe Tiffany would get a leg cramp. Anything that might stop them from showering.

Tiffany's hand snaked behind the shower curtain and turned on the water. Cold water flooded Jo's shorts. Tiffany adjusted the temperature.

"I like it really hot and steamy."

No kidding. She'd gone from freezing Jo's tush with cold water to almost parboiling her butt. A flick of Tiffany's wrist and the shower rained down on Jo's head.

Still she didn't give away her position. It wasn't over till that curtain opened.

Tiffany ripped open the curtain.

Jo stood. She infinitely preferred being eye-level as opposed to crotch level with Brad's dictaphone and Tiffany's unfettered mountains, given their naked state. Both looked as if they'd seen a ghost.

Tiffany recovered first.

"You perverted bitch!" she screamed in outrage. "You've been in here the whole time?"

"No, I just flew in on my broom. Did I miss something?" Jo could have possibly overlooked the middle-aged comment, but *perverted bitch?* Tiffany had just tossed the final straw to break this particular camel's back. Jo clicked on the video camera. "Perverted bitch, did you say? I'm not the one who just had sex on top of my boss's desk. By the way, smile." Jo jiggled the handheld video camera. "Did you want to say hi to Max and Cici?"

10

"Jo, YOU WERE MAGNIFICENT. And you showed admirable restraint. I thought you might deck her when she called you a perverted bitch." Sloane leaned against the railing of the upstairs landing.

"Thanks for abandoning me. I thought you were backing me up."

"Baby, the only danger you were in was getting run over by Tiffany and Brad when they hightailed it out of there." He teased her, his eyes crinkling at the corners the way she loved…whoa. It was late. She was tired. That hadn't gone through her mind. She didn't *love* anything about him. Liked. Lusted. But not loved.

She leaned against the wall for support. Exhaustion swamped her—the mind-numbing variety that followed intense adrenaline surges. And Jo had experienced several adrenaline rushes today. She glanced at her watch. Technically, yesterday.

Before she mustered the energy to walk the five steps to her bedroom and collapse, she had to ask Sloane one thing. "Did you watch, you know, while Tiffany and Stud Boy…"

He laughed outright as she stumbled through her question. "No. There wasn't anything to look at that interested me." His green gaze flicked over her with the intimacy of a lover, warming her. "Did you?"

She returned his look. She'd had male perfection. Brad

the Stud Boy was a callow youth in comparison. "Ditto."

"Good answer."

She fought to stay awake, propped against the wall. Sloane took her arm and led her to her room. "Go to bed, Jo."

What a lovely idea. She dropped to the mattress, her feet still on the floor, incapable of further movement.

Sloane knelt beside the bed, removing her wet shoes and shorts. He swung her legs and feet onto the bed, his warm touch gentle and comforting. In the vague recesses of her mind not yet succumbed to sleep, she registered the fact that he tucked her covers around her. But surely she imagined the tender brush of his mouth against hers.

"THIS BETTER BE DAMN GOOD if you're calling my house at two in the morning. Lucky for you, I'm an insomniac," said Vic.

Sloane relayed Tiffany, Brad, and Jo's role in the evening's events, leaving out salient points such as Jo discovering his identity and handcuffing him to the bed.

"So did the secretary and her date know you were there?" Vic quizzed.

"No. Never."

"Well, we know the secretary just dropped by to boff her boyfriend on the boss's desk. What was the Calhoun broad doing there?"

"She was definitely staking the place. There wasn't any real danger tonight except maybe when the secretary called her a perverted bitch. You should've seen Jo's face."

"Jo?"

"Cheltham's sister-in-law. Anyway, I went through

some more files. It's a distinct possibility someone's setting Cheltham up. "He shared the information in detail.

"I need motive and suspect, not theory, Matthews."

"I know. I'm close. I can feel it."

"Good. I'm glad to hear it, 'cause we're coming down to the wire." Vic paused on the other end. "You're not going Gallagher on me with the sister-in-law are you?"

Sloane thought about the cop who'd blown an operation by getting involved with a woman.

Was he involved with Jo? Hell, yeah. Was she "safe"? He'd bet his life on it. "No, I'm not going Gallagher on you."

"Good. Now close this case."

Jo sat up in bed, the idea in the back of her mind pulling her from sleep. Of course. It was as plain as the nose on her face.

She jumped out of bed, still wearing her T-shirt from the night before. She tugged on a pair of panties and shorts, brushed her teeth, dragged a brush through her severe case of bed-head, and hotfooted it downstairs.

Sloane, unshaven and with his hair standing on end, still struck her as incredibly sexy when he looked up from pouring a cup of coffee. "Hey..."

Jo flew past him, flinging a directive over her shoulder. "Pour me a cup, too, and then meet me in Tiffany's office."

She punched in the code on the mudroom door.

"Hold the door. I'm right behind you. I was going to bring a cup up to you." The aroma of fresh coffee wafted over her shoulder.

She turned and took one of the coffee cups, charged simply by the brush of his hand against hers as she took the mug. Seconds dragged by as she lost herself in the green of his eyes.

Sloane blinked and the moment was lost. "What in Tiffany's office has you in such a hurry this morning?"

They walked down the hall together. "You said money and revenge were the two major motivations for criminals, right?"

"Yep."

"So, where better to start looking for revenge than with disgruntled employees?"

Sloane looked at her with admiration as they passed through Max's office. "You may be on to something."

Within a matter of minutes Sloane had accessed the company's personnel files. Sloane sat in front of the computer screen and Jo peered over his shoulder. They started with the most recent terminations, scanning the files for any one piece of information that might stand out or offer a clue.

Jo tried to pay attention. She really did. Unfortunately she found the stubble shadowing his jaw and the fresh, male scent of him seriously distracting.

"Jo." He turned his head fractionally, bringing them into intimate proximity.

"Yes?"

"I can't concentrate because all I can do is think about kissing you." His eyes took on the hard, glittery edge she found so arousing.

Her breath caught in her throat. "Oh." That made two of them.

He cupped the back of her neck in his hand, his thumb rubbing the sensitive spot he'd discovered. She leaned against his shoulders to compensate for her sudden loss of knee support.

"Maybe we should just go ahead and get that kiss out

of the way,'' he suggested. Sloane pulled her closer, until she felt the slight abrading of his beard against her cheek. ''Then we can concentrate.''

Concentrate? Concentrate on what? Jo rested her forehead against his. Oh, yeah, the employee files. ''Do you really think it'll help?''

His eyes smiled sexily. ''Not really. But we might as well give it a try.''

He twirled around in the office chair and pulled her down onto his lap, capturing her mouth beneath his. He tasted of coffee and passion and tenderness. He nipped at her lower lip with a newfound playfulness before he released her.

''How would you feel about taking some dictation?'' He parodied Brad from the night before, shifting suggestively against her bottom.

Jo slid off his lap, laughing. ''Oh, I don't think so, Slug Boy. We've got files to go through.''

Sloane lowered his brows menacingly. ''That's Stud Boy, thank you. And dictation sounds like a lot more fun.'' He spun the chair back around to face the monitor. ''But we'll do it your way.''

An hour later Jo's lightheartedness had almost dissipated along with her conviction that they were on the right track, when a name caught her eye. ''Back up, Sloane. Go back to that last page.''

Jo didn't recognize the name Rocky Dorfman, a stevedore who'd been fired and sent to prison five years ago for smuggling. But she did recognize the name listed as his next of kin. Gwendolyn Price. She couldn't believe it. ''Mrs. Price?''

Sloane nodded excitedly, jotting down notes. ''It looks that way. It's certainly a motive.''

''So Max is cleared?'' Relief flooded her.

"Not quite. It's all supposition and circumstantial at this point. We still need solid evidence."

Confident it was just a matter of time until they found what they needed, Jo headed for the door. "Then let's go find some solid evidence."

NORA AND THE KIDS trooped in just as Sloane and Jo left the office.

Molly and Tara swarmed first her and then Sloane, offering kisses and hugs.

"Busy night?" Nora winked at her over the girls's heads.

"You could say that," Jo answered. Nora didn't know the half of it.

"Where's Connor?" Sloane looked out the back door.

"The Marcums next door to me had their little grand-daughter, Melanie, over. He stayed to play with her." Nora poked her head inside a cabinet. "They'll bring him home later."

Jo had no idea why news of Connor playing with Melanie Marcum brought such a big grin to Sloane's face. "Guess he decided to punt."

"Huh?"

"It's nothing. Just a guy joke."

Jo shrugged. After the belching thing, she'd really rather not know.

The girls settled themselves and their caged rat at the table. Mephisto appeared and licked his lips at Hermes.

Molly doled out crayons and paper. "We're gonna make cards for Mommy and Daddy for when they come home today. Aren't we, Tara?"

Tara nodded, scribbling on the blank paper.

"I'm going to make some cookies," Nora announced.

Jo shuddered, thinking about her grandmother's culinary skills, or rather, her lack thereof.

"You sure you feel okay? You're not light-headed or dizzy, are you?" Jo asked as Nora gathered ingredients for baking cookies. She'd tease Nora out of her domestic funk. Otherwise they'd have to eat her cooking.

"What? Can't a body make cookies in this house?"

"Oh, sure. A body can. It's just seeing your body doing it that's so unusual. The closest you've ever come to making cookies was standing in the check-out line with a bag of ginger snaps at the grocery store."

"You've got a smart mouth going there, Josephina. You're not too old for a little soap to wash it out."

Sloane helped Tara and Molly at the kitchen table.

Molly stopped coloring. "Mama says Norrie's cooking is deadful."

"Dreadful. The word is dreadful. Although, deadful isn't too far off." Jo set the record straight.

"Go ahead, girls. Enjoy a little jest at Norrie's expense. We'll see who's laughing when Sloane and Tara are eating my cookies."

Jo looked at them with fake sympathy. "Our condolences."

Nora plugged in a hand mixer and eyed all the ingredients she'd laid out on the counter with a puzzled frown.

"A bowl." Jo offered. Things were bad when *she* had to offer culinary guidance. "A mixing bowl."

Nora huffed into the pantry.

Jo almost swallowed her teeth when Mrs. Price bustled through the back door. She tried to act normal, wondering if she was facing the woman determined to ruin her family. "Mrs. Price, what are you doing here on a Sunday?"

"I wanted to make sure everything was shipshape for Mr. Max and Mrs. Cici's arrival." She cast a territorial eye on Nora's cookie ingredients laid out on *her* counter. "But I can see someone's making a mess. What's going on here? You know I don't allow anyone in my kitchen, dear." Her kindly expression no longer struck Jo as quite so kindly.

Out of sorts, Nora yelled back from the pantry, "What does it look like? I'm going to make some ding-dang cookies."

Mrs. Price planted herself in front of the cookie supplies. "Not in my kitchen."

Jo moved to stand in front of the children while Sloane nonchalantly moved to the back door.

"Listen, you harridan, back off the '*my* kitchen' business. You can't even keep a decent mixing bowl in here." Nora emerged from the pantry, a misshapen clay bowl in her hands.

All the color in Mrs. Price's florid face drained away, leaving her an unbecoming shade of gray. She lunged for the bowl. "Give me that. It's mine."

Nora snatched it out of reach. "How can it be yours if it's here?"

"I'm just keeping it here."

"Well, I think I'll hold on to it so I can show Cici what kind of junk you're storing in her cabinets."

"So, that's yours?" Sloane asked with casual interest.

"Yes, it's mine." Mrs. Price said, snatching at the ugly thing again. "Give it to me."

"How about this? Since you just told all of us this bowl belongs to you and it's a pre-Columbian artifact stolen two weeks ago, you, Gwendolyn Price, are under arrest for receiving stolen property. You have the right to remain silent..."

For an older woman carrying quite a bit of weight, Mrs. Price moved surprisingly fast. She yanked a handful of Nora's hair in one hand, jerking Nora in front of her. She snatched up the hand mixer, flipping it to high speed. "Hold it right there." She brandished the wildly spinning beaters toward Nora. "If I go, the old bat goes with me."

Adrenaline surged through Jo. Caution and concern for Nora kept her still. She silently urged Sloane to go easy. Jo knew he could tackle Mrs. Price, but she also feared how much damage the mixer might inflict on Nora before he could wrestle it from the madwoman.

"No one needs to get hurt. Let's make this easy." He spoke in a low, soothing tone.

Mrs. Price remained wild-eyed, inching the rotating beaters ever closer to Nora's head. "I knew you weren't a nanny. Them kids's clothes didn't even match."

Sloane didn't shift his attention from Mrs. Price. "Let's make a deal."

"I've already got your deal. You and Jo are gonna round up those kids."

Jo glanced around frantically. Where were the kids? They'd been at the table coloring just a minute ago. Where were they now? She spotted them crawling along the wall, sliding Hermes cage ahead of them. Mephisto stalked along beside them.

"Then, real nicelike, the four of you are gonna get in the pantry. If everyone behaves, Grandma gets to join you. Understand?"

Molly lifted the door to Hermes cage. The rat ran straight across Mrs. Price's foot with Mephisto in hot pursuit. Mrs. Price emitted a blood-curdling scream, flinging the hand mixer across the room while making a mad dash for a chair. "Get that rat away from me."

Nora fluffed at her hair. "It's a mouse, you silly old bag."

Sloane grabbed Mrs. Price by the wrist.

Nora looked from Sloane to Jo. "Is someone going to tell me what's going on here?"

Tara and Molly grinned triumphantly as they retrieved Hermes from the pantry and returned him to his cage. Molly turned to her great-grandmother.

"Now can you make them cookies, Norrie? Rescuing makes me hungry."

"I SUPPOSE EVERYONE would like to know what Mrs. Price did and why she did it."

Jo sat on her end of the sofa and watched Sloane command the room. Instead of a ball game, everyone had assembled for some answers. Cici and Max had arrived as the patrol car carried Mrs. Price away. Vic Finelli, the department head and Sloane's boss, had stayed behind to smooth things over with Max. Molly and Tara sprawled on top of Cici in the armchair. Max paced the length of the room. Nora, still shaken by her hostage experience at the hands of a Whip-o-Matic-wielding lunatic, for once sat quietly.

A classic denouement, lacking only Poirot or Holmes.

"Four years ago, Cheltham Shipping fired and prosecuted a stevedore for stealing. Rocky Dorfman was sentenced to five years in prison." Sloane looked to Max for any sign of recognition.

Max shook his head and shrugged. "It's a big company. It doesn't ring a bell."

Sloane continued. "Gwendolyn Price is Rocky Dorfman's mother. Dorfman swore he'd been set up, despite incriminating evidence. Gwendolyn swore revenge. She plotted and schemed and waited until an opportunity presented itself. She devised a plan to implicate Mr. Cheltham in smuggling and stealing pre-Columbian artifacts. Gwendolyn wanted Mr. Cheltham and his family to suffer as her family had. She almost got away with it—she'd planted some very convincing evidence against you—except she got greedy in the end and decided to sell one of the artifacts herself. When Nora found the bowl, her game was over.''

Cici fanned herself. ''I think I'm gonna hyperventilate. I still can't believe it was sweet Mrs. Price. She made the best chicken and dumplings.''

Max patted her hand and then addressed Sloane. ''We went to South America because I suspected a problem on that end. All the time the problem was under my nose. What about the airport mugging? Did Mrs. Price have anything to do with that?''

''Not that we know. She didn't mention it, and she was spilling her guts pretty fast and furiously.'' A rueful smile quirked his lips. ''I don't believe in coincidences, but it was one of those odd coincidences.''

''Did the old witch push Jo into Max's desk?'' Nora asked.

''She heard Jo coming down the passageway and jumped behind the door. Jo definitely surprised her.

''She would wait until Mr. Cheltham was out of town on business. Then she'd access his office after hours. There was a pattern. If you look at his schedule and the entries in the computer, you'd notice that every time he was out of town, the entries were slightly skewed.

''Ms. Calhoun definitely surprised her that night.''

Ms. Calhoun? He'd torn her purple panties off with his teeth while he was handcuffed to her bed and he couldn't even call her Jo? There was professionalism and there was the big kiss-off. Welcome back to the real world. ''What about my car not starting, or was that just coincidence, as well?''

For the first time since Sloane had read Mrs. Price her

rights, he looked at Jo. It was the impersonal regard of a stranger. Except that a stranger couldn't break her heart with a dispassionate look. "She didn't seem to know anything about it."

Nora suffered a coughing fit. "I might've had something to do with your car. You know, I thought it might be a good idea if you spent some time here." She cut her eyes toward Sloane in a not-so-subtle message.

Vic Finelli glanced at his watch and took the floor. "We'll keep you informed, Mr. Cheltham, as we find additional information. Please accept our apologies for any inconvenience this might've caused you and your family."

Max clasped Sergeant Finelli's hand. "Just doing your job." Max pulled Finelli aside to the window, their heads together.

Molly wiggled out of Cici's lap and ran over to tug on Sloane's pant leg. "Mr. Sloane, can we go look at them clouds again?"

Tara toddled behind and danced around him as if he were a maypole.

Sloane looked stricken, as if they'd slapped him instead of invited him to play. He knelt to their level, and wrapped an arm around each child. "Girls, I'd love to look at the clouds with you, but I have to go."

Molly gazed at him with trusting, adoring eyes and patted his hand. "That's okay. We'll do it when you come back. I like looking at clouds with you."

The pain reflected on his face made Jo ache inside.

Tara dashed out of his embrace and dived at the bottom of the couch. She pulled a pair of black panties from beneath the edge of the furniture, plopped them on her head, and danced around the coffee table.

Molly clapped her hands. "Look. Tara's a thunder-cloud."

Max and Sgt. Finelli stopped their conversation to watch.

Cici laughed in delight at Tara's antics as she plucked the underwear off her baby's head. "Where in the world did these come from? Just as well Mrs. Price is gone if that was the kind of housekeeper she was."

Jo wanted to take the easy way out and say nothing. Instead she took the underwear from Cici and stuffed it into her pocket. "That's my fault. I was careless."

She held her head high and dared anyone to question her. She'd played a foolish game of pretend and been careless with her heart.

Molly, true to form, had not yet begun to fight for her way. "So can we look at clouds when you get back? Pretty please. With sprinkles on top."

Jo caught a momentary glimpse of moisture in Sloane's green eyes before he composed himself. He hugged Molly to him. "You know how you like to play dress-up and pretend?"

She nodded eagerly. "Yeah. You wanna do that? You can be the prince."

"That's the problem, sweetheart. I'm not a prince and I'm not a nanny. I'm a policeman. I was just pretending. I can't play pretend anymore. I have to go back to being a policeman."

I was just pretending. Sloane's words shattered any lingering illusions Jo might have had. They'd all spent the last week pretending to be things they weren't. Sloane was right. She'd had her fling, now it was time to return to the real world. None of them could play pretend any-more.

"But I loves you. I don't want you to go." She cut through his objections with a child's simplicity.

Tara waddled over and slopped a wet kiss on his cheek.

Their declarations of adoration flayed Jo, giving voice to the machinations of her own fickle heart as she sat quietly on the couch and died inside.

"I bet you'll get a new nanny you really like." Even Sloane didn't sound convinced.

Molly lost her patience and stamped her foot. "No. We want you." Her blue eyes flashed at Jo. "And Aunt Jo gots nobody else to dance with."

Sloane lurched to his feet, as if he couldn't withstand further entreaty. He cleared his throat. "Maybe I can drop by for visits and your mom can bring you down to the station. Would you like to see a police station?"

One pair of blue eyes and one pair of brown eyes welled with tears and gazed up at him. "Please, please don't leave us, Mr. Sloane. We really, really loves you." Molly's pitiful whisper echoed in the dead silence of the room.

Sloane, his countenance bleak, looked at Vic Finelli. "Are you ready?" Vic moved toward the door. Sloane nodded curtly to Max. "I'll come over this afternoon to clear my things out and explain everything to Connor." He barely looked at the girls. "Goodbye, girls."

Tara and Molly flung themselves against this legs, clinging to him. Deep, wrenching, sobs wracked Molly's thin shoulders. Tara wailed inconsolably. Jo wanted to join them.

Cici, visibly upset over her children's distress, pulled Molly. Nora took Tara. Both girls held out their arms for Sloane, tears flooding their faces, soaking their clothes.

Sloane strode from the room without even as much as

a glance in Jo's direction, the hollow echo of his steps mingling with the children's misery. Mingling with Jo's own silent misery.

Cici cooed soothing sounds to Molly, rubbing the child's back in an attempt to bring comfort. Tara hiccuped against Nora's shoulder.

Jo tried to fix things. For them. For her. "He was only here a week. That's not very long. Give them a few days and they'll get over him."

Nora looked at Jo, her blues eyes sad and without their customary sparkle. "A week. A day. A year. Time doesn't matter. They love him, and you don't get over love, Josephina."

Jo read something else in her grandmother's eyes— something she'd never seen directed at her before and almost didn't recognize. Disappointment.

11

"THEY'RE KIDS, they'll get over it. You'll get over. So will the broad with the great tush. Or maybe not."

Sloane stared out the car window and brooded. He did not want to discuss the kids or Jo with Vic. And he sure as hell didn't want to hear Vic comment on Jo's tush.

He'd handled Jo and the kids poorly—especially Jo. He'd fallen back on his habit of walking away from a woman before she walked away from him. He wanted to meet up with his old pal Jose Cuervo and pull an all-nighter, so he could forget about playing pretend and how much he'd enjoyed it. But, as he knew from long-ago experience, a night out with Jose meant facing the same issues the next morning—with a hangover.

No. He needed to bury himself in work. "What's my next case?"

"How about a little R and R? I'm giving you a break, Matthews—a week off."

"I'd rather work."

"Tough. Ya got time off."

"What am I supposed to do with a week off?"

Vic shrugged. "Wrap up this nanny gig. Take a walk on the beach. Get in touch with your inner child. I dunno. What do I look like, a social director?"

"No. You look like a fat, short cop who's lost most of his hair and picked up a bad attitude."

Vic stabbed a stubby finger in his direction. "I'm

gonna let you slide on that comment, Matthews. On account of you being in that miserable state of love.''

Denial sprang to his tongue. He snapped his mouth shut. If he responded, he opened the subject up to further commentary. Instead, he ignored Vic.

"Let me tell you a story. It's the story of how me and Gladys met."

"I always wondered how a nice lady like Gladys got stuck with a guy like you." Maybe it'd take his mind off of Jo.

"Today's your lucky day. I'm gonna take the mystery out of it for you. Not too many people know the story. I was a rookie cop working a beat in the Bronx—a real go-getter. Anyways, Gladys was a working girl I hauled in one day."

He could've sworn Vic just said "working girl" in conjunction with Gladys, the canonization candidate.

"Close your mouth, Matthews, before you catch some flies. Yeah, Gladys was a hooker. A young and scared hooker. Her old man liked to knock her and her mother around. So, one day she up and leaves, figuring it can't be any worse on the street than getting roughed up every day at home."

Vic paused to bite the tip off of a cigar. "My life wasn't the same from the first time I looked in her eyes."

"So you married her and that was it?"

"Eventually. But I had to get her to go out with me first. I asked her out to dinner every day for a month. Every day for a month, she turned me down. Said hanging out with a hooker wasn't gonna further my career as a cop and hanging out with a cop would definitely hurt her business."

"So, how'd you get her to go out with you?"

"I bought her. I took every penny I'd saved and gave

it to her. Told her I figured that paid for at least two months."

"And she took your money?"

"Gladys is a nice woman, but she's no dummy. Of course she took the money. So, from then on we were on my time and she could finally sit down and have a cup of coffee with me. I asked her if she could do anything in the world, what would she want to do? She got sorta misty-eyed and said she'd like to have babies and a husband and a cozy little house where everyone felt safe."

"Damn." Sloane felt pretty misty-eyed himself.

"Yeah. I know. Some broads mighta wanted diamonds or to go on fancy vacations or maybe be some Broadway star, but my Gladys wanted a safe house filled with babies and a husband who came home sober every night."

"So she married you?"

"It took a while. She had some crazy notion about being unlovable. She figured if her own parents hadn't cared about her, nobody could."

Sloane ached with an onslaught of recognition. How many times, deep inside, had he wondered how anyone would ever love him if those closest to him—his parents—hadn't loved him? He'd always kept relationships at arm's length, so he'd never have to face and fail once again the test of his own lovability. Just as he'd turned his back on Jo today.

Oblivious to Sloane's introspection, Vic continued his story. "Eventually she saw the light and we moved here to start fresh. We been married twenty years next month. I figure I'm the luckiest man I know."

"Maybe Gladys didn't get too bad a deal, either."

"Can the suck-up, Matthews. I got the prize and we all know it."

"Why are you telling me all this, Vic?"

"'Cause when you find the prize, you better catch it and hold on to it."

JO TOSSED the last pair of shorts into her carry-all and zipped the bag.

Cici came in and threw herself across the bed. "Whew. They're finally napping."

"Are they okay?" Molly and Tara had sobbed for some time after Sloane left. The only thing worse than a little girl with a broken heart was a big girl with a broken heart who should've known better.

"They're exhausted, but I told them Mr. Sloane would stop by this afternoon. They were willing to rest so they could see him. They obviously adore him." Cici studied the tips of her nails. "Of course, he's eminently adorable. Don't you think?" She widened her baby blues at Jo.

"Mmm-hmm." Jo refused to be drawn into that particular conversation. She began to pack up her laptop.

"You know you could stay a couple of days. You don't have to go home just because we're back," Cici said.

"I've got a project due next week I need to focus on. My week's vacation is up. I need to go back home and get back on track." She needed to get her head screwed back on straight. It was time for the real Jo Calhoun to return from holiday.

"Nora's going to stay and help me for a few days since we don't have a housekeeper or a nanny. I've been thinking, I might slow things down a bit. I don't think I'm going to bring another nanny in. At least not for a while. Max and I will just have to cut back on our social engagements. I think our kids need us more than we realized.''

''I think that's a wonderful idea.'' Jo shared Connor's school woes and subsequent belching solution with Cici.

''That settles it. I don't want Max to be a stranger to his own children.''

''They're great kids. You and Max are very lucky.''

Cici looked at her consideringly. ''You could have the same thing, Jo. I just never thought you wanted it.''

''I set a different course, Cici.''

''So set a new direction.''

''We are what we are.'' Jo shook her head. ''It's not that easy.''

''Usually the things worth having aren't.''

SLOANE PULLED INTO the circular driveway. No little red car. Before he could get out of his car, the front door opened and the kids spilled out of the house. Cici Cheltham followed at a more leisurely pace. Sloane easily painted himself and Jo into this domestic scene.

''Mr. Sloane. Mr. Sloane. We missed you.'' Molly flung herself at his legs as if it had been weeks rather than hours since he'd left. Tara followed right behind her.

Connor grinned. ''Mom says you're a policeman. She says we were all part of an undercover operation. That's cool. Real cool. Wait until the guys hear.''

Sloane laughed in relief at Connor's enthusiasm. The girls had darn near killed him this morning with their pleading and sobbing. Subconsciously he'd worried about Connor's reaction.

''Now that you've mobbed him, why don't ya'll let Mr. Sloane come in?'' Cici smiled at the kids.

Now that they'd seen him and knew he'd stay awhile, they were content to scatter and play. Sloane followed

Cici Cheltham into the house, surreptitiously looking around for a sign of Jo.

Without turning, she informed him. "Jo's not here. She left this morning."

"Oh." How'd she do that? "I need to return something that belongs to her." He thought about the panties from that first night in the gazebo tucked away in his upstairs drawer. Maybe he'd just keep them.

Cici led him through the house to the kitchen. General chaos reigned. Pots burbled on the stove. Dishes were piled in the sink. "I don't run as tidy a ship as Mrs. Price. Maybe they'll put her in the prison kitchen. Will she have to go to jail?" A frown knitted her brow.

"She'll probably be in prison for some time. You know, that's what she wanted for your husband." Didn't she understand the situation?

"I know. But she didn't succeed and I can understand why she did it. Someone threatened her family." She shoved a plate of hard, dark cookies—at least he thought they were cookies—at him. "Have one of Nora's cookies. Wait. Let me get you some milk. They chew best if you soak 'em first." She poured up a short glass and passed it to him.

He hefted one of the weighty discs and dunked it as instructed. He gnawed at the wet cookie. A chunk broke off, and he damn near choked. He recovered and chewed valiantly. It reminded him of rubber.

"Nora taught Jo and I everything we know in the kitchen." She nodded at him sympathetically across the table. "Just thought I'd warn you."

"I'm not too bad at turning out a meal." He remembered the smorgasbord he'd pulled together in this very kitchen. He pictured himself and Jo in a kitchen, working together on a feast for their family. He'd teach her everything he knew.

Nora breezed into the kitchen. She beamed at Sloane and the cookies. "Hey. Pretty good cookies, eh?"

Yeah, if you were looking for a puck to play street hockey with. "Unique texture."

"You won't find any like that in the grocery store."

"That's for sure."

Cici and Nora exchanged a mysterious glance. Cici spoke up. "As the monarch of our..."

Nora interrupted her. "That's matriarch, dear."

"Oh, okay. As the matriarch of our family, Nora has a question for you."

She turned to her grandmother. Nora drew herself up regally. "What are your intentions toward Jo?" She asked.

He thought about his earlier conversation with Vic. He knew just what Vic had meant when he said he'd never been the same from the first time he'd looked into Gladys's eyes.

"You know, when you first look at her eyes, they just look brown. But if you really look, they're more like milk chocolate flecked with caramel."

Two pairs of blue eyes waited expectantly.

Vic's message had been a two-parter. First, you had to have enough gumption to figure out when a prize stared you in the face. Second, the prize didn't always come willingly. He'd licked the first part. "She's a prize."

Nora nodded. "We know that. Darn good thing you've figured it out, too. But what are you gonna *do* about it? You need a plan, man."

Sloane laughed. "You know she'd be spittin' mad if she knew we were sitting around talking about her." He could just see her brown eyes flashing fire and her sexy upper lip downturned in a pout. "She's so cute."

Cici smiled her satisfaction. "No one's called Jo cute since we were five years old."

He scowled. "How could they not? The way she's got that dusting of freckles over her nose…"

Nora waved her fingers in front of him. "Hey, snap out of it. Okay, she's cute. What's the plan?"

He wasn't the most original guy in the world. And he also wasn't above using an idea that worked. "I'm going to take her out for a cup of coffee and ask her what she wants most in the world." Sloane sat up a little straighter. They'd be impressed.

Nora and Cici exchanged a considering look. Nora faced him, shaking her head. "It won't work. Gotta come up with something better."

They weren't impressed. He didn't have something better. And he wasn't so eager to give up on this one. "What's wrong with it? Why won't it work?"

"Jo's got a heart of gold. But she's sort of quirky." Cici attempted to explain her sister.

Sloane rather thought it a case of the pot calling the kettle black.

"Jo's got mono vision."

His heart raced at the thought of her suffering an illness. "Whatever it is, we'll face it together."

Nora and Cici exchanged a telling glance.

"What is it?" Sloane asked.

"She's stubborn. With her it's either black or white. She doesn't see things in shades of gray."

"Oh." He felt foolish. She didn't have an illness, just an attitude. "Well, we'll face that together, too."

"The point is, if you haul off and ask the girl what

she wants, she's likely to give you some cockamamy answer 'cause I'm not so sure she really knows,'' Nora said.

"Any suggestions?" They were women and they were her family, surely they knew more than he did.

"It won't be easy," Cici warned.

"I'm ready."

Nora slapped him on the back. "That's the spirit. I've got faith in you. Anyone that can get Jo out of not just one, but two pair of panties…. The girl will put up a heck of a fight, but she's history."

12

JO TRIED TO IGNORE the empty feel of the house. She'd only been back from Cici's for a day, but she couldn't shake this despondency. As soon as she received the overnight package containing her new client's specifications, she'd have lots of work to keep her busy. She loved her work. It fulfilled her. Gave her satisfaction. And having accomplished absolutely nothing in the office this morning, she'd elected to work from home this afternoon.

Sloane pushed his way through every mental block she erected. Images of a different type of fulfillment and satisfaction flashed through her head. She shoved away from the keyboard, annoyed with herself. It had been a pleasant, fleeting interlude. An escape from her everyday life. And it was over.

A sudden gust blew in through the open window, scattering the papers on her desk. Jo put a paperweight on top of the remaining stack and dove beneath the desk to retrieve the others.

Footsteps pounded up the front stairs and the doorbell rang. Bad timing, but she was glad the documentation had arrived. Scooting around on the floor, she yelled to the delivery guy, "Just leave it on the front porch."

"That's probably not the best idea." Sloane's voice floated back through the open window.

Startled to hear Sloane, Jo sprang up, thunking her head. "Ow."

She crawled out from under the desk. Sloane stood on the other side of the screen, watching her crab imitation. She'd planned to be cool and composed when she saw him again, not face him on all fours.

"What are you doing here?" She scrambled to her feet. So she sounded rude and surly. She felt rude and surly. He wouldn't even look at her yesterday and today he shows up on her porch? Wasn't it enough that he plagued her mentally, now she had to deal with him in the flesh—impressive, wonderful-to-behold flesh?

"It's good to see you, too. Aren't you going to ask me in?"

Just why the hell should she? Jo pulled herself up to her full height. "Is this official police business?"

"No. This is personal business."

"Then, no, I'm not going to ask you in. We don't have any personal business." She sat at her desk and began to organize the papers, summarily dismissing him.

Sloane shrugged his defeat. But instead of walking off of the porch and out of her life, as she'd intended, he backed away from the window and sat on the porch rail. "Okay. Have it your way. Don't let me in. But you're wrong, Josephina Wilhelmina Calhoun. There is personal business between us. Intensely personal, unfinished, unresolved business." He deliberately raised his voice until he practically shouted. A quick glance confirmed he'd captured the attention of at least two of her neighbors and a couple walking on the beach.

"Go away, Sloane."

He raised his arm. A pair of white panties dangled from his fingertip. "Not until I've returned your panties."

Within seconds she flung open the door and dragged him into the house.

Furious, she snatched at her underwear. She was furious he'd made a spectacle of himself on the front porch. Furious that her heart had shattered into a million fragile shards when he'd walked away a stranger yesterday. Furious she was so aware of the crisp hair on his arm, beneath her hand. Furious his mere presence turned her world topsy-turvy. Furious that she of calm, cool demeanor was…well, *furious*.

He held her panties out of reach.

"Give me my darn panties and get out," she shouted.

"You're making it damned hard to talk to you," he yelled back.

She lowered her voice. "Good. Catch a clue, Mr. Hotshot Detective. I don't want to talk to you."

"You're behaving like a child, Jo."

The worst of it was, he was right. "And what? You're the model for mature, adult behavior—waving my underwear about like a teenager?"

He looked sheepish. He tossed her panties onto her desk. "You're right. I'm sorry. Could we just sit down and talk?"

Her temper deserted her as quickly as it had appeared. Silently, she led him out of her office and across the hall to the den. She waited until he sat on the couch, then she dropped into an armchair. No more of that couch-sharing stuff.

The gentle whir of the ceiling fan mingled with the cry of a gull. Sloane braced his forearms on his knees and threaded his fingers together.

Jo broke the silence. "I'm sorry I was so rude. It's no excuse, but I was surprised to see you."

"What? You thought I'd just walk away from us?"

Jo pulled her knees up to her chin and wrapped her

arms around her legs, having learned her lesson well. "There is no us, Sloane."

"I was there. And so were you. That makes an us."

"Everything was a pretense. You lied about who you were. I wasn't exactly myself. None of it was real."

"Jo, I was doing my job. I had assumed an identity. That doesn't mean everything else was a pretense."

To her way of thinking it was. "At least be honest about this."

"Maybe we could go out and grab a cup of coffee."

She shook her head, resolute.

Sloane levered to his feet. "I'll go now. I can tell there's no reasoning with you."

Jo followed him to the door. She opened it and stood aside for him to leave. She swallowed hard at the implacability stamped on his face and the anger lighting his eyes.

"Is this where I'm supposed to tell you to have a nice life without me? Okay. Have a nice life. And since none of it's been real, you won't mind this." His arm wrapped around her back, pulling her tight against him. His mouth captured hers. It was a kiss driven by anger and fed by his frustration, yet tempered from brutality by an underlying tenderness. He withdrew as abruptly as he'd descended. "Pretend that didn't happen, if you can."

Jo sagged against the door and watched him walk away. Again. And even though she sent him away this time, it didn't hurt any less.

CICI FACED JO DOWN across the wrought-iron table on the patio. Molly and Tara chased each other in the backyard, while Connor and a friend raced remote-control cars on the brick pathway.

''You look awful. You've got dark circles under your eyes. You're not sleeping at night, are you?''

Jo shook her head. ''No. Not really. But thanks for the ego boost.''

Cici threw her hands up in the air. ''I don't get it. You're miserable. He's miserable. He's crazy in love with you, why won't you at least talk to him?''

''We talked. There's nothing more to say.'' How dare Cici take that exasperated tone with her? ''You just don't get it, do you? It's not me he's in love with. He's in love with someone I'm not, someone I can't be. I tried that 'thinking outside the box.' That was the girl who surrendered her panties. Not plain, practical me. That's the woman he wants, and I can't be her.'' Jo ended the statement with a whisper, the words barely sneaking past the enormous lump in the back of her throat.

She shrugged off Cici's comforting hand. She was teetering one fractional step away from a crying jag.

''Poor, Jo. I wish you could see it isn't mutually exclusive states of being.'' Cici's soft, sympathetic tone dislodged a tear, which gave way to another. And still they continued to come.

Jo gave up trying to stem the tide.

Cici shoved a tissue into her hand. ''Pretense is giving a false impression of being something you're not. Thinking outside the box isn't a pretense. It's tapping into another part of yourself. It is you, Jo. Just as much as the practicality you work so hard to maintain and take such pride in. The world isn't black and white, Jo. There are wonderful shades of gray in between. And you miss so much of the world because you can't see them. I hope you don't wait too long.''

Jo sniffled and stared at her sister in something close to amazement.

"What? I'm not a total airhead, you know. Actually, I've discovered I have quite a resourceful side. It's rather nice being considered capable."

Maybe, just maybe, Cici had a point.

NORA GATHERED CICI and the kids in the kitchen after Jo left.

"Okay, troops. Desperate times call for desperate measures. Jo has made a royal mess out of her relationship with Sloane." Nora shook her head in disgust. Sometimes her granddaughter was downright obtuse. "Looks like we get to be the cleanup committee cause we're family and that's what family does. If two people ever belonged together, it's those two, but it looks like we're gonna have to give them a little push." Nora rubbed her hands together in gleeful anticipation.

"Will Sloane be our uncle?" Connor asked.

"If we have anything to say about it, he will," Nora answered.

"Yahoo!"

"Are they gonna gets married and have babies?" Molly asked her mother.

"I certainly hope so," Cici added, looking adoringly at her own offspring.

A giggled escaped Molly. "Then they're gonna kiss."

"Kiss. Kiss. Kiss." Tara banged her sippy cup in rhythm with her chant.

"Yuck." Connor made gagging noises.

How did Jo and Sloane stand a chance in the face of so much enthusiasm on their behalf? "We've got to help them turn off their brains and turn on their hearts. They're thinking too much and feeling too little." Nora gathered her troops into a tight circle around the kitchen table. "Now, I've got a plan...."

SLOANE CHECKED HIS WATCH. Five minutes late. He would have made it on time if Blakely hadn't pulled him over and given him a warning. Of course, Blakely would've laughed his ass off if he'd known Sloane was about to spend his Friday night baby-sitting the Cheltham kids.

Cici had called, frantic. She and Max had a last-minute engagement and no baby-sitter. Nora had line dancing with Leona tonight and Jo had other plans. His gut clenched, wondering what those plans might be.

Cici had said the kids would love to see him. She'd asked if he might watch them for a bit. So, why not? He was damn depressed. His visit out to Jo had been a wash. He'd hoped all week she'd come to her stubborn senses and call him, but she hadn't. Connor, Molly, and Tara were fun. They'd lift his spirits.

He parked in the circular drive. Max waved from the driver's seat of his SUV. Cici ran down the steps before he reached the front door. "Gotta run. The kids are in the kitchen. Thanks so much, Sloane."

He closed the front door and followed the lilt of childish voices down the hall.

He walked into the kitchen, only to be sucker punched. Jo sat at the table with the kids. She appeared surprised, as well. And none too pleased to see him.

"What are you doing here?" What was he doing here? What was *she* doing here? She'd made him miserable all week. She had some nerve showing up here now.

"This is my sister's house. I'm here to baby-sit."

"I'm here to baby-sit, so you can leave."

"I'm not leaving. They're my nieces and nephews. You go."

Molly screamed—a piercing high-pitched shriek. She jumped up and down, pointing at the pantry.

"Mephisto chased Hermes in there. He's gonna eats him. Stop him, Aunt Jo-Jo. Stop him, Mr. Sloane. Quick afore he bites his head off."

Jo ran into the pantry. Sloane followed her and flipped the switch. "The bulb must be burned out."

He peered over Jo's shoulder to the far corner. He didn't see the cat but it was difficult to spot a black cat in an unlit room.

Jo turned around and stopped short of running into his chest. She ignored him and yelled over his shoulder. "Molly, are you sure—"

The pantry door slammed shut, pitching the room into total darkness. A key turned in the lock outside. Sloane tried the knob just to be sure. It wouldn't budge.

The little devils had trapped them in the pantry. "Connor? Molly? Unlock this door right now," Sloane called.

"Kids, this is Aunt Jo. If you unlock the door, we can go to Chuck E Cheese's." She muttered under her breath, "Right after you come off of being grounded for life."

A key scraped against the lock only to be snatched away again. Connor's voice rang on the other side of the door. "No, Molly. It's a trap. Isn't it, Norrie?"

It was a trap, all right. And he and Jo were the ones snared.

"Jo. Sloane." Nora definitely had *his* attention. "Make yourselves comfortable. Given the ridiculous state of affairs between the two of you, you've left us no choice but to intercede. We're going to the den now. We'll watch a double episode of Rugrats, then we'll be back. That gives you an hour. If you two are still at odds, we'll give you another hour and so on and so forth until you work things out."

"You can't do this, Nora," Jo called.

"But, dear, I just did."

"Are Hermes and Mephisto in here?" He felt her anxiety in the dark.

"No. They're both upstairs. Now get busy sorting things out between you. You've got plenty of snacks. We'll check on you in an hour. Toodles."

A general shuffling sounded through the door and then the footsteps grew fainter as the cohorts in crime moved down the hall. True to her word, Nora had left them locked together in a room that really qualified as a closet.

"We might as well sit down. I don't think they'll be back before an hour's up." Sloane lowered himself to the floor, bracing his back against the door.

Jo sat in the dark, somewhere in front of him.

The silence between held an almost companionable quality. He sat in the dark and absorbed the essence of Jo—her own unique scent, the rhythm of her breathing.

"God, I've missed you this week." Sloane spoke spontaneously, without measuring his words or her reaction.

A sharp intake of breath was the only indication she'd heard him. An intimacy fostered by the darkness encouraged him to speak from his heart.

"I'm sorry, Jo. I'm not sorry I did my job. But I'm sorry I had to lie about my profession. And I'm even sorrier I walked out that day without making things right with you. I was so afraid you wouldn't love me that I just walked away. I never meant to hurt you, baby. But I swear to you, that's where the pretense stopped. I'm the same man now I was last week." He took a deep breath and forged ahead, thankful for the cover of darkness. "For what it's worth to you, I love you. Just like I loved you last week. Just like I'll love you next year. And the one after that."

He'd said his piece. He'd pitched his inning. It was her turn to step up to the plate.

She sniffled. He might've missed it had it not been so quiet in the pantry. There it was again. Another sniffle.

"Jo?"

"Yes?" Her voice quivered.

"Are you crying?"

"Yes." A bona fide sob followed her affirmative.

Instinctively, he reached out and gathered her to his chest, nesting her between his outstretched legs. Tears flowed freely down her cheeks. She sobbed openly.

"Hush, baby. Please don't cry. I didn't mean to upset you." He smoothed her hair and made shushing noises against her forehead. "Please, honey, don't cry. Shh."

She settled between his legs and leaned her head against his chest. Her sobs gradually subsided. He rested his chin against the top of her head. "Want to tell me why you're so upset?"

"Because you love someone who doesn't exist. That woman who slipped her panties off wasn't me. Not really. And the handcuffs—I don't do things like that—"

Sloane stopped her with a finger to her lips. "Honey, is that the problem? You think I don't know the real you?" He brushed his finger against the soft fullness of her mouth. "I believe I know you better than you know yourself. All I'm asking is that you give me a chance. Give us a chance." She nibbled at the tip of his finger and he grinned in the dark. The sound of her breathing became more pronounced. He felt the subtle yet telling shift in the way she moved against him.

"I think you aren't used to doing things like shucking your underwear on request. I'll let you in on something. I've never asked before. But I think you liked it. I know I did." She rubbed her head against the underside of his chin. "Honey, even if you never take your panties off again—a decision that would greatly inhibit lovemaking between us—I'd still love you. Panties on or panties off—it doesn't matter. You fill in a blank I didn't even know I had."

She sniffled.

"Jo?"

"Yes?" Ah. It was that quivery, watery sound.

"Do you love me?"

"Yes."

He'd never been so relieved to hear a sobbed "yes" in all his life. "Do you think you could tell me? Maybe if you quit crying?"

She laughed as she threw her arms around his neck. She showered him with a sweet and salty mixture of kisses and tears. Being a smart man, he returned her kisses until the tears went away.

"I love you, Sloane Matthews. Whether you're a cop or a nanny." She pressed a kiss against the corner of his mouth.

"Jo?"

"Hmm?" She nibbled a series of tiny kisses along his jawline.

"Do you think you might…no, never mind. I shouldn't ask."

"What?"

"Would you consider…forget it."

"Sloane, just ask whatever it is you want to ask." Exasperation punctuated her words.

"Well, feel free to say no, but how would you like to slip your panties off?"

NORA LEFT THE KIDS parked on the couch in front of the big screen. The only noise as she walked down the hall to the kitchen was the echo of her own footsteps against the hardwood floors.

A faint thud followed by a giggle sounded on the other side of the pantry door.

"So, have you two finally come to your senses?" she quizzed through the closed door.

"Actually, Jo's being quite stubborn. I've almost convinced her to change her position. We're making headway, but we're not there yet." Sloane's muffled reply brought a smile to Nora's face.

"Well, that's too bad. You're in there for another hour."

"I'm counting on it," Sloane replied.

She began to walk back to the den but stopped at the kitchen door to call out.

"Jo, don't do anything that I wouldn't do."

And didn't that just leave the whole thing wide open?

Epilogue

Six months later

Jo FOLLOWED Tara, Molly, Cici, and Nora down the brick path toward the gazebo in Cici's backyard. Sloane awaited her at the steps, with Connor, Max, and Vic Finelli beside him.

White ribbons festooned the gazebo. Surrounding flower beds provided a riot of color and scented the warm air of the spring afternoon for the guests seated in folding chairs.

Just how practical had it been to arrange an outdoor wedding in mid-April without backup plans? Not very practical. But very, very lovely. There was a lot to be said for this thinking-outside-the-box approach.

If the dark cloud rolling in on the horizon would slow down.

Jo beamed at the guests as she strolled down the path, immeasurably happy. Her parents sat on one side, Sloane's on the other. Several of Nora's friends had come. A large contingency of Savannah's finest was also in attendance. Gladys Finelli, very pregnant with baby number eight, sat amid her brood of seven. Most of Jo's employees were clustered together.

But the most important people in her life—in particular the one who'd awakened her slumberous heart—waited patiently for her to complete her journey. Sloane watched her as if she were a prize he'd won at the county fair and still couldn't believe his good fortune. The crazy besotted man who'd shown her several different sides of herself.

Jo came to the end of the path and joined hands with Sloane. Off to her side, Cici surreptitiously wiped at her eyes and sniffled. Molly and Tara copied their mother. As the minister began the ceremony, Cici began to cry in earnest. The girls cranked up their waterworks.

Sloane grinned at her as the minister shouted to be heard above the wailing. He queried the guests rhetorically to speak now or forever hold their peace if they knew of a reason Jo and Sloane should not be joined in holy wedlock.

"Cici, you and the girls need to stop the waterworks. We can't hear out here," Nora bellowed above the crying.

Cici mopped at her face but quit sobbing. Molly and Tara quieted, as well.

The minister cleared his throat to continue. As he opened his mouth to speak, an enormous belch echoed through the yard. Stunned, he snapped his mouth shut.

"Wow. Tara, that was a ten," Molly pronounced in a loud, clear voice.

"Eight," argued Connor from behind Sloane.

"Kids," admonished Cici.

"We'll let Uncle Sloane decide since he's the most impotent member of our family now," Molly argued.

Someone snickered in the office contingency and the mirth spread like wildfire.

Sloane closed his eyes, shook his head, and laughed out loud.

"Hey, put a lid on it, fellows. We got a wedding to

get through up here," Vic ordered from his position next to Sloane.

Finally, with a little additional crowd control, the minister continued with the ceremony. Just as he presented them as husband and wife to the guests, the heavens opened and offered their own benediction.

Everyone except the bride and groom scattered and dashed for shelter in the Cheltham house.

Oblivious to the rain, Sloane pulled Jo into his arms. Droplets glinted in his lashes and dripped off his chin. Jo tightened her arms around his solid strength. Moving as one, they danced in the soaking shower.

"Hey, look everybody, they're mattress dancing." Molly's voice floated down from the terrace.

"It's the cha-cha, you dummy," her brother corrected. "Mom…"

Sloane nuzzled his lips against the corner of her eye. "Your makeup's running, darling."

Jo stepped on his toe. "Thanks for making sure I know, honey."

The big goof just grinned down at her, his green eyes shining. "I love you, Josephina Wilhelmina Calhoun Matthews."

She stared up at him. "I know you do."

And she did know. He loved the practical pragmatic Jo and he loved the mischievous Jo. He loved her whether she was inside the box or outside.

She judged the moment right to impart the news she'd waited all day to tell him. "And I'm not wearing any panties."

Moonstruck

Sandra Paul

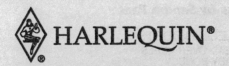

HARLEQUIN®

TORONTO • NEW YORK • LONDON
AMSTERDAM • PARIS • SYDNEY • HAMBURG
STOCKHOLM • ATHENS • TOKYO • MILAN • MADRID
PRAGUE • WARSAW • BUDAPEST • AUCKLAND

Dear Reader,

I've always been the timid sort. Just the thought of making a fool of myself before strangers makes me cringe with embarrassment. Yet somehow I manage to do so, invariably egged on by my writer friends.

Like the time Elda Minger convinced me to enter a dancing competition along with her on a taping of *The Leeza Show.* The grand prize was a souvenir T-shirt. Carried away by her enthusiasm and persuasive arguments (you can never have too many T-shirts), I never noticed when Elda, who was behind me in line, slunk back to her seat. In fact, it wasn't until I was up on stage, hopping around like a demented Snoopy, that I even remembered, "Hey. I can't dance."

So I can understand how Dee, the heroine in my book, ends up in such a terrible predicament because of one foolish, impulsive act. As a dysfunctional dancer who's performed before a studio audience, I know better than most insanity is often just a step away!

Happy reading,

Sandra Paul

Books by Sandra Paul

HARLEQUIN DUETS
12—HEAD OVER HEELS
31—BABY BONUS?

SILHOUETTE ROMANCE
883—LAST CHANCE FOR MARRIAGE
1016—THE RELUCTANT HERO
1087—HIS ACCIDENTAL ANGEL

For Mooners everywhere

1

FUNNY HOW INSANITY CAN strike—so suddenly and without warning. Especially with friends nudging you gently over the edge.

To be fair, Dee's friends didn't know she'd just been through a hellish Friday, capping an even more hellish work week. They knew she'd joined them in one of the company's carpool vans because her car had died in the parking lot; they didn't know she suspected the bill to get her vintage Volkswagen bug going again would be beyond her meager savings. They knew her job as secretary for the big boss, Jason Masters, was difficult at the best of times; they didn't know Masters's temper had been hair-trigger all day as he worked to close a major deal.

They certainly didn't suspect their remarks on her love life would feel like salt on a raw wound. The five women had all been friends since high school and commenting on Dee's love life—or more often, the lack thereof—was a common pastime among the group.

Marlene was the one who started the round this time with the innocent query, "What are you and wonder-boy Stewart planning to do this weekend, Dee?"

"Nothing," Dee answered briefly, trying to ignore the pang of hurt the mention of Stewart's name caused in her chest.

She had sat in the back seat of the van hoping the

others would sit at the front near Andrea, who was driving. Elizabeth and Bonnie had unconsciously complied with her unspoken wish but Marlene—the one Dee had hoped to avoid the most—had sauntered down the aisle to flop in the seat directly in front of Dee.

She didn't even put on a seat belt, Dee noticed disapprovingly, automatically tightening her own as the van hit a bump in the road. Instead Marlene leaned back against the window and stretched her long silky legs out on the bench seat. She looked sleek and sexy, from the top of her spiky blond hair down to her polished toenails displayed in strappy sandals.

"You're not going to get together to hold hands chastely on the sofa tonight?" Marlene prodded, idly inspecting her immaculate manicure while continuing her inquisition.

"No," Dee answered. She deliberately kept her answer curt so that some people—say, those with a modicum of sensitivity—would sense she didn't feel like talking.

But Marlene was known for her alluring walk, comehither green eyes and "live for the day" attitude. And although she had many admirable character traits, sensitivity wasn't among them. Without shifting her gaze from her maroon nails, Marlene pressed, "What do you mean nothing? Don't you and Stewie have a standing date to eat prunes and watch the news every Friday evening?"

"We eat popcorn," Dee corrected her, staring out at the cars speeding along the crowded L.A. streets on their way to the 405 freeway.

"Prunes would be better. You both need something to loosen you up."

The other three women chuckled at Marlene's teasing remark. Usually Dee would have laughed, too, before launching into her ongoing debate with her friends on why the sedate courtship she and Stewart had embarked on three months ago was preferable to the weeklong flings that Marlene indulged in.

But not tonight. Tonight, merely the thought of the way Stewart used to solemnly munch his popcorn while watching *World News Tonight* caused tears to burn behind her eyes. Knowing that Marlene wouldn't stop teasing unless she confessed what had happened, Dee finally admitted, "Stewart broke up with me today."

For a second, silence filled the van. Then everyone spoke at once. "The jerk!" "What a loser he is!"

"Why on earth did he do that?" Andrea asked. Andrea always wanted to know the whys and wherefores of things and now was no exception. Her steady brown eyes met Dee's in the rearview mirror as she added, "You two seemed to be getting along so well."

"That's what I thought," Dee said, averting her gaze. She pulled out her handkerchief—Dee always carried a handkerchief, they were much more practical than tissue and better for the environment—and blew her nose. "But I guess I was wrong. He said I was too conservative, too boring, to keep up with his wilder lifestyle."

Andrea snorted, lifting a hand from the steering wheel to tuck a strand of golden-brown hair back behind her ear. "The only wild lifestyle Stewie has is in his head. This is probably just another pitiful attempt to emulate Masters—*he* certainly goes through women fast enough." She signaled for a left turn before adding, "Stewart's a bum. You're better off without him."

"Easy for you to say," Dee muttered. Andrea—indeed, *all* the other women—never had any problem finding men. Unlike Dee. She blew her nose a bit fiercely as another wave of regret rose in her chest. It had felt so good to have a boyfriend, someone to talk about when her friends mentioned the different men they were going around with or her mother asked who she was dating. Having Stewart as a boyfriend had made her feel *normal* somehow—like a regular woman rather than the quiet, retiring, destined-to-remain-a-virgin-forever oddity that deep in her heart she knew she really was.

"Well, be glad you never slept with him," Marlene said, as if in answer to her unspoken thought. "If you had—"

"If I had, maybe he wouldn't have broken up with me," Dee burst out. "But he never even tried to have sex with me. Not once!"

The thought shouldn't have hurt so much. She knew she wasn't the kind of woman to inspire lust in a man. After twenty-six years of living with her medium brown hair, common gray eyes, and short—not fat, but not thin, either—figure, she'd come to terms with the realization that she was basically nondescript. But still...

"Obviously I wasn't even worth the effort," she said, voicing the fear uppermost in her mind.

Once again silence filled the van. Then Andrea said, "Oh, come on, Dee," in a bracing voice, taking her eyes off the brisk evening traffic long enough to frown at her in the rearview mirror. "That's not true. You never seemed that turned on by him, either. You probably didn't give him any encouragement."

Dee stiffened in surprise. "Yes, I did—or at least, I didn't *discourage* him."

"Maybe not verbally, but I bet you froze him off just the same," Marlene drawled. "You do it all the time...you've *always* done it—even in high school. You stand there with that 'I'm-purer-than-driven-snow, Miss-Goody-Two-Shoes-is-a-whore-compared-to-me' aura that makes men freeze in their tracks."

"I do not!" Dee declared, shock and indignation at this unexpected attack momentarily replacing hurt. "I'm *very* approachable."

"Sure you are," Elizabeth agreed in her soothing voice, sending Marlene a reproving look. "To animals and little children. But men…" She hesitated.

"Men want something more," Bonnie chirped in to explain, bouncing a little in her seat. Bonnie always bounced when she got excited—a habit no doubt leftover from her cheerleading days, Dee reflected. Bonnie bounced again, making her shoulder-length red hair flip up and down as she added earnestly, "Men want the chance, the hope, the merest possibility that someday—"

"They might see you naked," Marlene concluded.

"Very crudely put," Andrea said dryly. "Still, Bonnie and Marlene have a point. *Sexy* is the word we're looking for here. You have to think sexy to get a man to make a move. You need to appear available—"

"Cheap," Marlene said.

"No, not cheap," Elizabeth insisted, her blue eyes narrowing thoughtfully as she absently braided a lock of her shiny, shoulder-length dark hair. Elizabeth did thoughtful very well—achieving an expression Dee always thought of as her Maternal Goddess look. Elizabeth's eyes were filled with solemn female wisdom now as she explained, "Men don't want someone who's easy, just…persuadable. As if you might be talked into doing something…impulsive."

"I can be impulsive. *Very* impulsive." Dee knew her friends were only trying to help, but they were beginning to annoy her. "I've done lots of impulsive things in my life."

"Oh, yeah?" Marlene inquired. "Name one spontaneous, crazy thing you've done in the ten years we've known you.''

"I've…I've…well, I bought those three-inch red heels. And they weren't even on sale!''

Marlene's lip curled. "Wow, how daring. Especially since you've never gotten up the nerve to wear them.''

"They make me wobble,'' Dee admitted. "I'm afraid I might sprain an ankle in them.''

"Why doesn't that surprise me? Let's list the other stuff you've been afraid to do.'' Marlene held up her hand, bending down a slim finger. "You wouldn't try out for the drill team with the rest of us….''

"I'm not very coordinated.'' The thought of everyone watching her try to march and dance made Dee's armpits prickle with nervous perspiration even now. Oh, her parents had insisted she take ballroom dancing as a preteen, the kind they'd always enjoyed. As a result, she could waltz, do the two-step and even tango with the best of them. But none of those dances were popular with her peers, and she'd never gotten the hang of the loose-jointed, sexy moves everyone else enjoyed so much. So instead, she'd stood alone on the sidelines at each school function watching her friends perform.

Marlene bent a second finger back. "You wouldn't go to Jimmy Hopkins's party.''

"Because Jimmy did drugs.''

Marlene gave a delicate snort. "He tried pot. One time—the presidential way. He didn't even inhale.''

"Well, I was afraid he'd have marijuana—or worse—at his party.'' Dee had wanted to go; she'd wanted to go very badly. Jimmy's was the first "in'' party she'd ever been invited to. But instead she'd stayed at home, unable to overcome visions of police swarming in on a raid, and somehow catching her with a joint in her hand. "I thought the police might come..."

Marlene's mobile mouth pulled down in a disgusted look. "His parents chaperoned it! It was just a small teen-age gathering." She bent back another finger. "You wouldn't go away to college...."

"My parents wanted me to commute." Dee hadn't protested their suggestion. Her parents were elderly and she knew they'd wanted their only child close by. She added, "Besides, Cypress has such a nice junior college, it would have been a waste to spend the money to go away."

"It would have been a blessing," Marlene declared. "Cypress is the boringest city in Southern California. Its only claim to fame is as the place that cute golfer, Tiger Woods, couldn't wait to get out of. And *you* are a perfect example of the kind of person such a sleepy suburb breeds. Why, you wouldn't try even *one* drink when we took you out for your twenty-first birthday."

Dee clenched her hankie in her fist and lifted her chin. "I don't like to be out of control."

Marlene raised her arched eyebrows. "How would you know? You've never *been* out of control."

"Now, Marlene..." Elizabeth said, trying to intervene.

But Marlene was beyond being stopped. Her gaze locked with Dee's as she pressed on relentlessly. "You wear conservative clothes, read conservative books, don't drink, don't smoke—you even stay away from sugar be-cause it's 'bad' for you. You always buckle your seat belt and chew thirty times before swallowing—and you insist on pulling your hair back in that damn bun. For God's sake, let it hang *loose* sometimes."

Defensively Dee lifted a hand to her head. "It tends to frizz. It's neater this way."

Marlene rolled her eyes. "And heaven forbid you should look a little messy. I swear, Dee, sometimes I think you're physically incapable of doing anything mad and impulsive—a wild, crazy act just for the sheer hell of it. I'll bet that not once in your entire life have you ever strayed from the safe and narrow."

"So what's wrong with being safe?" Dee demanded.

"Nothing, as long as you're not operating from some Chicken Little mentality that the sky is going to fall down if you let go and live a little."

"I live a little...."

"That's exactly my point!" Green eyes blazing, Marlene leaned closer, saying earnestly, "What you need is to learn to live a *lot*. To show Stewart and all the guys like him that they don't know the first thing about the *real* Diana 'Dee' Edith Evans."

Dee blew her nose again, hiding behind her handkerchief a moment to escape the intensity of Marlene's gaze while she considered what her friend had said. She hated to admit it, but maybe Marlene had a point. Maybe she needed to learn to be more spontaneous, to let go, to develop a bit more backbone—

Her thoughts were interrupted when Andrea said suddenly, "Speak of the devil, isn't that Stewart's car coming up on the right?"

Bonnie turned to the side window, her nearsightedness and vain refusal to wear glasses causing her to squint as she peered through the glass. "You're right. It *is* Stewart," she declared, confirming the sighting.

Backbone forgotten, Dee scrunched down as far as possible. "I can't bear to have him see me," she groaned.

Marlene rose on her knees to glare down at her over the back of the seat. "What are you *talking* about? *He's* the one who should be embarrassed, not you. *He's* the one who threw you over—and for what? For being too conservative? Too boring? *That's* what he complained about?''

Dee nodded.

''Well, you'll show *him*,'' Marlene declared. ''You're going to do something so reckless, so daring, so down-right outrageous, that ol' Stewart 'I'm-too-wild-for-you-babe' Paxton will just die from stupefied shock.''

Dee was perfectly willing for Stewart to suffer such a fate, but she really didn't see how she could bring it about. ''What do you want me to do?'' she asked, risking a peek out the window at the black Lexus edging up next to the van.

''Moon him.''

''What!''

''You need to moon him.''

Dee felt as if she might die from stupefied shock herself. ''I can't do that.''

Marlene raised her perfectly plucked eyebrows. ''Why not?''

''Because...because it's immoral...and—and childish. And I'm almost certain it's illegal—why, yes, it would have to be,'' Dee added on a more positive note, ''because I'd need to take my seat belt off.''

''Exactly!'' Marlene declared triumphantly. ''It's the *perfect* revenge. It'll show Stewart that he was wrong about you—and that you think he's an ass—all at the same time.''

''Put like that, Marlene almost makes sense,'' Andrea said dryly.

Bonnie certainly thought so. Bouncing wildly, she sang out in the ringing, cheerleading tones with which she'd extolled their 0-wins high school football team on to victory, ''It's a *great* idea! Do it, Dee! Do it for all the women who've ever been labeled boring! Do it for women everywhere who've ever been dumped!" On a rising crescendo, she cried, "Come on, Dee! Do it for the Gypper!"

Dee wasn't sure exactly who the Gypper was, but she was *certain* she didn't want to moon her ex-boyfriend for his benefit. She opened her mouth to say so.

But before she could get the words out, Marlene took one look at her expression and flopped back into her seat. She said resignedly, "Save it, Bonnie. She won't do it. Mooning someone is too daring for proper little Dee to ever consider."

"No, it's not," Bonnie said loyally, but Dee could see the doubt filling her big blue eyes, her previous enthusiasm ebbing away. The same doubt was mirrored on Elizabeth's pretty face and Andrea's somber one as well.

They didn't think she'd do it, Dee realized. They didn't think she had enough guts to pull off such a bold prank. Just like Stewart they thought she was too predictable, too conservative, too...boring.

A small spark of rebellion, which had simmered unnoticed for twenty-six years, suddenly flared up inside her. Who were *they* to think they knew her so well?

"Oh, my goodness!" Bonnie said, peering out the window again. "I think there's someone in the car with Stewart. It looks like a woman."

Dee's friends turned as one to glance at Dee, pity on their faces. It was an expression Dee knew well. She'd seen it often in high school, in college, and especially during the last few years. She'd even seen it on Stewart's face now and again—the two-timing jerk!

Darn it, she was tired of being pitied. She was tired of being "the voice of caution," the party pooper, of being proper little Dee. Why *shouldn't* she show Stewart exactly what she thought of him? He certainly had no regard for *her* feelings!

The rebellious spark burst into a conflagration. She unbuckled her seat belt, her resolution hardening as Elizabeth's eyes widened and Bonnie gasped. If she could elicit that kind of reaction from her friends, then imagine how shocked Stewart would be.

Inspired by the thought, Dee rose to her feet while the other women watched her with excited trepidation. They'd never looked at her like that before and the amazement on their faces filled her with elation. She felt reckless, she felt brave—she even felt a little noble with the fate of jilted women everywhere resting on her shoulders. She'd prove to everyone she wasn't afraid. And after tonight, Chicken Little Dee would be gone forever!

The Lexus was pulling up alongside them now. Dee slid down her nylons and white cotton panties. Turning around, she grasped the back hem of her three-inches-below-the-knee-length skirt.

''She's going to do it,'' Bonnie said, awe in her voice.

Dee's palms felt damp with sweat. Terror and excitement were making her head swim. From the corner of her eye, she could see the dark-haired driver start to look over. Taking a deep breath, she flipped up her skirt—

—just as Elizabeth gasped out, ''That's not Stewart! Oh, my God—*it's Jason Masters!*''

2

AT THIRTY-FOUR, Jason Masters had pretty much seen it all.

From the time his mother died when he was twelve, Jason and his three brothers had run wild, losing their innocence and broadening their cynicism at a rapid pace. Robbed of her gentle guidance, they grew up doing what they wanted, when they wanted and how they wanted.

Their father certainly made no effort to curb them. Born in England into a hardworking, pragmatic family, John Masters had traveled to America to study the latest advances in electronics; he stayed after uncharacteristically plunging in love and marrying an Irish-American waitress from L.A. When his wife died, John drowned his grief by immersing himself in his work. He emerged long enough to try marriage a second time, but retreated again when he realized loyalty and faithfulness—not to mention monogamy—were concepts alien to his new wife's narcissistic nature.

Loneliness for his first wife, disillusionment about his second, soon completed John's emotional isolation. As long as his sons made it through school, didn't do drugs, kill anyone and—most importantly—didn't disturb his absorption in the predictable scientific world he found so comforting, John figured they were doing just fine.

Since all four boys were highly intelligent, making it through high school and then college hadn't presented any problems. But the same smarts that helped them ace tests without studying bred a restless curiosity that all too often led them into trouble. Before their father's business took off, they prowled the rough streets of L.A. with arrogant confidence, unimpressed by the gangs that claimed the area. The quick temper they'd inherited from their Irish mother landed them in plenty of fights. The shrewd intelligence bestowed by their practical English father guaranteed they came out on top. When John's business became a success and money started pouring in, his sons changed their venue without altering their behavior in the least. They prowled through the gatherings of the rich and famous throughout the world with the same cockiness they'd displayed in the low bars and dives of L.A.

Jason was the oldest. He was also the wildest. His mocking blue eyes smoldered with a hot restlessness that lured the daring and frightened the cautious. His time was spent pursuing whatever new diversion came his way. His extensive mechanical knowledge insured he had the fastest cars. His dark good looks and muscular build attracted the fastest girls. He rode the machines and women alike with a hard energy that made the car engines hum and the women purr.

The hearts he broke meant no more to him than the engines he burned out. He walked away from both with an uncaring shrug, unconcerned about the reputation he was earning as a heartless, unpredictable playboy. At twenty-eight, he didn't think about the future, or the possible repercussions of his actions. He didn't give a damn what anyone thought of him or his way of life.

But all that changed the day his father died.

Within twenty-four hours of his father's heart attack, Jason learned his father's company, Masters Inc., was on the verge of bankruptcy, its assets depleted by his step-mother's unceasing demands on his father's wallet. Within forty-eight hours, he'd bought her off and assumed control, resolved not to let the company go under. John Masters had been a neglectful father, but he'd loved his sons and the electronics firm he'd poured so much of his life into was their legacy. Jason was determined to build it into a profitable one.

He used his brawling instincts to fight off his competitors. He used his shrewd intelligence to make executive decisions that were quick and successful. He used his good looks when necessary to charm the ladies and his tall muscular build to intimidate the men. When he realized his reputation for wildness wasn't good for business, he tried to bury it beneath a cold, conservative film of icy control.

For the most part, he was successful. When—as it did every now and then—that control melted under the heat of his quick temper, he pushed twice as hard to overcome the setback, applying the same unrelenting determination that he'd used all his life to get his own way.

If sometimes it seemed life consisted simply of business, he didn't let it bother him. If sometimes he felt lonely, he ignored that, too, determined not to make the same mistake his father had. He preferred the hard reality of business to illusions of affection.

He set goal upon goal for the company, and his stratagems worked. In a mere six years, Jason had restructured his father's business into an international concern that was growing more powerful daily by allowing nothing and no one to get in his way. In the process, he'd been threatened, pleaded with, cussed out and swung at more often than he could remember.

But Friday evening was the first time in his entire life that Jason Masters had ever been mooned.

And he didn't like it. Especially from a company van.

Circumstances had prevented him from pursuing the offender right then, but doing so was at the top of his agenda on Monday morning. Pacing past his wide ebony desk he paused to slash through the item "Take care of Mooner" with a firm, broad stroke of his gold pen. He'd handle *that* infuriating matter as soon as his private secretary—Diana Edith Evans—arrived.

When he finally heard her enter the adjoining office, a grim smile curved his mouth. Stabbing at the intercom button with a long finger he demanded, "Come in here as soon as you've put your stuff away."

He didn't bother to wait for her reply. He knew she'd obey his command. She always obeyed promptly and unquestioningly, and damn efficiently, to any order that he gave. She was the perfect secretary—quiet, unassuming—a bland piece of machinery that never gave him trouble nor a moment's second thought. Until today.

In the outer office, Dee jumped and stared at the small intercom unit on her desk as if it were a snake waiting to strike. In the circumstances, she wished it were a snake—a large poisonous one. Then her death would at least be less painful than the one Jason Masters might have planned.

She sank into her chair with a low moan. "He's going to kill me."

It wasn't the first time she'd uttered the phrase. Her early demise had occupied her mind the entire weekend.

"I'm going to die," she'd informed her friends when they gathered in the living room of her little house on Friday evening, still shaken after their unexpected "encounter" with their boss.

"No, you're not," Andrea had replied in her practical tones. "You only mooned the man—you didn't commit a drive-by shooting. You can't die from flashing your bottom at someone."

"I can," Dee declared, lying on her flowered couch with her hand pressed to her aching forehead. Horror at what she'd done seized her every few minutes, making her flush with heat, then shiver with shock. How could she have committed such a disgraceful act? She cringed every time she thought of it.

Glancing at the concerned faces grouped around her, she said, "I'll never, *ever* be able to face him again." She considered the matter a moment, then added with a shudder, "Or turn my back, either."

"Of course you will." Elizabeth sat down beside her to pat her shoulder comfortingly. "Maybe he didn't even realize what you were doing. Andrea speeded up almost immediately—but perhaps you don't remember that part. That's when you fell, wasn't it? And bumped your head?"

Andrea leaned over Elizabeth's shoulder. Pulling Dee's hand away from her forehead, she studied the swelling bump on her friend's right temple judiciously. "My goodness, you did get whomped didn't you? Bonnie, hurry up with that ice!"

"Here it is," Marlene said—the only remark she'd made since helping Dee regain her seat in the van. Marlene looked pale, but belligerent—a sure sign, Dee knew, that her friend was upset. The blonde held out a green bag, adding in a gruff voice, "It's not ice exactly—you don't have any, Dee—but this bag of frozen brussels sprouts should work just as well."

Bonnie wrinkled her dainty nose and perched on the

coffee table next to Fluffy, Dee's furry white tomcat. "Yuck, brussels sprouts. How can you eat the things?"

"They're good for you." Dee sighed a little as Elizabeth gently laid the plastic bag against the bruise on her temple.

"Do you think she'll have a black eye?" Bonnie asked, her own eyes widening with dismay at the thought.

Elizabeth started to say, "Maybe—" but Andrea cut her off. "No," Andrea declared, her firm tones brooking no argument. "She'll only have a colorful bruise. She's just lucky she didn't get hurt worse."

"I should say." Bonnie gave a little bounce, startling Fluffy who jumped indignantly down to the floor. "The way she tumbled over and over I thought she'd break her arm at the least. It was a good thing she landed on her head. Accidents always happen when you don't wear your seat belt," she added piously, leaning closer to shake her finger reprovingly at Dee. "You should never have taken yours off."

"She should never have listened to me—that's what she should never have done," Marlene suddenly burst out. With a violent sweep, she knocked Dee's numerous throw pillows—her legacy from an industrious great-aunt—from an overstuffed armchair, and threw herself down on it. "Now we'll *all* get fired—and dammit!" Marlene pounded on the chair's arm with her clenched fist. "I don't want to lose this job. I really enjoy it."

Tears burned Dee's eyes, hidden beneath the plastic bag. She didn't want to lose her job, either. But when Marlene, in a voice husky with remorse, added, "I'm so sorry I started all this," Dee managed to swallow the lump in her own throat and say, "It's not your fault. I knew better—it was just…"

Her voice trailed off. How could she explain the reckless euphoria that had seized her? Looking back, it seemed insane to have done what she did. A low moan escaped her. "Oh, what's the use in talking about it? It's no one's fault but my own. I'll just explain that none of you had anything to do with it."

She tried to tell herself Masters would overlook it; maybe even laugh about it. Her efforts were fruitless. Picturing her boss laughing over such a juvenile prank by one of his employees was a mental picture beyond her abilities to imagine. Maybe—if she pleaded hard enough—he wouldn't fire her friends, but Dee knew she'd lose her job for sure.

The thought made her throat constrict even more. She loved her job. She'd started with Masters, Inc. while still in college, working her way from department to department until less than a year ago, she'd finally been promoted to Masters's private secretary. And—darn it!—she was good at the position. She enjoyed the challenge of handling the myriad details the job involved, as well as the challenge of keeping up with Jason Masters.

Oh, she'd been a little afraid when she started, worried about triggering Masters's famous quick temper, and at first he *had* seemed to bark and growl a lot. But soon she'd developed the knack of reading his mood, often intervening at exactly the right moment in a business meeting with a question or a comment, giving him the time he needed to rein in his anger. Lately she didn't need to say a word; he'd shoot her a look and calm down all on his own.

In fact, they'd become a good team—so good, that she'd hoped to earn the title of assistant in another year or so. And why not? She might lack self-confidence when it came to social situations, but when it came to her work, she knew precisely what she was doing. She was self-assured, responsible, knowledgeable—not once in the entire time that she'd worked for Jason Masters had she ever made a major mistake.

Except for mooning him from the company van, of course.

"It doesn't matter what you tell him, I know he'll fire us all," Marlene said bitterly, interrupting Dee's thoughts. "When Masters takes action, he always makes a clean sweep of things. Remember when he took over that company and fired everyone from the CEO down to the mail clerk? The truth is, we're all in this together."

A gloomy silence fell over the group. Dee blinked back tears beneath her melting plastic bag, while Elizabeth frowned and Marlene kicked at an innocent throw pillow lying by her feet. Bonnie gave a forlorn bounce, but Andrea didn't move a muscle as she stared with narrowed eyes at the yellow wall opposite. Fluffy, disgusted with the grim atmosphere, indicated his disapproval by jumping up on Dee, who gave a surprised grunt as the cat landed on her stomach.

The small sound seemed to break Andrea's preoccupation. Straightening her shoulders, she suddenly said, "Wait a minute, everybody. This situation might not be that bad."

Dee lifted a corner of her sprouts bag to stare at her. The other women all stared, too, eyebrows raising in surprise.

Marlene demanded, "What are you talking about?"

"I mean we're jumping to conclusions here. Like Elizabeth said, maybe Masters didn't realize what Dee was doing—or even see her." Andrea's brown eyes narrowed as she looked around at the others. "I was only paying attention to the road. Did anyone else catch his reaction?"

The women were silent a minute, considering. Dee cuddled Fluffy closer, taking comfort from his small warm body as she tried to remember exactly what had happened. *She* certainly hadn't seen Jason. All she'd seen was the floor of the van coming up to smack her in the face. Apparently no one else had caught his reaction, either.

"I didn't," Marlene admitted. "I was trying to catch Dee."

"Neither did I," Bonnie said.

Elizabeth twirled a strand of her dark hair thoughtfully. "I know I didn't see him. But don't you think if Masters *had* seen Dee's...gesture, he would have chased the van down right then and there and fired us all on the spot?"

Pushing Fluffy off her stomach, Dee sat up, struck by the truth of what Elizabeth was saying. She lowered the soggy bag of sprouts to her lap, not even flinching at the icy dampness seeping through her skirt. Of course he would have. Jason Masters always reacted swiftly and decisively—especially when he was angry. And he certainly would have been angry in this situation.

Maybe he *hadn't* seen her.

The thought gave her hope. And her friends built on that faint hope to persuade her to return to work on Monday as if nothing had happened.

"Just act normal," Andrea told her.

"Try to be extra cheerful," Bonnie advised.

"For God's sake, don't act frightened—or let him see that guilty look!" Marlene said. "He'll definitely know something is up if he sees that expression on your face, whether he caught your act in the van or not."

"Think pleasant thoughts before you go in to see him," Elizabeth had recommended. "Picture a peaceful lake, full of ducks floating on the calm waters."

Remembering Elizabeth's suggestion, Dee put her purse in a desk drawer, then took another moment to take a few deep breaths, trying to ease her tension and make her expression serene. She'd pictured a lake and was struggling to visualize a few ducks—should she go with plain white ones or would mallards be better?—when once again the intercom clicked.

"Miss Evans!"

The lake evaporated and the ducks fled squawking. Perspiration dampened Dee's palms. Automatically snatching up the contracts she had ready for him to sign and her notepad and pen, she hurried to his office. Opening the door, she paused, peering cautiously inside.

White walls provided a stark contrast to the ebony desk and chairs in the room, as well as the vast expanse of black marble floor. Sculptures, composed of twisted curves of metal and rock, were placed on pedestals between the high arched windows. To Dee, the postmodern pieces always seemed stern and unyielding, and for the most part, unfathomable. But no more stern and unyielding than the dark suited figure standing by his desk with his back to her, gazing out a window at the city below.

She swiftly scanned Jason's rigid figure, from the top of his thick dark hair down to his polished shoes. Her heart sank. He was mad, all right. No mistake about it.

To her experienced gaze, the signs of an incipient explosion were all there. Tension tightened his broad shoulders, and he'd thrust his hands—fisted no doubt—deep into his pants pockets. Perhaps the worst sign of all was that he didn't even turn around at her entrance. She knew he'd heard the opening of the door. Jason Masters heard all and knew all when it came to his company.

Why on earth had she thought he wouldn't have seen her mooning him?

Dee pressed the notepad and papers against her breasts, and tried to still the trembling in her knees. She wanted to turn and run, to escape before he could see her. Oh, how she hated angry voices—especially angry voices directed at her. But she refused to give in to the impulse to flee. She'd promised her friends to do her best to hide her crime or, if that wasn't possible, to try to explain. She'd come prepared to apologize, to plead with him not to fire her—or at the least, not to fire her friends—and she wouldn't let them down.

Taking a deep breath, she began walking across the endless black marble floor to her usual chair in front of his desk. Jason neither turned nor acknowledged her presence. In the silence, her flat heels hitting on the floor sounded unnaturally loud, the dull clacks affecting her sensitive nerves like bullets. She walked faster. The clacks became louder, making her wince. Finally she reached the black leather chair in front of Jason's desk. She sank into it with a sigh of relief.

Jason hadn't moved. He still didn't turn. The oppressive silence lengthened.

Dee shifted. She shifted again, rearranging the notepad on her lap, taking a firmer grip on her pen. Then she stared at that unyielding broad back, feeling more nervous by the second. Oh, goodness—this was worse than she'd expected. Even confession had to be better than this unending tension. Her apprehension increased until the heavy thudding of her heart made her almost feel sick.

Suddenly she knew she couldn't bear the silence any longer. She opened her mouth to try to explain but before she could force out a word, Jason suddenly spoke.

"How long have you worked for me, Miss Evans?"

His voice emerged on a low growl that made the fine

hairs rise on the back of her neck. The desire to explain fled. All she wanted to do was to get this dreadful interview over with as quickly as possible so she could slink away and lick her wounds in the privacy of her little house.

He still hadn't looked at her. She wasn't certain whether to be sorry or thankful about the omission. Swallowing to ease the dryness in her throat, she managed to croak, "I've worked six years for the company. Eight months as your private secretary."

He spoke again, sounding even more menacing. "And would you say I've been a fair employer?"

Her voice dropped to a husky whisper. "Very fair."

Another long silence ensued. Through the window he was facing, the sky looked gray and cloudy. Perfectly appropriate, Dee decided, for the way she was feeling.

She jumped as his low growl came again. "And would you say that, as a fair employer, I'm entitled to at least the token respect of my employees?"

"Of course you are."

He nodded, then rocked ever so slightly on his heels. "So, if you were in my position, what would *you* do to an employee who had the impudence—the insolence— the sheer gall—to *moon* me from a company vehicle?"

Dee swallowed the lump in her throat, humiliated by the icy contempt in his tone. There was only one true answer she could give. "I suppose I'd fire the employee, sir," she said in a whispery voice.

"Good answer."

He swung around to face her. Dee's heart leaped in alarm. Oh, my goodness! Jason Masters wasn't just angry—he was *furious!*

His dark blue eyes burned with rage, and the harsh planes of his tanned face looked sculpted from stone. His jaw was locked so tightly that a small muscle pulsed in his cheek. His big hands were clenched into fists.

She hugged her notepad tighter, trying to subdue her rising panic. She'd seen him angry before, more times than she could count. Never had she seen him as angry as he was now. And this time his anger had been caused by *her*.

He braced his hands on the desk and leaned forward. Dee cowered back in her chair.

"In fact, that's the perfect answer, Miss Evans," he said between clenched white teeth. "Because firing the Mooner is exactly what I plan to do—"

Dee shut her eyes in dread, waiting for the blow to fall.

"As soon as *you* find the culprit."

3

DEE'S EYES POPPED OPEN. She stared at Jason in astonishment. "Me?"

"Yes, you."

"I'm supposed to..." She couldn't even finish the sentence, her surprise was so great.

Masters finished it for her. "I'm putting you in charge of finding the perpetrator. Whatever resources you need to accomplish that goal, I'll provide personally."

For a moment, Dee was afraid she was going to fall off her chair she felt so dizzy. Taking a deep breath, she tried to calm her crazily racing pulse as one thought whirled over and over through her mind: Her friends had been right—he *didn't* know she was the Mooner.

A gasp of relief escaped her. The small sound caught Jason's attention and he glanced at her, then really seemed to focus on her for the first time that morning.

His blue eyes narrowed. "What have you done?"

Alarm leaped again in Dee's breast. "Done?" she repeated. *Oh, good Lord, had she somehow given herself away?*

"To your hair," he added, gesturing impatiently toward her head.

Immediately Dee's hand flew up to the unaccustomed, layered curls bouncing around her face. The new hairstyle had been Bonnie's idea. "If you pull your hair back into your usual bun, he'll see that bruise for sure," the redhead had stated. "What we'll do is cut your hair a little—and let your natural curls hang loose. Then he won't notice a thing."

Unfortunately the plan seemed to have backfired. Jason was staring at her so intently that Dee squirmed uneasily in her chair, dropping her hands from her head.

"You've never worn it like that before," he stated.

"I know."

He added, almost accusingly, "You cut it."

"Just—just a few inches." Okay, maybe more like six or so, but who was counting? Bonnie certainly hadn't been as she'd hacked away.

"And you've let it go wild."

Dee stiffened a little, her hands tightening on her notepad. *Go wild?* He made her hair sound like an untended hay field. Before she could respond, however, his gaze narrowed even more. Coming swiftly from around his desk, he walked over to her.

Dee gasped as he caught her chin between his thumb and forefinger and tilted up her face. His blue eyes darkened as he stared down at her. What on earth was he doing now? He was so *close*—he'd never been this close before. She could see a small pulse beating in his clenched jaw beneath the faint shadow of his beard. His fingers felt warm against her skin, and the tangy scent of his aftershave surrounded her. Disturbed by his proximity she shrank back in her chair.

He ignored her reaction, tilting her face up farther to study her closely.

Her cheeks flushed with heat. They burned hotter as he carefully brushed back the curls by her temple, his callused fingertips sliding into her hair. "You've hurt yourself."

Her stomach dropped. His rough tone was filled with

so much uncharacteristic concern, she nearly forgot to breathe. Trying to move away, she reached up to grasp his strong wrist. "It's nothing."

He ignored the comment along with her attempts to escape. Holding her gently but firmly, he examined the bump. "Did you see a doctor?"

"Of course not. I told you it's nothing."

"How did it happen?"

Uh-oh. *There* was a question she didn't want to answer. Involuntarily her eyes met his. Alarmed at the intentness of his blue gaze, she hastily looked away, and he finally released her. "I fell—"

"You fell?"

Dee pulled herself up short. *What was she saying?* "No, I mean—well, actually, something smacked me."

His brows drew down and his stern mouth hardened. "A man?"

"No! Of course not!" How on earth had he reached *that* conclusion? Frantically she tried to think of an explanation that would satisfy him without revealing the truth. "I was... Swimming!" Yes, that was it! "In the ocean. And a big wave smacked me." She almost cringed as the words left her mouth. Now not only was she an exhibitionist, but a liar as well.

And obviously not a good one. He leaned back against the edge of his desk and crossed his arms, his eyes still fixed on her face. "Are you trying to tell me *water* caused a bruise like that?"

"Yes. I mean, no. It wasn't the water exactly that bruised me, but—but…my surfboard."

His eyes widened slightly with surprise and Dee drew a breath of relief, thankful to have thought of a plausible excuse. "Yes, that's how it happened. I was swimming when my surfboard, which was floating on a wave of water, smacked me on the head and caused the bump.''

A skeptical expression flitted across his lean face. ''You surf?''

''Mmm-hmm.'' Dee looked down at the notepad she was clutching in her lap, praying he'd believe her. Her cheeks were flaming hot, and her hands were trembling. Oh, how she hated lying—and how dreadfully bad she was at it! Hoping to avoid any further questions she added, ''But I'd really prefer not to discuss that anymore. It, er…brings back bad memories.'' *That* was certainly the truth.

For a long, unnerving moment he merely looked down at her with an inscrutable expression. Then to Dee's immense relief, he straightened and returned to his chair.

He sat down. ''All right. Let's get back to the business at hand. As I said, I've decided it's best for you to handle this affair.''

Of course he would, Dee realized, subduing an almost hysterical desire to laugh. Lately Jason had begun passing on to her the situations he was too annoyed to handle. And he was more than annoyed now.

He must have read her thoughts in her expression because he nodded. ''You can be more subtle, make inquiries more discreetly among the employees, than I'd be able to do. And…'' He bared his white teeth in a humorless smile. ''You won't be tempted to tear the culprit into tiny strips.''

No, she wasn't tempted to do that at all. And he was right about the first part of his statement as well. No one ever noticed her. But Jason commanded everyone's attention by his mere presence alone.

Relief and increasing dismay warred in Dee's breast as she considered the situation. Her elation that Jason didn't realize she was the Mooner was fading fast at this new, unexpected glitch. She didn't want to be in charge of hunting down...well, herself. It was a situation where she just couldn't win.

She took a deep breath. "Mr. Masters, I appreciate the—the confidence you have in my ability to find this offender, but I'm not sure I'm the right person for the job."

He frowned. "Why not?"

"My regular duties keep me very busy..."

"We'll suspend your regular duties for a while. Give you an assistant."

He continued to stare at her, making it hard to think. Stalling for more time, she asked weakly, "Ah, when and where did the...incident occur?"

"Near the corner of Alphonsus and Gassendi. Right before sunset on Friday evening."

Dee was trying to think of another question or reason to refuse the assignment when Jason added, obviously irritated at her reluctance—she'd certainly never argued about an assignment before—"Is there a problem here?"

Plenty of problems. "Yes," she blurted out. "I mean, no. That is, I'm not sure that this is even worth pursuing. After all, what real harm did this Mooner do? Other than offending your dignity, of course," she added hastily as his expression darkened.

Her final comment didn't appease him in the least. "It's not my dignity that I care about, it's this company," he said flatly. "Antonio Dialti—of Dialti and Sons—was in the car with me."

"Oh," Dee said in a hollow voice. "You didn't mention that."

Smiling sardonically at her aghast expression, Masters said, "Didn't I? Well, he was and he saw the whole thing—and he passed the news on to his father. As you know, the elder Dialti is very conservative and old-world European. Now they're reconsidering that limited partnership deal we'd proposed. This 'trivial' incident may cost our company a potentially twenty-million-dollar deal.''

A sick feeling swamped Dee's stomach. This mess just got worse and worse. Not only had she put her own job at risk—along with those of her friends—but she'd put the entire company in jeopardy as well.

Guilt tightened like a band around her chest. She couldn't do it—she couldn't perpetuate this lie any further. Maybe if Dialti knew that the Mooner had been fired, he'd go ahead with the deal. She'd confess the whole thing and—

"So as you can see, Miss Evans, this was no mere prank." Merciless resolve hardened Jason's voice. "Exposing your buttocks in the state of California is a crime, you know. I plan to not only fire, but press charges against the culprit.''

Dee could actually feel the blood drain from her face. Terrifying images arose in her mind. Herself out of work, broke, probably out on the streets. Unable to feed Fluffy, and forced to push her cat and all her belongings around in one of those metal shopping carts with the wheels that always jammed. Fluffy would never stand for that; he'd probably run away. Then Dee would be all alone—in jail at the worst, and at the least, labeled a Mooner and publicly scorned for the rest of her days.

Her nausea increased. Her sweet, elderly parents would be horrified to learn their only daughter was a criminal. She couldn't let that happen. She couldn't let *anyone* find out!

"I'll do it," she said bleakly. "I'll find the Mooner."

"Good." Jason wasn't surprised at her agreement; he'd obviously expected no less. After all, she always obeyed his decrees. "Do you have those contracts?"

Dee laid them on his desk.

A satisfied expression crossed his hard face. He nodded dismissal.

Dee rose to her feet. She trekked slowly across the endless marble floor, weighed down by a disheartening realization: Not only was she a liar, an exhibitionist, and a criminal, but she was a coward as well.

At the door she paused, one final hope emerging from the cloud of despair surrounding her. "Mr. Masters..."

He glanced up. "Yes?"

"You do realize it might be impossible to ever find the guilty party. We have no proof and one, er..." Heat flamed in her cheeks again. "...*derriere,* does look pretty much like another, after all."

Even before she finished speaking, he was shaking his head. "We'll be able to recognize this particular derriere, I promise you," he said, grim satisfaction in his voice. "This bottom has a crescent moon-shaped mark, right in the middle of the left cheek."

Without another word Dee left, closing the door quietly behind her.

Jason was still staring thoughtfully at that closed door a few minutes later when it suddenly opened again and his youngest brother walked in.

Jason frowned. He'd requested, more than once, that his brothers wear suits to work, to help promote a proper business image. The twins—James and Justin—usually complied with his request; Jon never did. Today he was dressed in Levi's. He'd thrown a lab coat on over his white, pullover shirt and his dark hair—worn too long in Jason's opinion—was tousled.

Jason tapped his pen impatiently on his desk. "What do you want?"

"To find out what's happening, of course," Jon said, undeterred by his brother's deliberately discouraging tone. "Where's Dee?"

"Dee?"

"Diana. Your secretary."

Jason's frown darkened. How had Jon known his secretary's nickname? *He'd* certainly never heard it before. Hell, half the time she still called him Mr. Masters—like he was seventy years old or something. "Diana—*Dee*—" If his brother could use her nickname then why shouldn't he? "—is probably on a short break." He checked his watch. "Yeah. Nine o'clock. Right on time."

Jon ambled across the room and appropriated the chair Dee had recently abandoned. Leaning back, he linked his hands behind his head and stretched his long legs out in front of him, before cocking an inquiring eyebrow in his brother's direction. "She go for it?"

"Yeah."

"She suspect anything?"

Jason shrugged. "I'm not sure. I couldn't quite figure out how much of her reaction was due to embarrassment at the subject under discussion, and how much was fear that the malefactor might be caught."

"She gets embarrassed just talking about a mooning?"

"She's conservative. Kind of old-fashioned about stuff like that."

Jon shook his head in mild wonder. "Hard to believe in this day and age, isn't it? Not too many woman like that around anymore."

"They're not likely to be found in the types of bars and strip joints you hang out in," Jason said dryly, but he knew what his brother meant. These days most women were as blasé as any man when it came to discussing sex.

But not his secretary. He remembered how red her cheeks had been when she'd used the word "derriere."

Jon interrupted his thoughts. "I still think you're going to an awful lot of trouble making her track down the Mooner. What if it's not one of her friends like you suspect?"

Jason smiled grimly. "Trust me on this. The van was eastbound, and only two of our vehicles would be traveling in that direction, on that street, at that hour. According to the parking lot attendant, only one of those left before I did. That's the van headed to Orange County—the one that Dee's friends travel on."

"Okay, but why involve Dee? Why don't you just fire the person who did it yourself?"

"Because then I'd be the bad guy."

Since Jon looked blank, Jason explained impatiently, "Diana went to a great effort to get those women hired on. She went to each of the department heads personally to put in a good word for them. She might even quit over the issue if I'm the one who nabs whichever of her friends did it. But if she's in charge, and *she* discovers the culprit…" He shrugged. "She can't blame me in that case."

"Why is that so important?"

"Because she's the best damn secretary I've ever had. She's efficient, reliable, discreet—and even more importantly—she's never come on to me."

"And that's good?"

Jason threw his brother an exasperated look. "If you'd been through what I've been through before Dee you wouldn't even have to ask. The older women I've hired haven't had the stamina the job requires, while the younger ones all seem to view me as a prospective husband.''

"But not Dee."

"I could be a robot giving her orders and it wouldn't make any difference to Diana. She's no more sexually attracted to me than I am to her."

Jon nodded approvingly as if that were a mark in both their favors, before adding, "Yeah, it's well-known you're a die-hard bachelor. And she's probably too enamored of Stewart Paxton to pay you any attention."

Jason glanced up sharply. "Paxton?"

Jon nodded. "In accounting. I hear they're dating."

How did his brother do it? Jason wondered. Like their father, Jon had a scientific mind and would disappear for weeks, even months, in the company's research labs, totally absorbed in some project. Yet, when he emerged, Jon always seemed to know the latest gossip. Even something so obscure as who his brother's secretary was dating.

Jason certainly hadn't known Dee was involved with anyone. He'd thought she was content being alone, the kind of woman that a hundred years ago would have been considered a dedicated spinster. Obviously he'd been wrong.

But *Paxton?*

"Why did she choose that wimp?" he asked aloud, irrationally annoyed by the thought.

Jon raised a dark eyebrow. "You have someone better in mind?"

"Hell, no. She shouldn't have a boyfriend at all—"

Jon's eyebrow climbed higher.

"Then she'll want to get married. And start a family. Then quit her job to stay home with the kids." Jason had no doubts on that score. Diana was precisely the kind of woman who would do such a thing. Somehow, the realization annoyed him even more. Dammit, her loyalty belonged to *him*—to Masters Inc.

Both Jon's eyebrows were raised now. "It's normal for a woman to want a family," he pointed out. "I know this is hard for you to understand, bro, but there's more to life than this company..." He added beneath his breath, "For some of us, anyway."

"Yeah, well, don't let me keep you away any longer from your women and beer." His patience exhausted, Jason pulled the pile of papers on his desk closer, signaling to his brother that their chat was at an end.

Jon stood up, taking a long, leisurely stretch. "Just one more thing..." He met his brother's frowning eyes. "How do you know Dee will tell you who the Mooner is, once she finds out?"

"Diana Evans is the most predictable employee at this company," Jason stated. "She's also the most honest." All the Masters brothers valued honesty; Jason most of all. He'd been old enough to realize how often his stepmother deceived his father to hide her extramarital affairs.

He told his brother, "Dee has never lied to me. I doubt she ever would. But even if she doesn't tell me which of her friends did it, I'll be able to read the answer on her face." Dee had the most open expression he'd ever seen, he reflected, adding confidently, "She hasn't surprised me once in the eight months she's worked for me and I'm positive she'll do exactly as I expect in this instance, too."

His tone was firm with conviction. Yet, as the door closed behind his brother, Jason was uneasily aware that what he'd told him wasn't quite true. Dee *had* surprised him. Today in fact. And more than once.

He'd thought he knew her completely. He knew she came to work at eight and, unless he asked her to stay, left precisely at five. She always wore neutral colors—beige, brown or navy blue outfits memorable only for their complete lack of style. She kept her purse in a lower desk drawer and watered the plants on her file cabinet on Mondays, Wednesdays and Fridays without fail. She took a bathroom break at nine, and a coffee break at ten, trotting down to the company cafeteria to daintily sip one cup of decaffeinated coffee—no cream, no sugar—for fifteen minutes before returning to her desk by ten twenty sharp. She could type 120 words a minute, was an expert on the computer and could spot a grammatical error or typo in a letter from fifty yards away.

But it wasn't only her office skills that made her so valuable, but her delicate sensibilities. She usually had a pretty speaking voice, but she squeaked when alarmed and she stammered when she was nervous. She cringed at loud arguments and crude language made her wince. At several important business meetings lately, just as he'd been about to blast someone, either her soft voice making a timid inquiry or the apprehension in her gray eyes would pull him up short. She'd become, without him quite knowing how it had happened, his own private barometer of when he was about to go over the line.

Yeah, he was definitely attuned to her reactions whenever they were in a room together. He was aware of her—but not really *aware* of her. Not in a sexual sense.

Until today.

He rapped on his desk impatiently with his pen. It was that damn haircut—that was the problem. He couldn't believe how much the simple change altered her appearance. She'd looked…vulnerable, with the tousled curls framing her face. More…touchable.

Not that he'd intended to touch her; he'd just been trying to see how badly she'd been bruised. The unexpected surge of lust he'd felt when he'd looked down into her startled eyes had taken him by surprise. The feeling was the result, no doubt, of being without a woman for far too long. And maybe—just a little—from the feel of her baby-fine skin. She had the prettiest skin he'd ever seen. So clear and silky. Unbelievably soft. Not mucked up with the makeup that most women layered on. No, he couldn't deny that today he'd been aware of her—just for a second, of course.

And she'd been aware of him, too. His eyes narrowed in unconscious satisfaction. No mistake about that, either. Her breath had caught, then come a bit more quickly when he'd brushed his fingers across her cheek. The pupils of her gentle, silvery-gray eyes had darkened and expanded. He'd been around too many women not to recognize those small signs of arousal—even if she hadn't.

He leaned back, thinking that over. Like he'd told his brother, she'd never shown any awareness of him before...so why now? His satisfaction faded as the most likely explanation presented itself. Maybe Paxton was responsible. Maybe Paxton had awakened her sexually, and her reaction to himself was merely a side effect—sexual runoff so to speak. Jason scowled. The thought was revolting. Hell, the thought of Paxton involved with Diana at any level was revolting. But there was no doubt that she'd been acting differently today. Skittish—like when she'd first started working for him. And somehow wary.

Especially during that story she'd told of how she'd gotten the bruise on her temple. He'd swear that she'd been lying. His frown deepened. But why would she?

Unless… A grim stillness crept over him. Unless *Paxton* had hit her, and she was merely trying to protect the jerk.

If so, the guy was toast.

The next minute or so passed pleasantly as Jason imagined various ways to take Paxton apart. Then an unwelcome thought intruded. Paxton simply wasn't the physical type. Oh, he might *whine* a woman to death, but as for being violent…no, it just didn't fit. Nor could Jason imagine Diana ever putting up with such a situation. His secretary might be reserved, but she wasn't a fool. Disgust welled up inside him. Crap, he'd have to let Paxton live, after all.

But that still left the question of how she'd gotten that bruise. He simply couldn't imagine her surfing. He couldn't even imagine her in a swimming suit. She probably wore one of those old-fashioned jobbies, with a high bodice and a skirt down to her knees. Judging by the old-lady clothes she sported at work, she'd want something that would hide her figure.

Not that her figure was bad, he supposed. He'd never really thought about it before. He had no idea if she had a small waist or not, or if her legs were decent—and good luck rating her breasts. She always walked around with a notepad pressed up against them like some kind of protective breast shield, keeping them safe from the eyes of men.

Still, now that he considered it, maybe her figure was okay. After all, she wasn't fat. Nor anorexically thin. Maybe she did wear a more modern suit—a sleek one-piece. Or even a bikini. And maybe she really had tried surfing, too. He straightened a little. Maybe she'd tried surfing with Paxton and the wimp's board had gotten away and hit her. Maybe that's what she'd lied about—in order to protect her new boyfriend.

Jason's grip on his pen tightened. She shouldn't be surfing and she *certainly* shouldn't be surfing with Paxton. How could she concentrate on her job, if her thoughts were on swimsuits, or surfing—or sex on the beach?

The gold pen snapped, ink spilled on his fingers. Jason stared at the shattered metal pieces in amazement for a second, then threw them away in disgust. He opened a drawer and pulled out a tissue to clean his hands. Hell, he was getting worked up over nothing. Diana wouldn't have sex with a wuss like that. Paxton—if she really was dating the jerk—was probably just a friend. Diana was a career woman to the bone, completely dedicated to Masters Inc. Staid, loyal, trustworthy—hell, the woman was so scrupulously honest that she could hardly live with herself if she thought she'd done something wrong. Once when payroll overpaid her fifty dollars on her check, she'd practically run all the way down to their offices she'd been so anxious to correct the error.

Talk about a perfectionist. Still, her perfectionist tendencies would be a boon in this case. They'd drive her to find the Mooner as quickly as possible. Then her sense of loyalty to the company—or her honest face—would reveal the culprit, who would then be fired and prosecuted.

Jason tossed the tissue into the trash. He picked up the first contract on the pile she'd left, satisfied with his analysis of the situation. There was nothing to get stirred up about here; everything would be settled just as he planned. Like he'd told his brother, Dee Evans was the most predictable woman he'd ever known.

At that precise moment, Jason's predictable secretary was standing in a stall in the women's bathroom, her heart pounding in dread as she waited for the room to empty.

Finally the last chattering group filed out, leaving her alone at last. Dee unlatched the stall door. Turning, she climbed up on the toilet seat, balancing carefully on the edge as she pushed down her panty hose and underwear.

She glanced over her shoulder. Taking a deep breath, she lifted her skirt—teetered—then thankfully regained her balance. She looked again at her bare white buttocks reflected in the bathroom mirror behind her. Her breath emerged on a sigh.

No doubt about it, Jason Masters had the eyes of a hawk. There, as clearly visible in the middle of her left cheek as if it had been painted on, was a distinct, tan-colored crescent moon.

She was a birth-marked Mooner.

4

"HOW COULD YOU FORGET you have a birthmark?" Bonnie demanded when the women gathered at Dee's house that night for a "debriefing" of her encounter with Jason Masters. Since Dee had to work late, she'd taken the bus instead of riding with her friends in the van. But they were all waiting when she arrived at her door.

"I didn't forget exactly. I mean, I've seen it on those 'bare-baby-on-a-bearskin-rug' pictures that my mom thinks are so clever, but I thought the mark had faded by now—like one I used to have on my leg. I certainly never thought to check it." Dee spread her hands helplessly, looking around at the group who settled in her living room. "Who bothers to look at their own bottom?"

Bonnie started to answer, but Marlene cut her off. "Never mind about that. The important thing is that Masters doesn't suspect you." She gave Dee a thumbs-up. "We're off the hook."

"I'm not sure we are," Dee said, feeling a twinge of regret as her friend lowered her hand. She didn't get very many thumbs-ups from Marlene. Setting aside the bone china her mother had passed on when she and Dee's father had moved to Leisure World, Dee opened up the box of pizza her friends had brought. After doling out slices onto the pink flowered dishes, she handed them around as she added, "Jason's bound to suspect something is wrong when I don't produce a Mooner."

Finished with serving, she picked up her own pizza slice. The pepperoni on it all looked like eyes, staring at her accusingly. She set it down again. "I can't believe I lied to him—or that I got away with it. I felt so guilty. My face burned like it was on fire." She pressed her hands to her cheeks. "Oh, if only I didn't blush so easily! It makes me feel like such a fool."

Andrea patted her shoulder, saying reassuringly, "Don't feel bad. Blushing is completely natural in this situation."

"It is?" Dee glanced at her hopefully.

"Of course. It's simply your body's physiological response to an attractive male who you feel vulnerable around."

Bonnie bounced in agreement. "Andrea's right. Blushing is your body's way of saying to a man, 'Hey, look at me—I'm all red. I'm either scared or hot for you, so you'd better stay away.'"

Dee stared at her in horror. "Surely Jason doesn't think I'm interested in him?"

"Bonnie's exaggerating," Elizabeth said. "I'm sure Jason didn't even notice your reaction."

"How could he help it when I turn as red as a beet?" Dee picked up Fluffy, who was edging toward the pizza, and hugged him to her chest. "Darn it, all this lying makes me feel so nervous around him—like when I first became his secretary. All jumpy and queasy. And when he touched me—"

"He touched you?"

Fluffy's claws shot out and Dee flinched as all four women shrieked the question at once. The cat leaped to the floor. Dee looked at her friends, surprised by their reaction. "Well...yes."

"When? Where?" Marlene demanded.

"Today. In his office."

Bonnie bounced impatiently. "Not where like that, silly! Where did he touch you?"

Dee's eyes widened. "Nowhere he shouldn't have, for goodness' sake! Just on my face. He was concerned about my bump."

No one spoke. Dee glanced around. "What's wrong now?" Her voice rose defensively. "Why are you all so quiet?"

"We're assessing the situation," Elizabeth explained absently, deep in Maternal Goddess mode. When Dee still looked blank, she elaborated, "We're trying to decide if he was making a pass or not."

"Well, stop it! All of you." Dee jumped to her feet to confront them, indignation rising in her breast. "For goodness' sake, the man's my boss. He wouldn't do that—nor would I let him. What kind of a woman do you think I am?"

"A normal one—underneath that coating of proper etiquette your mother plastered on," Marlene said. "Any normal woman would have to be a little interested in Jason Masters."

"Well, I'm not. I mean—I'm normal, of course, but that doesn't mean he appeals to me sexually." Dee pushed aside the memory of the way her stomach had dropped when his fingers brushed her cheek. That had been pure fear—nothing more. Feeling the need to emphasize the point, she added, "I'm not interested in Jason Masters—and he's certainly not interested in me. Nor any other woman as far as I can tell."

Marlene gazed at her in patent disbelief. "Oh, pul—leeze. The women he's dated are legion. The man's definitely a player."

"Maybe he used to be, but a person can change. I

don't think one woman has called the office in the past six months.''

"Just because a wolf is silent for a while, doesn't mean his howl is gone. It might simply mean he's on the prowl.''

The other women nodded in agreement with Marlene's remark, but Dee shook her head, irritated by their insistence on seeing Jason as some kind of perpetual playboy. The man was intimidating, quick-tempered and autocratic, but that didn't mean he was a sexual predator. Why couldn't they give him a break?

She looked around, intending to hold up the blue pillow embroidered Judge Not, Lest Ye Be Judged, but since Bonnie was sitting on it, continued without the visual aid. "He's never made a pass at me in all the time I've worked for him. Why would he start now?"

"Well, that's true," Elizabeth admitted.

"It certainly is," Dee said, pleased to have made her point. She added firmly, "All he ever thinks about is work—and finding this Mooner. So let's concentrate on what's really important. Like what I should do now."

Andrea, chewing thoughtfully on her pizza, was already working on the problem. "You need to stall," she announced after swallowing. "Maybe after awhile he'll get tired of the whole thing and give up."

That wasn't going to happen. "Jason never gives up when he wants something," Dee said flatly. "And what he wants is every problem to be solved yesterday."

"Stalling will at least buy you a couple of days," Andrea insisted, "give you some time to prepare for the next step." She took another bite and frowned, considering the situation more deeply. "Your game plan should be to delay, divert and—as a last resort—distract."

Dee sat down again. Fluffy was out of reach, so she

picked up a pillow that Great Aunt Diana had embroidered with lavish purple pansies, and hugged that to her chest. "Okay, the delay part is clear enough, but what do you mean by divert?"

"Divert him from his goal of finding the Mooner. Convince him that he didn't see what he thought he saw. Make him think he was mistaken."

Dee stared at her disbelievingly. "Jason never makes mistakes."

"Sure he does—everyone does. And the people who make the most mistakes are the people who take the most risks. No one takes more risks than Jason Masters," Elizabeth stated. "The trick will be to get him to believe and then admit he made an error in this case."

Dee gave a mirthless laugh, running her fingers along the pillow's purple fringe. "Some trick."

Elizabeth nodded, a sympathetic expression on her face. "I know, but what other choice do you have? Unless you're planning to confess—and I'd think Masters would be even more angry now to find out that you not only mooned him, you lied to him as well."

Dee buried her face against the pansies, shutting her eyes in dread. Oh, good Lord, Elizabeth was right. She remembered what he'd said about tearing the malefactor into tiny strips. She *couldn't* confess now, but...

She lifted her head. "What about Dialti?" she asked, remembering Jason's passenger. "Jason said he saw the mooning, too."

"If you can convince Jason Masters he was wrong, believe me, he'll do the same with Dialti," Andrea told her.

"And I think you can do it, Dee," Marlene put in.

Dee glanced at her. Was she kidding? The task was impossible. She started to say so, then paused as Marlene

added, "After all, you survived your first interview with
him without admitting anything—or him discovering the
truth. And well, to be honest…" A faint pink stained the
blonde's high cheekbones, but she met Dee's gaze
steadily. "I don't know if I could have done that. You
have more guts than I realized."

Dee stared at her, struck by the truth of what she was
saying. Why, she *had* survived that interview without being unmasked—or uncovered, as the case might be.

She looked around at the expressions on her friends'
faces. They really thought she could do it. They actually
thought she had a shot at making Jason Masters doubt
the evidence of his own piercing blue eyes.

A small glow of surprised pleasure blossomed in her
chest. How could she possibly give up now? They were
depending on her.

She set her pillow aside. "I'm not sure I can do it,"
she admitted. "But I'll definitely try my best. Now help
me figure out what to say…."

JASON WAS REVIEWING a report from the research division a week later when a discreet knock broke his concentration. He looked up. "Yes?"

Dee peered around the edge of the door. Her slim eyebrows lifted questioningly. "Do you have a minute? I
have the information you requested. On the…er, mooning incident."

"Of course. Come in." Jason pushed the papers aside,
pleased his expectations had been correct. Just as he'd
told his brother, Dee obviously had gotten right on the
project and was prepared to present him with the culprit
already. And to think, he'd actually begun to wonder if
she was working on it at all. She hadn't appeared to be.
But right when his patience had worn thin and he'd de-

cided to have a word with her sometime today, here she was, report in hand.

He watched as she crossed the room to her usual chair, clutching her notepad shield against her chest. Her hair, curling around her head, bounced with every step. He still wasn't used to her new cut. He wanted her to go back to her old way of doing her hair. Her prissy bun hadn't been so damn distracting. The curls she wore now altered the line of her face, making her features look softer, her eyes bigger. Even the color of her hair seemed different. He'd always thought of it as plain brown. Now he could see that the wayward tresses were streaked with shades of chestnut, gold, even a few strands of blond.

He frowned. Had she gotten those blond streaks from the sun while surfing?

She sat down, shifting slightly to get more comfortable. Planting her flat-soled shoes on the floor, she pressed her legs together, and smoothed her skirt over her knees. Unable to help himself, Jason's gaze followed the movement, skimming curiously down over the line of her calf and ankle. From the little he could see she wasn't tanned at all, but dammit, her legs looked pretty good. Her calves were slim, but sweetly curved. She had nice ankles, too. So narrow that he'd bet he could wrap his fingers around them and lift—

"Mr. Masters?"

His gaze jerked up. She was watching him, her head cocked, a puzzled expression on her face. "Is this a bad time? I can come back later...."

"Now is fine." Irritated with himself for the direction of his thoughts—and with her for causing them—his frown deepened even more. He quickly replaced it with a businesslike expression, trying to pretend he hadn't been having slightly lascivious thoughts about her and forced himself to concentrate on the subject at hand. "What have you discovered?"

She looked down at the notepad in her lap. "I drove the route to the place where the sighting occurred..."

Very thorough, Jason thought. Unnecessary, but still thorough. She was a perfectionist, all right, and just as predictable as he'd expected. The thought reassured him somehow.

"...and I noticed several streetlights in the area. Round, low, *white* streetlights," she added, lowering her voice in a significant fashion.

She was looking at him expectantly, yet a couple more seconds passed before Jason could bring himself to believe she was actually suggesting what she seemed to be. "I did not see a streetlight," he said flatly.

"Oh." She looked slightly disappointed. She stared down at her pad again, then straightened her shoulders. His gaze dropped but the shape of her breasts was indiscernible beneath her loose, navy-blue jacket. He forced his gaze away.

"I also made enquiries at a party shop down the same street," she added. "The proprietor told me a few balloons escaped Friday night from the bunch he hangs outside the door."

She checked her notes. "First, a red one—with happy birthday written on the side in blue letters. Then a Mickey Mouse shaped one—you know, the kind with the big ears? And..." Again that significant pause. "A plain white one. Perfectly round, about twelve inches in diameter."

His jaw tightened. "I didn't see a balloon either."

"Oh." Again, she looked disappointed...but also more determined. Her chin jutted forward just a little. She had a small, firm chin. Funny, he'd never noticed before how stubborn it could appear.

She met his gaze. Her gray eyes were serious, concerned. "Mr. Masters, sometimes a person's mind can play very strange tricks on them."

He raised his brows at the unexpected comment, but didn't argue. She had a point. Ever since he'd talked with his brother, images of his secretary, questions about her, would stray through his mind at the oddest times. He'd find himself thinking of the graceful way she moved, or how she'd pucker her smooth brow in concentration whenever she took notes. How appealing the intent expression on her face could be. In fact, at this very moment, he couldn't help thinking that she appeared strangely fetching, almost innocently sexy with her flushed cheeks and solemn tone. Her clear eyes were earnest as she added, "It can happen to *anyone*—even someone as intelligent as you appear to be—"

Jason straightened in his chair. *Appear* to be?

"—Especially when the person is under a lot of stress. And you have been under a lot of stress, haven't you?"

Jason nodded cautiously, unable to resist the hopeful plea in her eyes. Yeah, he was probably under stress. Not that stress bothered him, but still...

"And it's not necessarily a sign of insanity, you know."

Jason stared at her blankly. Somewhere between the intelligence estimate and stress talk, she'd lost him. "What's not a sign of insanity?"

"Seeing things," she said brightly. "Although insanity is a possibility, of course."

A big possibility, Jason decided. Because suddenly he had the insane urge to stop her rather insulting suggestions by kissing her senseless. Which was ridiculous. His prim, proper secretary wasn't the kind of woman he kissed—or even imagined kissing.

"...I believe there is medication available for this condition—but I don't recommend it in this case," she added hastily, as his eyes widened. "The more natural remedies available to help a person relax are really much better." She consulted her notes again. "Such as—"

Having sex.

"Meditating." She looked up again and met his eyes. "Chanting might help you there—or relaxing in a Jacuzzi. Or if you don't have one of those, a hot bath. You can splash the water around a bit, or let the faucet run— I always do," she confided, "and I add lots of bubbles as well. It's not as relaxing as a real Jacuzzi, of course, but still..."

A vision of Miss Evans, naked, with her curls piled on her head, bubbles strategically popping revealing her soft skin, appeared full-blown in his mind.

"...scented candles can be relaxing, too. Or scented lotions. Lemon is good, but according to my friend Elizabeth, if you rub chamomile all over your body—"

He had to stop her. "Miss Evans."

She paused in midsentence, her lips shaped in an enticing pink circle. He *was* going mad. He'd never noticed her mouth before—or thought about making love with her. What the hell was going on? This was his secretary, for God's sake. His quiet, unassuming, basically invisible *secretary*.

Clenching his jaw, he said with forced patience, "I don't soak in bathtubs. I prefer a hot shower—" Or a cold one, when the situation called for it. Like now for example. "And I am not under stress." Unless, you counted his sudden awareness of her. Forcing the strange attraction from his mind, he added, "Are you finished?"

His tone was biting, a clear warning that a prudent woman shouldn't try his patience any further. And he knew that no one was more prudent than Diana Edith Evans.

So he could hardly believe his ears when she replied, "I do have one more suggestion, Mr. Masters."

"Yes?" He drawled the word out in a deliberately menacing fashion, but his secretary—usually so sensitive to his every mood—didn't even hesitate.

"Yes," she said, her chin lifting even higher. She met his gaze resolutely, her eyes narrowing with determination. "This last possibility might appear a bit far-fetched, but I've always believed you're a man with a remarkably open mind."

Yeah, too open, if the thoughts he'd been having lately were any indication. He nodded in cautious response to the compliment and waited, determined to keep his mind on business.

She took another deep breath. Her jacket gaped. Triumph surged through Jason as his gaze zeroed in on the firm, full curves pressing against her blouse. *Ah, ha! Just* as he'd suspected. She *did* have nice breasts. Now if he could only see her waistline—

"In Roswell—New Mexico to be precise—strange phenomena have occurred...." Dee's soft voice jerked his attention back up to her face. "Several people living there have claimed to see spaceships. Some of these people have actually talked with the alleged aliens involved, and it seems they—the aliens, of course, not the people— have very strange faces. They are round, very white, and their mouths run straight down the middle—"

"*Diana!*"

She raised her brows in inquiry.

He spoke slowly and distinctly. "I did *not* see a balloon, or a street lamp, nor was I hallucinating. But most of all, I did not—I repeat, *not!*—see a fanny-faced alien! I saw human buttocks framed in that van window. To put it in words of one syllable, I was *mooned*. Do you understand?''

It was a mild rebuke by his standards, but usually it would have been enough to make his meek secretary instantly apologize. Or at least excuse her outlandish proposals.

But not today.

With something akin to amazement he watched her purse her lips. She tilted up her small, stubborn chin. She even had the effrontery to say in a reproving tone, ''Of course, I understand. There's no need to raise your voice. I know that as the Moonee, you must feel—''

''As the *what?*''

''*Moonee*—victim of a Mooner.''

''I'm not a victim and I'm sure as hell not a *Moonee!*'' he barked, slamming his fist down on his desk for emphasis. Ignoring her reproachful expression, he added, ''Now do you have any *viable* suggestions for finding this person or should I put someone else on the assignment?'' He held up his hand to forestall the comment he could see hovering on her lips. ''And I repeat, it was a *person* I saw.''

She must have finally recognized his patience was at an end. ''Since you seem…unreceptive to my initial suggestions, I do have another plan to propose.''

He regarded her suspiciously. ''Yes?''

''I thought it might be a good idea to have a party.''

His brows snapped together but before he could blast her, she added primly, ''A *small* party consisting of the employees who ride in the company vans. We'll say it's a gathering to discuss the carpool program and hold it here, in your office.''

"And why would I want to do such a thing?"

"Because I believe the malefactor—when placed in your presence—might reveal himself.''

His brows lifted. "By mooning me again, you mean?"

Her cheeks reddened. "Of course not—that would be ridiculous. I mean they might be...well, nervous. And s-stutter, or something like th-that.''

She stopped, biting her lower lip. She had such an absurdly anxious expression on her face that Jason's anger eased a bit. Obviously this wasn't easy for her—pointing the finger of blame at one of her friends. If she wanted to go through the charade of a party, and have him do the dirty work of identifying the culprit, why the hell not?

"Fine. Set it up for Wednesday afternoon.''

She seemed relieved by his decision. Not an unexpected reaction, Jason decided. In fact, it was about the only normal one she'd had so far today. Yet something in her demeanor made his eyes narrow in suspicion. Somehow she seemed *too* pleased. Jason didn't claim to have his brother's skill at reading people—and heaven knew this woman was turning into more of an enigma than he'd ever imagined—but there was no mistaking the satisfaction on her face as she gathered up her notepad, rose and headed to the door.

Jason watched her departure thoughtfully, his gaze fixed on her slim back. Her shoulders were straight, her step brisk. Her whole bearing exuded a sense of success, rather than the worried or deflated attitude he would have expected of her after basically failing an assignment—not to mention wasting his time. Even those damn distracting curls of hers seemed to bounce with an extra jaunty air.

A warning was clearly in order.

He waited until she reached the door. "Dee..."

She turned immediately, her hand on the knob. Her eyes were wide with surprise. They widened even more as he stood up and strolled toward her.

She didn't retreat but she stiffened, one hand tightening on the doorknob, the knuckles of the other turning white from the clench she had on the notepad pressed against her breasts.

He stopped less than a foot away. Her gaze flashed across his face then skittered somewhere over his shoulder.

"Dee," he said again.

"Yes?" Her voice squeaked. She wouldn't meet his gaze.

He reached out. His fingers brushed her cheek then caught her chin—how had he ever missed its defiant slant?—and he gently but inexorably tilted her face up to his.

For just a second, he was distracted by the sweet berry scent of whatever perfume she wore; the feel of her silky skin beneath his fingers. His eyes drifted to the dark mark on her temple. "How's your bruise?"

Her gaze shifted again. Her lids fluttered. Then her dark lashes lifted and her eyes reluctantly met his. "It's fine. Almost gone."

"Good." He dropped his hand. Assured he had her full attention, he said, "I'm determined to find this Mooner. I don't want an employee who'd do something like that running loose in my company."

He paused, watching as the apprehension in her gray eyes turned wary. Satisfied she was finally taking him seriously, he added, "Don't try to put me off with any more tricks."

For a fleeting second, a guilty expression crossed her face. Then with a brief nod of acknowledgment, she hurried out the door.

5

THE PARTY WASN'T A *TRICK* exactly, Dee kept telling herself the following Wednesday afternoon as she straightened the napkins and silverware the caterers had laid out in Jason's office. It was simply a carpool brainstorming session, a friendly business meeting, a logical step in the Mooner hunt, a—

Her rationalizing crumbled. Who was she trying to kid? Herself? Because it sure wasn't working. Her conscience kept reminding her this party was actually another delaying tactic. A diversion device—which Jason would probably see through in a second.

She began to fold the napkins into neat triangles, piling them next to the finger-size sandwiches. Then again, maybe she was being too pessimistic. After all, she'd brushed through the conversation in his office fairly well. Much better, in fact, than she'd ever anticipated. He hadn't dismissed her from ''the case'' as she'd secretly feared; nor had he quite lost his temper. That was almost a miracle in itself.

She could hardly believe even now that she'd dared to suggest he'd been hallucinating. Or was insane. Or might have seen an alien. An irrepressible smile played on her lips as she thought of that last suggestion. She had to admit, she'd almost enjoyed proposing that one. Just the memory of the stupefied look on Jason's face filled her with satisfied glee every time she thought of it. He certainly hadn't expected her to say anything like *that!* Never had she seen him so astonished.

Her smile faded. But she hadn't been completely successful in her mission. She hadn't raised any doubts in his mind about what he'd actually seen; nor had he decided to abandon the hunt as she'd hoped he would. He'd also given her a fright. He'd never called her Dee before. The sound of her nickname spoken in his deep, husky voice had literally stopped her in her tracks. And although his touch on her chin had been gentle, there'd been a definite warning in his dark blue eyes: Jason Masters wasn't known for his patience, and her Mooner "report" had pushed him almost to his limit.

She clasped her hands together, praying that this party wouldn't shove him over the edge. That somehow he wouldn't notice the obvious—that no women were present. She'd cut the women carpoolers from her invitation list on purpose, of course. She wouldn't put it past Marlene—or indeed, any of her friends—to sacrifice themselves if they thought Dee was in danger, and she didn't want to take that risk.

Besides, Jason had never *specifically* stated that the Mooner was a woman. So he might believe it when she told him she'd assumed the culprit was a man, wouldn't he? She certainly hoped so.

But even if he didn't, she'd have a short reprieve before finding out. When she'd arranged for this gathering, she'd also scheduled a second meeting at the same time for him with a prospective buyer. Earlier this afternoon, she'd informed him of her "mistake," stammering through an explanation that was barely coherent, much less believable.

But the ploy had gotten the job done. Since the buyer was one he'd been working on for months, Jason hadn't been able to pass up the chance to meet with him. With a grim, ''We'll talk about this later,'' he'd headed out to keep the appointment and with any luck, he'd be awhile before returning. At the least, the conflicting meeting would make him late to this gathering. At best, he might miss this party altogether.

Clinging to that hope, Dee greeted the arriving employees with a serene smile on her lips. They entered rather warily at first, some in suits, others in the white coats worn in the research department, still others dressed in the denim pants and casual shirts worn by those on the assembly lines. None were quite sure what to expect. But as soon as they spotted the food and the small bar by one of the windows—and were informed the boss hadn't yet arrived—everyone started to relax, breaking up into small groups to laugh and chat together.

Dee knew most of those present; she'd worked in so many of the departments at Masters Inc. that she knew almost all the employees at the company. She went quietly from group to group, pausing to exchange a word or two and offering refreshments. She was carefully measuring out a Scotch and soda for one of the researchers when someone said her name.

''Stewart!'' she said, looking up in surprise from behind the small bar where she'd retreated to act as impromptu bartender. ''What are you doing here?''

''I'm socializing, that's what I'm doing—no thanks to you.'' The hurt expression on his long face deepened as he added, ''I know that you're upset that I broke up with you, Diana, but I never believed you'd be so spiteful as to exclude me from a party with the boss.''

Pride stiffened Dee's spine. ''I wasn't upset,'' she protested automatically—then realized with a slight shock that it was the truth. In fact, with all that had happened lately, she hadn't given Stewart a thought since last Friday night. "And I certainly didn't exclude you out of spite," she added more firmly. "This party is for the company's carpoolers."

The disdainful sniff he gave told her he didn't believe her; Stewart was an expert at arguing without uttering a word. He'd merely look disbelieving, or make a dismissive gesture, if you said something he didn't like. And if you protested, or called him on his reaction, he'd assume a bewildered expression and declare he hadn't intended to disagree at all. If that failed, he'd quickly change the subject. Or cough like he was sick. Stewart hated arguments, and refused to "bicker" as he called it.

Since Dee hated arguments, too, she'd always respected his feelings in the past, keeping any of her contradictory opinions to herself. But right now, with Jason's arrival looming, she had more important things to worry about than Stewart's sensitive psyche. "Look around," she told him, picking up a liquor bottle. "No one else from your division is here."

"Oh." Stewart looked disconcerted at first, whether at her impatient tone or by the information, Dee wasn't sure. But his narrow shoulders relaxed a little as he followed her advice and scanned the room. After a few seconds he said, "I must say, I was wondering why some of the workers were invited."

Workers being the ones who weren't wearing suits, Dee thought, interpreting the disdainful note in his voice. Stewart liked to classify people by what they wore, or the jobs they did, the cars they drove—basically by their financial or social status in general.

Which made her wonder suddenly why he'd ever gone around with her in the first place. At the time she'd been too grateful for the attention to question his interest, but now that she thought about it, she wasn't the type he enjoyed being seen with at all. She wasn't pretty, or rich. Her clothes were dowdy—unlike his own. Her gaze skimmed his suit. "Dress for success" was Stewart's favorite motto, and he followed the dictum faithfully, wearing suits and crisp shirts as closely resembling Jason Masters's as possible.

Dee frowned thoughtfully, setting down the Scotch bottle she'd been holding. But when Jason wore an Armani suit, a woman only noticed the man—the breadth of his shoulders in the tailored garment; the way he moved with such primitive grace.

When Stewart wore Armani, a woman noticed the suit.

"I'm going to go mix, network a little," Stewart announced, as if he was sure she'd been standing there with bated breath, dying to know his next move.

"Good," she said briskly. She thrust the glass she'd filled into his hand. "On your way, take this to Tom Watson over there by the door, will you?"

She could tell by Stewart's affronted expression he wasn't pleased by her request, but of course, he didn't argue. Dee studied him as he walked off. No, even in his expensive suits, Stewart never made the impact on a woman's senses that Jason did. She tried to figure out why. It wasn't that Jason was more handsome exactly, she decided, picturing him in her mind. His tanned features were too roughly hewn, his blue eyes too shrewd. More often than not, Jason's dark brows were drawn down with impatience, and he was more likely to wear a scowl than the uneasy smile Stewart had pasted on his face as he circulated.

Perhaps the petulant thrust of Stewart's lower lip was what made him look less handsome. Or the uncertain, self-conscious expression in his pale green eyes—or were they blue? She'd never really noticed. Stewart's posture didn't help his image, either. Jason always strode across a room like a man who knew where he was going, never doubting that people would get out of his way—which they did. Stewart, however, walked with his shoulders hunched, edging around the groups that never even glanced up at his approach. Jason's shoulders were so straight, and wide. And his arms were much more muscular than—

—Oh, good Lord, what was she *thinking?* Was she actually comparing Stewart to *Jason*—to her ex-boyfriend's detriment? Had she actually been having appreciative...she swallowed...almost *yearning* thoughts about her curt, demanding boss?

That was ridiculous. She'd *never* been attracted to Jason. Not in the slightest. He wasn't the kind of man she wanted. He wasn't restful, or attentive. He was impatient and dictatorial—why, he yelled at people whenever he felt like it. Talk about alarming! Her heart speeded up when he simply came close. She'd have to be crazy to develop a crush on him. That would be the stupidest thing she'd ever done in her life—even more stupid than mooning him.

And she wasn't *that* dumb. Not at all. Maybe she was unconsciously bitter about Stewart dumping her. Maybe that's why she'd been so critical of him. Because surely Stewart had *some* features she liked better than Jason's.

Feeling strangely panicky, she tried to find one. She watched Stewart as he frowned at a mushroom on his plate, sniffed it, then put it back down. Stewart's hair...no, too thin and too blond. It couldn't compare at all to the thick, silky dark brown of Jason's. Stewart's mouth—no, not that, either. Stewart's was a little weak, whereas Jason's was firm, and nicely sculpted. Why the mere thought of kissing those lips made—

Oh, dear, oh, dear! She had to stop this! There had to be *something* about Stewart— Oh! His hands! That was it! Stewart had much nicer hands than Jason's, she realized in relief. Stewart's hands were smooth and white, his nails discreetly polished. Jason's hands, however, were tanned, and small white scars marred the backs. He'd noticed her looking at them one day, and had told her he'd gotten the nicks while working on old cars as a kid.

Jason's lean fingers were scarred, too, and his palms and fingertips were callused. His nails were clean and short, but never buffed. He also had the bad habit of thrusting his fists into his pockets whenever he got angry, which ruined the lines of his expensive suits.

Stewart would *never* do such a thing. He never made fists. He was proud of his hands and took care of them. He also gestured with them often—maybe a little too often, she thought, as he waved at her from across the room before starting back toward her. Sometimes Stewart's hands reminded Dee of restless white doves, fluttering in front of her face. She'd often had the irrational urge to bat them away.

He reached her side again. She was turning to face him when from the corner of her eye, she saw one of his hands fly out toward her. She jerked back out of reach.

"You have something on your temple," Stewart said, clearly offended by her involuntary recoil.

"It's the remainder of a bruise," Dee told him. "I got it while surfing."

Her life of crime must be affecting her more than she'd realized, she decided. She blushed and stammered when lying to Jason, but with Stewart, the words came out with no trouble at all. Nor did she feel a twinge of guilt, saying them.

"Surfing? You? In the ocean?" Stewart looked dumbfounded. "I don't believe it," he blurted, shock making him forget his dislike of controversy. "You've never surfed in your life."

How dare he call her a liar, Dee thought indignantly—even if she was one. "It's true. I do surf," she said, smug with the knowledge that this time she was telling the truth. She'd signed up for lessons the day after she'd told Jason about her pretend hobby, partly to alleviate her deception and partly as penance for the lie. In fact, she'd been to two surfing lessons already. If she'd spent more time during the sessions dragging her board across the sand than she'd spent in the water, it really wasn't any of Stewart's business. Nothing she did anymore was his business, she thought with a sudden sense of release. Pleasing him was no longer even a remote goal in her life.

She glanced at him. He still looked as if he didn't believe her. Simply to emphasize how trendy she'd become, she added, "I got this bruise when my surfboard hit me."

"Let me see." He reached up suddenly and touched it.

"Ouch!"

"I didn't mean to hurt you."

But he *had* hurt her. His hands might be soft, but they lacked the gentle care that had been in Jason's calloused fingertips when he'd examined the mark. And Jason's hands had been warm. Stewart's were kind of clammy.

Dee stared up at him resentfully. Why, not only wasn't she heartbroken over him, but she was actually glad, glad,

glad those clammy hands had never stroked her body. "Don't touch me again. I don't like it," she told him.

"You've always made that clear enough."

He sounded sulky—and definitely full of dislike. Had he ever cared for her? Dee wondered. Which brought her back to her original question. "Why did you go out with me, Stewart?" she asked.

He stared at her in surprise, then glanced away. Looking out across the room, he mumbled, "Why not?"

Now there was a reply to make a woman's heart beat faster. Did he really think he could get away with a non-response like that? Dee's eyes narrowed. She'd committed a *crime* because of this man. She deserved some real answers.

Before she could question him further a faint commotion occurred by the door. Dee turned. Her heart jumped as she caught a glimpse of a dark head and broad shoulders. Then the small crowd shifted again and her pulse settled back down to normal. It wasn't Jason, but Jon, who had arrived.

She watched the researchers eagerly crowd around him and shook her head in faint wonder. The two Masters brothers might look startlingly alike—same intense blue eyes, wide shoulders and thick dark hair—but they couldn't have been more dissimilar in their personalities. Jason pursued his goals with concentrated focus, barely noticing the people around him unless they got in his way. Jon, on the other hand, was an easy-going mixer. Oh, he got his way, too—Dee had realized that quickly enough during her stint in the research department—but Jon preferred to make allies, not enemies on his route to success. He took the time to talk with people. Time Jason usually wasn't willing to spare.

After chatting with a few of the researchers, Jon

grabbed some of the finger sandwiches and headed to the door. Looking up, he caught her gaze on him. He winked, then wandered back out of the office.

"What was that all about?" Stewart demanded beside her.

"Nothing."

Stewart's expression turned sulky again. "Oh, come on, Diana. I saw the way Jon Masters looked at you."

An odd note in his voice—one she'd never noticed before—caught Dee's attention. She stared at him. "Are you implying something is going on between Jon Masters and me?"

Her direct question made him nervous. His gaze dropped. "No, of course not—"

"Well, if you are, then you're a fool. Jon is friendly with everyone."

She made no effort to keep the contempt from her voice and Stewart's full lips tightened. Resentment brought his gaze back up to meet hers. "Well, *Jason* Masters isn't—but he sure is friendly with *you*," he said in a snide tone.

Her eyes widened. "What are you talking about?"

"Anyone can tell he wants you. He watches you all the time at meetings, he listens to what you say. He doesn't even yell at you like he does the rest of us."

"And because of that, you think he—he's interested in me? My God, you *are* a fool!" she declared. What was going on with everyone? First her friends, now Stewart. Determined to set him straight, she said, "Jason Masters is my boss—we simply work together. If he watches me at meetings, it's probably to make sure I'm getting everything down. And as for yelling, if I'm doing my job correctly, why would he need to?"

Stewart wasn't convinced. "He's different around

you,'' he insisted, his full bottom lip thrusting out stubbornly. ''And you're different around him. Prettier.''

''I'm not pretty,'' Dee protested, taken aback by the remark.

''Whenever Masters is around you are. You...I don't know. Light up somehow.''

Light up? ''What on earth are you talking about?''

''You sort of come alive. You tense. Your eyes brighten and your cheeks turn pink. You even move quicker.''

Dee stared at him in disbelief. Good Lord. He'd interpreted her anxiety in her boss's presence as a sign of sexual tension. ''If I move quicker, it's to provide a moving target,'' she said flatly. ''I'm usually afraid he's going to bite my head off.''

''The point is, he never does bite your head off. Not like he did with all his other secretaries. Why do you think no one else ever lasted long?'' Stewart's voice held uncharacteristic conviction as he added, ''I think you two are having an affair.''

An *affair*—her and *Jason?* How could Stewart even think that?

And if he did believe it, then why on earth had he gone out with her himself?

Suddenly it all became blindingly clear. ''That's why you started dating me,'' she said, her voice breathless with amazement. ''You dated me because you thought I was one of Jason's alleged women.''

Stewart's pale eyes bugged. ''I—no. I didn't—''

''Yes, you *did.*'' His expression more than gave him away and a strange feeling swept over Dee. It wasn't until red dots swam before her eyes that she realized the odd emotion was rage. Why had she wasted three hours a night, three nights a week, for *three whole months,* going out with this jerk?

Her fists clenched and her voice rose. "Why, you *used* me!"

Alarmed at her rising voice, Stewart tried to sidle away. "No. No, I didn't."

She grasped his arm to stop him. "Yes, you did," she repeated. "You try to copy everything Jason does. You copy his clothes, bought a car like one of his—and you decided to date me simply because you thought I was a woman he wanted."

She took a step closer, feeling fiercely pleased when Stewart tried to step back. Her grip tightened. "Well, you *are* a fool. A bigger fool than I ever realized. Jason Masters isn't interested in me—and I'm certainly not interested in him," she added emphatically. "He's obviously a confirmed bachelor, and a bad-tempered one at that. Why would any woman seeking a long-term, meaningful relationship waste her time on him?"

To Stewart, this was blasphemy. He mumbled, "All women—s-supermodels—want him—"

"Oh, *pul-leeeze,*" she drawled, borrowing one of Marlene's favorite phrases, and rolling her eyes for good measure. "Don't you know better than to believe everything you read in the papers? All Masters ever thinks about is business—"

"But—"

"But nothing. Those rumors about his sexual prowess are probably no more truthful than this imaginary affair you've dreamed up between him and me. Why, even if the stories aren't totally false, they're definitely exaggerated. The man's getting too old to party all night and work productively the next day."

Stewart made a gasping noise, and clutched his throat as if he was choking.

But Dee refused to be stopped by one of his pitiful attempts to avoid arguing. It was time he heard the truth! "Even if he was a player when he was younger—which I doubt—he's *way* past that sort of thing now. And you should be, too, you—you—Jason Masters copycat!"

Stewart blanched.

Dee paused, the exhilaration coursing through her veins tempered by doubt. Maybe she'd gone a little too far with that copycat remark. Righteous anger was one thing, cruelty another. She released Stewart's arm. Now that the red haze was clearing, she could see he looked horrified. Crushed even. Who would have thought a scolding from her would have such an effect? she thought, torn between pride and alarm. He almost looked ready to cry.

Then the fine hairs rose on her nape. A tingle skittered down her spine. She felt as if someone was standing directly behind her. Breathing heavily. Okay, practically breathing fire if the warmth flowing down on the back of her head and neck was any indication. Still, another second passed before realization struck.

She wasn't the reason Stewart looked so scared.

She turned around. No, the reason Stewart was frozen in place like a sickly green Popsicle was standing right behind her.

Six feet two inches of angry Jason Masters.

Dee froze, too, hunching her shoulders. It was an instinctive reaction, one a small animal might have when confronted by a predator. She'd had excuses, explanations all ready to divert him, but her mind had gone blank. All she could do was stand there, desperately trying to remember what she'd just said about him to Stewart. Surely nothing too bad.

But nothing too good, either, judging by his simmering expression. Dee braced herself to withstand the storm she could see brewing in his eyes, but to her surprise, she wasn't the one Jason went after—but poor hapless Stewart.

"What are you doing here, Paxton?"

Stewart looked ready to faint. "I…ah, I heard there was a party—gathering and I, ah…."

"And you immediately decided to leave your work undone and join the fun."

Stewart's Adam's apple bobbed up and down frantically as he tried to swallow. "No! I, ah—"

"Have you finished the analysis I requested on the Stickler account?"

Stewart obviously didn't want to answer. He tried to give one of his noncommittal shrugs, but Jason simply repeated the question in an even harsher tone. "I asked if you have that analysis ready?"

"No," Stewart admitted miserably.

Dee couldn't help but feel sorry for him. Now that her temper had cooled—doused by shock at Jason's arrival—she realized Stewart hadn't been the only one at fault in their so-called relationship. He'd made the mistake of using her to try to be like Jason, but she'd made an equally bad one in thinking any boyfriend was better than none.

Besides, for a man who hated confrontations, Stewart was really having a bad day. Jason looked ready to go for his throat. She looked around for help, but Jon had left and the rest of the employees were huddled at the opposite side of the room practicing the first law of corporate survival: Get as far away as possible when the boss is on a rampage.

Dee straightened her shoulders, realizing it was up to her to try to help Stewart. "I'm sure Stew—Mr. Paxton simply misunderstood the purpose of the gathering," she said in the quiet tones that were usually so successful in calming Jason down.

They failed today. Jason cast her such a coldly furious glance that she took a step backward, and Stewart winced.

Jason told him, "If that analysis isn't on my desk by noon tomorrow, you'll be collecting your final paycheck, Paxton. So I suggest you put down that drink and get out of here and back to work!"

Stewart left without a word. Dee watched him scurry away, pity welling up again inside her. Jason needn't have been so hard on the poor man! Especially since she'd just finished tearing a strip off him herself.

Her concern about her ex-boyfriend fled, however, ousted by concern over her own skin as Jason turned her way.

"As for you, come with me."

Dee wanted to argue, but standing up to Stewart was a different proposition than dealing with Jason. He took hold of her elbow and steered her toward the door—and out of sight of potential witnesses to her murder. His grip wasn't painful, but it brooked no resistance, and she prudently didn't try. His hands were as warm as she remembered—even warmer actually. She could feel the imprint of each finger burning through her suit.

She breathed a sigh of relief when they finally reached her office, and he closed the door on the employees gaping after them.

Releasing her, Jason began to pace. For a moment, Dee

stood where he'd left her with her back against the door. Then she started to sidle to the safety of her desk.

Immediately Jason halted, his piercing gaze pinning her in place. "What exactly are you trying to pull?"

Dee froze, not positive which of her recent transgressions he was referring to. She swallowed. "Pull?"

Jason's eyes narrowed to angry slits. "You're not fooling me with that innocent look, not anymore." Through clenched white teeth, he added, "Let's get one thing straight. I don't care how chummy you and Paxton are, when you're at work, you—your attention—belongs to *me*. And I expect you to direct it toward the projects I've assigned you—like this Mooner hunt—no matter how unpleasant you might find them. Pursue your *personal* pleasures with your boyfriend on your own time."

Dee's mouth dropped open. She'd expected him to be angry, but not about this! "Stewart isn't a pleasure—I mean, he's not my boyfriend," she stammered, rattled by this unexpected attack. Indignation dawning, she added, "And I'd never pursue a…personal relationship on company time."

The rigid hostility in his bearing didn't ease. "Then why was he here?"

"He didn't realize this meeting was only for carpoolers. Jon was here, too, for a while."

She'd hoped to dilute his annoyance by mentioning his brother, but if anything Jason's expression hardened even more. "Jon? You call my brother by his first name?"

She stared at him in surprise. "Why…yes. He asked me to when we worked together in research and I agreed. After all, it would be confusing to call you both Mr. Masters."

"So instead of calling me by my first name, you call my brother by his."

Dee was bewildered. What did he mean by that? He sounded accusatory—as if she'd done something wrong. Unsure how to respond, she kept her mouth shut.

His angry eyes scanned her face restlessly, and his lips tightened. He returned to his original contention. "So what did Paxton think this meeting was about? Did you tell him about the Mooner?"

"No! I didn't tell anyone about that." And if she could help it, she never would. Trying to avoid getting Stewart into any more trouble, she said, "He…he assumed the gathering was to discuss the status of the Roberts project—" her gaze dropped away from Jason's skeptical stare "—and that the memo inviting him had gone astray."

Jason's eyebrows lifted. He said sarcastically, "And I suppose missing invitations are the reason half the carpoolers weren't there, either." He gestured impatiently toward the closed door. "Other than you, I didn't see one woman in there."

Now *this* was the accusation she'd been expecting. Dee tried out the surprised expression she'd been practicing all week in front of the mirror. "Women?"

"Yes, women," he repeated, his grim tone telling her he didn't buy her performance for a minute. "Where were they?"

"I didn't invite them." His shoulders tensed and she added hastily, "I didn't think I needed to. Surely the Mooner was a man?"

"He—*she*—was a woman."

"But you can't be sure—"

"I may be way past my prime, too old for late nights or getting it on anymore, but believe me, I can still recognize a woman's *derriere* when I see one."

Dee's face flamed. So, he *had* heard at least part of

what she'd said to Stewart. But she hadn't intended her remarks in that way at all. "I'm sure you can—I mean, I'm sorry. I didn't mean to imply—"

"I know exactly what you meant. And I'm also well aware that all this is an attempt on your part to delay the inevitable." A pulse throbbed at the side of his jaw. He ordered through gritted teeth, "Get the women in here now."

Dee feebly tried to rally. "They've left for the day. Maybe I can gather them together next week. Or the week following—"

"Tomorrow afternoon. In my office. Four o'clock and not a second later." His expression was implacable, his tone unyielding. "It's time to end this Mooner hunt once and for all."

6

THERE WERE BIG BOTTOMS, there were slender bottoms, there were normal-size bottoms. Yes, there was quite a variety in the lineup of Mooner suspects Dee ushered into Jason's office at precisely four o'clock the following day.

Along with her friends Dee had rounded up the three other women who used the company vans: Mrs. Staples, who had been with the company from its inception; Bertha Ann, head cook in the company cafeteria who was almost as wide as she was tall; and Heather, a voluptuous brunette from product sales.

None of the three knew, of course, why they'd really been summoned to Jason's office. Using the same excuse she'd given to the men, Dee had merely told them the gathering was to discuss the carpooling program. But her four friends knew the truth: they were there to be evaluated as possible Mooners.

Dee was anxious about the confrontation, especially since she hadn't had a chance to confer with them about the best possible course of action. Jason had kept her working late the previous night, and requested she come in early this morning. So she'd only had time to make a quick call to Elizabeth informing her of the meeting and asking her to pass the information on. Nor had Dee had the opportunity to tell them about her faux pas and how coldly Jason had been treating her since.

But upon entering his office, all her friends immediately realized from Jason's grim expression that the situation had turned dire. They exhibited their anxiety in a variety of ways that only added to Dee's own. Not that Elizabeth's or Andrea's demeanors were all that upsetting, she decided. Only someone who knew them well would recognize the worry in Elizabeth's eyes, or the distant aloofness on Andrea's patrician face as they shook hands with their boss. But Marlene's hostility was unmistakable. Her nod in response to Jason's polite greeting was so brief as to almost be insulting, and the way she immediately turned away to the refreshment table equally so.

But even worse than Marlene's defensive antagonism was Bonnie's dramatics. She'd obviously interpreted Jason's anger toward Dee to mean Dee had become a suspect. She confided to Dee in a hurried whisper that she would "throw the wolf off the scent." She'd worn black—a fluttery, chiffon dress more suited to a cocktail party than an office event—and she drifted around the room with a coffee cup in one white hand, staring at Jason out of big, frightened eyes as if she'd indeed committed the crime. In fact, she played the role of persecuted criminal so well that Dee began to worry Jason might buy her act, especially since Bonnie had the build most similar to her own.

All in all, Dee could only be thankful the three other women carpoolers were there, to provide a bit of distraction and keep Jason busy. They were obviously pleased that their opinions were being sought by the "big boss" as Bertha Ann called him, and they weren't shy about sharing their insights.

"I just love riding in those vans," Bertha Ann told him, as the women gathered around him in a semicircle talking. "Comfy—you just bet those seats are the best

I've ever sat on. Not too soft—just firm enough for a woman of my size,'' she added, her chubby body shaking with her good-natured laugh.

"It's a very innovative program," Heather interjected, drawing Jason's attention. Meeting his gaze, the brunette smiled slowly, adding in an almost purring voice, "I've been impressed with the many innovative ideas you've implemented in all areas, Jason."

She smoothed down her tight blue skirt as she spoke, and Dee watched Jason's eyes follow the movement. Lately Dee had noticed Jason frowning at her own hem lines, displeasure on his face. She knew he wanted to present a conservative image at all times, and in an effort to placate him, today she'd worn her gray pantsuit to the office. All her outfits were restrained, but this one was even more subdued than usual, with its loose pants and waist-length jacket. It still hadn't seemed to appease him.

But he wasn't frowning at Heather's hemline—and the brunette's dress was extremely short. Instead pure speculation narrowed his gaze as it roved up to the brunette's curvy hips. Oh, dear. Did he think Heather had done the dastardly deed?

Dee could only be grateful that he looked away when Mrs. Staples said, "Jason and all his brothers are like their father. Clear-thinkers, and years ahead of their time."

Jason's gaze softened as he glanced at the elderly woman. All the brothers treated the little white-haired lady with a gentle respect Dee had never seen them use toward anyone else.

"Thank you," Jason replied now with one of his rare slow smiles. But the smile disappeared and his expression hardened again as he added, with a flicker of a glance in

Dee's direction, "I'm glad one of my employees doesn't think I'm beyond it—at least when it comes to the company."

Dee could feel her cheeks heat, her chest tightening. Why couldn't he forget those stupid remarks she'd made? Ever since yesterday afternoon, he'd been throwing either sarcastic remarks or frigid glances her way every chance he had. And each small verbal dart increased her feeling of guilt.

Dee knew she should stay with the group, to try to monitor the situation, but mingled anger and distress made her too restless to remain still. She wandered over to one of the high arched windows and glanced out at the late-afternoon sky.

No clouds could be seen, but the muffled boom of thunder sounded in the distance, and the shimmering air had the leaden cast that often presaged a summer storm. In the west, the sun hung heavy on the horizon, glowing an angry orange-red. Toward the east, facing the sizzling sun, was a cool slice of crescent moon—a huge, distant replica of the one on her bottom. Not a good omen, Dee decided, her edginess increasing.

"Are you okay?" a voice whispered next to her.

Dee turned her head. Elizabeth had joined her and was holding out a drink. Dee automatically accepted the icy glass, replying in an equally low tone, "Yes—I guess so."

Elizabeth cast a quick glance over her shoulder. "Masters looks so grim—especially when he looks at you." Her worried eyes met Dee's. "Do you think he suspects you're the Mooner?"

Dee shook her head. "No. He's been mad at me since yesterday when he overheard me talking about him to Stewart."

Elizabeth's eyebrows lifted in surprise. "That doesn't sound like you to be so indiscreet. What did you say?"

Glad to have someone she trusted to confide in, Dee told her about the confrontation with Stewart and its unhappy result in a hushed whisper. She started out calmly enough, but ended on a defensive note, her guilt increasing at the growing horror on Elizabeth's face. "I know I shouldn't have been talking about him, but for goodness' sake—I didn't say anything *that* bad."

Elizabeth's eyes were wide with disbelief. "Are you kidding? You could hardly have said anything worse. Not only did you call the wolf a good doggy, you patted him on the head then announced to all and sundry he's now neutered."

"No, I didn't—"

"Yes, you did. You hit Jason in a man's most vulnerable area—his ego. That's why he's so mad." Her eyes narrowing, Elizabeth glanced back at the group and added, "It also explains why he's not discouraging Heather's advances. He probably wants to prove he hasn't lost it."

"Lost it?" Dee frowned, turning to follow her gaze. "What are you talking about?"

"Haven't you noticed the way she's been flirting with him? Or the way he's responding? Why, he has her practically licking her chops."

"No, he isn't—and neither is she," Dee protested. For some reason, the suggestion increased her uneasiness— and her anger as well. Why did her friends always think the worst of Jason? "I certainly don't see it."

"You never see anything you don't want to," Elizabeth pointed out. "Look how surprised you were when you discovered Stewart had been using you."

Dee couldn't honestly argue about that. But just because Elizabeth was right about Stewart, didn't mean she was right about Jason and Heather. Dee glanced at them again. Why, he wasn't paying any attention at all to the brunette, who had moved over to stand by his side. His entire attention was fixed on the women across from him.

Dee followed his gaze and suppressed a groan. "Things don't look good. Marlene must be scared—she looks like she wants to hit something. And Bonnie appears about to swoon."

She watched a second longer, tensing up as Jason's gaze roved from one woman's hips to another. "We're doomed," she said in a despairing tone, as he evaluated Marlene. "I just know he's going to accuse one of them of being the Mooner."

"I'm sure he won't. He's not stupid enough to make an accusation like that unless he's totally positive he has the right person."

"Then why can't I shake this feeling of impending disaster?" Dee demanded. She glanced at the window again and suppressed a shudder. "If that moon was full, I swear I'd be about to turn into a werewolf. My skin feels too tight for my body, and I'm so jumpy, I can hardly stay still."

"That's caused by nerves, not the moon," Elizabeth declared. "I should have brought some chamomile, but since I didn't, take a swig of this."

She tapped the glass Dee had forgotten she was holding. Obediently Dee lifted it to her lips and took a huge gulp. Sizzling liquid sunshine filled her mouth, then swirled down her throat in a burst of fire that exploded in her stomach. Warmth flared, sweeping out along her limbs.

She gasped and choked, her eyes tearing so heavily

she felt like she was underwater. "That's awful," she wheezed, thrusting the glass back at Elizabeth.

Jason's head jerked up and he glanced in their direction. Dee covered her mouth, trying to stifle her coughing and hide the fact that she'd just been poisoned. "What *is* that stuff?"

"Whiskey and water. I thought it might calm you down."

Before Dee could disabuse her friend of this misguided notion, Jason strolled over to join them, his unreadable gaze fixed on Dee's face.

"Are you all right?" he asked in a brusque tone. He hesitated a second, and then reached out, firmly rubbing her back as her coughing continued.

Dee's pulse quickened at the feel of his warm hand moving up and down her spine in long, soothing strokes. "I'm fine," she managed to say, adding hoarsely, "I just swallowed the wrong way."

Still coughing, she stepped away and his hand dropped. He nodded, his expression settling back into a frozen, unrevealing mask as he turned to rejoin the group he'd left. But the women had trailed him like a pack of curious hounds, and Bertha Ann was blocking his path. Before he could go around her, Heather glided closer, too.

The brunette lightly touched his forearm. "My goodness, what fascinating artwork you collect," she said, staring at a nearby sculpture. "So riveting."

Jason politely glanced toward the piece. Dee did, too. He'd once told her the work was a Hvostal creation—a marble of ebony and ivory, entwined in a bewildering blend of curves and angles.

Everyone gathered around it.

"What's it called?" Heather asked.

"It's an untitled piece," he told her.

"What's it supposed to be?" Mrs. Staples wanted to know, her wrinkled brow creasing even more in curiosity.

"It's a cat," Bonnie decided, after frowning at it for a few seconds. "See? There are its whiskers. And the stub of a tail."

"No, it's not." Heather cast her a condescending glance, then leaned closer to Jason to get a better view of the work, her hand still resting on his arm. "Can't you see it's a killer whale, leaping out of the water?"

"Not a whale—a panther. Attacking a white deer."

An argument broke out. Dee stood silently, barely aware of the voices raging around her, her attention fixed on the man standing by her side. Jason was close, so close that she could feel the warmth radiating from his strong body. She shivered as the fine wool of his jacket brushed against her hand.

As if he felt the small movement, he glanced down at her, then away.

Her stomach twisted. She wanted to say something, to apologize somehow. She hadn't meant to be rude—or to dent his male ego, as Elizabeth had suggested. Ever since that terrible Friday night, it seemed she just made one mistake after another with him.

Until she'd lost it, she hadn't realized how much she valued the working relationship they'd shared. The silent communion that made everything run so smoothly. Now all she wanted was for things to be right between them again. So they could work together once more without all this constraint.

"Mr. Masters..." she said in a low tone.

He didn't seem to hear her. She gave his sleeve a furtive tug. "Jason..."

He glanced down at her again, his blue gaze unreadable. Dee thought he was going to ignore her, but after a second of hesitation, he bent his head to hear what she wanted to say.

"I'm sorry," she said, her low tone barely audible through the conversational din around them. "I shouldn't have been talking about you with another employee."

He gave her another enigmatic look. Dee waited, wondering if he would accept her apology. Then Heather pulled on his other arm, drawing his attention away again.

"Come on, Jason, tell us. What does the piece represent?" Heather demanded, looking up at him from beneath long lashes.

He shrugged. "Obviously different things to different people." He glanced down at Dee, and said in a tone only she could hear, "What do you think it is, Miss Evans?"

Miss Evans...so he was back to calling her that, was he? Dee gave the work a distracted glance. "I don't know." She'd never understood any of the art in Jason's office.

But he didn't let her off that easily. "Look again," he ordered quietly.

The command in his voice sparked an unexpected surge of resentment. Fine. He was the boss—she'd look again. Dee stared at the work, trying to choose between the proposed kitten or whale. She really couldn't see either, but just as she'd decided to cast her vote for Bonnie's choice, something happened.

Under her amazed gaze, the curves and angles seemed to shift. The lines of the polished stone moved, flowing into perfect clarity. Dee blinked—then blinked again. She couldn't believe she'd never seen it before: the sculpture was unmistakably that of a man and a woman embracing.

The man's dark head was lowered, his mouth fastened to the woman's full white breast. The woman was bent back in ecstasy, her rounded leg curved around his lean hips, his muscular arm locked around her tiny waist.

And as for that stub...well, it certainly wasn't a cat's tail!

Startled, Dee jerked her gaze away. Her eyes locked with Jason's. A hot blush rose under her skin, scorching her from toes to cheeks. Outraged virtue narrowed her eyes.

Jason met her glare, his eyebrows lifting in silent question. Then his stern mouth tilted up at the corner. Pure wickedness widened his white, mocking smile.

Dee's lips pressed firmly together and her slender fingers curled into fists. Unreasonable anger rose up inside her, making her feel hotter still. Until that moment, she hadn't realized how much she'd been hoping he *had* changed—that he wasn't the player he used to be, that everyone thought he was. That he'd settled down, *calmed* down, enough to appreciate a woman for her character and brain, rather than the size of her bust.

But he hadn't changed, not at all. Not if he could put something like this in his office where anyone could see it. What a fool she'd been, defending him to her friends—and even Stewart! Worse yet, she'd apologized to Jason himself, feeling bad for denting his tender ego. Ha! She couldn't dent his ego with a one hundred pound sledgehammer! Marlene had been right all along. He was a howler, all right.

For the first time, the guilt Dee had been carrying around for the past two weeks eased. Okay, so maybe she was a Mooner—a *full* mooner. But at least, she'd only done the deed once. Jason, on the other hand, hadn't abandoned his disgraceful ways at all. He was still a full-time wolf. All he'd done was hide the evidence—in plain view!

How could she have been so blind? She'd trotted through this room, hundreds—thousands—of times, so intent on her job and wary of Jason, she'd never really noticed anything else. But if she'd missed this sexually suggestive statue, what else hadn't she seen?

At that moment Heather moved closer to him again, bumping him gently with her shoulder, causing him to look down. Dee looked at Heather, too—and remembered what else Elizabeth had said. Heather and Jason *were* flirting with each other. Heather's glances lingered on him much longer than was necessary, and she didn't miss a single opportunity to draw his attention with a light touch or a teasing remark.

Well, who cared? He could do whatever he wanted, Dee told herself. But her restless tension kept growing, fed by worry over the Mooner situation, but even more by an increasing anger at the subtle byplay between the two. Every time Heather touched his arm, Dee's nails bit into her palms in the effort not to shove the other woman away. Or punch her in her jaw.

The last thought shocked Dee. Of course, she'd never *really* commit an act of physical violence. She was much too kind and gentle. Her eyes narrowed as Heather's high, tinkling laugh rang out.

She'd have to get Marlene to do it.

Not because she cared about Jason or was jealous or anything, Dee assured herself. Simply because the brunette's lack of correct office decorum was the most offensive thing Dee had ever seen.

But angry as she was at Heather, she was even angrier at Jason. If he was so concerned with preserving a conservative company image, then why didn't he do something to stop the brunette? Use that biting sarcasm that was practically his trademark? He'd never had any problem being blunt or off-putting—even downright rude—to anyone before!

As the small party continued, her anger and anxiety kept growing. Even the air felt heavier, stifling and oppressive as gray clouds gathered outside. Sullen thunder rumbled like a drum roll from the hills, heralding the approaching storm. All Dee wanted was for the "Mooner meeting" to end.

Finally, the clock struck five, and everyone prepared to leave. Dee held her breath as her friends moved slowly toward the door, wondering if Jason would suddenly pounce on one of them as a likely suspect.

But nothing happened; no accusations were made. After a whispered assurance from Dee that she'd join them at the van in a few minutes, her friends departed with no more than a nod and a brief farewell to Jason.

Bertha Ann left next, with Mrs. Staples right behind.

Which left only Heather.

Dee gritted her teeth, gathering up coffee cups as Jason and Heather dawdled by the door. She almost wished he *would* accuse Heather of being the Mooner. Good luck getting Dee to step forward to save *her*. Why didn't he say goodbye, and shove her out the office? Or at least, move away a little. The woman was practically standing on his shoes, she was so close.

Then Heather leaned even closer—*too* close. Her breast pressed against his arm. Dee, watching so intently, saw a knowing expression flash across Jason's cynical face.

Rage, mixed with a strange hurt, welled up inside her. Before she could hide her reaction, Jason's gaze flashed

to her face and Dee saw an odd satisfaction in his eyes.
Then he looked at Heather again.

He's going to ask the brunette out, Dee thought. No
doubt about it.

Heather cooed, "Thank you again, Jason. It's been interesting. I'd love to get together again to discuss
other...projects, whenever you'd like."

Dee waited for him to agree, to set a date. But he only
nodded and—finally!—moved out of reach. "Thank you
for your input," he responded politely.

And that was that.

Heather left with an annoyed swish of her hair, and
Dee resisted the urge to slam the door behind her. Good!
One problem gone. As her anger eased, anxiety rose to
the fore. Now, if she could only find out what conclusion
Jason had reached about the Mooner.

He'd gone to sit in his chair and was leaning back, his
preoccupied gaze fixed on a far wall. "Leave it," he said
abruptly as Dee began moving around, gathering glasses
and stacking plates. "The caterers will be back later tonight to clean up."

Dee knew they would; she'd made the arrangements.
But with a noncommittal murmur she kept working, using the small task as an excuse to hang around, feeling
almost desperate to know what he was thinking.

"I think it went rather well, don't you?" she ventured.

He grunted, still staring unseeingly into space.

Did that mean he agreed? Or not? She tried again.
"You've seen all the Mooner suspects now—both men
and women." She put the top on the creamer and set it
aside with trembling hands. She moved over to the Hvostal piece to remove a glass someone had put on the pedestal. "Have—did you recognize anyone?"

Another grunt.

Dee interpreted this grunt as a negative. It had a slightly lower tone. She breathed a little easier and said soothingly, "I suppose it's hard to remember—"

"There's nothing wrong with my memory."

She bit her lip and set down the glass. Uh-oh. *Another* soft spot. When had he gotten so sensitive? "No, of course not. But it still must be hard to uncover the culprit—I mean, to identify the bottom in question, when all the suspects are wearing clothes."

He didn't reply to that at all. Dee relaxed even more. It had worked; he hadn't been able to—

"Were all the suspects here?" he asked abruptly. "Every single person who's ever ridden in the carpool vans?"

This wasn't good. "Yes," Dee admitted. "I'm sure of it."

He nodded, his frown of concentration deepening. He rose from his chair and strode to the window behind his desk, shoving his fists deep into his pants pockets. For a long moment he stood there, staring out at the graying sky. Then he swung around again, and paced to the front of his desk. Leaning a hip on the edge, he crossed his arms, looking past her as he turned the possibilities over in his mind. "Eliminating suspects. That's the first step," he murmured. "That gets rid of Bertha Ann—definitely too wide, and Andrea—too tall and lean."

He paused. "That leaves Marlene, Heather, Elizabeth and Bonnie."

Dee could feel her heart thudding with a quick, heavy beat. She wasn't on that list. Neither was someone else. "You forgot Mrs. Staples."

He cast her a sardonic glance. "Give me a break. We're looking for someone young—and possibly angry. That eliminates your friend Elizabeth—she's too placid.

And I don't think Heather seemed angry, did you?'' he asked, his gaze sharpening suddenly as it fixed on Dee's face.

Dee fought to keep her expression as unrevealing as his. *No, Heather had been perfectly happy to be pawing at you,* she thought, but said only, ''Angry isn't how I'd describe Heather.''

He nodded in agreement, lapsing back into his thoughts. ''If we're looking for someone with a temper, Marlene seems the most likely suspect.'' He studied Dee's face again. ''Why is she so hostile?''

''Marlene always gets…upset, when she's nervous. I suppose she was simply worried about meeting you.''

He considered that, while Dee watched anxiously. He said finally, ''I definitely got the impression that she was mad at me personally, but—''

Dee held her breath.

''—it really doesn't matter because she's not quite right, either. Her derriere is much too flat. Not the inverted heart shape that I remember at all.''

Embarrassment and panic roiled inside Dee. She resisted the urge to cover her bottom with her hands. How humiliating that he had such a definite mental picture of her derriere—and how alarming, too.

''So that leaves Bonnie.''

Dee swallowed. Her mouth felt dry. They'd come to Bonnie, the most similar to Dee in build.

''She's the right height—just about your size,'' Jason said, confirming Dee's thoughts. He idly looked her up and down. ''Tall enough to be seen through the window, but not towering, either.''

His gaze settled lower on the hem of Dee's short jacket. ''Her hips appeared to be the correct width, too. But her waist…no, that wasn't right. The Mooner has a very small waist with a sharp indent between her hips and ribs. An old-fashioned, Gibson girl type figure."

His gaze lingered on her as he spoke, and he stepped closer. To her shock he reached out and placed his hands above her hips, gathering her jacket and blouse tightly against her. "Your waist is so tiny," he murmured, his husky voice filled with an odd satisfaction. "My hands span it with no problem at all."

Neither moved. Jason appeared deep in thought; Dee was frozen with fright. Her heart was jumping, pounding against her breasts. Her muscles were tense with alarm.

She could almost see his brain ticking away like a mental time bomb. In another few minutes—seconds!— he'd reach the correct, fatal conclusion that she was the Mooner. And then he'd explode.

She had to stop him. But how? Oh, if only her friends were here—but they weren't. *It's up to you. Think, Dee, think!* she ordered herself fiercely. *At least get out of reach!*

She stirred, and his grip automatically tightened. Her terror increased. How could she escape? *Diversion! That was the answer!* Say—no! *Do* something!

She flew up on tiptoe, and flung her arms around his neck. Her fingers slid into his thick hair, pulling his head down until his lips were within reach.

Then, she kissed him.

7

MOUTH TIGHTLY CLOSED, she kept her lips pressed against his and simply hung on. It was an act of desperation, a frantic, impulsive attempt to halt his line of reasoning. Dee knew almost immediately that she'd made a big mistake.

His lips were rigid and unmoving beneath hers. His eyes were wide-open—total shock reflected in their blazing depths.

She drew in a shaky breath, inhaling the scent of his skin and aftershave. Her lips quivered beneath his. She wasn't any good at this—why had she tried such a thing? She shut her own eyes, unable to look at him any longer, and waited miserably for him to end this awkward torture.

His hands came up and grasped her waist again, slipping under her jacket and settling warmly against her thin blouse. Dee loosened her stranglehold on his neck, certain he was about to push her away.

But instead his grasp tightened. One arm clamped around her waist to pull her closer, pressing her breasts against his hard chest. His other hand slid up into her curls, tugging her head back even more. He increased the slant of his mouth, his lips urging hers to part. Dee's pulse raced with alarm. Stewart had never kissed her like this. Their kisses had been brief, a quick brushing of dry lips. He'd been polite, tentative—anxious to pull away when she did.

There was nothing tentative about the hungry urgency of Jason's mouth, nothing polite in the way he ignored her fingers clutching his arms as she tried to keep her balance. His heat enveloped her. Confusion clouded her brain. All she knew was that she had to stop this. Think about what was happening.

She parted her lips to protest...but never formed the words. Because Jason immediately deepened the kiss, his questing tongue seeking her own. He explored the secret inner softness of her cheeks. Then he nipped gently at her lips and ran his tongue teasingly over them again and again, until the sensitive curves were swollen and throbbing with need.

Dee whimpered, alarmed at the responsive tightening of her breasts and belly, the desire rising inside her.

Hearing her small sound of distress, Jason broke the kiss, his warm lips roving up her hot cheek to her temple. He pressed his lips against her tender skin, rocking her gently against him. "It's okay. It's okay," he soothed, his warm breath flowing along her cheek, his hand stroking her hair.

The words didn't make much sense. It wasn't okay for him to be kissing her like this, Dee knew. She just couldn't quite remember why. Yet, his tone calmed her. The familiar, spicy scent of his body reassured her somehow. Though they'd never been intimate, she'd spent almost every day for nearly a year with this man. She'd absorbed his scent unknowingly as she'd stood next to him, discussing business and taking notes. She'd never touched the muscles beneath her hands, but her eyes had instinctively recorded their breadth and strength.

He was so warm, and she was so cold. Small shivers

shook her body, and instinctively she burrowed against his hard chest, craving the comfort of the heat radiating from his healthy body. He gave it to her, folding her closer still until she felt like she was melting against him. Into him.

This time when his mouth covered hers, her lips parted immediately. She welcomed the taste, the secret excitement of feeling his tongue inside her. Shyly she touched it with hers. He groaned, his arms tightening until she could hardly breathe he'd crushed her so close.

But Dee didn't need to breathe—she only needed him to keep kissing her. She felt light-headed, as if she was floating away, anchored only by the secure strength of his arms around her as a tidal wave of pleasure rippled through her.

He lifted his mouth a fraction of an inch, and she moaned again, this time in protest. Her arms tightened around his neck, her fingers clutched at his silky hair. She didn't want to let him go, even for a second. He made her feel things she'd never felt before. Never had she been so aware of her body. The blood humming in her veins. The small flashes of excited heat exploding low in her tummy. The way her nipples tingled, and her lips throbbed. How every inch of her skin quivered, yearning for the touch of his callused hands.

"You taste so good," he murmured against her mouth. The tip of his tongue swept the swollen curve of her bottom lip, as if he really was tasting her, preparing to eat her up.

She did? She leaned her head on his shoulder, sweet dizziness making her weak. "The whiskey," she mumbled, remembering the drink Elizabeth had given her. He liked whiskey—of course he'd like the taste of it in her mouth.

She lowered her arms from his neck and wrapped them around his waist under his jacket, enjoying the feeling of his hard chest pressed against her breasts, his heart thudding against her ear.

He hugged her in return, dropping a kiss on her forehead. She shivered as his lips moved down along her cheek. His jaw felt raspy, like fine sandpaper against her skin.

"And you smell so sweet," he whispered huskily, his warm breath tickling the shell of her ear. "Like berries."

Berries? She wasn't wearing perfume, or anything that smelled like... Oh. Her deodorant was berry scented.

The thought startled Dee, jerking her out of the sensual haze she'd been sinking into. She pulled away from him slightly, blinking as if she'd just woken, embarrassment heating her cheeks. It seemed so personal. So *intimate* that he could smell her deodorant. Even if he did like it.

She moved away a little more. He definitely didn't like that. His warm hands glided down her hips to grip her bottom, clenching lightly to hold her still. Dee stiffened. This was even more intimate. No one had *ever* put their hands there before. She moved again. With casual possessiveness, he altered his grip to cup and lift her against him, pulling her lower body snugly against his.

Dee's eyes widened. Her breath caught. One of his hands was resting right on her crescent moon birthmark. Not a good sign.

But even more alarming was the part of him pressing against her hip and stomach—the big, *hard* evidence that the Mooner was no longer the main thing on Jason's mind.

Dee began trembling. This was a dangerous man—an *experienced* man who expected only one outcome from all this kissing and petting. And that outcome was *sex!*

Probably right here on his hard marble floor. Or maybe his desk—she really wasn't too sure on that point.

But she *was* sure she wasn't up to his speed—not as fast as he was moving. His hands were stroking her warmly, firmly molding her soft curves to his hard muscles. His mouth was exploring her neck again; kissing, nuzzling—even biting her gently in a way that made her nipples stiffen and her insides dissolve. She was fairly certain—okay, she was positive, she amended as he drew on her skin, causing a corresponding aching tug low in her belly—that she wouldn't be able to withstand this delicious torture much longer without surrendering her virtue. To a man who, when it came to women, didn't know the meaning of the word!

She took a deep breath. She'd accomplished her goal of diverting him. It was time to get out, to escape before it was too late.

She tried to step back, but bumped into the pedestal holding the marble sculpture. She stopped, caught between the proverbial rock and his hard—well, it wasn't a *place* exactly, but she was caught nonetheless.

She pushed at Jason's shoulders. Reluctantly, he stopped kissing her neck. He lifted his head to look down at her, his eyes heavy-lidded and dark with desire.

"I—I need to go," she stuttered.

"Go?"

"Yes. Please. Excuse me, will you?"

His arms tightened for a long, unnerving moment. But when she pushed insistently at him again, he loosened his hold, slowly releasing her.

Dee didn't hesitate. She turned and headed for her office, forcing herself to resist the urge to break into a run. Walking slowly but steadily, she went through Jason's door, past her desk, and out her own door and into the hallway.

There panic kicked in. He wasn't coming after her yet, but instinct told her it was just a matter of time until he did. She sped past the other offices and out of the building at a brisk trot that evolved into a sprint before she reached the parking lot.

There she paused. The sun and moon had disappeared behind the clouds. The storm had broken. Raindrops fell on her like warm tears as she looked desperately around. To her relief, she spotted the carpool van with her friends waiting patiently inside, parked in a far corner beyond her Volkswagen.

She raced across the asphalt. The van door flew open. Without slowing, Dee leaped on board. She kept her head down, letting her hair hide her face, as she rushed to the far back seat and flung herself onto it.

She'd deliberately chosen that one, hoping that her friends would stay at the front near Andrea who, as usual, was driving. But Bonnie, Marlene and Elizabeth all left their places to trail her to the rear, claiming the seats around her.

''Buckle up,'' Andrea called over her shoulder, as she pulled out into the street.

Everyone promptly complied. Everyone, that is, except Dee. She sat with her back against the side of the van, her feet planted on the seat and her arms wrapped around her legs. She buried her face against her updrawn knees, her damp hair falling like a curtain along her cheeks.

Her lips felt strange. Swollen and full—almost pouty, as if they still yearned for the crush of Jason's kiss. Dee pressed her mouth against the linen of her pants, trying to ease her lips' throbbing sensitivity.

''So how did it go?'' Marlene drawled, from the seat

next to her. "Did he say anything?" She paused, and when Dee didn't answer her voice rose slightly in alarm. "Dee? Elizabeth, something's wrong with Dee."

"Give her a minute to catch her breath," Elizabeth admonished, reaching back to put a comforting hand on Dee's shoulder. "Are you all right?" she asked, giving her a small pat.

Dee nodded without lifting her head. She just couldn't face anyone for a few minutes. Her mind was too full of Jason. She still quivered from his touch, she could still smell his spicy scent on her skin and clothes.

She stifled a groan. How could she have done such a thing? How could she have thrown herself at Jason—her boss!—and kissed him like that?

She'd acted out of desperation, of course. She'd had to stop his line of reasoning. But that wasn't what kept her huddled with her head down, her stomach churning with anxiety. What kept her frozen in place, a flush rising in her cheeks, was the inescapable knowledge that stopping Jason wasn't the *only* reason she'd kissed him. She'd also desperately wanted to.

The thought shook her. Oh, good Lord, she *was* attracted to him, despite all her denials, her unwillingness to see him as anything more than her boss.

"He knows you're the Mooner, doesn't he?" Marlene said, her voice tight with tension. "Oh, Dee, did he fire you?"

"Did he fire all of us?" Bonnie wanted to know.

"What's happening back there?" Andrea called. "Should I pull over?"

Dee knew she had to say something. Her silence was upsetting them. She answered wearily, "No, you don't need to pull over, and no, he doesn't know that I'm the Mooner."

Taking a deep breath, she lifted her head. Her friends were all looking at her in concern. Even Andrea was shooting anxious glances in the rearview mirror as she maneuvered through the evening traffic. Dee decided she might as well let them know the worst immediately. "But I can't go back there. I can never, ever face Jason Masters again."

"Why?" Marlene demanded. "For God's sake, Dee, tell us what happened!"

"I kissed him."

The van swerved wildly. Her friends gasped and clutched at their seat belts. Dee slid off the seat and onto the floor. "Ouch!"

"Don't say another word," Andrea ordered grimly. "Not until I find a place to park."

Tires squealing, she swung into a grocery store parking lot and switched off the engine. By the time Dee had climbed back onto her seat, Andrea had joined the group, squeezing in beside Marlene.

"Now," Andrea demanded, her steady eyes fixed on Dee's face, "start from the beginning and tell us exactly what happened."

"Just what I said. I kissed Jason Masters."

"But why?"

"I had to." Her hair, her cheeks, were damp from the rain. Dee searched for her hankie, but remembered she'd left her purse in her desk. She used her sleeve instead, wiping at the drops as she added, "He was making comparisons between the Mooner's build and mine and I did it to distract him."

Her friends maintained a respectful moment of silence at the enormity of her daring. Then Elizabeth asked in a subdued tone, "Was he very angry?"

"No. He wasn't angry exactly."

"What did he do?"

Dee shifted in her seat, wrapping her arms around her legs again. "He—he started kissing me back."

Everyone straightened. Marlene let out a low whistle, and Bonnie's eyes widened as she leaned closer. "He did? Then what?"

"Well, we kissed and then we—we kissed some more. And he forgot about the Mooner. And I forgot about the Mooner. Then—" Dee pressed her mouth against her knees, adding in a muffled voice, "Then he said he liked my deodorant, and I ran out."

Her friends exchanged glances. Marlene flopped back in her seat in disgust. "Well, I for one don't blame you. If that isn't the worst line I've ever heard—"

"No! I didn't run because of that," Dee protested. "He just…surprised me. But then he put his hand on my bottom, right on my birthmark and of course, I knew *that* was a bad omen."

Another silence fell.

"I'm not up on omens," Andrea said doubtfully, "but personally, it sounds to me as if you overreacted to what was simply a clumsy pass."

"I *am* up on omens and I think Andrea's right," added Elizabeth.

"No! You don't understand. Jason's not clumsy at all. In fact…" Dee's tone lowered as she admitted, "He's *good*. He's a very, *very* good kisser."

Her expression must have convinced her friends that she wasn't exaggerating. Bonnie said knowingly, "A real toe-curler, huh?"

Dee nodded. But after considering the matter a moment, added for the sake of honesty, "That is, I'm sure mine *would* have curled if I hadn't been standing on tiptoe. And if my shoes weren't so tight."

"So what's the problem here?" Marlene demanded. "If he liked it, and you liked it—"

"That *is* the problem. I liked it too much." Dee glanced around at her friends again and swallowed a lump in her throat. "I was afraid it might go too far. And then where would I be? After all, you guys are the ones who keep telling me what a womanizer Jason is. That he goes through women the way I go through—through—"

She broke off, unable to think of an adequate comparison.

"Dish soap!" Bonnie supplied.

Everyone looked at her. "That's all I could think of," the redhead said defensively. "Dee doesn't do anything to excess except clean."

How true, Dee thought. And how sad. Not that she'd done much cleaning lately—she'd been too busy. Worrying about the Mooner hunt, taking her surfing lessons. Kissing Jason.

She should have stopped at the surfing. If she'd never kissed him, she never would have realized what she was missing. She'd still be content to date men like Stewart— only ones that weren't quite so annoying, of course. But how could a woman be content with a regular man, after being in Jason Masters's arms? "It was such a mistake to kiss him," she said fiercely. "What was I thinking?"

"You were thinking of a way to save all our butts," Marlene said. "No pun intended. And I don't think you made a mistake at all. It worked, didn't it? Jason was diverted. He forgot about the Mooner."

"But what's he going to think now? Especially since I ran out on him? He'll be so confused."

Marlene's eyes lit up. She hit her palm with her closed fist. "And that's just how you want him to be," she declared, her tone firm with conviction. "The more time he spends trying to figure you out, the less time he'll have to think about the Mooner. You didn't make a mistake, Dee—what you made is *progress*. All you need to do now is keep to the game plan and divert him some more.''

Dee stared at her in disbelief. ''Are you kidding?'' It would be like playing with fire—and she'd heard plenty of warnings against *that* growing up. ''He might want to make love with me.''

''So?'' Marlene arched her slim brows haughtily. ''Let him want. You're not obliged to oblige him.''

That was true, but… ''It doesn't seem fair,'' Dee said. ''I don't want to lead him on like that.''

Marlene rolled her eyes. ''Give me a break. He's what? Thirty-two? Thirty-three? He's obviously a dedicated bachelor. He can take care of himself.''

Even though she'd told Stewart almost the same thing, it still didn't feel quite right to Dee.

Reading the doubt in her face, Marlene added, ''Do you think he's sitting home worrying about leading you on? I don't think so.''

Dee didn't think so, either. But it really didn't matter. ''I don't think it would work anyway.''

''A few weeks ago, I would have agreed,'' Marlene admitted. ''But you've changed, Dee. Put on some new clothes, a Wonderbra—and I promise he'll sit up and take notice. After all, you've already gotten off to a great start kissing him. He seemed interested then, didn't he?''

Very interested, Dee thought, remembering the hard length of him pressed against her. She could feel herself blushing as she admitted, ''Yes, but I'm still not sure about this.''

''Well, it's up to you,'' Andrea said. ''Only you can

decide if you want to keep going forward with this or not.''

The women fell silent, giving Dee a chance to consider her options. Even Marlene pressed her lips together, sitting back with her arms folded. But Dee knew they wanted her to continue—to try to lead Jason on.

But they didn't know what they were asking. What if she appeared foolish, dressing in a new style? What if she did something even more foolish than kissing him? What if—

She pulled herself up short.

Her whole life had been defined by those two fearful words…what if. She was twenty-six years old—she'd mooned a man, she'd taken surfing lessons, she'd kissed Jason Masters. Darn it, she was long overdue for leaving old fears, old worries behind.

For once in her life, she was going to take a risk. She was going to try to make Jason see her as more than a secretary, to see her as a desirable woman. And divert him from the Mooner hunt, all at the same time.

The only question left was—could she? ''Will you help me?'' she asked, looking around at her friends. ''With the new clothes, new makeup and stuff?''

Without hesitation, Elizabeth and Andrea nodded.

''Of course. It'll be fun dressing you up,'' Bonnie said, giving an excited bounce.

And Marlene gave her a slow thumbs-up. ''Don't worry, Dee. When we finish your makeover, Jason Masters won't know what hit him!''

8

WHERE WAS SHE?

She was late—and Dee was *never* late, Jason fumed, sitting in his office the following morning.

He'd been in there since 7:00 a.m., waiting for her to arrive. Eight o'clock had come and gone without a sign of her, and it was now 9:10.

He resisted the urge to stand up and pace—he'd done plenty of that for the past hour. Instead he glanced again at his watch: 9:11...it was now 9:11, dammit! Which meant Dee was an hour and eleven minutes late. Was she even coming to work at all?

She'd better be, Jason decided, tapping his pen impatiently against the desk. He wanted some answers. Like why had she run out like that? Why hadn't she stayed to talk?

Why had she kissed him in the first place?

Maybe seeing him with Heather was what had caused her to act so precipitously. He leaned back in his chair, staring unseeingly out the window. He'd suspected he'd seen jealousy in Dee's eyes when he'd been talking with the brunette and it appeared he'd been right. And he had to admit, he was glad Dee had suffered a bit watching Heather flirt with him. She'd deserved it after the wringer she'd put him through the past couple of days.

He frowned, remembering how annoyed he'd been seeing her with Paxton. How dare she discuss him with that wimp? And even more, how dare she make him sound like some kind of soggy noodle that had been left on the boil too long? He hadn't settled down—he still had it, dammit! He'd just been too busy with work the past few months to take the time to use it.

And lately, he'd also had the Mooner situation to contend with, not to mention Dee's unusual behavior, as well. Both had claimed even more of his attention.

In fact, Dee had claimed his *entire* attention yesterday. Why had she suddenly grabbed for him? Jealousy couldn't have been her only reason. She, too, must have felt the sudden surge of recognition, of desire, that he'd experienced when their eyes had met across the top of the Hvostal sculpture. He'd known without a doubt that she'd seen exactly what he did in the piece. Sex. Passion. Completion.

Considering the way she'd flung herself against him and wrapped her arms around his neck, she must have been feeling the same driving need that he'd been feeling for her for the past two days.

But why had she broken off the embrace? And why had she run? At first, he'd thought she'd merely retreated to the women's rest room, and he'd left her alone, giving her a few minutes to recover her composure. Hell, he'd been shaken by that kiss, too. Who would have thought cool little Dee would burn with such hungry passion in his arms?

But when she hadn't returned, he'd gone to check on her, only to discover she'd left the building. He'd waited by her Volkswagen in the parking lot, but that had been a dead end also. Bob, the parking attendant, had come by and told him that her car had been parked there for a while. The elderly man had been almost positive Dee had taken the carpool van home.

But she hadn't answered when Jason tried to ring her house. He hadn't persisted, figuring she must be staying with a friend. He'd planned to talk with her when she arrived at work in the morning, but she hadn't come in and he had no idea where she might be—or what she was thinking about what had happened.

Maybe he'd moved a bit too fast, and she'd gotten scared. Maybe she'd had second thoughts. If only he could see her, he was sure he could convince her—

A sound from her office interrupted his thoughts. He jumped to his feet and strode to the door, flinging it open. But instead of his errant secretary, Tony Dialti was there, standing by her desk.

The Italian's dark brows lifted in question as he noticed the frown on Jason's face. "Am I early? Our appointment is for today, is it not?"

Jason nodded, and stepped forward to shake the man's hand, cursing inwardly. He'd forgotten about the meeting, which Dee had set up a week or so ago. She'd worked hard to arrange it, anxious to try to repair the rift between the two companies.

He was anxious for that, too, of course. But not right now. Right now, nothing seemed as important as talking to Dee, as learning how she felt about the kiss they'd shared. Instead he'd be stuck here for another hour or so with Dialti.

They went into Jason's office and sat down, Jason at his desk, Dialti in one of the chairs across from him. After the initial pleasantries were exchanged, Dialti immediately launched into a rambling monologue about the growth of Dialti and Sons. Jason nodded now and again, pretending he gave a damn, while inside he seethed with impatience. He stole a glance at his watch. Nine-thirty!

More time wasted. Couldn't the man simply get to the point and leave? Jason wanted to go find Dee, to—

At a sound from her office, he stiffened, and lifted his head. It was her! It had to be this time. Dialti had paused and was watching him, his expression confused. Jason ignored the other man, using all his willpower to resist rising from his chair. He wanted to storm in there—to demand some answers. But he didn't want to startle her, or scare her away as he had last night. Maybe it would be best to wait until she came in with the mail, as she always did.

He was waiting, straining to hear more sounds, when Dialti said with false casualness, "By the way, what was the outcome of that unfortunate incident that occurred during our last meeting?"

Jason glanced at him blankly.

"You remember," the Italian prompted. "The employee who displayed such disrespect toward you while we were driving to the restaurant?"

Oh, the Mooner, Jason thought, comprehension dawning.

"My father..." Dialti shook his head sadly. "He couldn't believe it when I happened to mention what had occurred. Of course, I wouldn't have said anything if I'd known he'd be so affronted."

Yeah, right. Jason stared at him with cynical understanding. Dialti had probably skipped up the steps of the Dialti mansion, thrilled to give his father the news in person. Despite the other man's attitude of sympathetic regret, Jason had no doubt at all that the Italian had told his father of the mooning to try to put Jason—and thus Masters Inc.—at a disadvantage. He also knew Dialti was bringing the subject up now to try more of the same.

Jason opened his mouth to tell Dialti to take a hike,

then paused. Now that he thought about it, an update on the Mooner hunt might not be a bad idea. Not only would it shut Dialti up, it also gave Jason the perfect excuse to call Dee into the room—and get her talking to him.

"I have my secretary working on that," he said coolly, and flicked on the intercom. "Would you please come in here a minute, Miss Evans?"

He flicked the button off, then waited, his muscles tightening. It seemed like an eternity before the door opened, and when it did, he forced himself not to immediately look over at her. To act normal, and nonthreatening. As if nothing had changed between him and Dee.

Then he noticed Dialti. The man was slowly rising to his feet, an astounded expression on his face. What the—?

Jason turned. Then somehow, almost without realizing it, he, too, was standing. He couldn't help it. The woman framed in the doorway was simply the kind that forced a man to take notice and straighten up—in more ways than one.

Dammit, it couldn't be... It was! *Dee* was the woman standing there, staring at Dialti with wide eyes. And she was wearing the most revealing outfit Jason had ever seen.

Okay, maybe not, he grudgingly admitted to himself a moment later. But definitely the most revealing he'd ever seen on *her*.

She'd been transformed, from the tousled curls piled on the top of her head down to her toes, daintily clad in high heels—bright red, three inch heels that accentuated her small arched feet and slim, shapely legs.

Jason's astonished gaze traveled upward. Her legs looked so long—an illusion caused, no doubt, by those totally inappropriate shoes and her minuscule, black skirt—which was *definitely* much too short and way too tight. Why, he could clearly see a few inches of her silky thighs, the womanly curve of her hips. For God's sake, what was she thinking?

But worst of all was her top. Like her shoes, her top was red—a deep cherry color that pinkened her cheeks and made her brown curls gleam. At first glance, the knit top didn't seem immodest, but a second, *longer* scrutiny revealed how slim her arms appeared in the tight, wrist-length sleeves. That the V neck was low enough to show a hint of shadowy cleavage. The clingy material also displayed to advantage the deadman's curve of her waist, and her full, firm bosom.

Jason stared at the swell of her breasts, outrage building inside him until he felt ready to explode. Didn't she realize another man was in the room? Staring so hard at her chest that his damn Italian eyes were in danger of popping out from his head? *Where on earth was her breast shield?*

"You've forgotten your notepad," he barked.

Dee jumped, looking startled. "Oh, so I did," she said, running her palms nervously down her skirt. She turned back into her office.

Jason gritted his teeth as Dialti craned his neck to keep her in sight as she disappeared through the door. He ground them even harder when Dee reappeared. She stepped forward—and wobbled on her heels. The misstep made her bounce. Not only her curls, but the tops of her white breasts, just visible above her notepad.

Regaining her balance, she started toward them again. She walked slowly, placing each foot on the slick marble floor with deliberate care. The result of her caution was a leisurely, strolling pace that caused her hips to sway enticingly back and forth—back and forth—in a way that made Jason's skin burn and his fists clench. Never had the black expanse of floor seemed so endless. Never would Jason have believed that he'd miss her plain suits and flat-soled shoes so much.

He glanced at Dialti and scowled. The guy had threatened to pull a contract on morality issues, yet here he was, drooling over a woman in a short, tight skirt. Yeah, Dialti was conservative, all right.

Finally she reached them. Dialti, who hadn't taken his eyes off her for a second, sprang forward to gallantly hold her chair. "Here you go," he said, flashing what Jason considered to be a blatantly false smile.

Dee, however, didn't seem to notice its insincerity. Instead of freezing the Italian with a look, or refusing to take the chair—actions Jason considered perfectly appropriate under the circumstances—she merely smiled shyly in return. "Thank you," she murmured as she sat down.

Dialti sat down, too, scooting his chair closer to her. Close enough that he could rest his hand on the back of Dee's chair, just behind her sensitive nape. He might have to kill Dialti, Jason thought, watching as the man stole a lingering look downward at Dee's cleavage. Even the fact that her breast shield was up didn't mitigate Jason's anger.

Jason sat and scowled at her. Not only was she dressed differently, but she'd done stuff to her face, too. He was so busy noting the changes—her darkened lashes, the cherry lipstick on her pretty mouth—that it wasn't until Dee cleared her throat, saying tentatively, "Did you want me to take something down?" that he realized he'd been staring at her in silence for who knew how long.

"Actually..." Actually he was sorry he'd called her in. But since he couldn't admit that, he said, "Tony was wondering what progress we'd made on the mooning incident. I called you in here to make a brief report.''

''Oh.'' Dee clutched her notepad tighter, and turned to face Dialti, who leaned closer, an interested expression on his face. ''Well, Mr. Dialti—''

''Tony, please.'' His white teeth flashed in another wide smile. ''So much formality makes me feel unwelcome.''

''Tony, then,'' Dee responded, with a small smile of her own—a smile that disappeared when she glanced in Jason's direction and met his stony stare. She cleared her throat, and began again, saying, ''So far we—I haven't been able to locate the Mooner....''

Tony's mouth turned down in sympathy.

''Although we have eliminated several suspects. In fact, we've eliminated everyone who usually rides on our vans.'' She glanced at Jason, an unconscious plea in her eyes. ''Didn't we, Mr.—Jason?''

He hesitated. He still couldn't shake the notion that she knew who had done the deed; that it had to be one of her friends. But he couldn't put her on the spot right now, with Dialti watching so intently. Finally he compromised with a nod. ''Almost everyone,'' he said dryly. ''But we still have a few to reconsider, don't we, Diana?''

He intended the question as a warning to her that he still had no intention of dismissing the incident, whether one of her friends was involved or not. She appeared to understand his meaning, because a worried expression flitted across her face before she slowly nodded.

Seeing the anxiety in her eyes, Jason relented a little. He hadn't intended to upset her. He started to say something to reassure her, but before he could, Dialti leaned closer and touched her hand.

"I can see this incident has distressed you," the Italian said, patting her soft skin. "I will be glad to offer my services, Diana, to help you find this disrespectful employee. Why don't we discuss it over dinner this evening?"

Jason's eyes narrowed. Dee's widened. She removed her hand from Dialti's reach, stammering, "W-why—"

"Thank you, Dialti, but I assure you Miss Evans doesn't need any help in solving this problem," Jason said, cutting her off. "It should be cleared up in the next day or so." He glanced at Dee and rose. "That will be all, Miss Evans. Thank you for your input."

Dee stood up, barely noticing that Dialti had, too. Bewildered by Jason's curt dismissal, she responded to the Italian's goodbye automatically, hardly aware of what he'd said. With a brief nod that encompassed both men, she hurried back into the safety of her office.

Reaching her desk, she sank into her chair, her knees feeling shaky as she fought to suppress the hurt growing inside her. Until she'd seen Jason, she hadn't realized how much she'd hoped their kiss had changed things between them. That he'd greet her with a smile instead of a scowl—or at the least show some concern as to why she'd been late although truthfully, putting together her new "look" had simply taken longer than she'd expected. Instead he'd glared at her in a way that had made her heart sink all the way down into her red shoes. Obviously she'd been right to wonder if she had what it took to hold his interest. He hadn't even noticed she was wearing a new outfit. All he'd noticed was she didn't have her notepad with her.

And if facing Jason wasn't hard enough, she'd also had to face Tony Dialti. When she'd walked in and saw the Italian, she'd been too stunned to move for a moment.

She'd been so embarrassed—and so terrified. Thank goodness the man seemed to have no clue that she was the Mooner.

The phone rang, jolting her out of her thoughts. She picked it up, her voice quivering a little from reaction as she said, "Jason Masters's office, Diana speaking."

"Why hello, Diana," a deep masculine voice drawled in her ear. "This is Justin. Is my brother around?"

"He's in a meeting with Tony Dialti."

"Good. This concerns the Dialti deal—he wanted me to check up on a patent the firm holds. Let me talk to him."

Justin was an attorney, and like Jason and Jon, he was used to unquestioning obedience. But Dee hadn't dealt with the Masters brothers for the past several months without learning to resist such blunt commands. "Just a second please," she said, then buzzed Jason and passed on the request.

"Put him through," Jason told her, and she did.

Barely had she set down the phone when Jason's office door opened. Her pulse sped up, then slowed again as she looked up and met Tony Dialti's brown eyes.

He stepped into her office, closing the door behind him. "Ah, there you are," he said, with a pleased smile.

Dee uncertainly returned the smile, wondering where else he'd expected her to be than in her office. She was Jason's secretary, after all.

His smile widened in response to hers, and he strolled over to her desk. "You left so quickly. We didn't get a chance to arrange a time and place to meet. I think it would be best to send my limousine here to pick you up, right after work—say, six o'clock? We will make a long evening of it. Have dinner. Perhaps go dancing, if you so desire."

Hadn't he heard Jason's refusal? "I appreciate your offer, but I wouldn't want to take up any of your valuable time," Dee said.

But instead of accepting her refusal and departing with good grace, Dialti sat down on a corner of her desk, swinging one beautifully shod foot slowly back and forth. "I don't think it would be a waste of time. I am eager to discuss this oh-so-daring person with you."

Dee had been staring at his Italian leather shoe, absently thinking how small it was for a man, and worrying about Jason. But something in Dialti's voice brought her gaze up to his face.

It was a handsome face, tanned and lean with high cheekbones, an arrogant Roman nose and liquid eyes. He had a slim, elegant build as well. Dee knew that as heir to the Dialti fortune, Tony was considered a very eligible bachelor. So was he insisting on taking her out because he habitually came on to every woman he met, and he was used to their attention? Had her new outfit, the Wonderbra Marlene had convinced her to wear, caused her to distract the wrong man by mistake? Or...she swallowed to relieve the sudden, by now almost familiar tightness in her throat...was the real reason for Tony's sudden interest because he recognized her as the Mooner?

She suppressed a groan. *Oh, please, not that. Not another complication.* But the feeling of dread rising inside her was all-too familiar, too. She couldn't take the chance that Dialti was merely too conceited to take no for an answer. If he had recognized her as the Mooner she needed to know—to discover what he planned to do about it.

So when he reached down and picked up her hand, saying once more, "I believe an evening in my company will be very informative," she had no choice.

"All right," she replied. "I'll go out with you."

Just as she finished speaking, the door to Jason's office swung open. Dee looked up, directly into Jason's stunned gaze.

9

DEE JERKED FREE of Dialti's grasp, but she knew Jason had seen the Italian fondling her hand again.

Jason's expression turned menacing. Dialti hopped off Dee's desk with less grace and more haste than he'd used climbing on. "I will see you later then," he said quickly. With a brief nod at Jason and Dee, he disappeared out the door.

For a long moment Jason didn't speak. Neither did Dee. Then he said bluntly, "I don't want you going out with him."

Dee pretended to be busy, straightening the mail into a neat pile. "Why not?"

"He's pretty slick. A real player."

"But I thought his firm was ultraconservative."

"The firm is. But not Tony Dialti."

Dee considered that a few seconds, then shrugged. "So? It's just a dinner date. He thinks he can help me find the Mooner."

"Fine." Jason started walking toward her, his stride slow and deliberate. "Then let him tell you what he knows here—in the office."

"Tony wants to go out to talk."

Jason's eyes flared. He came closer, planting his fists on her desk as he leaned toward her. "Let's get something clear. You kissed *me* last night. If you hadn't run away, things would have gone even further. While we have this thing going on between us, I don't want you dating other men.''

This *thing?* Dee stared at him. And what exactly was that? Attraction? Proximity? Lust? He didn't even know what to call it.

Budding indignation stiffened her spine. He'd used that tone of arrogant demand with her before, of course, plenty of times. And she'd obeyed without question. But those demands had concerned work. This one concerned her personal life. Did he really think he could boss her around about that, too? After treating her like a virtual *nobody* just now in his office?

Her hands tightened on her notepad. ''Are you saying that *you* won't be dating other women?''

He straightened abruptly. The startled, disbelieving expression on his face was so identical to the one he'd worn when she'd suggested that preposterous alien theory that Dee would have laughed...if it hadn't hurt so much.

He scowled. ''No, of course not. That's a different issue entirely.''

Dee remained silent, marveling at her own naivete—and his arrogance. To think, she'd actually worried about leading him on, hurting his feelings. How ridiculous could she get? Jason didn't have any feelings—at least not for her. He was simply used to controlling everything and everyone around him.

''I see,'' she replied. And she did. Their kiss hadn't meant anything to him. The hurt she'd felt at his lack of response to her new clothes—her new look—hardened into anger. She had no trouble at all meeting his gaze when she asked, ''Do you still want me to discover who mooned you?''

''Yes, but—''

''Fine.'' She picked up the mail again, and stood up.

"Since I have plenty of work to do, and *Tony*—" she stressed the name, feeling a fierce pleasure when Jason's expression darkened even more "—had other appointments to keep, it simply makes sense for us to conduct our business over dinner."

"I said—"

"I heard what you said, just now and a couple of days ago as well. If I remember correctly—and I do—you told me then not to pursue my personal relationships on company time. This way, if a little pleasure gets mixed with business…" She shrugged again, rolling her shoulders more than usual so that her breasts lifted and fell with the gesture. "It will be on my time. So no one loses. Not the company. Not me—and definitely not you."

His gaze had dropped to her breasts. They lifted at her final remark and narrowed on her face. "Dee…" His tone was threatening.

But anger, Dee discovered, could be a very empowering emotion. It allowed her to brush by him without a qualm to take a break and when she returned, to ignore his obvious displeasure as the day wore on. She replied calmly to his barked demands. She ignored his glares, making a face at his closed door when he finally slammed into his office. At six o'clock anger enabled her to gather up her purse when the parking attendant called up to say Tony Dialti was waiting, and to walk out of her office without a single glance in the direction of Jason's closed door. Why should she bother to tell him she was leaving? It was after five; she was on her own time now.

But once outside, her guard lowered, and hurt threatened to overwhelm her again. She climbed into the limousine, replying to Tony's greeting with a forced smile. Her heart felt heavy as she leaned back against the leather seat.

"We have reservations at The Eclipse," Tony told her.

Dee nodded, wishing she could summon up some enthusiasm. She'd always dreamed of being taken out in a limo, to some high-priced Hollywood club by a handsome man. But none of that mattered, she realized, when you weren't with the right man.

She felt so unhappy. She wished she could go back in time—before she'd mooned Jason and become involved in this miserable deception. Before their kiss had awakened all these unfamiliar yearnings inside her. It had been so easy when everything was black-and-white. So safe traveling alone along that straight and narrow path where there weren't many choices, but there weren't so many possible potholes to avoid, either.

Where she didn't have to worry, she added silently, eyeing Tony's classical profile, if someone suspected she'd committed the mooning.

That worry—along with insuppressible thoughts about Jason—dominated Dee's thoughts to the exclusion of almost everything else. The club Tony escorted her into a short while later had an air of old-world elegance, quite unlike the more contemporary clubs Marlene often described after her various dates. The music playing discreetly in the background even had the "elevator" quality so abhorred by her friends. But Dee had grown up listening to such music. Neither that nor the fancy table settings, nor the richly dressed people surrounding them really impinged on her consciousness. All she could think about was the threat Tony represented to her job—and Jason's opinion of her.

She played with her silverware, wondering if he'd left the office yet, and if he'd been angry to find her gone. "Is this where you and Jason dined the last time you were in the city?" she asked, more from the painful pleasure of saying Jason's name than because she really cared.

Tony shook his head. "This is a private club, one my father has been a member of for many years." A smile of satisfaction curled his lips as he added, "I do not think Jason Masters is a member. Nor, I believe, do we require his presence to discuss this exhibitionist employee."

But whether they required Jason's presence or not, they soon had it. Barely had their waiter taken their order when Jason strode in, a hard, determined expression on his face.

"So I was wrong. Masters is a member," Tony almost hissed.

Dee tensed, her grip tightening on her linen napkin. Energy surged through her, her pulse quickening as her senses tingled to high alert. What was he doing here? He paused in the doorway, his gaze immediately locking with hers. For a brief second of mingled alarm and happiness, Dee thought that he was going to join them. Tony obviously thought so, too, judging by the wariness on his face. But after giving them a brief businesslike, almost formal nod—the kind Dee imagined a duelist would bestow, right before shooting his opponent—Jason followed the maître d' to another table situated about ten feet away and a little behind Dee. He sat down and accepted the menu he was handed, not bothering to look their way again.

Dee's pulse, however, was still speeding. Why had he followed them? Because he truly didn't want her dating other men? Or simply because he was annoyed she'd disobeyed an order?

Probably the latter, she decided, as the evening wore on without him once approaching them. She was careful not to look in his direction, but somehow she knew every time he glanced at her. Her nape would prickle. Heat would rise up under her skin, then subside, leaving her cold and shivering from the reaction.

At first, Tony seemed overly conscious of Jason, too. He kept shooting wary glances his way, and his conversation was a bit disjointed, as if his entire attention wasn't on what he was saying, but on the man nearby. But as dinner continued, and Jason made no move to join them—and Tony imbibed more and more of the expensive French wine—the Italian relaxed. He seemed to dismiss the other man, his focus settling on Dee...or more specifically, she realized wryly, on her breasts.

It appeared Marlene had been right. A Wonderbra could do...well, wonders when it came to attracting male attention. That seemed to be the case with Tony—so maybe her fears about him seeing her in the van were for nothing.

And if he hadn't seen her, she certainly didn't want to tip him off. So she didn't bring the subject up, either, simply nodding now and again as he talked on and on. Tony was smooth, she gave him that. The compliments from his lips flowed as fast as the wine into his glass. But she couldn't relax. Never had she felt more uncomfortable, or more unsure what to do, with Jason glaring at her back, while Tony perused her front.

"Let us dance," Tony said, between the main course and dessert. Dee had been sitting silently for the past few minutes, fighting the compulsion to glance in Jason's direction. "I am sure you are a dream on the dance floor."

None of the bored boys in her dance classes had ever thought so, but Dee didn't argue. The dance floor was across the room near the outside patio, which meant she'd be a little farther from Jason and the temptation to stare back at him. So she allowed Tony to lead her onto the floor.

A simple two-step was playing, but in less than a minute, the music changed to a tango. With Latin grace, Tony moved to the erotic rhythm, appearing delighted when Dee followed along without missing a beat. For once, Dee was thankful for the endless hours of dancing lessons her mother had made her endure, especially when people paused to watch them, spurring Tony on to even more demanding steps. She managed to keep up, but was thankful when the dance ended—despite the dramatic dip Tony maneuvered her into at the end.

Draped over Tony's arm Dee glanced up, directly at Jason's face across the room. Even upside down, she could see the anger in his expression as his eyes swept from her face to her bosom, which was practically falling out of her red top. Dee was thankful to look away from that accusing stare as Tony brought her upright once more.

Tony drew her back into his arms as another, slower dance started. He danced her toward the French windows leading to the patio outside. "It is so warm," he said. "Let us dance a little out here, in the cool darkness."

That sounded just dandy to Dee. Something in Jason's stare had made her feel oddly shaken. She didn't want to be alone with Tony, but the desire to get out of Jason's sight for a while, overcame her reservations.

She followed Tony into the night. The deserted patio was lit with torches that cast a flickering light over the flowers in big white pots lining the floor. The sweet scent of jasmine drifted on the air. It would have been utterly romantic if she'd been with…someone else.

But she was with Tony. He gave an expert whirl, pulling her a little closer at the same time. "You are so lovely and so graceful, *cara.*"

"Diana," she corrected automatically.

For a second he looked confused, then his expression cleared. "No, no, I have not forgotten your name. How could I when it is so beautiful?" He looked deep into her eyes. His, she noticed, were a little bloodshot. He leaned closer. His breath—which smelled like wine mixed with breath mints—brushed against her cheek as he added in a throaty voice, "You were named after a goddess, of course."

"A goddess?" She jumped as his warm, slightly damp hand slid up beneath her top, settling on the bare skin of her back.

"Diana—the huntress."

Dee paused in her attempt to shrug off his hand to stare up at him blankly.

"From Roman mythology," he explained.

"Oh, her." Dee wasn't sure quite what to say or do. Even she—inexperienced as she was—could tell Tony was making a pass. She didn't want to offend such a potentially important client—again!—but she didn't want him sneaking his hand beneath her blouse, either. Maybe distraction was the key once more, but this time she'd try a different dose of distraction. She was tired of lying; she refused to do it anymore. Instead she'd use the truth to set her free.

She took a deep breath. "Well, actually I wasn't," she explained, trying to step back from him. "My father named me in honor of my great-aunt—who was, however, named after the Roman goddess you're talking about. Unfortunately the goddess thing seemed to have gone to her head."

She twisted but his hand didn't move. "As a child, all

my great-aunt ever talked about was going on a safari to Africa, and when she reached twenty, her parents—they were really rich, you know—let her go.''

She twisted the other way. His hand didn't move. Dee's chin lifted, and she continued grimly, ''Unfortunately the trip didn't turn out as planned. She killed a rhinoceros—poor thing, they're on the endangered species list now, I believe—but while she was posing on top of it, a pack of lions came up. Very _hungry_ lions.''

Tony's hand finally dropped. Dee gave a small sigh of relief and kept talking. ''Well, my great-aunt had forgotten to reload her gun. She managed to get to the truck, but her guides ran off and she was stuck there for over eight hours with the lions leaping and roaring around her. She was never quite the same after that, poor thing. She had a terrible fear of cats—even kittens terrified her—and she ended up staying indoors all the time to avoid them, keeping busy by embroidering pillows and stuff. Which was hard on her parents, of course—you can only use so many embroidered pillows—but that's what comes, my mother always told me, of being overly indulgent with your kids.''

She inhaled deeply, feeling breathless after all that talking. But it appeared her plan had worked. In fact, there was almost a foot of space between them now. Tony was still dancing, but his movements had slowed almost to a shuffle. She glanced up at him, thankful he'd finally backed off.

But when her eyes met his her relief evaporated. Cold speculation was in his gaze. ''That is so interesting about your ancestor,'' he said, his eyes narrowing even more. ''But are you trying to tell me you lack courage, too? Like your aunt?''

Was she like her aunt? Dee had always thought so—

except, she liked cats, of course. But in fact, she'd been worse than her aunt. At least her aunt had pursued her dream, albeit unsuccessfully, before retreating from the world. Dee, however, had lived her life in fear without even trying to venture forth, hiding from imagined dangers that might not even exist.

But never again, she decided, lifting her chin in determination. From now on, she was going to face danger head on. "I have courage," she said, and proved it immediately, stiff-arming him as he once again tried to pull closer and thereby preventing the intimacy.

For a second, his mouth tightened and an ugly expression crossed his face. Dee's uneasiness grew. The feeling increased as he gave an indulgent laugh, murmuring, "Do you? Then you are indeed Diana...Goddess of the Moon."

Dee's wary eyes met his knowing brown ones. "What are you talking about?" she asked, but she already knew.

He made a tsking sound, and again tried to pull her closer. "Did you think I would not recognize you? How could I ever forget such beauty? I noticed you, *cara,* even before you stood up and made such a...provocative gesture. I have known all along."

Dee wanted to die. She wanted to be sick—all over his suit, and expensive shoes. She hated the thought that he'd seen what he had.

And she hated him as he proceeded to make it clear exactly how he planned to use the information. "Obviously you have no great fondness, or respect for this employer of yours. And who can blame you? Jason Masters is low class, his manners those of a barbarian. But I would make a very good employer indeed. And I'd be willing to pay you well for certain information."

"What information?"

"Any information you might care to give me about Masters Inc. Especially information that might help in our negotiations concerning this limited partnership."

Now Dee understood his sudden interest in her. "You want me to pass on company secrets," she said bluntly.

Tony winced. "That is so crude. I merely ask you to share with me your business concerns, your evaluations...as good friends so often do."

Good friends? She stared at him in disgust. They weren't friends. She didn't even like him. She had to end this bad habit she had of going out with jerks.

But it seemed Tony liked her well enough. Emboldened by her silence, his hand slipped down again...and settled directly on her bottom.

She pulled away, but he yanked her back. "I won't do it," she said firmly. "I won't tell you anything and I certainly don't want to be your friend."

He shrugged, unperturbed by the anger in her tone. "You don't want your boss to know, do you, *cara,* that you are this Mooner he is trying so hard to find?"

She didn't answer. She didn't need to. They both knew she didn't want Jason to know. Tony's voice became even silkier as he added, "I will not give away your secret, as long as you—" she flinched as he pinched her bottom "—are willing to share some of Masters's."

In Dee's opinion, that pinch clinched the whole thing. This was it. The end of the line. She was almost glad that Tony knew; she was so tired of all the deceit. He'd tell Jason, of course. He'd have to. Because no way on earth was she going to be *friends* with this scum. Or endure his touch for another minute.

He held her right hand in his; her left arm was caught between them. She struggled, trying to move away, and to free her hand from his, but his grip tightened.

"Let me go," she said quietly.

Instead he pulled her even closer, chuckling at her attempts to escape. "You don't mean that. Think of the disgrace. Of losing your job."

"I said, let me go!" Her voice rose higher, and she tried to kick him.

"But, *cara*—"

"Let her go, Dialti. Before I take your head off."

Startled, Dialti and Dee both looked up at Jason, who was standing in the doorway. They'd been so intent on their argument, Dee realized, neither had seen him arrive.

But they sure couldn't miss him now. His shoulders were tensed, the planes of his face looked hard as stone. Blazing rage shone from his blue eyes.

Tony tried to force a smile. "You misunderstand, my friend, this woman—"

"No, *you* misunderstand. I *said* let her go."

Tony's arms dropped. He even took a step back in reaction to the menace in Jason's voice. Shuddering with relief, Dee moved to Jason's side as he came closer.

But Tony wasn't finished yet. Frustration in his voice, he said, "There is something you don't know, Masters."

"Oh, yeah? What's that?"

"This woman—this secretary of yours, is no better than a whore. She—"

But he got no further. Possibly because it was hard to speak with Jason's fist slamming into his mouth.

Tony keeled over. His arms flailed as he went down, so he took a couple of flowerpots along with him. Dee covered her mouth, her eyes wide with horror as she looked down at him lying there, dirt and gardenias covering his suit. He was a mess. This whole situation was a mess.

She waited in dread for Tony to get up. Jason was

waiting, too, his fists clenched, his expression filled with anticipation. Glancing at him, Dee wasn't surprised that Tony elected to stay where he was. Jason was clearly just waiting for the opportunity to hit him again.

But Tony didn't move nor say a word, not even when Jason growled, "You wanted to tell me something?"

The Italian looked at him appraisingly. Then slowly shook his head.

"Fine. Then let me tell you something. The deal's off. I don't want you near my company—or Diana—ever again. And if I hear you've been talking about her, saying anything at all, I'll hunt you down and finish what we started here tonight. You have my word on it."

He paused, but Tony apparently had nothing to reply. Satisfied, Jason held out his hand to Diana. "Let's go."

"Go?" She stared at him in bewilderment. "But how can we? He's hurt...and he broke all those pots." She gestured at the flowers and dirt lying around their feet. "Shouldn't we at least help clean up a little? Wait for the police to arrive?"

Jason stared at her, then shook his head. Trust Dee to want to tidy things up. "Believe me, I've been in enough fights to know you don't want to hang around once the job's done." Patience at an end, he caught her wrist. "So come on."

He began walking, heading back into the restaurant. And since he had hold of her wrist, she had no choice but to follow, hurrying along as fast as she could on her high heels. He only paused a second at her table so she could snatch up her purse, then he strode on again, aiming for the exit. As they passed the maître d', Jason told him, "There was an accident—out on the patio. See to it, will you, Roberto? And bill me—no, bill Tony Dialti—for any damages."

Jason didn't wait for Roberto's reply. He wanted to get Dee alone as quickly as possible. They definitely had plenty to settle between them.

At the entrance, he handed over his ticket and the valet hurried off to get his car. Finally alone, Jason glanced down at the woman at his side. Her hair was tousled, her eyes looked stricken. He could feel her fingers trembling in his hold. The anger he'd felt when he'd discovered her struggling in Dialti's arms simmered higher, and he fought the urge to go back and punch the bastard again. "Did he hurt you?" he asked bluntly.

She shook her head.

"I saw him grab you, but I didn't catch what he was saying. Did he proposition you? Say something obscene?" he asked, half-hoping she'd say yes, so he'd have an excuse to finish what he'd started.

Again she shook her head, saying as the valet pulled his car up in front of them, "What a nice Lexus."

"It's a Porsche. The Lexus is what I drive to work," he said dryly, undeceived by her blatant attempt to change the subject. He tucked her in, then went around to the driver's side, climbed in and immediately took off.

She didn't say a word as he drove. Neither did he. But when he turned onto the 405 freeway she asked in a subdued voice, "Where are we going?"

"Home."

He felt more than saw the quick, almost frightened glance she shot at him. "Your home," he elaborated.

That seemed to reassure her. She relaxed a little in her seat, and gazed out her side window at the other cars. And when he finally pulled up in front of her house, she reached for the door handle before he even had a chance to turn off the engine.

"Thank you," she said, "I appreciate all your help

with Tony and everything and the ride home. I'll see you at work—''

''Not so fast.'' He flicked the door lock switch and turned to face her. ''We need to talk.''

She gripped her hands together, but nodded and sat back. ''I know.''

He couldn't tell what she was thinking. Her expression was shadowed, only dimly lit by a nearby streetlight. But he could almost feel the tension radiating from her figure. He said slowly, ''I've been thinking about what you asked me, Diana.'' In fact, he hadn't been able to think of much else all day. ''And you were right. It wasn't fair of me to expect you not to go out with other men, if I still planned to date other women.''

He reached out and picked up her hand. It felt so small in his. He gently ran his thumb across her delicate knuckles. ''But I don't. I only want you.''

He'd thought she'd be pleased. That maybe she'd throw her arms around his neck again, as she'd done yesterday.

Instead she simply looked shocked. Her hand twitched in his hold. Her eyes were huge, and even in the dim light he could tell that she'd paled as she turned her head to stare at him. ''You've got to be kidding.''

He frowned. This wasn't going at all as he'd expected. ''Why would I? Don't *you* want *me?*''

She blinked. Color flooded her cheeks. She pulled loose from his hold and linked her fingers together in her lap again. ''That's not the point.''

''It seems to me it is.''

She shook her head, her hair falling to half hide her face as she looked down at her hands. ''There's…stuff you don't know about me, Jason.''

She looked so solemn, so worried. Tender amusement

rose up inside him. Did she really think anything in her past could compare with his? Unable to resist, he ran a teasing finger along her warm cheek, tucked her hair behind her ear. "There's stuff you don't know about me, either."

She glanced at him, then looked down at her hands again. A small frown furrowed her smooth brow. "Well, yes. I suppose that's true. But this concerns work as well as…us. Our relationship, I mean."

He cast her a sidelong glance. He didn't have relationships, just brief affairs. But, of course, as he should have suspected she would, Dee was thinking in terms of a longer-lasting connection.

He knew he should set her straight. With any other woman he would have trotted out his patented speech about their liaison being temporary. But he couldn't; not with Diana. Her words warmed him. He found he liked the thought of having more than an affair, of having a *relationship*, however temporary, with her.

But she still looked troubled. She stumbled on. "I need to tell you something about—about the Mooner." Her voice dropped almost to a whisper. "And you aren't going to like it."

Ah, *now* he understood. The Mooner was one of her friends, just as he'd suspected all along. He started to reassure her that it wouldn't make any difference in how he felt about her, then paused, looking down at her. She was biting her lip, twisting her hands together in anxiety. And suddenly, he realized that it might make a difference to *her*. She was clearly upset. If she told him who the Mooner was—even if he didn't take action against the culprit—she'd have to live with the knowledge that she'd betrayed a friend.

And he couldn't make her do that. He knew how much

loyalty meant to her. He never should have set her on the task in the first place. Not only was he virtually forcing her to rat on a pal, but he'd also put her at risk. If she hadn't been hunting the Mooner, she wouldn't have felt compelled to go out with Dialti.

She was still wringing her hands, distress on her face as she struggled to tell him what he now realized he really didn't need to know. He put his hand over hers to still their anxious movements. "Dee…"

She looked up at him again, worry on her face.

He leaned closer, his grip tightening in reassurance around her slim hand. "Forget the Mooner. I'm abandoning the hunt. I don't want you to think about it anymore."

"You don't?" Her eyes widened, her lips parted in surprise. "Why not?"

Such pretty eyes. Such soft, sweet lips. He bent down and tasted her. She murmured something, and he deepened the kiss. When he finally lifted his head, her arms were clinging around his neck. Her eyes were dazed as she stared up at him.

"Because," he told her, "all I want you to concentrate on is me."

10
_____

Dee had intended to wave a white flag of surrender—
to tell Jason the truth about the Mooner. Instead she felt
as if she'd waved a red cape before a charging bull.

Because the hungry desire in his kiss left her breathless. His words made her heart race. It sounded wonderful—to concentrate only on him. In fact, being able to
concentrate on anything at all sounded pretty good, Dee
decided, considering the way her thoughts were spinning—not to mention her emotions. Surprise, relief, desire and confusion tumbled inside her, making it impossible to think straight. And she knew instinctively that as
long as she remained in his arms, the situation wouldn't
change.

Reluctantly she slowly pulled away. "I'll, ah, think
about that—concentrating on you, I mean," she said,
sounding as breathless as she felt. "But I'd better get in
now."

He didn't want to let her go. She knew that by the way
his arms tightened for the briefest second and by the frustrated expression on his face. But his voice was filled
with reluctant understanding as he said, "All right. Think
over what I said and I'll talk to you tomorrow."

Dee merely nodded, then climbed out of the car and
hurried into her house, locking the door behind her. Leaning back against it, she heard his car roar off. She'd

thought she'd feel calmer once inside and away from him, but her pulse continued to race with excitement.

He wanted her. She wrapped her arms across her chest, hugging herself in disbelief, allowing the realization to sink in. He was attracted to her as much as she was to him.

She paused, her excitement fading as logic crept in to cool her thrilled elation. Or was he? Maybe he'd simply been carried away by her new clothes and makeup. Or her Wonderbra—like that slimy Tony Dialti.

The memory of Tony brought up another depressing possibility. Maybe the passion she'd seen in Jason's eyes had merely been caused by the fight he'd been in with the other man. She'd always heard that men usually wanted sex after fighting—the leftover effects of adrenaline, or testosterone or whatever it was that made men so aggressive. Maybe Jason's ardor was simply due to that natural reaction.

She bit her lip, pushing away from the door to wander into the living room while she considered the possibility. Everything had happened so fast. She didn't want to make another mistake like she had with Stewart. If she was going to pursue a relationship with Jason, then she wanted to make sure it was really her—the *real* Diana Edith Evans—he was interested in.

She could hardly sleep that night worrying about the situation, but she arose the next morning at precisely the same time as usual and prepared for work. As she looked into her closet, her hand wavered over another new dress her friends had persuaded her to buy, but then she resolutely pushed the garment aside and donned a navy blue skirt—with a three-inches-below-the-knee hem—and a loose, matching jacket.

With the same determination she ignored her new

makeup, and simply touched up her lashes with a little mascara and ran a colorless, moisturizing lipstick over her lips.

Her hair, of course, refused to be tamed, and she finally abandoned her attempts to secure it into a bun. Yet, in spite of the curls haloing wildly around her head, the figure in the mirror looked dismally subdued to her worried, critical eyes when she was finally dressed. Before she could change her mind—and her clothes—she left the house, waiting outside for her friends to arrive in the company van.

When they did, she didn't confide any of what had happened the previous day nor mentioned how she'd gotten home, merely replying noncommittally to their questions until they moved on to the subject of Bonnie's latest conquest. She wasn't quite sure why she kept the information to herself. Possibly because she was too excited to share the news of Jason's sudden interest; possibly because she was afraid his interest wouldn't last once he saw her again in her "normal" clothes.

That probability seemed depressingly certain and refused to leave her mind. She didn't hurry to her office; she wasn't late. Yet her palms were perspiring by the time she reached her desk.

Putting away her purse, she forced herself to take a few deep breaths before picking up the mail and her notepad and tapping on his door. But any serenity she might have gained evaporated at the sound of his deep voice, bidding her to come in.

She did so, closing the door behind her. She even managed to take a couple of steps forward before she met Jason's gaze across the room.

Her knees went weak. She wobbled on her almost flat heels. All the hungry passion that had been in his eyes the previous night was still burning in his intense blue gaze. He didn't seem to notice her bland clothes or unmade up face. All he seemed to see was her.

And all Dee could see was him. In fact, it wasn't until a discreet cough broke the silence that she realized Jon was in the room, sitting across from Jason's desk. Heat rising in her cheeks, she strode forward, nodding in greeting to both men before she laid the papers she'd been clutching on Jason's desk.

"Here's the mail," she said, sounding self-conscious and breathless, as if she was saying something intimately sexy.

"Thank you, Dee," Jason responded, his voice as husky and seductive as if he was replying to her unspoken thoughts.

Helplessly her gaze lifted to his once again—and remained caught until for a second time, a small cough from Jon broke their absorption. This time the cough sounded suspiciously like a stifled chuckle. Blushing even more furiously, Dee turned and headed back out the door.

For the rest of the day she managed to maintain at least a semblance of composure. For the most part, anyway. Okay, maybe her heart continued to race whenever Jason came near. And a tingly, aching feeling would blossom in her belly whenever he spoke. But although Jon had had a distinctly knowing expression in his eyes when he left Jason's office, none of the other employees coming and going seemed to notice anything amiss.

For the entire day, Jason said nothing out of place, nothing that could be interpreted at all as flirtatious. But Dee wasn't surprised when he paused by her desk as five o'clock neared. Her newly awakened woman's intuition had assured her he'd be asking her out. What she wasn't expecting was for him to mention her disabled Volkswagen, long neglected in the company parking lot.

"Bob told me your car broke down," Jason said, sitting on a corner of her desk and laying down a folder. Casually he caught her hand as she reached for it, adding, "It's quitting time. Why don't I take a look at your car for you, then we'll go out to dinner?"

Dee stared at his tanned hand, wrapped around her pale fingers, as she tried to marshal her thoughts. She'd forgotten about the car—forgotten about the whole mooning incident all day, totally distracted by her new awareness of Jason. Even now she could hardly think as he stroked the mound of her thumb with his finger, before making a tickling motion on her sensitive palm that made her stomach drop.

"My car..." she repeated absently, her attention fixed on the way he was playing with her hand.

He laced her fingers between his, and laid her hand on his hard thigh. "Yeah. I thought I'd see if I could get it going for you. You don't want to have to ride in the company van forever, do you? Especially with the mad Mooner still on the loose."

His words were teasing, but Dee blinked, her heart dropping. Even though he'd said he no longer cared about finding the Mooner, his comment tweaked her conscience. She pulled her hand away. "You don't need to do that. I'll call a mechanic."

But she protested in vain. Jason, it seemed, had decided to take care of her car and as usual when he'd made up his mind, nothing was going to stop him. Less than ten minutes later, Dee found herself out in the parking lot, holding his jacket, his tie—and finally his dress shirt—as he stripped down to his white T-shirt before lifting the back hood to check out her engine.

She tried not to stare at how broad his chest looked in the thin white cotton, how the short sleeves stretched over the muscles in his upper arms. He'd retrieved a toolbox from his sleek car's trunk and when he opened it an amazing variety of wrenches, pliers and other tools were revealed. He proceeded to use them with callous efficiency on her poor little bug's innards.

"How did you learn so much about cars?" Dee asked, hugging his jacket closer as she peered over his broad shoulder, trying to see what he was doing.

"I used to buy, rebuild and resell old cars while I was in high school and college, to make extra money," he told her absently. "Can you hand me those needle-nose pliers?"

Dee glanced down doubtfully at the box, then shifted his clothes to her other arm and gingerly selected a likely looking tool. Apparently she'd picked the right one, because he accepted it without comment and went back to work.

"Did your brothers help you?" she asked.

He shrugged. "Sometimes. James and Justin were usually off doing their own thing. Jon would usually hang around, though. He loves engines and working on them with me kept him out of mischief."

He glanced up in time to catch her surprised glance, and his mouth turned down wryly. "Yeah, I know. That sounds funny considering my reputation for trouble. But I could handle the messes I got into, and the twins watched each other's backs during fights they stirred up. Jon, though, was still a kid when my mother died, with more attitude than brains. Whenever I could, I tried to keep him under my eye."

He fell silent, fiddling with some wires, and Dee remained quiet, too, thinking over what he'd said. She'd always wished for siblings—a sister to talk to, an older brother to watch out for her. What would it have been like to grow up with someone like Jason around to stand up for her, to help her overcome her fears? Jon had been lucky to have an older brother like him, she decided, clutching his jacket and shirt a little tighter.

"So why didn't Paxton fix this for you?" he asked suddenly.

She turned to look at him, startled by the question. "It broke down after we'd already parted." Not that Stewart would have fixed it anyway, she thought to herself. Stewart didn't like to get his hands dirty.

"You were pretty serious about the guy, weren't you?"

The intent way he was watching her made her nervous for some reason. She wanted to lie—the truth made her sound so foolish—but she'd resolved never to lie again. "I thought I was," she admitted, "but I was wrong. I just wanted to fall in love. To be part of a couple. To be committed."

"Trapped is more like it," Jason said. "Believe me, love is overrated."

She stiffened. "Why do you say that?"

He shrugged. "Because I saw my father make a fool of himself over a woman—my stepmother, Wanda. Wanda the Witch, we used to call her. Man, did she hate that."

"It wasn't very nice," Dee felt compelled to point out.

"Yeah, but we weren't nice kids—and she wasn't a nice person, anyway. My dad was still grieving for my mom when she caught him on the rebound, and for three years she led him around by his—" he paused, slanting her a sideways glance "—nose."

"Maybe they cared about each other."

"You don't lie to someone you care about, and she lied to my dad plenty." The cynical expression she so hated crossed his face. "All Wanda cared about was Wanda. She wanted money, plenty of men to prove how sexy she was... Hell, she even came on to me once." He shook his head in disgust.

Dee felt disgusted, too...but she also felt guilty. His comment about lying to someone you cared about pricked her conscience once again. Was it still lying— still wrong—when he'd said he didn't care about the truth? She wanted to believe not, but a little voice inside her told her she was kidding herself.

She was trying to outargue the little internal nagger— who was proving frustratingly stubborn—when the sound of her hood slamming down jolted her from her thoughts.

Jason dropped his tools back in his box and picked up a rag. Wiping off his hands, he said briskly, "Okay, that should do it. Let's fire this baby up." He strode over to the driver's seat. Cramming his long legs in under the steering wheel, he turned the key.

The engine started immediately and a look of satisfaction softened the hard planes of his face. "Not a bad little car," he said. "But you should think about getting something safer."

Dee glanced involuntarily over at his car, which crouched at the other end of the parking lot like a big black beast. "And your car is safe?" she asked, raising her brows.

He grinned reluctantly. "No, but sometimes you have to choose between safety and excitement. I'll choose excitement every time."

Of course he would, Dee realized, handing over his clothes as he turned off her car and climbed out again, watching as he shrugged on his shirt, then slung his jacket over his shoulder. The safe, predictable path would bore Jason in no time. She'd often thought that was why he grew impatient so often and lost his temper. He didn't worry about being cautious, doing the prudent thing. It was hard for him to understand people who did. People like her.

"I'll follow you home, then we'll go out to dinner," he said.

It was a statement, not a question, and Dee thought once again about how fast he could move. She thought about prudence and safety—and her lie about the Mooner. But foremost in her mind was his stated aversion to commitment.

"Are you sure?" she asked slowly. "I don't drive as fast as you. You might get irritated at how slow I decide to go."

His eyes gleamed with understanding. He dropped a quick, hard kiss on her mouth, making her lips tingle. "Don't worry, honey. We'll take it as slow and easy as you like."

DEE'S SUSPICION THAT Jason's definition of taking it slow was very different from hers turned into a certainty during the following few days. That first day set the pattern for those that followed, and Dee was swept up in the rush, carried helplessly along by his will.

In fact, it wasn't until the following Saturday, sitting alone on her couch, that she found the chance to catch her breath, to think through this sudden change in their relationship. Not that he seemed much different at work, she decided, hugging a pillow to her chest. At least, not on the surface. He never kissed her there. But his eyes would send her messages so sexually explicit she'd literally shake from embarrassed excitement. Like yesterday, during a break in a sales brainstorming session. Jason had been standing next to the marble sculpture, idly resting his hand on the white leg of the woman as he'd chatted with the marketing director. Dee had been absently watching, half-mesmerized by the contrast of his warm tanned hand against the cold white marble when she'd glanced up—to find him looking directly at her, a knowing expression on his face as he'd watched her turn bright red.

It was as if they could communicate without saying a word. She'd watched him for so many months, learning to read his moods, that of course she often knew what he was thinking almost before he did. Now it seemed he could do the same with her. Whenever someone said something odd, or funny, she'd involuntarily glance his way to find the same amusement in his eyes that she felt. And when she thought about his kisses…he *definitely* sensed that. His eyes would linger on her face, then her breasts until she felt weak with the longing to slip into his arms. It didn't seem to matter if she was wearing her drab suits—or the shorter, tighter outfits that Bonnie and Marlene had selected. The desire in his eyes burned hotly for either.

But it was after work that things really heated up. Although he'd gotten her Volkswagen running smoothly once again, he insisted on picking her up for work every day and driving her home in the evenings. They'd have dinner together, sometimes going out, sometimes staying in. But every night without fail, they'd end up on her couch. Making love.

Well, not quite all the way, but almost, she thought, a small smile playing around her lips. She stroked the cushion next to her, glad that her couch was so soft and cushiony. Yet big enough so they could both lie on it together.

She always ended up on top of him, of course. His shoulders were too broad to fit next to hers. But she liked the feel of his hard body beneath hers—she liked it a lot. He'd kiss her mouth until she felt dizzy and boneless with desire, then he'd slowly move down her neck to her breasts.

She hugged the pillow tighter, the mere memory causing her nipples to tighten. She'd been startled at first when he'd kissed her there. She'd known she should stop him. But who could resist such heart-stopping caresses? The feel of his sandpapery jaw against her skin was so dangerously exciting. The tug of his mouth on her nipple made her forget her own name—much less all those warnings her mother had given her about a man not needing to marry the cow if the milk was free.

No, it wasn't the free-milk-worry that always made her pull away just as his hands began exploring below her waist. What made her stop—the *only* thing that kept her from seeking the completion he was coaxing her toward—was the knowledge that if he finally did get all her clothes off, he'd find the Mooner mark on her bottom.

She wanted to tell him. She hated having this secret, this lie, between them. She'd been brought up with the knowledge that "honesty was the best policy," and she longed for complete honesty between them. It hadn't felt right to lie to him from the beginning, and her guilt increased even more the closer they became. He'd been right in what he'd said, the day he fixed her car. You didn't lie to someone you cared about.

She traced an embroidered rose on the pillow with an absent finger. She already should have told him she was the Mooner. It wasn't as if she hadn't had opportunities. She could have gone on with her confession that very first night when he'd said that he wanted her. Or at the least the one following. Or the first time he'd come to her house.

But she'd lulled her conscience with the reminder that *he* was the one who'd abandoned the hunt. *He* was the one who'd wanted her to concentrate solely on him. But deep inside she knew the real reason she hadn't confessed was that she feared his reaction. She dreaded the thought that this new intimacy between them might end.

Putting aside the flowered pillow, she stood and wandered toward her real roses in a crystal vase on her mantel. Pausing, she touched a velvety red petal with wonder. She'd never received red roses from a man before—nor flowers of any color or kind. Jason had known she didn't need them. She had more than enough flowers from her garden to fill a dozen vases. But picking them herself, she'd discovered, wasn't the same as receiving them as a gift. Just looking at them made her feel special. *He* made her feel special. Like the kind of woman who wore sexy underwear, instead of practical white cotton. Who lit candles, and sipped white wine, without worrying about becoming dizzy. Who slept naked during the long, hot nights, dreaming of the man she loved—secure in the knowledge he was dreaming of her, too.

With Jason, she felt reckless—she felt wild. Was it so wrong to want to savor such feelings, just for a little while? To enjoy feeling beautiful, desirable—and yes, even needed—as long as she possibly could?

Because Jason did need her, and not only in a physical way. He needed someone to talk to in the evenings about work, as he'd done this past week. Someone who understood his frustrations and could soothe his anger. He needed someone to listen when he confided his hopes and dreams for the future, like he did when they snuggled together on her couch. His memories of his family before his mother had died, his worries about his brothers.

But most of all, he needed someone to laugh and play with, to help him realize there was more to life than Masters Inc.

Someone like her.

Because she did make him happy. Surely she wasn't mistaken about that? This past week, the impatience, the tension had disappeared from his expression. He'd been more relaxed than she'd ever seen him before. Best of all he smiled more often—especially at her. A slow, crooked *wicked* smile that told her he was thinking of all those fantastically forbidden things he did with her on her little flowered couch, and that he was waiting to do more.

His smile, that look on his face, never failed to make her stomach drop. She'd get tense—almost as tense as he was when he left her house at night, following those amazing, frustrating almost lovemaking sessions.

Fluffy entered the room, and strolled over to twine his furry body around her legs, greeting her with a plaintive meow. She bent down to stroke him, saying somberly, "You don't know how lucky you are to be neutered, Fluff."

Fluffy strutted off as if he didn't agree, but Dee knew she was right. Life had been far less complicated before she'd known how compelling sexual desire could be. Sooner than she'd ever thought possible, she'd reached the point where her guilty pleasure at Jason's attentions, couldn't compensate for the pain of pulling away from his slow, coaxing hands and his hot, hungry mouth.

In fact, she couldn't go through it again—not one more time. She didn't *trust* herself to go through it again without succumbing. She'd have to tell him tonight that she was the Mooner, praying that it wouldn't make a difference.

She picked up Fluffy. Cuddling him close, she tried to build her confidence for the ordeal. She brushed her cheek against his fur, then paused as a sudden thought occurred.

Maybe she could use her new feminine wiles to soften the blow when she told Jason. She'd make a delicious dinner to put him in a good mood. She'd use candles, her best china—even champagne to relax him. What man could resist all that? And, in case he could, as a pièce de résistance, she'd wear a new dress—one that Marlene had persuaded her to buy as part of her "transformation." A slinky, sexy dress in Jason's favorite blue.

She gave Fluffy a hug, then set him down as he wiggled in her arms. Maybe all wasn't lost. Maybe Jason would understand…and forgive…and forget.

Well, she'd know in a few hours. Because tonight would be the night that she'd confess.

FROM THE MINUTE DEE opened her door to him, Jason knew: after a long frustrating week, tonight would be the night—*finally*—that they'd make love.

The clues were all there for a man experienced enough to read them. Candlelight glowed in the living room behind her. Soft music played on the stereo. Delicious aromas wafted from the kitchen. All signs that she'd set the stage for romance.

But the most important clue was Dee. The pretty blue dress she'd donned, of some kind of silky material that skimmed her sexy figure. The half-scared, half-determined expression on her face as she closed the door behind him. The twin spots of pink high on her cheeks.

The way her eyes couldn't meet his for more than a second.

"Hi," she said. She glanced fleetingly up at him, then stared at his shirt.

It was a nice shirt, a dark blue pullover. But it didn't merit the intense scrutiny she was giving it. "Hi, yourself," he said huskily, and cupped her chin so he could see her eyes. A serene clear gray, they were the color of the sky just before the sun rose at dawn. The most beautiful eyes he'd ever seen. As they met his, they slowly lit up with a smile. Something inside him twisted, the way it always did when she looked at him like that. He bent and touched her mouth with his.

Her soft lips trembled, then parted. After a minute or so, he broke the kiss before things got out of control and rested his forehead against hers. Already he was hard with need. He wanted to steer her over to the couch— no, forget the couch, he wanted to carry her into her bedroom, which he'd never even seen, and keep her there, making love over and over for at least another week.

But Dee was new to all this. During the past week he'd realized just how new. For a woman of twenty-six, she was amazingly inexperienced. In fact, he'd never been with anyone so virginal before. To be truthful, he'd never wanted to be. He'd never been interested in the small gestures of romance—buying a woman candy, flowers, spending time with her when they weren't in bed. His affairs had been as straightforward as his business transactions. His goal—and the woman's goal as well—had been sexual satisfaction.

Inexperienced women, however, were apt to get emotional, to expect more than sex from a man. To think they were in love. To cling. He'd sure as hell never wanted any part of that.

But to his surprise he'd realized he enjoyed giving things to Dee. To see her eyes brighten when he handed her flowers. To feed her chocolate, watching her blush as he placed the candy between her half-open lips. He'd even realized he wouldn't mind too much if she clung a little. At the least, it would keep her away from men like Dialti or Paxton. He didn't like it, but he couldn't help feeling possessive about her, in a way he'd never had about any woman before. He wanted to protect her, take care of her. Make sure she was happy.

Dee was...different.

Simply holding hands with her felt somehow satisfying. Talking with her, playing with her soft curls, feeling her gently stroke his shoulders and the muscles of his back. Simply kissing was a big deal to Dee—and because she enjoyed it so much, it felt like a big deal to him, too.

Yeah, he wanted to make love with her. But he'd been patient—remarkably patient—for a whole damn week, willing to savor everything along the way as well. No sense in blowing it now, when she was finally ready to let down the last of her defenses.

So he wrapped an arm around her and led her into the living room. ''Hey, this is nice,'' he said, looking at the candles she'd put on just about every available surface.

The first time he'd seen the inside of her house, Jason had been stunned. For a woman who wore such drab, bland clothes the variety of colors she used in her home had come as a shock. Her walls were a soft melody of blue, lavender, yellow and pink, gently blending into one another, outlined with broad, white molding. Everywhere, there were flowers—the print of her couch, the pictures hanging on her walls, not to mention on her assorted throw pillows.

Her home was as different from his as possible, yet he'd been struck by a strange sense of familiarity the first time he'd entered. It wasn't until his third visit, however, that he realized why: her house reminded him of his home during his childhood, before his mother died.

It wasn't the way Dee decorated that caused the similarity—his mother had preferred an almost spartan look, probably a wise choice with four active boys tumbling around. Rather it was the scent, the atmosphere of both houses that was the same. Both smelled clean and fresh and inviting—the tangy scent of lemon polish mixing with the mouthwatering aromas of baking cookies and home-cooked meals. His father had hired plenty of housekeepers through the years—heaven knew Wanda had no intention of cleaning up after four boys—but only this past week had Jason realized what a difference small, loving touches made in turning a house into a home.

Dee had that kind of loving touch. Her furniture might be old, but it gleamed with care. Her mirrors and windows were crystal clear. Just as he'd suspected, Dee was as competent at homemaking as she was running his office.

He glanced down at her, unable to resist pulling her into his arms again for another kiss. He cupped her cheeks, his fingers sliding into her hair, enjoying the way the silky strands curled around his fingers. His blood pressure rocketed as this time—for the first time—she deepened the kiss before he did, slipping her tongue between his teeth to incite a small duel of her own.

He groaned, forgetting his good intentions, his vow to be patient. Leaning against the back of her couch, he pulled her between his thighs. His hand slid up the silky

material of her dress to find her breast. She sighed into
his mouth, and he got even harder. With rising excitement, he brushed his thumb across the erect peak of her
nipple.

Her breath caught. For just a second, she thrust the
plump mound more firmly into his palm, then she slowly
drew away. Her eyes were bright, but her lids looked
heavier, drowsy with the beginnings of sexual languor as
she glanced up at him. "I made chicken…"

He tugged on her full bottom lip with his teeth. "I
love chicken."

"And apple pie…"

He nibbled along her jaw. "My favorite."

"And I bought some champagne…"

Champagne—this was new. Reluctantly he lifted his
head. Dee wasn't a drinker; she *had* gone to a lot of
trouble to make this evening special. He wanted it to be
special, too.

He dropped a kiss on her soft hair, and slowly released
her. "Then why don't you go get it. We'll toast our
new…relationship."

Another smile lit up her face. "That's a wonderful
idea. I'll get down my crystal goblets."

He smiled back, and his lips remained curved upward
as he watched her hurry off into her kitchen. Women.
Always going crazy over stuff like crystal, and flowers
and embroidered pillows.

He shook his head, glancing at the array heaped on
Dee's couch. She had a ton of pillows, some with flowers, most with embroidered sayings. They reminded him
of stuffed caution signs, warning Dee about every con-
ceivable moral danger. No wonder she always tried to be
so prim and proper. Duty Is Heavier Than A Mountain
one declared. It's Not The Stone You See That Trips You

On Your Nose another stated. A Secret Spoken Finds Wings a blue one warned. Still others prohibited lying, vanity, stealing—there was even one against sex.

He was burying that one at the bottom of the pile when he felt something brush against his ankle. He glanced down at her cat. As a rule, he didn't care much for cats, but he had to admit he had a secret compassion for this one. He reached down to scratch its furry neck. "Fluffy, huh?" he said sympathetically, as the tom purred under his hand. "What kind of name is that for a male?"

The cat tolerated his touch for another couple of seconds, then sashayed off into the kitchen in search of his mistress. Satisfied with his rearrangement of her pillows, Jason wandered over to her bookshelf.

She had an eclectic selection of books—mysteries, horror, romances—fiction and nonfiction lined up in neat even rows. On a lower shelf, she'd stored her photo albums. Jason pulled one out and opened it, smiling at the solemn little Dee in pigtails, standing between her parents. Judging by the gaps in her front teeth, she was only about six or seven in the picture. Her parents, both stout and conservatively dressed, looked more like her grandparents than her mother and father. He flipped through the pages. Almost every picture was of Dee—and almost every one showed her primly, solemnly posing, hands folded in front of her, like a miniature little old lady.

Not a hair out of place, not a stain or tear in any of her clothes. Jason remembered how wistful she'd seemed as she'd listened to him talk about his brothers. He shook his head, mentally comparing her image to the scattering of pictures of his brothers and himself as children. If they weren't making faces or scowling at the camera, they were usually brawling. The only time they appeared halfway decent was when their mom was standing next to them, within disciplining distance.

Yeah, his brothers were a pain…but at least he'd had someone to pal around and spar with, he thought, staring down at Dee's pictures, in which she was almost always alone. What had it been like for her, he wondered, growing up an only child with elderly parents? No wonder her friends were so important to her. No wonder she tried to be perfect, to do everything right. She'd obviously had plenty of practice as a kid.

Oh well, it didn't seem to have hurt her much, he decided, shoving the album back into its place. He pulled out another, a quick glance informing him that this one contained her baby pictures. Even if her childhood had been fairly restricted, it didn't mean she couldn't learn to loosen up now, he thought, flipping through page after page featuring a pink clad, bald infant. In fact, it had probably been good for her. Her staid childhood might be the reason she was now the sweetest, the kindest—he turned a page—

—then glanced up as she reentered the room. Her eyes were fixed on the tray she was carefully carrying. Fluffy sauntered at her heels.

"I thought we'd use my Waterford goblets," she said, walking over to the coffee table to cautiously set the tray down. Picking up the frosty bottle, she added, "I chilled this. I hope that's right." She glanced fleetingly at him, her eyes shy. "Do you still want— *Omigosh!*"

The bottle went flying—Dee went flying. The wine landed on the couch, and Jason watched in amazement as Dee practically vaulted a chair to get to him. Before he could figure out what was going on, she'd grabbed the album from his hands.

Dee was trembling, adrenaline pumping through her as

she clutched the open album to her breast. She didn't need to look down to know what page he'd turned to. Her quick glimpse had revealed it all. Indelibly printed on her brain was the image of her least favorite baby picture—herself at three months, drooling happily as she lay naked on her stomach on a bearskin rug, her moon-shaped birthmark clearly visible for all the world to see.

I'm never going to forgive you, Mother, for taking that darn picture, she vowed silently. She'd always feared it would embarrass her someday. She definitely didn't want it to be the way Jason discovered her horrible secret. Not before dinner! Not before champagne!

She shut her eyes a second, sending up a silent prayer of thanks she'd gotten the book away before he could see the photo…then paused in mid-prayer. At least, she didn't *think* he'd seen it. She cautiously opened one eye, then the other…and sighed with relief. No, she was safe. He was frowning but the expression on his face was puzzled, not angry.

"What was that all about?" he asked, reaching down over the back of the couch to retrieve the bottle she'd thrown. He strode to the tray to set it down and turned to face her again. "Why did you grab that book away from me like that?"

"I—I didn't want you to see these photos. I don't take a very good picture." When his frown didn't ease, she added weakly, "They say the camera adds ten pounds, you know."

"Those are your *baby* pictures I was looking through."

"Even worse." She grimaced, hugging the book against her chest. "Nothing's uglier than a big, fat baby."

Jason stared at her, silently shaking his head. He'd

heard of low self-esteem, but this was ridiculous. How ugly could a baby picture be? He decided he wanted to find out. "Let me see."

Her eyes widened, and her clutch on the book tightened. "No." She backed away a step. "I'm—I'm naked in the picture."

Ah, ha! *Now* he understood! No one could be that repressed—not even Dee. She was learning to loosen up, as he'd thought she should. She simply wanted to play a little, make him come after her. To chase her. Okay, he was up for it.

He took a step toward her. "Let me see," he repeated.

"No!" She took a step back. "Jason, we need to talk."

"No. No talking now." He bared his teeth and growled menacingly, getting into the spirit of the game. "I want to see you naked."

Oh, good Lord, he wasn't going to give up, Dee realized, panic growing. What a time for him to suddenly turn playful. She felt as if she'd teased a lion—like the ones who had frightened her great-aunt. Somehow she'd aroused his hunting instincts, and now he was determined to get the book.

She took several steps away, backing into the hall leading to the front door. "You can't. I'm not kidding, Jason," she added in her sternest voice, ending the sentence with another retreat as he came after her.

But his strides were long. He was getting closer. "Neither am I. I want to see you—in all your naked, fat baby glory," he declared, flashing his wicked, white smile. He reached out and grasped the top of the album, giving it a threatening wiggle. "Give me that book!"

She jerked it away, backing up faster as he tracked each step. "No!" She bumped into something, and realized her back was to the door.

He reached out again. She hugged the album tighter—

Then squeaked in alarm as her doorbell rang out behind her.

Jason's teasing expression disappeared. His mouth straightened into a thin line. "Don't answer it."

But Dee wasn't going to disregard a friendly act of fate. "They know I'm here, my lights are on," she told him, ignoring his frown. She unlocked the door and opened it.

Two of her friends were standing there. Marlene was holding a video and Bonnie hefted a pizza box up like a waitress serving drinks.

"Hi, Dee. Long time no see. Are you up for an impromptu pizza and video party?" Marlene asked cheerfully.

But Bonnie's gaze had traveled past Dee into the hall. The box wavered, and the redhead gasped, "Oh, my God, it's Jason Masters!"

11

ONCE AGAIN SHE'D LOST HER nerve. Dee sat alone in her house a couple of hours later, berating herself for chickening out once more. The scare over her baby book, the sudden interruption by her friends, had unnerved her, making her panic. Marlene and Bonnie had wanted to leave right way but she hadn't let them. With a surreptitious squeeze of Marlene's arm, she'd invited them in.

Her friends had responded to her silent signal—and so had Jason. After waiting for a half hour or so, he'd left when it became clear they wouldn't be departing until he did. Marlene and Bonnie had left soon after, shaken by the unexpected encounter with their boss, respecting her desire not to go into the details. Dee had discovered she no longer needed their advice. She knew what she had to do. She simply had to carry through with it.

In fact, barely had they departed, when Dee began regretting her cowardice. She'd called up Jason, intending to ask him to return, but no one answered. She tried his number again and again, finally giving up at eleven, wondering where he could be.

She'd call him in the morning, she decided. And ask him to come over the next day. And this time, nothing and no one, would stop her from telling him the truth.

WAKING UP IS NEVER EASY after an all-night bender. Waking up to a phone call at eight o'clock was especially tough, Jason discovered the next morning.

More to stop the infernal ringing than because he cared who was on the line, he grabbed for the receiver. "Hello," he growled, the rough sound of his own voice making him wince. He clamped a hand to his forehead, trying to ease its pounding ache.

"Jason?" a feminine voice asked uncertainly.

His eyes opened. Dee—definitely the last person he'd expected to hear from this early. "Yeah?"

Silence...guilty silence, Jason decided. Yeah, she should feel bad, dumping him like that last night for her friends. Especially after the candles and the unopened champagne. He'd had big expectations last night—and not just concerning sex. He'd realized after he'd left her house how much he'd begun to enjoy just being with her. Talking. Discussing stuff. Cuddling on her couch.

He'd wanted to spend the entire night with her. To wake up with her in his arms, and see her dawn-colored eyes smile up at him in the morning.

Anger and irritation had led him to the nearest bar. The discovery that the liquor didn't compensate for not being with her had finally sent him home and to bed, wondering if she was missing him, too.

Now it seemed that she had. Just when he'd thought she might have hung up, she said, "I'm sorry about— about the interruption last night. I didn't expect my friends to come over like that."

"But you didn't ask them to leave, either, did you?" he asked dryly, not trying to hide the accusation in his voice.

"No, I didn't," she admitted. "I wasn't quite sure how to without sounding rude." Even over the phone he could hear her take a deep breath, before she added, "But I'm hoping I can see you again tonight. There's something very important I need to tell you, and I've put it off too long as it is."

Jason leaned up on his elbow, running his hand through his rumpled hair as he tried to concentrate. What was she talking about now? "So tell me," he said bluntly.

Another pause. "It's, um…something I'd rather tell you in person. It's kind of…personal."

The frown wrinkling his brow cleared. Personal. Tell him in person. He sat up straighter, finally understanding where all this was heading.

She obviously wanted to tell him she was a virgin.

Now he understood the reason she'd been holding back all week; why she'd gotten cold feet last night. This was another big deal to her. She obviously wanted to be truthful with him before they went to bed.

A tender ache swelled his chest. It was really kind of sweet when he thought about it—how much she cared about his reaction, wanted complete honesty between them. He couldn't help but feel…touched.

The disappointment he'd been nursing since the previous evening disappeared. "Okay." He cleared his throat to ease the huskiness in his voice. "I'll see you tonight."

"Great." She sounded relieved. "Just come to my house at eight and—"

"No." He wasn't going through that again; take the chance of her friends arriving unexpectedly. He used to think that Dee was the tagalong of the group, but he'd realized lately she was actually the lynch pin. Her house was the one everyone always met up at. Her stable, traditional background and morals provided a home base the others appeared to rely on. "You come to my house this time," he said decisively. That way he'd be sure they wouldn't be interrupted.

"But—"

"And bring your swimming suit," he ordered with sudden inspiration, remembering her lecture on relaxing in a hot bath. "I've got a pool and a spa. Maybe we can take a swim." That would be one way to get her clothes off. And help her relax at the same time.

She didn't answer, and for a heart-stopping moment he thought she'd refuse. Then she drew a deep breath and agreed. "All right. Your house. Eight o'clock?"

"That's fine."

And she hung up.

HE WAS WAITING FOR HER when she arrived. He answered his bell on the first ring, and when he opened the door, Dee was standing there.

Jason greeted her with a slow smile he was unable to suppress as his gaze ran over her. She was wearing a loose, filmy sort of skirt in a soft shade of pink with a matching top, just transparent enough for him to see the darker outline of her bathing suit underneath. "Come in," he invited, unable to keep a husky note from his voice.

Her answering smile was a little uncertain, but she did as he asked and went past him into the living room. He shut the door and locked it, then followed at a more leisurely pace, pausing in the doorway to watch her as she looked around.

His home was much different from hers. He wondered what she thought of it. Her house was small; his was spacious, with cathedral ceilings that added to the grandeur of the rooms. As in his office, he preferred dark furniture with strong clean lines, that provided a contrast to his white walls and carpet. A few abstract sculptures were scattered here and there, and a bright Joel original in primary colors hung on one wall, but other than that the place was bare of decoration.

But Dee gave no indication what she thought of his home. She stood in the middle of his living room, her shoulders stiff, her hands clasped in front of her, a nervous expression on her face.

Not good, he decided. As tense as she was, she'd probably bolt before they could get to…the good stuff.

"Come with me," he told her, making an abrupt decision. He reached out and laced her fingers between his. "You're wearing your bathing suit under that, aren't you?"

"Yes, but—we need to talk."

He frowned, feeling the trembling in her fingers. Hell, she *was* uptight. "So we'll talk in the hot tub."

Without giving her a chance to refuse, he turned and walked across his living room toward the glass doors leading to his deck, towing her behind him. She didn't pull away, but her steps were slow and reluctant as he led her out into the cool darkness.

The high wall and aspen trees lining his property provided privacy, shielding it from curious eyes. The trees shivered in the night breeze, their leaves rustling like whispering murmurs. Light from the full moon shone down from the clear, star-filled sky.

Releasing her, he left her standing by the spa while he went to the control panel. The water was already hot. A misty cloud of steam drifted gently upward. As he hit the jets, the water surged to life, frothing and bubbling invitingly.

Jason didn't turn on the lights before returning to stand by the water. He didn't want to alarm her. Just being near to her, knowing that they'd soon be making love, already had him hard with arousal. Prudently he kept his back to her as he stripped off his shirt and shed his pants and shoes. He wanted to discard his black briefs as well, but he knew she wasn't ready for that. So he kept them on as he stepped into the water.

It was hot, but he was even hotter. He sank down into the liquid heat and draped his arms along the sides of the spa, the cool breeze flowing against his warm skin. He glanced up at Dee.

She still stood on the deck where he'd left her, shifting nervously from foot to foot. "It's so big," she said. "The biggest one I've ever seen."

She startled him for a moment. Then he realized she was talking about the size of his spa. "Yeah. I bought the biggest I could find."

He'd gotten such a huge one for the parties he used to throw, in his rash and reckless twenties. But he didn't tell her that; it wouldn't be a smart thing to mention to a woman he was hoping to seduce. No, not seduce, he realized, looking at her face, which glowed softly in the moonlight. He wanted her to desire him, too.

Hell, if she desired him even half as much as he did her, he'd be doing pretty good, he thought wryly. Never had any woman been so tense and nervous simply at the prospect of joining him in the water. Even in the shadowy darkness, he could see the uncertainty in her stance.

"Come in," he said coaxingly. "The water's fine."

For a long moment she didn't move. He held his breath and remained still, sensing she was about to refuse or make an excuse to stay where she was. Then she seemed to sigh, and her tension eased a little. She slipped off her shoes. She undid the waistband of her skirt, and it slid down to her feet. Then slowly—oh so slowly—she lifted up her top. She drew it over her head and dropped it onto the deck.

Jason set his jaw to keep that from dropping as well. Now he was so hard he almost hurt. The tiny black triangles of her suit top barely supported the inviting fullness of her white breasts. Her skin glowed with a pearl-like luster. His gaze traveled downward, past the sharp indent of her waist, to her hips and slender legs. Tiny beads of sweat broke out on his forehead. Her breasts and hips were rounded and lush. Although he'd always gone for women who were tall and model thin, he now knew without a doubt lush was definitely what he preferred.

"That's a thong, isn't it?"

She slowly nodded.

His jaw tightened. "Is that the suit you go surfing in?"

"No." She cleared her throat, suddenly looking self-conscious. "I bought this one today. I wear another suit under my wet suit when I surf."

Good. He was glad to hear it. He was also glad she'd chosen *this* suit to wear for him. He watched, unable to look away, as she walked slowly to the edge of the water and tested it with a cautious toe.

"It's so hot." She drew back a little.

"Sit on the edge." He cleared his throat, trying to erase the huskiness from his voice. "Let your body get used to it. Before you tell me whatever it is you need to discuss, I want to go over a few details of the Robertson deal with you."

She did as he suggested, at first sitting primly upright, back straight, knees together. But he was careful to stay at his side of the spa, and to keep the conversation on business.

The ploy worked. Gradually she relaxed, lulled by the

heat of the water, the mundane details about the business contract. After a few minutes, she leaned back on her hands, lazily kicking her legs through the swirling ripples as she became engrossed in the discussion. "You might want to recheck that clause defining patent limitations," she said, frowning earnestly.

He nodded, his gaze fixed on the teasing movements of her legs, the way her foot played with the water, idly splashing up and down.

"I believe you could raise our percentage on some of the other options as well...."

She kept talking, but he stopped listening. All he could hear was the seductive whoosh of the water and the pounding of his heart. God, he wanted her more with every second that passed. He'd never wanted a woman so intensely. His mouth went dry as her foot circled near his leg, then retreated in another lazy arc.

"And we'd better review the limitations...."

The mist had dampened her hair. Tiny tendrils clung to her moist cheeks and temples, forming delicate, upside-down question marks against her soft skin. He resisted the urge to brush them back. To let his lips wander along the fragile arch of her collarbones with their enticing hollows. To nibble the slender column of her neck, the plump curves of her breasts...

Her foot brushed against his thigh—and his control snapped. He caught her ankle, chaining it with his fingers. It was as narrow as he'd thought.

She gave a tiny gasp. "Jason?"

"What?" He caught her other one.

Her eyes widened as he moved closer, her pupils expanding until they seemed as black as the sky above. "We need to talk. I have to tell you something."

Hell, the virgin thing. He couldn't believe it bothered

her so much. To save her from stumbling through what was to her an obviously embarrassing revelation, he said simply, "I already know what you want to tell me."

Her eyes grew even bigger. "You do?"

"Yeah. I figured it out this past week. Actually I suspected even before that, but I wasn't quite sure." Gently but inexorably, he parted her legs. He stepped closer, waist deep in the water, nestling his torso against the cradle of her thighs. "But I want you to know, it doesn't bother me in the least."

Her mouth dropped open. She closed it, then opened it again to ask, "It doesn't?"

"No. And you shouldn't let it bother you, either." Since she was sitting above him on the deck, from this position she couldn't feel his hard arousal—but damn, could he ever feel her softness. Her soft, silky thighs clasping the sides of his waist. Her full, soft breasts pressing against his chest as he drew her closer for a kiss. He could feel her nipples through her wet suit. They had tightened into hard, tiny berries. Her soft—oh, so soft mouth—was swollen and sweet.

He kissed her again, then drew away to look at her. He tucked a tiny, damp curl behind her ear. "Believe me, it's not that big a deal."

"Oh, Jason." Her breath emerged on a broken gasp of relief. "I'm so glad that you feel that way. I've been so worried about telling you."

Her hands were resting on his shoulders. They felt cool against his hot skin. The moonlight slanted across her face, shining in her eyes as she added almost shyly, "But I shouldn't have been. I think you must be the most understanding man in the world."

He shook his head in faint amusement at the statement. No one had ever said that to him before. He couldn't believe how worried she'd been. Didn't she realize most men would be more than understanding, be thrilled in fact, to learn they would be the first—the only—with the woman they cared about?

And he did care about her, he realized suddenly. They fit together; she felt right in his arms. In his life.

He dropped a kiss on her nose. "And I think you're the most beautiful woman in the world." He added huskily, "I want to make love to you, Dee."

"Oh, Jason." Shy excitement flashed across her face, transforming her expression. Her eyes lit up. She stroked his arm gently. "I want that, too."

Her admission caused his desire to surge higher, sweeping away the remainder of his control. He gathered her tightly against him and bent to kiss her mouth again. Her lips immediately parted, allowing him to explore the delicate softness inside. He groaned, his muscles tightening even more at her willing response. She flung her arms around his neck.

She tasted so good. She smelled so clean and enticing. He loved the feel of her slender arms locked around his neck. The softness of her mouth beneath his, the way she eagerly returned his kiss. A wild, fierce feeling expanded inside him. She was his—only his.

He needed her even closer. Without breaking the kiss, he slid his hands beneath her bottom and lifted her. Her arms instinctively clasped his neck more securely, her legs tightened around his waist. Jason groaned at the sweet agony of his hardness pressed against her as he drew her down into the water.

Dee didn't resist. She was lost, drowning in sensations. The hot water seething around her. The cool night air caressing her wet skin, playing with her hair. The hard flat feel of his lean abdomen between her thighs and the glistening, powerful muscles in his chest and shoulders beneath her hands. And most of all, the joy humming through her veins at the hungry, secret urgency of Jason's callused hands beneath the water on her back, on her bottom.

Then his hand swept up along her spine. Dee felt the slight tug as he pulled at the swimsuit tie around her neck. Another tug at her back and her top floated free. Jason tossed it aside. He lifted her higher, out of the frothing water. She braced her hands on his strong shoulders as he leaned away to look at her.

Her nipples tingled and puckered in the cool breeze. A shiver chased along her skin, causing tiny goose bumps. She felt vulnerable as he held her there, but she felt wonderful, too. Fully gloriously female as he slowly bent his dark head to her breast.

Dee gasped as he drew her nipple into his mouth. Her fingers clutched his hair, and she arched back in ecstasy, her eyes drifting shut. He suckled gently, making her breasts swell, her womb clench with painful pleasure. Instinctively she tightened her legs around his waist. She leaned back even farther, thrusting her breast more fully against his mouth.

His lips tugged at her nipple, then released it to roam down to her stomach. She lay back in the water, relying on his arms for support as the miniature waves foamed around her, pulling at her hair.

She opened her eyes and looked up at the sky. Above her floated the moon, full and glowing and surrounded by an endless armada of twinkling stars. She felt like she could reach up and touch it. As if she were floating, too, rising into the air on the misty steam rising from the water. Jason's warm, exploring mouth on her wet, sensitive skin was inciting her to madness—moon madness, she thought hazily.

Her stomach muscles contracted as his lips brushed lower near the elastic of her suit. Her hands tugged at his thick hair, but he lingered, probing her indented navel, teasing her into a mixture of alarm and excitement, before his hot mouth traveled back up her midriff.

He lifted her out of the water again and his lips closed around her other nipple. Her arms cradled his head and she looked down at him, watching his mouth drawing on her breast. Water flowed from her hair in small, warm streams over her shoulders, down over him. The delicious, aching torment at the core of her built higher. He'd thrust his leg between hers. Dee pressed against him, riding his thigh in an effort to relieve the unbearable yearning growing inside.

He pulled away, ignoring her whimper of protest and buried his face against her neck. "You're driving me crazy." His voice was ragged and rough. His breath flowed hotly against her skin. "Let's get out of here and into a bed before things get out of control."

Dee felt as though she was already out of control. She didn't want to leave his arms even for a second, but he didn't give her any choice. He carried her across the Jacuzzi, and hoisted her up to sit on the edge again. Anxious to get into his bed—and back into his arms—she rose and turned to go into the house.

"What the *hell?*"

His harsh tone stopped her in her tracks. Startled, Dee's arms instinctively flew up to cover her bare breasts. She turned to look at Jason.

"There—on your left cheek." His eyes narrowed to slits. *"You're the Mooner."*

12

DEE WAS BEWILDERED, the sudden transition from hot passion to cold shock making it hard to think. She stared at him in confusion. "I know—you know, too."

"What are you talking about?" he demanded. Even in the dim light, she could see how his features had sharpened, how taut the sculpted planes of his cheeks and jaw had become. "I had no idea it was you."

"But just a while ago—before we started kissing. I started to tell you and you said you'd already figured it out."

"Oh, God." He raked a hand through his hair and swore. "I wasn't talking about that—I haven't even thought about it for days. I thought you were trying to tell me you were a virgin."

Dee could feel a heated flush rising beneath her skin. Her arms tightened across her breasts. "No, I—I never even thought about telling you that."

His gaze narrowed, searching her pale face in the moonlight. "No? Well, I guess that shouldn't come as a surprise. You certainly didn't tell me about the 'grand gesture' you made from the company van," he said with an edge to his voice. "I suppose your friends are all in on this, too."

She shook her head, the wet strands of her hair whipping across her cheeks. "No," she said as convincingly as she could. No matter what he thought of her, she had to protect her friends.

"No?" His expression hardened as his gaze scanned her face. "Are you saying you thought of this brilliant plan all on your own—and for what, might I ask? To humiliate me in front of Dialti? To show your contempt?"

"No!" How could he think that? "I didn't mean to moon you at all. I thought you were Stewart. I wanted to explain but—but one thing led to another and telling you just seemed to get…more and more difficult."

"Yeah, I'm sure it was a lot easier to let me make an idiot of myself trying to find the culprit, than to tell me the truth." He shook his head in self-disgust. "I can't believe I didn't see it sooner. It's all so clear now—your car sitting in the company lot. Dialti's sudden interest in you—" His mouth twisted as that thought led to another. "*Your* sudden interest in me. What a fool I am."

"No! You don't understand—"

"Don't I?" Jason stared at her, his disillusionment increasing by the second. Oh, he understood, all right. Better than she knew. He knew all about women who used desire to blind a man to the truth.

His tone harshened. "It seems perfectly clear to me. You started coming on to me to save your job, to make me forget about the stunt you pulled. That's why you came over tonight, wasn't it? To ask me to forgive you?"

"Yes— No! It wasn't like that," Dee protested. But her voice lacked conviction. She *had* started this whole thing to try to save her job. She *had* hoped that he'd forgive her—and that they'd end up making love tonight.

And Jason knew she was lying. He could see it in her face. Hear it in her voice.

Pain—unrelenting and unquenchable—welled up inside him. God, he *was* a fool—the biggest one that ever lived. He'd thought she cared about him. That maybe, she even loved him a little. When in truth, she obviously didn't care for him any more than she had Paxton—less in fact. With Paxton at least she'd been hoping for love, for commitment. With himself, her main concern had been to save her job.

The pain he was feeling spread, burning through him like acid. The fact that she was *still* lying added hot anger to the mix. But what made him angriest of all was the knowledge that even now, he had to fight the urge to go to her. To take her in his arms and beg her to say she loved him, too.

Even if that was the biggest lie of all.

His jaw clenched harder. His muscles tightened till they ached. But he refused to play the fool any longer. Nor to let her know she'd hurt him. So he almost welcomed the rage building inside him. It was a familiar tool to block the hurt, a shield for his pride. A weapon to fight back with.

He couldn't accuse her of misleading him about love. She'd never mentioned love—not once in all the time they'd spent together. So instead, he hit her with the one accusation she couldn't deny or explain away. *"You cost me a twenty-million-dollar deal!"*

Dee bit her lip to still its quivering. His eyes blazed. His mouth was set in a cold, unforgiving line. "I didn't mean to. I made a mistake."

"Yeah, you made a mistake all right," he agreed, "but I made a bigger one thinking you were something special. That I was something special to you."

Shocked by the bitterness in his tone, Dee stood there trembling. How could he talk to her like this after what they'd just shared? When he'd been about to make love to her?

After the heat of the water, the breeze was freezing cold against her skin. After the heat of his embrace, his words were freezing her heart. It felt brittle, ready to break in her chest. But what hurt most of all was the knowledge that it wasn't his fault—it was hers. There was no excuse for what she'd done. Nor for failing to tell him the truth sooner.

Still, she whispered, "It wasn't like it seems, Jason. I didn't…kiss you in hopes that you'd forgive me. Or just to save my job."

His gaze scorched over her. "Are you saying you *don't* want me to forgive you?"

"Well, yes, but—"

"I thought so." He shrugged, his wet shoulders gleaming in the moonlight with the movement. The cynical expression she disliked so much settled on his face. The one that made him seem like such a stranger. "Well, don't worry. Your job is safe. There's no need to keep up the pretense anymore."

"It wasn't a pretense," she said, her throat so tight she could hardly speak.

She could tell by his face he didn't believe her. She wondered if he'd ever believe her again.

"Another lie, Dee?" he asked, confirming her thoughts. He gave a brief laugh, so grating that it made her wince. "And to think, I once thought you were the most honest person I knew." His gaze ran over her and he added sardonically, "And the most modest."

Agony pierced her. "I am modest." Even as she said the words, Dee realized how ridiculous they sounded, with her standing almost naked above him. Her throat constricted, and she fell silent.

There was nothing left to say. She was in a nightmare; her worst fear had come true. She'd made a fool of herself. Jason didn't care about her. He didn't seem to even like her. She'd risked her pride, her hopes—her love—for nothing.

She wasn't cold anymore. She felt numb. Her hands dropped. What did it matter if he saw her breasts? What did anything matter?

She picked up her blouse and slipped it on. She reached for her skirt and put that on, too, while he simply watched without saying a word, steam rising up around his still figure.

She gathered her shoes, then turned and started walking toward the door. When she reached for the knob, he suddenly spoke. His voice was rough, as if the words were forced out of him. "If you leave now, I'm not coming after you."

She paused, and looked him directly in the eyes. "Good," she said, and left.

13

JASON WAS STILL ANGRY the next morning.

He sat in his office, fighting to control the emotion. To get his mind off Dee and her deception and back on business. But he couldn't. Every few minutes a turmoil of emotions would surge up inside him in a relentless, almost overwhelming wave.

He hadn't felt like this since the loss of his parents. He wanted to take off—to roam the world and distract himself with meaningless pleasures and risks, the way he had when his mother died. Or submerge himself in the sterile, logical world of business where he had some control, like he'd done at the death of his father.

But instead, he could only ride his emotions—rage, pain, grief—tumbling his thoughts into confusion where only one thing was clear: She'd lied to him. She'd led him on. She'd played him for a fool.

Exactly the way Wanda had played his dad.

The realization continually cycled through his mind, feeding his hurt, his anger with Dee and with himself. He'd planned to never fall into that trap—to be caught by a woman's lying wiles, the way his father had. But he'd done exactly the same thing. He'd let desire blind him to the truth for weeks. He'd been deceived by her soft eyes, her sweet kisses, into believing that she loved him.

Unable to sit still, he rose to pace around his office.

He passed one high arched window, then another, the view beyond the glass nothing more than a blend of meaningless shapes and colors.

He paused before the Hvostal sculpture, remembering how shocked Dee had been when she'd first realized what it represented—how a few days later she'd smiled at him and blushed, when their eyes met over the cold marble. He'd thought they shared some kind of affinity; a silent communication. How wrong could he be? He stood there, his hands clenching and unclenching as he fought the urge to pick it up, to hurl it through a window or smash it on the floor.

And suddenly he knew he couldn't go about business as usual. That the only reason he'd come to work at all was because of the faint, secret hope she'd be here.

God, did he never learn?

Cursing under his breath at his own stupidity, he turned toward the door to leave. But before he could take a step, the door opened. His pulse jumped. But it was only his brother Jon standing there.

"What do you want?" Jason asked. He strode back to his desk and sat down.

His brother's eyebrows lifted at his surly tone, but he didn't retreat as Jason hoped he would. Instead, he strolled into the room and took the chair opposite.

Dee's chair.

"I just stopped by to see how things were going," Jon said, leaning back and stretching out his long legs. "Did you find the Mad Mooner yet?"

Jason's jaw clenched. His grip tightened on his pen, then he forced himself to relax. Jon would find out sooner or later; he might as well tell him now and get it over with. "Dee was the one who mooned me."

For once, he caught his brother by surprise. For a full

ten seconds Jon stared at him in amazement. Then he suddenly burst out laughing. "Dee? Your secretary, Dee? You've got to be kidding me. And then you put her in charge of finding herself?" Jon laughed again, and shook his head, still chuckling. "Who'd ever guess she was such a joker. I gotta talk to her about this." He half rose from his chair. "Where is she? On a break?"

"She isn't here." It felt strange to say the words, but Jason forced himself to add, "And she's not coming back. We had an argument last night, and I think she's quit."

"You think…?" All traces of amusement disappeared from Jon's expression. He sank back into his seat and eyed his brother in silence. "Jase, Jase," he said softly. "What did you do?"

"Me?" The injustice of the question made Jason rise from his chair. Angrily he began to pace his office again. "*She's* the one who mooned *me*—from a company van, no less. Did you expect me to applaud her performance?"

"No, but I wouldn't expect you to be this angry over it."

"That's because you have no sense of proper behavior. Or what's due this company. What kind of woman does something like that?"

Jon considered the question. "I dunno. Dee's kind I guess. Are you saying it's some sort of habit with her? An addiction? That she does it often?"

"Of course not," Jason said, enraged all over again at the light view his brother was taking of the matter. "Don't be an idiot. She only did it once. She told me she was aiming for Paxton, and got me instead."

Jon's mouth quirked. "A miss-mooning, huh? No wonder you're upset. That's a pretty bad mistake to make."

"Yeah, make jokes. That little mistake cost our firm a twenty-million-dollar deal," Jason reminded him bitterly.

Again Jon looked surprised. "It did? That's odd. I thought Justin said Dialti came around last week, that he was ready to go forward on the patent deal."

"Yeah, but—" Jason broke off, unable to argue. Dialti *had* still been interested—until Jason landed a left to his jaw.

"Well, maybe there's still hope in salvaging the partnership," Jon said, pursuing his own line of thought. "It's not like you to give up without a fight. Why don't you try talking to Dialti again and—"

"No!" The word escaped with more force than Jason intended, but he didn't take it back. After the way Dialti had put his slimy hands all over Dee, refusing to let her go, no way on earth was he going to do business with that scumbag ever again.

His eyes met his brother's.

Jon had a knowing look on his face. "So, it seems Dee isn't the one nixing the Dialti venture—you are. So what's the real problem here, bro? What's really bugging you?"

"I don't know what you're talking about." He turned to look out the window. "Okay, maybe she wasn't responsible for losing the Dialti deal, or at least not completely. She still made a fool of me." His throat tightened, making his voice harsh as he added, "Anyone would be angry, to find out a woman they…cared about had done something like that."

For a long moment, neither spoke. Then Jon said in a thoughtful voice, "You know, I always felt sorry for Dad, having a wife like Wanda. But even worse than what she did to him, is the number that she pulled on you."

Jason stiffened as if he'd taken a bullet in the back. He whirled around, his eyes wide with shock before they narrowed on his brother's face. "What the hell are you talking about? I never cared about that bitch!"

"No, but she's sure made you doubt your own judgment when it comes to women."

The thought that Wanda had affected him in any way was intolerable. "Bull," Jason said roughly. "I've been with plenty of women."

"Yeah, fleeting affairs, with no real emotions involved. You always move on before things get serious, before you can make a mistake—like Dad did." Jon paused, then added quietly, "But you're not Dad, Jason."

"I never—"

"You don't retreat from life the way he did. You've always been there—for Justin, James—" his mouth turned down wryly "—and especially me."

Jason stared at him, not knowing what to say.

Jon met his gaze steadily. "And you know, deep in your heart, that Dee isn't Wanda, either."

Jason opened then shut his mouth, his brows lowering. Of course Dee wasn't Wanda. He knew that. The comparison was ridiculous. Dee was loyal. She was sweet, and kind. She didn't care about money, or status. She cared about people—the other employees. Her parents. Her friends. Him.

He swallowed, trying to ease his suddenly dry throat. At least, she *had* cared about him…before he'd taken her head off, overreacting to a simple prank.

In a vain attempt to justify his actions to himself even more than his annoying brother he said, "But I never thought she'd do something like that—or lie about it." He wondered if the excuse sounded as feeble to Jon as it now did to him.

Apparently so. Jon straightened in his chair. "Is *that* what this is all about? You're angry because you cared about her...and then discovered she'd done something wrong? She hurt your pride—and proved that she's not perfect?"

"I never thought that she was perfect!" Jason said, glad to be able to dispute at least one mistake.

Jon snorted. "Pretty near. You told me yourself she was the perfect secretary—quiet, unassuming. I bet you decided she had to be the perfect woman, too."

"That's a bunch of crap," Jason declared, but he shifted uneasily, shoving his fists into his pockets. Okay, maybe the perfect secretary. And maybe he'd been pleased she was so ladylike. And so sweet. And yes, he'd been glad she was a virgin. But he knew she wasn't perfect. No one was.

Yet, the first time she'd done something he didn't like, he'd decided she must be like Wanda—bad through and through. He'd been defining Dee's whole character on his stepmother's actions. He raked his hand through his hair, beginning to sweat. How could he have done that? he wondered, the truth of Jon's accusation becoming clearer and clearer. He knew what Dee was really like. He'd worked with her nearly every day for almost a year. He'd been even closer to her this past month.

And then he'd pushed her as far away as he could with his anger.

Oh, God, Jon was right. Except Jason was worse than his father. At least his Dad had taken the chance of falling in love—had had a good relationship with his mother. Jason had never let himself get close to anyone but his brothers. And then, when he'd fallen in love in spite of himself, at the first excuse, he'd reverted to character and chased her off.

"Yeah, well I can see why you got rid of her," Jon was saying in an annoyingly agreeable voice, disturbing Jason's concentration. "She's definitely a bad influence on the place. Especially since she started wearing more sexy clothes—"

Jason swung around to glare at him.

Jon smiled smugly. "Oh, yeah, brother. I noticed. Every man in this building noticed. She's become quite a distraction. Let her go disrupt some other firm." Jon rubbed his chin. "I wonder if Dialti and Sons has an opening?"

"Shut up," Jason growled.

"Or maybe she'll decide not to work anymore at all. To get married. Even Mooners fall in love, right? I bet it won't take her long to find another lover—maybe he'll be a Mooner, too, and they can go out on mooning sprees together. He wouldn't have your high standards, of course. But then maybe he won't have your temper—or your past—either."

"I said shut up."

But Jon never had listened to him. He didn't now. "It's kind of funny when you think of it. You, with your wild background, outraged because the woman you love—" He lifted his brows as Jason glanced at him sharply, then continued blandly when his brother remained silent. "Did one, foolish, outrageous act—probably the only one she's ever done in her entire life. Yeah, you were wise to get rid of her. She's a real—"

But Jason didn't hear the rest of his aggravating brother's remark. He was already out the door.

JASON COULD MOVE FAST when he wanted something. Less than forty-five minutes later he was knocking at Dee's door.

He waited. No one answered. Impatiently he knocked again, louder this time.

A few seconds later, the door opened, just a few inches. Just enough for him to see Dee, staring at him stonily. "Yes?"

"Can I come in?"

"No."

"No?" Jason was dumbstruck. Never in his worst imaginings, had he thought she wouldn't even listen to him. He barely recovered his wits in time to grab the edge of the door, holding it open as she tried to push it closed. "I want to talk to you."

"I don't want to talk to you." She shoved at the door again.

"Dee…" Jason lowered his voice to a warning tone. "If you don't let me in, I'll…"

"Do what?" she prompted when his voice trailed off. "Fire me? Prosecute me for being a Mooner? Yell a lot? Well, go ahead."

She pushed harder. Jason held on, almost getting his fingers caught. "Dee, stop this nonsense and let me in."

"No!"

"Why not?"

"Because I'm cutting you out of my life."

Her words pierced him as sharply as a knife slicing into his chest. His shoulders hunched in pain. The door shut a little more. "Dee—please don't," he begged huskily. "Just listen to me a moment."

She froze, then stepped away. She headed into the living room, saying over her shoulder, "Fine. Come in and talk if you want to. But I think you said it all last night."

She sounded so cold. So remote. As distant as she'd been when she'd first started as his secretary. But not at all as meek, he realized.

He took a step toward her, but paused when she stepped away. "I didn't say it all last night. All you heard last night was my damnable temper getting out of hand. I'm sorry about that, Dee."

Her mouth quivered, then she pressed her lips together. She turned away, and picked up some clothes lying on her couch and began folding them. "I'm sorry, too," she said gruffly. "I never should have mooned you—or tried to moon anyone else for that matter. Or lied to you after I did it. Now if you'll excuse me, I'm packing."

"Packing? Packing for where?" he asked sharply, for the first time noticing the open suitcases on the floor, the clothes stacked in neat piles on her furniture. "Where are you going?"

"I'm not sure. Hawaii, I think. Or maybe Jamaica. I haven't decided yet."

His heart sank. He knew without asking that she was traveling so far, simply to get away from him.

His fists clenched. She couldn't leave him; not now. Not ever. "Please. Don't go."

She went on packing, keeping her back turned toward him.

"We need to talk."

She still didn't answer.

"Dee, I need you." He drew a deep breath. "We belong together."

Her shoulders sagged, her hands dropped. For a second, she just stood there and then she turned around to face him again. And now, he could see the pain in her clear eyes. "We don't belong together, Jason."

"Yes, we do."

She shook her head.

His jaw tightened. "It's my temper, isn't it? I scared

you, lashing out at you like that last night. That's why you won't give us another chance.''

She shook her head. "No, of course not. You've never scared me. Not really. Not even last night. You had a right to be angry. And I knew, deep in my heart, that your anger wouldn't last and that you'd forgive me. But the truth is, Jason, that I'm not good enough for you.''

"That's a bunch of—''

"No. It's true. I thought about it, all last night." She picked up a pink sweater lying on a cushion, and then sat down, holding it in her lap. She absently ran her hand over the yarn as she told him, "You're brave. You love taking risks, doing exciting things. I'm not very courageous at all. You don't worry about anything. I worry a lot. Just about all the time, in fact. And worst of all, I've recently developed a new bad trait.'' She plucked at a loose thread in the sweater, looking down at it as she admitted, "I—I'm impulsive. And it makes me do dumb things. Like mooning you. And kissing you.''

"I'm *glad* you kissed me. I'm even glad you mooned me.''

She looked up at him, her expression doubtful.

Determined to convince her, Jason added, "It made me see something I've never seen before.''

She stiffened, hurt indignation freezing her expression.

"I mean, I've seen bottoms before—'' *Good Lord— don't go there, you idiot!* "What I'm trying to say is I never really noticed you before—this Mooner hunt started.''

Jason wiped at the perspiration on his brow. *Great— really smooth.* He'd never had any trouble talking to women. Why, when this was the most important thing he'd ever wanted to say in his life—to the one woman he'd ever cared about—was he bumbling around like this?

He took a deep breath. Well, smooth talker or not, he wasn't going to leave until he'd convinced her he was telling the truth.

Making a decision, he walked over to her and got down on bended knee. He'd read somewhere—probably on one of her pillows—that a woman never ignored a man kneeling at her feet. And he wanted her complete attention for what he needed to say. Never had he meant anything more.

He took her hands in his and looked into her clear gray eyes. "Dee, the truth is, you're too good for me. And if you don't believe me, ask my brother. Ask any of my brothers or any of the employees at the company. Ask anyone who knows us. They'll tell you it's the truth."

She started to shake her head, but he frowned in admonishment, saying firmly, "Oh, yes, unfortunately it is. I'm not perfect, and far less so than you. And I'll never be perfect, and I certainly wouldn't want you to be," he added, remembering Jon's taunting. His hands tightened around hers. "As for being brave...nothing could be farther from the truth. I've been running scared, Dee, my entire adult life. I've never let myself fall in love because I didn't want to get hurt, like my dad was hurt."

He took a deep breath, saying the words he'd once vowed never to say. "But I love you, Dee. I love you with my whole heart and soul. And I always will, no matter what."

Her eyes widened, but she didn't say anything. Her eyes remained locked with his.

Her silence made him even more desperate. He searched for words to convince her he was telling the truth. "I love *all* of you—everything that you do, everything that makes you Dee. Like the way you bite your lip when you worry. The way you look so guilty when you lie—and make up such unbelievable stories. The way you were just crazy enough—to fall in love with me.''

His grasp on her hands tightened. ''You do love me, don't you, Dee?''

Dee stared down into his blue eyes and read the demand there…and the entreaty. A part of her wanted to say no, because falling in love *was* crazy. It made a person vulnerable to hurt, to loss. It meant placing your heart in another person's care.

But despite her recent record, Dee had been brought up to tell the truth. ''Yes, I love you,'' she admitted.

His eyes flared. ''And you'll marry me?''

''Yes.''

And then he rose, pulling her up into his arms for a long and passionate kiss. He only broke it long enough to say huskily against her mouth, ''You won't regret it, sweetheart. I'll leave Jon in charge of the company for a while—he deserves to suffer a little—and we'll travel the world. Just tell me where you want to go.''

Dee pretended to consider the question. ''Well, there's one place…''

He hugged her closer. ''Name it. Hawaii? Aruba? The Bahamas?''

Leaning her forehead against his, she whispered soft and sweet, ''The bedroom.''

Jason didn't need to be told twice. Lifting her in his arms, he carried her off…to paradise.

INDULGE IN A QUIET MOMENT
WITH HARLEQUIN

Get a FREE
Quiet Moments Bath Spa

with just two proofs of purchase from any of our four special collector's editions in May.

Harlequin® is sure to make your time special this Mother's Day with four special collector's editions featuring a short story *PLUS* a complete novel packaged together in one volume!

Collection #1   Intrigue abounds in a collection featuring *New York Times* bestselling author Barbara Delinsky and Kelsey Roberts.

Collection #2   Relationships? Weddings? Children? = *New York Times* bestselling author Debbie Macomber and Tara Taylor Quinn at their best!

Collection #3   Escape to the past with *New York Times* bestselling author Heather Graham and Gayle Wilson.

Collection #4   Go West! With *New York Times* bestselling author Joan Johnston and Vicki Lewis Thompson!

Plus Special Consumer Campaign!

Each of these four collector's editions will feature a
"FREE QUIET MOMENTS BATH SPA" offer.
See inside book in May for details.

Only from

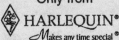

HARLEQUIN®
Makes any time special ®

Don't miss out! Look for this exciting promotion on sale in May 2001, at your favorite retail outlet.

Harlequin truly does make any time special. . . . This year we are celebrating weddings in style!

A Walk Down the Aisle

WEDDING CELEBRATION

To help us celebrate, we want you to tell us how wearing the Harlequin wedding gown will make your wedding day special. As the grand prize, Harlequin will offer one lucky bride the chance to **"Walk Down the Aisle" in the Harlequin wedding gown!**

There's more...

For her honeymoon, she and her groom will spend five nights at the **Hyatt Regency Maui.** As part of this five-night honeymoon at the hotel renowned for its romantic attractions, the couple will enjoy a candlelit dinner for two in Swan Court, a sunset sail on the hotel's catamaran, and duet spa treatments.

A HYATT RESORT AND SPA

MAUI
the Magic Isles™

Maui • Molokai • Lanai

To enter, please write, in, 250 words or less, how wearing the Harlequin wedding gown will make your wedding day special. The entry will be judged based on its emotionally compelling nature, its originality and creativity, and its sincerity. This contest is open to Canadian and U.S. residents only and to those who are 18 years of age and older. There is no purchase necessary to enter. Void where prohibited. See further contest rules attached. Please send your entry to:

Walk Down the Aisle Contest

In Canada
P.O. Box 637
Fort Erie, Ontario
L2A 5X3

In U.S.A.
P.O. Box 9076
3010 Walden Ave.
Buffalo, NY 14269-9076

You can also enter by visiting www.eHarlequin.com
Win the Harlequin wedding gown and the vacation of a lifetime!
The deadline for entries is October 1, 2001.

HARLEQUIN®
Makes any time special ®

PHWDACONT1

HARLEQUIN WALK DOWN THE AISLE TO MAUI CONTEST 1197
OFFICIAL RULES
NO PURCHASE NECESSARY TO ENTER

1. To enter, follow directions published in the offer to which you are responding. Contest begins April 2, 2001, and ends on October 1, 2001. Method of entry may vary. Mailed entries must be postmarked by October 1, 2001, and received by October 8, 2001.

2. Contest entry may be, at times, presented via the Internet, but will be restricted solely to residents of certain geographic areas that are disclosed on the Web site. To enter via the Internet, if permissible, access the Harlequin Web site (www.eHarlequin.com) and follow the directions displayed online. Online entries must be received by 11:59 p.m. E.S.T. on October 1, 2001.

   In lieu of submitting an entry online, enter by mail by hand-printing (or typing) on an 8½" x 11" plain piece of paper, your name, address (including zip code), Contest number/name and in 250 words or fewer, why winning a Harlequin wedding dress would make your wedding day special. Mail via first-class mail to: Harlequin Walk Down the Aisle Contest 1197, (in the U.S.) P.O. Box 9076, 3010 Walden Avenue, Buffalo, NY 14269-9076, (in Canada) P.O. Box 637, Fort Erie, Ontario L2A 5X3, Canada.

   Limit one entry per person, household address and e-mail address. Online and/or mailed entries received from persons residing in geographic areas in which Internet entry is not permissible will be disqualified.

3. Contests will be judged by a panel of members of the Harlequin editorial, marketing and public relations staff based on the following criteria:

   - Originality and Creativity—50%
   - Emotionally Compelling—25%
   - Sincerity—25%

   In the event of a tie, duplicate prizes will be awarded. Decisions of the judges are final.

4. All entries become the property of Torstar Corp. and will not be returned. No responsibility is assumed for lost, late, illegible, incomplete, inaccurate, nondelivered or misdirected mail or misdirected e-mail, for technical, hardware or software failures of any kind, lost or unavailable network connections, or failed, incomplete, garbled or delayed computer transmission or any human error which may occur in the receipt or processing of the entries in this Contest.

5. Contest open only to residents of the U.S. (except Puerto Rico) and Canada, who are 18 years of age or older, and is void wherever prohibited by law; all applicable laws and regulations apply. Any litigation within the Province of Quebec respecting the conduct or organization of a publicity contest may be submitted to the Régie des alcools, des courses et des jeux for a ruling. Any litigation respecting the awarding of a prize may be submitted to the Régie des alcools, des courses et des jeux only for the purpose of helping the parties reach a settlement. Employees and immediate family members of Torstar Corp. and D. L. Blair, Inc., their affiliates, subsidiaries and all other agencies, entities and persons connected with the use, marketing or conduct of this Contest are not eligible to enter. Taxes on prizes are the sole responsibility of winners. Acceptance of any prize offered constitutes permission to use winner's name, photograph or other likeness for the purposes of advertising, trade and promotion on behalf of Torstar Corp., its affiliates and subsidiaries without further compensation to the winner, unless prohibited by law.

6. Winners will be determined no later than November 15, 2001, and will be notified by mail. Winners will be required to sign and return an Affidavit of Eligibility form within 15 days after winner notification. Noncompliance within this time period may result in disqualification and an alternative winner may be selected. Winners of trip must execute a Release of Liability prior to ticketing and must possess required travel documents (e.g. passport, photo ID) where applicable. Trip must be completed by November 2002. No substitution of prize permitted by winner. Torstar Corp. and D. L. Blair, Inc., their parents, affiliates, and subsidiaries are not responsible for errors in printing or electronic presentation of Contest, entries and/or game pieces. In the event of printing or other errors which may result in unintended prize values or duplication of prizes, all affected game pieces or entries shall be null and void. If for any reason the Internet portion of the Contest is not capable of running as planned, including infection by computer virus, bugs, tampering, unauthorized intervention, fraud, technical failures, or any other causes beyond the control of Torstar Corp. which corrupt or affect the administration, secrecy, fairness, integrity or proper conduct of the Contest, Torstar Corp. reserves the right, at its sole discretion, to disqualify any individual who tampers with the entry process and to cancel, terminate, modify or suspend the Contest or the Internet portion thereof. In the event of a dispute regarding an online entry, the entry will be deemed submitted by the authorized holder of the e-mail account submitted at the time of entry. Authorized account holder is defined as the natural person who is assigned to an e-mail address by an Internet access provider, online service provider or other organization that is responsible for arranging e-mail address for the domain associated with the submitted e-mail address. **Purchase or acceptance of a product offer does not improve your chances of winning.**

7. Prizes: (1) Grand Prize—A Harlequin wedding dress (approximate retail value: $3,500) and a 5-night/6-day honeymoon trip to Maui, HI, including round-trip air transportation provided by Maui Visitors Bureau from Los Angeles International Airport (winner is responsible for transportation to and from Los Angeles International Airport) and a Harlequin Romance Package, including hotel accomodations (double occupancy) at the Hyatt Regency Maui Resort and Spa, dinner for (2) two at Swan Court, a sunset sail on Kiele V and a spa treatment for the winner (approximate retail value: $4,000); (5) Five runner-up prizes of a $1000 gift certificate to selected retail outlets to be determined by Sponsor (retail value $1000 ea.). Prizes consist of only those items listed as part of the prize. Limit one prize per person. All prizes are valued in U.S. currency.

8. For a list of winners (available after December 17, 2001) send a self-addressed, stamped envelope to: Harlequin Walk Down the Aisle Contest 1197 Winners, P.O. Box 4200 Blair, NE 68009-4200 or you may access the www.eHarlequin.com Web site through January 15, 2002.

Contest sponsored by Torstar Corp., P.O. Box 9042, Buffalo, NY 14269-9042, U.S.A.

PHWDACONT2

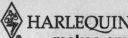

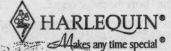